Carl Weber's Kingpins:

Greenville

Carl Weber's Kingpins: Greenville

Cedric Lewis

www.urbanbooks.net

Urban Books, LLC
300 Farmingdale Road, N.Y.-Route 109
Farmingdale, NY 11735

ISBN 13: 978-1-64556-681-6
EBOOK ISBN: 978-1-64556-695-3

First Trade Paperback Printing July 2025
Printed in the United States of America

10 9 8 7 6 5 4 3 2 1

Distributed by Kensington Publishing Corp.
Submit Orders to:
Customer Service
400 Hahn Road
Westminster, MD 21157-4627
Phone: 1-800-733-3000
Fax: 1-800-659-2436

The authorized representative in the EU for product safety and compliance
Is eucomply OU, Parnu mnt 139b-14, Apt 123
Tallinn, Berlin 11317, hello@eucompliancepartner.com

Acknowledgments

First of all, I would like to thank God for allowing me to go through trials and tribulations throughout my life. Without the trials, I couldn't have put all my pains, cries, sweat, and blood into this novel. There's Cane, Trapp, Kasha, Agent Jackson, and Fernandez all over the world.

I want to give James "Cat-Eye" Jamison a shout out for encouraging me to write this book. Gilbert Lewis Augusta's finest. Tim Griffin Green Line's finest. I want to thank Jamie Shell for helping me paint a perfect picture. Tommy Tally, Anthony Poole, Garnell "Boo" Strickland, and Mont Fant, my brothers from another mother, I love you guys for having my back through thick and thin.

A special thank you to authors, Justin "Amen" Floyd, author of *Anything 4 Profit,* and Belinda Hunter, publisher and author of *Waiting on My Cue,* for paving the way and putting Greenville on the map. Shout out to Racquel Williams; you're the best.

Portia Janee Sims, thanks for telling me to keep writing. Trust me, it's just the beginning, and I'm not going to put the pen down anytime soon. Wanda Kymetrian, thanks for always keeping me in your prayers and having faith in me.

I want to give a special shout out to my mother, Zelda Wallace, for loving me so much.

Last, but not least, I want to give a special shout out to all my friends and family: Kelly and Broderick Williams, Angela Dendy, Towanna Howard, Steven Poole, Kizza

Thompson, Tramayne and Travis Morris. Damian Taylor, Shannon Todd, Michael "Mike-Mike" Kennedy, Torasci Hendrix, Cavagio Chapman, Denese and Ashley Howard, Billy Walls, Patrick Tolbert, Tite Geer, Keela Anderson, Brittney Sizemore, Carlynn Burks, Tito Miller, Joseph Waters, Rico Evens, Gerald Pressley, Darrell and Angie Sims, Corey Rosemond, Rick King, Gregory Thompson, Celestine Kyabasinga, Alexis Williams, Love Elmore, Yolanda Neil, LB White, Shane Charles, John Goldsmith, Travis Smiley, Tanika Jones, Jacqueline and Traci Cummings, Al Harris, Mucci Robinson, Tekina Simms, NaTasha Phillips, Lena Chapman, Aunt Nette, Marcus Smith, Shannon & Shezmon Dendy, and Jordan Walls. If I forgot someone, don't blame me, blame the brain, and thanks for the support.

Chapter 1

Cane (2004)

Tyrese's voice serenaded the air from a mixed CD called *The Quiet Storm*. His single, "Signs of Love Making," had just been released, and it was hot! Cane couldn't help but smile to himself since he possessed the same chiseled chest, tattooed body, dark chocolate complexion, and bald head. People were always telling him that he looked just like Tyrese, which he took as a huge compliment. Tyrese was a hot commodity whom Cane assumed was most likely fucking all of the finest women in Hollywood, especially since Wesley Snipes had opened up the doors and brought the dark-skinned brothers back into style after his 1991 hit movie, *New Jack City*.

Over the music, he could hear Tina moaning out, "Don't stop now, ssssss. Oh, give it to me. Fuck me, daddy." All the groaning and moaning she was doing turned him on. He sped up his pace as sweat began to pour profusely from his face, neck, and back. Simultaneously, she aggressively rubbed his back with her hands in rhythm with his deep, hard strokes.

A cool breeze blew from the platinum and gold blades of the ceiling fan that hung above them. For him, the breeze was right on time. The cool air bouncing off of the trickling beads of sweat that poured from his back made him feel as if he were making love on the shore of a beach.

Through the window, he could see the shadows of the moon, which gave his room a darker, more sensual vibe.

He continued his strokes, glancing out of the bay window, noticing the moon was full and shining bright, just like in the movies. Cane knew he had to bring out the beast in him and make “thug love” to Tina. “Oh, shit, Cane! Oh, shit, I’m cumming.” Her body tensed up and jerked like a tractor trailer on a bumpy road. As her warm juices flowed, he released himself and came with her.

He rolled onto his back, gasping for air while holding Tina’s body tightly as they stared out of the skylight, watching the stars.

“Cane, baby, don’t ever let me go. My body feels so safe and secure with you holding me.” She paused for a few seconds and then exhaled, letting out a breath of fresh air. “Baby, just hold me in your arms forever and promise to never let me go.”

“I love you too much to let you go,” he said as he gently kissed her on the forehead.

“Damn, Cane,” she said, feeling a heat wave run through her body. She had to get her thoughts together. Tina swallowed her saliva to clear her throat. She really needed to tell him, and now was about as good of a time as ever. “Baby, we’ve got to talk about something.” She could tell by the way that he looked at her out of the corner of his eyes that he knew what she was about to say, and he didn’t want to hear it. But not hearing her wasn’t an option. She was going to speak her mind no matter what.

“What’s up, Tina?” He closed his eyes, preparing for the scolding that was coming.

“We need to talk about your retirement from this dope game if we ever plan to be a family,” she said.

“We’re already a family. Just because it’s not on paper yet, in my mind, you are my wife.” He opened his eyes, looking down at her.

Tina cleared her throat again. "No, Cane, a real family, because I'm pregnant," she blurted out.

His heart nearly came to a halt as he sat up, looking over at Tina, who was lying on her back, just looking at him, unsure.

"Pregnant! Damn, Tina, you're fuckin' pregnant?"

She was getting furious. "Yes, Cane, I'm fucking pregnant!" she said, allowing her cockiness to kick in, something she rarely had to do with him. "So, in six months, you're going to be a father."

He was still in a daze as he thought, *damn, a father? She's pregnant?*

Tina could see that he was clearly in shock. "Cane, seriously! Are you really upset about this? I thought you would be thrilled. This child will be born out of the love that you and I share for one another."

He had zoned out and was in a trance-like state. He didn't know what to think. Random thoughts consumed his mind about Tina's pregnancy, having a baby, and whether he was ready for such a responsibility.

"Cane, say something, please," Tina cried as she stared up at him.

He ignored her and turned his body toward his grandmother's picture. The anxiety inside of him caused his body to sweat, realizing that six months was around the corner.

"Really, Cane?" she asked again as she got up from the bed. "You have nothing to say about the situation?" She stood over him, sizing him up, hoping to break his silence.

"I am not ready for this!" he shouted while trembling and wiping sweat off of his face. "We can't be having any fucking kids. You're only nineteen. I'm twenty-one. We're both still in college. Shit, we haven't experienced life yet! I've only got one more semester before I can transfer to Florida State. This baby will ruin everything," he said as sweat continued to pour down his face.

"How in the fuck did this happen?" he asked as he took his fist and punched the wall.

Tears began to fall from Tina's face. "You fucked me without protection!" she screamed as she punched him in his chest. "Did you forget, Mr. I Wanna Feel My Dick Inside You? 'I don't like condoms'?"

"Okay! Okay! Just chill out! We'll figure this out together," he said after hearing enough of his own words.

He was too late. She was furious and crying hysterically. He took her into his arms and embraced her tightly, tugging her playfully, hoping to change her attitude. His touch smoothed her over. She giggled as they fell onto the bed. Trying not to apply pressure to her stomach, he rolled her to her side and placed his hands on her stomach, rubbing her belly in circular motions.

"I'm sorry, baby." He stared into her golden brown eyes, wiping away her tears. "You know I love you. I'll never turn my back on you or the baby." His heart was sincere, but his mentality was not ready. Financially, he could hold them down, but he was still living the fast life and was in no hurry to end his lifestyle just yet. He couldn't imagine giving up one hundred grand per week and buying the foreign whips he praised as trophies, aka eye candy.

He began tallying up all of the accomplishments he had achieved in life in a short period of time. He was a major drug supplier in the upstate of Greenville, and he was on top of his game, living a lavish lifestyle, like Scarface. Cane wanted to take over the world like Nino Brown did the Carter in *New Jack City*. The world was his oyster, and no one could tell him anything different.

He had built his dream house from the ground up. He had more than enough money to take care of Tina, the baby, and his family, but Tina wanted him out of the streets completely. He knew this day would come, but he was hoping for it to be after they were done with school. He loved Tina with everything in him, and although he wasn't ready to give up the game, he was not going to lose the best girl on earth for it. He opened his eyes, gazed directly into hers, and said, "It's over."

"What's over? Cane, I'm sorry! I love you. Please, Cane," she cried.

He couldn't do anything except smile on the inside. "It's not over with you, silly. I'm talking about the dope game and this lifestyle. I'll give up any- and everything for you, baby." He held her hand, letting her know she was safe and didn't have anything to fear.

She pulled her hand away from his hand and then slightly turned her back. "You've said that same thing before." Tina took a deep breath. "I just don't know if I can go through with this after the big scene you just made. Don't take this the wrong way, you know I love you more than anything, but I don't want my child being born into a drug-infested environment." She folded her arms across her stomach, watching him out of the corner of her eye, studying his body language.

Just a second ago, she was giggling. Now, tears seeped from her eyes. He felt in his heart that it was over, and he was being sincere with his decision. "It's over, Tina. A year ago, you weren't pregnant. A lot has changed since then. You know, just as well as I do, that street life is all I know. It's gotten me all I've ever wanted. It helped build me the family I've always wanted."

She wiped her tears away and faced him. "Cane, the game has been good to me and you. You have treated me like a queen and bought me the world, but don't let greed be your downfall. All of these years you have been blessed. Get out while you are ahead and never throw it in my face for wanting to keep you around."

"Just listen and trust me! I'm giving it all up for you, the baby, and myself. I don't want my child growing up the way I did. I don't want my child to be surrounded by drugs and guns. All I want is you. Marry me?" he said in a plea.

All of her tears ceased. She knew that he was serious.

"Cane? Are you serious, baby? Yes, Cane! I'll marry you." She kissed him softly.

All he could think about was that he actually had a child on the way, and Tina was going to be his wife. Yes, he had to get mentally ready to be the best husband and father he could be, but giving up the game for good was going to be hell, and most of all, explaining it to his CMB—Cash Money Brothers—clique that he was retiring for good would be difficult.

He was most definitely feeling good about himself. He wanted to call his favorite woman, his grandmother, and tell her the good news. Tina told him that, to hustlers, 3:00 a.m. was still young, but to ordinary folk, it was too early in the morning to be calling anyone unless it was an emergency. She advised him to wait until dawn.

The smooth melody of Sam Cooke's "A Change Is Gonna Come" played, and he was feeling the mood, pulling Tina to him as they danced to the rhythm. Tina squeezed him tightly. "I know that this will be the best thing for the both of us, just watch and see," she whispered into his ear. Her pussy was throbbing for his attention.

He was more excited than ever. Not the cars, money, or any other material thing could compare to the new life he had ahead of him. He always knew that he wanted to one day be a family man. He just didn't expect for it to be for another fifteen years. But what he did know was that, when that time arrived, he would hold down his wife and children. He had vowed to be everything that he had longed for as a child to his family. He knew that any fool could make a baby, but it took a real man to raise one.

"Baby, I'm sorry about everything that happened tonight." He held on to her as if his life depended on her. "I just wasn't in the right frame of mind when you hit me with the baby shit. You dropped a bombshell on me." He paused for a second. "I was being very selfish, and I'm about to be selfish right now. So, stop those tears from coming from your eyes, unless they're tears of joy."

Tears began to fall from his eyes. "Those better be tears of joy," she said in a joking manner.

"Yeah, babe, they are tears of joy. You're blessing me with my first seed. And most of all, you're committing yourself to being my wifey."

"Aw, babe, I wouldn't trade you in for nothing in the world. A man with a heart like yours is priceless." She wiped away his tears and gazed into his eyes. Just the look she gave him turned him on.

The twinkle in her eyes was bright and shined like a star. He started kissing on her, hitting the spots he knew made her hot. One hand gripped her fat ass and his other hand twirled her golden nipples.

"Stop," she groaned, using reverse psychology, hoping he would take what was his and make passionate love to her.

"Why? You don't want me?" he asked, knowing good and well that she really didn't want him to stop.

"Yes, I want you, big daddy," she groaned before an outside noise startled her. "Did you hear that noise?" she asked as she pulled herself away from him, looking toward the window.

"Baby, stop tripping. You're spoiling the moment." He pulled her back into his arms.

"I'm serious, Cane. I heard noises!"

"Stop tripping, babe. The alarm would've sounded by now if someone was back there."

Thinking about it, she said, "You're right, baby," as she tried to relax and get back into the mood. "Just got a lot going on in my head." She rolled over on top of him and started kissing on his chiseled, ripped chest. He loved the way she took control. He grabbed her ass and spread her cheeks apart, massaging her thickness.

In the heat of the moment, his eyes roamed in the direction of the bay window. He saw shadows reflecting from the spotlight. He tried to be as calm as possible, so as to not startle her. "Baby, move for one second," he said calmly, yet with urgency.

"I thought you loved it when I took charge. Am I doing something wrong?"

"Nah, you never do anything wrong when it comes to your lovemaking skills, sweetie. Just chill for a second," he said, putting his finger to his lips, shushing her as he sat up in the bed and squinted his eyes toward the bay window. At first, he thought his eyes were deceiving him until he saw more shadows reflecting from the spotlight of the neighbor's house.

"What's going on, Cane? You're starting to scare me."

She quickly rolled onto her side. He remained silent as he stood up and grabbed his 9 mm Glock out of the drawer next to the bed.

"Cane, baby," Tina whispered in fear. She leaned upright to see what was going on.

He could hear the fear in Tina's voice, but his mind was on what was going on outside. He had heard earlier in the week from one of his crew members that word on the street was that the Jack Boys were plotting to rob him. Knowing the dope game was one of the dirtiest games to be in, he knew off top that there were four things that he had to watch out for: the Jack Boys, the police, haters, and snitches.

He looked out the bay window fearfully, as any scared man would. The shadows were moving rapidly around the corner of the house. With it being dark, he didn't recognize who the shadows belonged to.

Tina finally got his undivided attention by crying out, "Cane, I'm scared! Please, Lord, don't let this be happening."

"Calm down, and put your clothes on," Cane demanded at once. He couldn't think clearly with Tina and the baby on his mind, and Tina's crying certainly wasn't helping him. His focus right now wasn't even about him. It was about protecting his family by any means necessary.

He placed the gun in her hands and commanded her to get under the bed and not come out until the police got there. She was in a trance, shaking in fear. "Did you hear me?" His tone rattled in her ears.

"Yes." She was terrified. She had seen plenty of guns before but never envisioned herself using one. Momentarily, she put her fear aside and began thinking about her unborn baby and what would happen if Cane was killed. She broke into tears. He grabbed her, hugging her tightly as if he was to never let her go. He looked into her tear-filled, scared eyes, and with one of his fingers, he wiped away the tears from her left eye while he kissed away the tears from her right one.

His grip was tight. She could feel his insides tremble with fear. Suddenly, he pulled away. She reached out and embraced him once again, kissing him as if it were going to be their last. "I've got to go, baby. Now, do what I told you to do, and don't come from under the bed unless it's the police." He knew that the jack game could be treacherous. "And don't come from under the bed for me either."

"Please don't leave me," she cried out. "Please don't leave me. I can't do this by myself."

"Yes, you can," he said, trying to build up her confidence. "You're brave, so stop it, and be the woman I know you are. I promise you, I'll never leave you. I'll be back. Now, get under the bed. We don't have much time."

He walked toward the picture of his late paternal grandmother that hung next to his bed. Once he reached it, he removed it and opened up the safe which hid behind it. He removed a semi-automatic with two filled banana clips that he kept there in case of an emergency. He closed the safe and then kissed his grandmother's face, imagining that she was there with him.

Placing her picture back on the wall, he muttered under his breath as he checked to see if Tina was under the bed and out of sight. "Back to business," he said with his Scarface game face on. "These motherfuckers want to play? Well, 'say hello to my little friend,'" he said just as Tony Montana did in the hit movie *Scarface*.

There was no way possible he was going to let the Jack Boys take him alive. His motto was to kill everything in sight. The sacrifices he had made to make his riches, he was not about to let anyone who hadn't paid the cost take away from him.

He heard what sounded to be about thirty or more footsteps pounding the outside deck. By the sounds, he could tell they wore combat boots. He peeked out the window but could only see shadows moving at a fast pace. "Damn, they brought the military to rob me?" He at first panicked and tensed before he became mad. His adrenaline was pumping, and he was ready for war! Whatever they had in store for him, he had in store for them. Right now, he was a one-man army—but he was ready.

Suddenly, a loud boom rang out from both the front and back of the house. Behind the explosion, a deep, raspy voice yelled out, "Cane! Come out! We know you're in there." His heart pounded as if it were being beaten with a hammer. He ducked into the hallway closet. By the echo of their voices, he knew they weren't close to him. He stood still and stayed alert while the raspy voices shouted "come out or else" scenarios.

His mind was made up. He wasn't going to let those low-life, jealous, hating-ass niggas with guns and ski masks take shit from him. He had hustled too hard, put in too much overtime, missed too many days of school, and wore the same clothes for too many weeks in a row in order to get on top, and he'd be damned if all that shit was going to be in vain. He wasn't giving up shit. They would get it over his dead body.

"Cane, don't make us tear up this house looking for you!" the voice sounded out with anger. Yet again, his worries worsened as he thought about Tina and the baby and how he had endangered their lives. Life for him was too good to be true with all the good news and Tina being pregnant. He couldn't believe how fast his day turned into a nightmare. A little relief came upon him when he didn't hear any gunshots coming from the room where Tina and his unborn child were.

He gripped the machine gun tightly in his hands. Although he never had to use one in the past, due to his Uncle Jack's reputation, he was ready to burn some people. The voice got closer. "Cane, come out wherever you are!" He aimed the gun at the door, ready to shoot anything or anyone who opened it. "Come out, Cane. We found your girlfriend," the voice pleaded once again. Instantly, his heart dropped to his stomach. Fearing that they may pistol whip Tina, Cane knew at this point it was kill or be killed.

"I'm all right, baby. Please come out before you get hurt. It's the police." Her voice was shaky, which confused him. Although he was happy to hear her voice, he was unsure if the Jack Boys forced her to call out his name and claim them to be the police or what. “I’m not hurt, baby, so come out.” He still lay low. “I don’t want to see you get killed, so, baby, please come out!” she pleaded. “Do it for me and the baby.”

He could feel the pain in her voice, and knowing that Tina would die for him, he knew she wouldn’t have called him out for the Jack Boys. He dropped his gun and stepped out of the closet with his hands pointing toward the ceiling.

Once his pupils dilated and the darkness from the closet escaped his eyes, he was shocked by what he saw before him. There were so many infrared beams pointing at him. He was lit up like a Christmas tree.

“Freeze. I’m DEA Agent Jackson. You are under arrest! Turn around slowly and put your arms behind your back.” Relieved it was the DEA and not the Jack Boys, he did as ordered. He could get out of this, but had it been the Jack Boys, he and Tina would have been killed on contact. “Now, get down on your knees, and if you try anything slick, I will blow your black ass into pieces.” Agent Jackson was ready to squeeze the trigger. His finger was itching to do so if Cane made the wrong move. To Agent Jackson’s disappointment, he obeyed, dropping to his knees.

As he lowered himself to his knees, a couple of agents rushed in and slapped handcuffs on both of his wrists while they forcefully pushed on his back, causing him to fall forward onto his face.

“Stop, y’all are hurting him. He hasn’t done anything to y’all!” Tina cried, rushing to his rescue, shoving her way through the agents.

“Get her the fuck outta here right now.” Agent Jackson’s face turned beet red as the agents attempted to remove her. Tina turned into beast mode and began kicking and screaming at every agent in arms’ reach. “Ms. Davis, if you don't want to go to jail with him, I advise you to get control of yourself," Agent Jackson said, giving her a stern look.

"Calm down, babe. I will be all right," Cane reassured her.

The agents stood him up and placed shackles on his ankles. "Curtis Griffin, aka Cane, you are under arrest for conspiracy of drug trafficking cocaine with the intent to distribute. I'm going to read you your rights. You have the right to remain silent—"

Cane cut Agent Jackson off. "I don't want to hear this bullshit."

Jackson was fuming, with his veins protruding from his neck. Cane loved every second of it.

"I don't care what you don't want to hear. I'm going to tell you what you need to hear." Agent Jackson continued to recite Cane his rights.

He ignored Jackson as ten agents began to escort him out of the house. He was somewhat shocked from the events that had taken place. Agents surrounded his house. He was astounded. They proceeded to a Ford Crown Victoria with ebony tinted windows. The doors were already ajar as if he were entering a limousine. His chariot had arrived.

Before he got into the car, he glanced over his shoulder, only to see the love of his life sitting in the back of a police car. He winked his eye at her as he whispered, "I love you." Although she couldn't hear him, she read his lips and said that she loved him also.

They backed the car into the road and began to drive off. He thought he was dreaming. There were four DEA agents in the car with him: a driver, Agent Jackson in the front passenger seat, and two in the back surrounding him. His worst dream had finally become a reality as the blood continued to run down his lips. The excitement was finally over, and his adrenaline was no longer pumping. His head ached in pain.

He caught himself sightseeing as the Crown Vic headed into town. He was noticing buildings that he had never paid attention to before. The car pulled into the parking lot of the bank. He questioned himself, *what the hell is this?*

Anxiety kicked in because he wanted to know what was going on. "Where in the hell are y'all taking me?"

Agent Jackson turned around with a victorious shit-eating grimace on his face. "Welcome to the major league, sport. This is our headquarters, and you've just earned yourself a free VIP pass." His facial expression spoke high volumes. He couldn't believe that the bank was the federal headquarters. And to make things worse, he was a loyal customer with his CMB clique. He got lightheaded, and his head started spinning, knowing a large percentage of his money was inside the bank.

The car pulled into the back of the bank. Agent Jackson rolled down his window and placed his hand on a scanner. "Hello, Agent Jackson," said an automated voice as the overhead doors rose, and they disappeared like a thief in the night into the building. "Have a nice day, Agent Jackson," the programming said as they proceeded through.

"What's so fucking nice about this day?" Cane thought out loud to himself, knowing it was the worst day of his life.

Agent Jackson smiled. "Oh, sport, play for now," he laughed out. "It's a very good day. We are locking your black ass up. Now, it doesn't get any nicer than this . . . sport."

Displeased with Agent Jackson's comment, he retaliated back. "Nah, what would be nice was if I had your white mama sucking my big black dick." He held back from laughing. "Now, that would be nice, right, fellas?" The agents sniffled while holding back their laughter.

Finally, they approached the interrogation room. Agent Jackson sat Cane down and began unlocking his shackles and cuffs. Thoughts of escaping crossed his mind, but with all of the technology, he knew he wouldn't get very far.

A familiar-looking Latina agent walked up, placing an identification card, black ink, and a camera on the table in front of him. Although it had been six years since he had seen the Greenville County Detention Center, this was a process that he knew all too well.

The female agent tried to hold a decent conversation with him, but he was not trying to hear shit she had to say. Once Agent Fernandez finished fingerprinting him and taking his picture, Agent Jackson escorted him into a holding cell. Before exiting the cell, Agent Jackson looked at him and said, "Yeah, we finally got you, Mr. Griffin. You're finished. History. You will be in prison for the rest of your life, you black son of a bitch."

His ears didn't miss the hateful, spiteful words Jackson let seep from his mouth. He tried his best to laugh it off, but his pride and slick tongue had to get the last word in. "Oh, I guess you're still mad about the mama comment, huh? Hell, I know you can picture her slobbering up and down on my dick." Cane could not hold back his laughter. Jackson's eyes turned firecracker red.

"We'll see who gets the last laugh, Mr. Griffin!" Agent Jackson said, exiting the room and slamming the door behind him.

He was still in disbelief that he had just gotten picked up by the Feds. Earlier today, you couldn't have told him that his night would end with him sitting in a holding cell that only had a toilet, sink, and no windows. He lay back on the cold steel bench and closed his eyes as he began meditating on how he got caught slipping.

Chapter 2

Kasha (1998)

She was making sure that her hair was on point as she looked into the mirror. She knew that, if not on any other day, today she had to be glamorous. It was her first day of public school. After two years of pleading, she had finally been able to convince her overprotective parents to allow her and her sister to attend public school. All of her friends who stayed in their neighborhood attended public schools. She had heard so much about Southside High that she was anxious to get in on all the hype.

As she waited on Ricky, she closed her eyes, reminiscing on how they had met at Cleveland Park. She could remember it like yesterday. She had on her Daisy Duke shorts, showing off her pretty, thick legs, and her butt cheeks were hanging out, showing her body, which was a sight to see. Every man out there had their eyes on her like she was a piece of candy. She knew she was eye candy and loved every bit of the attention.

The bitches were hating, and the men were trying to get at her as always, but she couldn't care less about those lame-ass niggas. When she saw Ricky walking her way, she was at a loss for words. He was about six three with a medium frame. His mixed Brazilian complexion and beautifully tanned skin made her body twitch like never before. She didn't hesitate to give him her number when he approached her real smoothly, unlike the other lames, and started a conversation. When he walked away, the ratchet, hating bitches were looking her up and down with turned-up noses.

As he headed toward his candy apple red convertible Mustang, it did not go unnoticed to her as a few females tried to get his attention. He spoke to those who spoke, giving them minimal conversation, and kept it moving. Once he was in his hot ride, he looked at her right before he pulled into traffic and held up two fingers to make a phone, indicating that he was going to call her. She was mesmerized by his smoothness and how fine he was. She smiled, showing off her pearly white teeth, forgetting she had a boyfriend. From the side of her eye, she could see the bitches rolling their eyes and hating on her even more.

Her heart raced when she heard the loud knock at the door. "Daddy, answer the door!" she hollered from the back of the house as she was slipping on her shoes. When she finally walked into the living room, she found her overprotective father drilling Ricky. She knew the direction the conversation was going, so she tried her best to hurry and get Ricky out of the house.

As they were walking out the door, her father trailed behind, adjusting his glasses. "Hold up, young man! You still didn't answer my question. What are your intentions with my daughter?"

"My intentions are to take her to school and bring her back home, sir. You have my word, nothing more. I respect her a whole lot, sir. Scouts' honor."

Noticing Ricky's ride, her father asked, "Where do you work, son?"

"Foot Locker at the Haywood Mall, sir."

"Foot Locker allows you to drive a car like this?" Mr. Davis asked while adjusting his glasses to see every feature the Mustang had.

She was really getting embarrassed with her father's questions to Ricky, as if he were a private investigator. "Daddy, stop it, please," she said playfully, but she was really embarrassed.

"You are my daughter, and I have every right to make sure that any man you show interest in is a stand-up kind of a man if he is going to be parading you around. Son, if you are involved in any criminal activity, my daughter is not the girl for you. And how old are you again?"

"He's seventeen, okay, Daddy?" she snapped without meaning to. How dare he accuse Ricky of being in illegal activity because he had a nice car? When she saw the disappointed look in her father's eyes, she turned and went to give him a hug. "Daddy, I'll always be your baby. Believe that you raised me right and trust that everything you instilled in me will prevail. I'm a smart girl, Daddy, and I would never date a guy who wasn't considerate or respectful to me or you. I love you," she said, putting on her best innocent look, the look that always won her father over.

He crossed his arms, still eyeing Ricky up and down. "Well, if he is so considerate, then he won't mind your li'l sister riding with y'all to school since y'all are going that way anyway."

"But, Daddy!" she whined. She wanted to scream to the top of her lungs. She didn't want anything to do with Tina. She wanted to be with Ricky alone and not have her little sister babysit her.

"Don't 'but' me!" her father interjected. "Tina!" He hollered for his baby girl to come out. "Come on out. You are—" His sentence was cut short by his wife, who told him to let the kids leave before they were late to school.

"Well, they are all going to the same place, so it makes no sense for me to take her. You don't mind, do you, son?" he asked Ricky sarcastically.

"No, sir!" replied Ricky with a quickness.

When they got to the stop sign, Cane, Trapp, and Shi were standing there, waiting on the bus. Ricky stopped and dropped his top, showing off his car and the fine ladies who occupied it. Kasha coolly nodded her head at her friends and old flame, Cane. She had dated Cane for a hot minute, but she had little remorse for how she had done him. Cane wanted a trophy girlfriend, but he had nothing to earn that trophy or to keep her from scouting. Kasha had been sheltered and shown the finer things that life had to offer. Her thoughts were that Cane didn't have shit going for himself—no car, job, or money. He depended on his uncle, and since Ricky came along, Cane was now a thing of the past. She was going to be the new hot chick in the school, rolling with a stud.

She looked at her sister sitting in the back seat and asked, "Are you sure you do not want us to drop you off with your friends?"

"No, ma'am," Tina said, giving her a smirk, knowing that she was annoyed that she had to tag along. "I'm good."

"Ugh, you get on my nerves," Kasha said, rolling her eyes and turning back to face forward.

"Well, you get on mine too," Tina retaliated.

"Apparently, I don't get on your nerves that much because every time I move, you are on my heels."

"Because Daddy put me on your heels, believe that. You are not that interesting to me," Tina said matter-of-factly.

Kasha looked at her smart-mouthed sister and rolled her eyes again.

"Don't blame me. Blame your daddy," Tina continued.

"Just shut up talking to me," Kasha said, not able to keep up with her sister's quick tongue.

"You asking me or telling me?"

"I'm telling you!" Kasha said, giving Tina a warning eye.

"Girl, I am not Cane. I don't do as you say and yet still be treated like shit. You know you've got me twisted, boo."

"I don't have you twisted. I know exactly who you are. You tag along on my coattail, hoping to get attention because you can't stand on your own. You love being in my shadows."

"Bitch, please! Why would I want to be like you when I know how dirty you are? And the way you did Cane is going to come back and bite you in your ass. You think your shit doesn't stank, but guess what? I smell it, and it's loud. And another newsflash for your conceited ass, I am not one of your fans, and I don't drop and play dead because you say so."

Hearing Cane's name, Ricky intervened. "Cane is in the past. I am her man now. Cane didn't know how to deal with a woman of her caliber. That's why he's assed out. It was time for a change, and Kasha is all woman. She doesn't need a little boy."

Kasha gave her sister a smug smirk and sat back, satisfied.

Waving off Ricky's comment, Tina said, "Whatever, if you say so. Just hurry up and get me to school. I don't want to be around y'all no more than I have to be. You two deserve one another." She mumbled to herself, "Just because you develop a little body over the summer, you go and get ahead of yourself, but you're no Janet Jackson or J.Lo, so stay in your lane." Tina could see the lustful look in Ricky's eyes as he scoped her sister's body from head to toe as he drove.

"I see that you are a hater as well. All I can say is join the party with the rest of them hating-ass hoes. And besides, you'll never have a body like mine and a man like I've got," Kasha said, rubbing on Ricky's arm.

"If there is a God, I sure won't," Tina said as she rolled her eyes and hopped out of the car once it stopped.

Kasha was relieved that they were finally rid of Tina and she now had Ricky to herself.

"I hope my daddy doesn't think she's going to be riding with us every day. I can't deal with her smart-ass mouth."

"Baby, I don't mind. I'll take your sister to school anytime," Ricky said, trying to do anything to impress Kasha so that he could tap that ass. He placed his hands on her thighs and then licked his lips. "Baby, I really am not feeling school today. We should go somewhere so we can be alone." He eased his hand farther up her thick, sexy thighs. She tensed up, feeling the same sensation she felt when she first met him at Cleveland Park.

"I can't skip school. My dad has us on probation, and if we mess up, it will be back to that boring-ass private school."

He looked into her hazel-brown eyes. "I thought you said that you wanted to spend some private time with me."

"I do, but you don't know my father. He can be crazy at times. I can't mess up my first week of school."

He pondered what she said for a few seconds. "I'm not tripping on you, but what's up with that li'l nigga, Cane?"

"Once again, for the hundredth time, I'm your woman, and you will never have to worry about another nigga being in my life. I was with Cane for six months and only have been with you for two months, but I love you more than I ever loved Cane."

"That's what's up," he said as he smiled, squeezing her thighs, already knowing he had her sheltered, simple-minded head fucked up. When he pulled a blunt out of the ashtray, her eyes lit up in awe. "Now, if you are going to roll with the big dawgs, you've got to loosen up a little, and I've got something to 'stimulate your mind,'" he quoted with his Chris Tucker tone.

After lighting up the blunt, he took two pulls and then passed it to her. She hesitated at first, but not wanting to seem like a naive, inexperienced little girl, she took it. She put it to her mouth and took a long pull as she had seen it done on television. Instantly, she started coughing, and then tears ran down her eyes. Ricky laughed as he asked, "You all right?"

"Yeah, I'm straight," she said after calming down.

As she continued to smoke with him, she mellowed out and was focused on everything around her. Tupac's song "Do for Love" had her vibing and relaxed. She thought she was tripping when she heard her own heartbeat thumping. She was so caught up listening to her heartbeat that Ricky had to shout out her name to ask, "You all right?" He knew she was high as hell.

"Yeah, baby, I'm good."

Kasha was really feeling herself as she sang along with Monica and Brandy's hit song, "The Boy Is Mine." She was waving her hands from side to side at the same time, thinking Southside High was going to be on and popping once she got there.

"I feel so good. Ricky. Drop the top back down?" she asked because he had put it back up when he pulled out the blunt.

"Nah, girl, that's not a good idea. You don't want to fuck up that pretty hairdo," he said, trying to make it seem as if he had her best interest at heart, but in reality, he didn't want the smell-good aroma to escape the car.

"It is sexy, isn't it?" she teased as she looked into the rearview mirror, checking out her 'do. She had the whole Mya thing going on, from feathers to hairdo.

She was thinking about what Tina had said to her about Janet and J.Lo. She didn't hesitate asking Ricky who looked better.

"Tina lied to you because the only thing Janet or J.Lo have on you is the fact that they have money," he said.

She looked at Ricky lovingly as she leaned over and kissed him before saying, "I love you so much, and if you ever do me wrong, you won't have to worry about my father because I'll kill you myself."

"You ain't 'bout that life," Ricky teased.

"Play with me," she said playfully, smacking his face.

"Home of the Tigers!" she read out loud as they parked and walked toward the front entrance. She grabbed his hand nervously, amazed at the size of the school. Walking in the gym, she knew that she wasn't in private school anymore and there were no more "Daddy's Little Girls." Public school was in her blood, and she was ready for whatever.

Right before they entered the gym, Ricky pulled his hand away from her. "Baby, this is high school, not elementary where your daddy has to hold your hand everywhere you go."

"I'm your girl, so it shouldn't matter!" Kasha snapped with an attitude.

"I know what you mean, but we don't do the holding hands stuff at Southside. It makes you look soft and wrapped."

She didn't let him get to her as she looked around through the thick crowd, looking for her friends. She didn't recognize anyone at first until Traci snuck up behind her, scaring the hell out of her. "Hey, girl. I've been waiting on you all morning."

"Girl, you wouldn't believe the nerve of my daddy this morning. He held us up, drilling Ricky, and then made us bring Tina to school. That fool is off the chain." She giggled out. "Oh, I'm sorry, Traci. This is Ricky, and Ricky, this is my bestie, Traci."

"Girl, you are the only new person here. Ricky and I have known one another since middle school." Traci and Ricky laughed. "I need some of that good shit you've been smoking on."

"I haven't been smoking on anything," she said as she sniffed her own clothes.

"Nah, shorty is good. She was in the car with me while I was. Sorry, babe," Ricky said, looking at her apologetically.

"Oh, my gosh. You can smell it?" Kasha asked, ignoring Ricky as she continued sniffing her clothes.

"Yes, I can smell it, but it's not that bad. Let's go to the bathroom to wash your shirt and blow dry it. It's thin. It won't take a minute."

"Good looking out, Traci," Ricky said. "I'll see you after school, baby," Ricky said, giving Kasha a friendly hug.

As soon as he walked off, Traci told her that she never cared for Ricky and he couldn't be trusted. Kasha thought, *not you too, Traci, hating. Well, join the damn haters' party because Ricky is a keeper.*

"You smell just like smoke. You sure you didn't smoke?"

"Nah, girl, that was all Ricky. I'll never smoke that shit. It'll kill your brain cells," she said, trying not to look guilty.

They split up in the auditorium. She walked past a group of males who started clapping their hands and singing out, "There goes the next fresh meat queen." She just rolled her eyes at the clowns. One of them had the audacity to ask, "Miss Queen, is you looking for a king?"

"Nah, player. I already have a king who sits on this throne." She did her best impression to shake what her mother had blessed her with as she walked to her first class.

As soon as she stepped into study hall, Ricky stood out like a sore thumb. He had his arms wrapped around a tall supermodel Naomi Campbell look-alike. She had one eyebrow raised as she made her way over to his table. "What's up, baby?" she said as she set her books down, holding her hands on her hips.

"Nothing much, just kicking it with some old friends. What are you doing here?" He freed his arms from around the girl.

"I have this class also." Her lips twisted as she stared the other girl in the eyes. "Come on, let's go sit by the window."

Ricky obediently followed her over to the table. She had just sat down when she spotted Traci walking into the class. "My girl has this class also! I'll be right back," she told Ricky as she made her way to Traci. She snuck up on Traci, grabbing her by the arms. She turned around, quickly grabbing her chest.

"Girl, you scared the mess out of me. Lucky it was you because if it was somebody else, I would've beat the hell out of them for handling me like that. You play too much," Traci laughed. "Girl, let me tell you this, you're not in private school anymore. These bitches around here are conniving and deceitful, so always watch your back."

"Tell me about it. Who is that female all up in Ricky's face? I just left his ass two seconds ago, and females are trying to holla already." Kasha exhaled.

Traci turned to see who Kasha was speaking of. This girl named Tyla was trying to be all up on Ricky, although Ricky was trying not to entertain her. Traci knew it was because he knew that Kasha was in the room and was most likely watching because if the circumstances were different, he would have had Tyla hemmed up against a wall by now. He was just as much of a whore as Tyla was.

"Oh, that's Tyla, just another slut around here. I owe her an ass whipping."

"Why?" Kasha asked with a giggle.

"Because she was sleeping around with my older sister's boyfriend, and when they were found out, he cut her off because he wasn't going to lose my sister behind a ho. Anyway, she started harassing my sister and even went to her house trying to fight her."

"What? She let her come to her house, talking trash, and she didn't whip her butt?" Kasha asked in disbelief.

"My sister is nothing like me. She is nonconfrontational, so she called the police on her, but then my sister ran into her at the mall. She followed behind my sister, talking shit, and said that my two-year-old niece looked like a gremlin."

"Oh, wow, she's really petty to talk about a child," Kasha said, looking over at her, checking her out.

"What her and my sister got going with that nigga doesn't matter to me because they choose to let him keep doing the stupid shit. And a nigga is only going to do what you allow. But my niece . . ." Traci said, shaking her head, getting mad all over again. "That little girl is my life! I will mess you up about her. Tyla had no idea that was my sister she was beefing with until I approached her after the mall incident. Of course, she denied it, but I let her know that I would fuck her up at the drop of a hat about my niece. Her ass bitched up until people separated us, and she started talking shit. The principal told us both that if we fought, we would both be suspended for ten days, and I never see the heifer off the school grounds. But her day is coming," Traci said. "But don't worry about her. Everyone knows how she is," Traci said. "Ricky wouldn't mess with her," she said, lying but not wanting Kasha to get into any trouble.

"Well, I am going to set some ground rules now. What Ricky used to do before I came is a wrap."

Kasha walked up on Ricky and Tyla, and she slipped her arm between Ricky's, letting them both know that she was there.

Ricky looked a little uncomfortable as he pretended to be having just a friendly conversation with Tyla, but he still had not introduced Kasha, so she put her hand out to Tyla, intending to introduce herself, but things quickly went south.

"Hi. I'm Kasha."

Tyla looked at Kasha's extended arm as if it were plagued. "Who is this, Ricky?"

"She told you who she was," Ricky said as he turned to go to his desk.

"Did you not tell her that you had a girl?" Kasha asked, looking at Ricky's back as he headed to his seat.

He stood there, looking crazy, stuttering, and trying to plead his case.

Tyla looked at Ricky and asked, "So, this here is supposed to be your girlfriend or something?"

"Yes, I am," Kasha said.

"Bitch, I'm not talking to you!" Tyla snapped, rolling her eyes and stepping into Kasha's face.

"Bitch?"

Traci stepped in and grabbed Kasha, pulling her back. "Don't worry about her, Kasha. As long as she knows that Ricky is your man, that's all that matters." Traci gave her a death stare. Tyla sucked her teeth and walked off.

Kasha then stepped to Ricky and asked, "Is there something I should know?"

"Baby, trust me, I am not seeing that girl. We are just friends. Yeah, she has a major crush on me, and I used to flirt around with her, but all of that ended when you and I got together."

Traci interjected, saying, "Look, if you're going to be with my girl, be with my girl, but all of this bullshit you do stops now. Kasha is my homegirl, and I'll be damned if I sit back and allow you to walk the dog on her like you have so many others. Know what you want."

Kasha knew Traci was as ratchet as they came. There was no chill button in her ghetto mentality. She had been born and raised in the projects and didn't take shit from anybody. She didn't discriminate. She would beat a nigga down as well as a bitch. Ordinarily, Traci would not have been someone Kasha would have hung out with, but their paths crossed when Traci's brother, Derrick, had solicited Traci to beat Kasha's ass because he was in his feelings. After Kasha explained to Traci that she had broken up with Derrick because she had caught him in a parked car, kissing another girl, Traci went off on Derrick. She and Kasha started talking, and a great friendship began. Kasha knew that she could always count on Traci being by her side at all times no matter what happened.

"Go get your books and chill out with us," she told Traci. After Traci walked off, she glanced over at Ricky just as he was sliding a piece of paper into his pocket. She bit her tongue with her mind already made up that she was going to keep her quick temper in check and not jump to conclusions. Give him enough rope and he would hang himself. He was a fine specimen, so quite naturally, he was going to have the females trying to be all over him, but he was going to have to learn that he didn't have to bite everything that put out a hook.

"You and your friend are off the chain. Y'all be wilding out. I expected that from her but not from you. You two seem like an unlikely pair," he said, shaking his head.

"Funny because our paths crossed in an unlikely way. Traci is cool. That's my dawg until the day I die," Kasha said. "She is as real as they come. Although we were introduced to fight one another, I am glad that our paths crossed," she explained as she looked over her schedule, seeing if she had more classes with Ricky.

"Introduced to fight one another? Why?" Ricky asked.

"Doesn't even matter. The point is that we didn't fight, and we are now great friends."

"Must've been about a nigga," Ricky said.

"Whether it was about a nigga we are fucking or taking up for, all girls' disputes go right back to a nigga," Kasha laughed.

Chapter 3

Cane (1998)

The loud sirens of the alarm clock almost made him jump out of bed and run for safety. He had forgotten that he had changed the alarm from the soothing sounds of Levert to the fire truck sirens. Once he realized that the house wasn't on fire, he reached over, hitting the snooze button as he lay back down for five more minutes. Twenty minutes later, he jumped up, racing to the bathroom after he had overslept. "Hurry up, Gina. I've got to get ready for school, girl!" He knocked on the door and then started pacing back and forth, getting impatient and frustrated.

When she didn't come to the door, he pounded on it harder. "Your mama needs to hurry up and get out of prison so y'all can go back home," he said, frustrated because he was always having to wait on the bathroom. His comments about her mother being in prison did not move her at all because, although his mom was not in prison, she was still worse off than Gina's mom. Gina's mom was in prison, but she was not strung out on drugs in the streets, tricking and living from pillow to pole as his mom was. He was the fourth grandchild out of ten living with his grandmother. Since he could remember, they had been living with her due to his mother's substance abuse and run-ins with the law.

Gina paid him no mind as she continued to take her precious time. He walked back to his room, checking out his new gear. His uncle Jack had taken him on a shopping spree because his grandmother couldn't afford to take care of necessities and get his clothes. She worked nine to five, paid all the bills, and made sure that they had food on the table and a roof over their heads. That was all she felt required to do. She bought clothes as needed and not for style.

After looking at his fresh gear, he was eager to get dressed and stunt. He walked back to the bathroom and started back beating on the door as he yelled out to their grandmother. "Grandma, tell Gina to let me use the bathroom."

"Please, gal, let that boy use the bathroom because he's driving me crazy," Grandma said.

She walked out with an attitude. "Dang, you happy now?" She sneered at him as he intentionally bumped her.

After brushing his teeth and washing his face, he stared into the mirror, making sure his haircut was fresh to death and his gear was tight.

On his way to the bus stop, he spotted Trapp and Shi. Trapp was his neighbor and had also been his best friend since they were in first grade. Trapp was the biggest one in their clique and a straight lunatic.

Shi had come to the school when they were all in third grade, and they had all been close since. People loved Shi because he was very laid-back, cool, and had mad swag.

"What's up, my niggas? It's our time to shine once again. CMB, you already know!" He gave them both dap while checking out their gear.

"You already know, CMB!" Trapp embraced him, showing thug love. "And, nigga, it's always about us." Shi nodded his head, agreeing with Trapp.

"Tru dat. That's love, fam." Cane felt the love Trapp had for him, and that was why he was his best friend. "And, I must say, y'all niggas are fly as hell."

"Shit, nigga, look at you, always shining like a star!" Shi said, speaking up for the first time. "Damn, I wish my uncle was as cool as Jack. He always shows love for his nephew."

"Hell, a nigga that has dope foreign whips, an exotic house, custom-made jewelry, and is caked the fuck up, he's supposed to show love every chance he gets," Trapp said as his eyes drifted when he saw Kasha walking out the door, sporting a white body dress that was hugging her hips. "Look who's coming," he said.

Seeing Kasha's beautiful face made his heart skip two beats. He tried to block Trapp's lustful-minded ass out, but it was hard. Cane couldn't help but notice her thickness and how her long hair looked like silk hanging down her back. She still reminded him of his favorite R&B artist, Mya. He was so caught up into her beauty he didn't notice that she was heading for a car until she got to it, and Ricky opened the door for her.

Trapp, thinking that Cane was hating on the fact that she was getting into the car with Ricky, which he was, said, "Fuck dat nigga, and fuck her trifling ass. She knows she's wrong for having them west side niggas over in our hood. And for Kasha to be fucking wit' that fake-ass, Brazilian-looking gorilla motherfucker tells what she's all about." Trapp balled up his fist, mad and ready to kick some ass. "Don't even sweat that nigga with his raggedy-ass car," Trapp said, seeing the pain in Cane's eyes.

"Don't sweat that bitch, bruh," Shi said, tuning in. "There are plenty of fresher fish in the sea."

"I'm not sweating either of them. Shit, like you said, there's plenty of fish in the sea." He said it as if he weren't sweating it, but in reality, he was heated as hell! Everything in him wanted to throw a brick through Ricky's windshield or, better yet, at their heads since he tried to show off and drop the top in front of them. But he couldn't let his boys see him angry over a female, so instead, he said, "It's time to go fishing, fellas."

The bus finally pulled up, and they all hopped on, walking to the back. He sat where he always sat, which was next to his partner, Calvin. "What's up, my dude?"

"Just another year of being a pimp, player. You know how we do."

"Hell yeah. Once again, it's our year to shine," he said as his mind quickly drifted back to Kasha. He looked out the window, thinking about how much he was still in love with her. He didn't hear Calvin calling his name until he felt a tap on his shoulder.

"Yo, man, snap out of it. Don't let that trifling trick get the best of you. That shit was fucked up though, my nigga. We will ride on that nigga, Ricky, in due time."

Calvin wrapped his arms around Cane's neck. "Shit, nigga, you built this shit. CMB. We all we've got. You can't fall weak on a nigga now."

"Nigga, we all we got!" He felt rejuvenated, realizing his clique looked up to him as their leader.

As soon as the bus pulled into the parking lot, everyone shouted out, "It's on and popping." They were dressed to impress, looking like a million dollars but broke as a joke. After picking up their schedules, Cane looked over it, seeing that he had first period with Calvin, second period and third period with Trapp, and last period with Shi. For the first time in forever, he was pleased with his schedule because he had one or more of his clique in every class.

The first period bell rang, so he and Calvin made their way to the gym. As always, all eyes were on them as they entered. Cane was very low-key and never cared for all of the attention that they received, but Calvin lived for it. Everyone respected CMB and wanted to be affiliated with them.

He caught a glimpse of Ray-Ray giving him an evil eye and instantly felt hatred in the atmosphere. He hated Ray-Ray and his clique, Poison Clan, with a passion. They were CMB's archenemies from the west side.

"Hey, Cane!" Tina yelled out, taking his attention away from Ray-Ray.

"What's up, sis?" he said, checking out how fly she was looking. He was going to have to protect her from these vultures here at Southside because, like her sister, Kasha, she was thick and cute as hell.

She smiled at him as she asked, "You all right?" as she nudged his arm as if to say, "Get your mind right."

"Oh, yeah, my bad. I'm good, just doing a little people watching." He felt embarrassed that she had caught him doing what he had vowed to never do again—wear his hatred on his shoulder.

"I'm not going to hold you up. I just wanted to speak to you," she said, giving him a hug before she and Tonya walked off to head to class.

"Damn, nigga, that's Kasha's little sister? She's cute as hell, but I know she ain't fucking," Calvin asked, nearly slobbering all over himself. "But who is her friend? Shawty's fine as hell. You gotta hook a nigga up."

"I'll see what I can do for you." Cane chuckled, glad that his attention was away from Kasha.

The whistle blew, getting everyone's attention. Cane was hoping that he got the fine-ass Ms. Williams as his gym teacher. She reminded him so much of Jada Pinkett Smith. Tina and Tonya's names were called by Coach Taylor. He crossed his fingers. When Coach Williams called Calvin's name, he thought, *please call me!* He kept hope alive until he heard Coach Eddie's voice. He uncrossed his fingers in disbelief.

He thought about what happened last year in the gym. Calvin's team was playing against Ray-Ray and his clique. Calvin was dropping them off, talking shit at the same time. Eventually, Ray-Ray got pissed because everybody was clowning his clique's ball skills. He intentionally fouled Calvin hard while he was up in the air taking a shot, knocking him out of the air. When Calvin hit the ground, members from Poison Clan started stomping the shit out of him. Cane came to the rescue with a bat in his hands, playing baseball with their bodies to get them off of Calvin. Coach Eddie had a hard time breaking up the fight, which ended in a week of suspension for all involved except for Calvin because Calvin did not have time to fight back. They were all on him before he knew what had happened.

Cane walked past Coach Eddie and smiled, reading his mind. "I can see the look in your eyes. Trust me, I'm not going to give you any trouble this year."

"I hope not, son, because you have unique talent in football and track and field that needs to be utilized and not go to waste. Son, you can be the next Deion Sanders, Carl Lewis, or Michael Johnson as long as you don't let Calvin Brown ruin your life. He's bad company. I advise you to stay away from him."

He walked off, blocking out Coach Eddie's words. He wasn't going to let Coach or anyone come between him and his clique. He heard a familiar voice yelling out, "Y'all CMB boys still got this shit on lockdown."

He turned around. There stood his homegirl, Shelia. He had not seen her all summer. Giving her a big hug, he said, "Fo'sho. Where you hide all summer?" She was looking as good as ever, and he didn't want to release her. He stepped back, looking into her dark brown eyes, checking out her beautiful features. She had always been just super cool, a homegirl since elementary school. She had never been anyone he would holler at, but once they got to high school, she blossomed. She was a real live showstopper.

"I worked all summer, so I didn't have time to hang out. Then, I went to visit with my gramps, but I hear that you had an eventful summer," she said knowingly.

"I bet you did. Word travels fast, but it's all good, payback is a mutha—"

She cut him off. "I already know where this is going. Don't let Kasha bring you down. The best thing that you can do is to let her go on and fuck with that no-good-ass nigga, Ricky." She shook her head in disgust. "Ricky will never be the man that you were to her. If him buying her shit is what makes her happy, then believe me, she is just a gold digger, and either way, you win. Ricky is sure not the one that's going to just be cuddled up, hanging out with her ass. Ricky is just an opportunist. Go for any opportunity to lay the next best-looking thing walking and then on to the next. It's her loss. Well, let me get to class. I will holler at you at lunch. I had to come show you some love, got all these fresh meat hoochies talking about how handsome you are. Be careful, boy, and control those hormones," she teased as she started to strut away.

His heart was racing. Her words took away his breath. He merely choked up. "Quit playing with me. You know that you are trying to make a nigga feel good, but it's not going to work," he hollered after he watched how good her ass looked in those jeans.

"Boy, I'd love to be in those jeans," he said, mimicking R. Kelly to himself. He would never say it to Shelia because he had too much respect for her.

"Well, from the way you are smiling, my job is done," she said, looking back, catching his eyes on her ass and giving him a sly smirk as she continued on to class.

"Hell yeah, you are doing a phenomenal job!" She was doing something to him at this moment. He was just confused on how he could ever approach his homegirl in any other way than just being his homegirl. He had shared so many things with Shelia that, hell, she might not want to fuck with him anyway. She knew how he operated, and she would run at the first hint of bullshit. He would have to come totally correct if he wanted her at all.

He went on to class but could not take his mind off of Shelia and how good she was looking. This was nothing new because she had been looking great for the past few years, but today, everything in him was saying, "You've got to have her!"

After class, he made his way in the direction that he had seen her going so that he could pretend to accidently bump into her. When he saw her, he snuck up behind her and picked her up really quick as she screamed out because she was caught off guard. When he put her down and she saw that it was him, she started laughing as she hit his chest and hugged him.

While they were hugging, she whispered into his ear, "We can't be hugging in public like this. Crazy folks will start rumors fast as hell, saying we fuck around." He was caught up in the moment. His chest was pressed against hers. He tightened up his grip to let her know that he didn't care what anyone said.

"All right now, sexual chocolate. Calm down, big boy." She backed away. "How does it feel to hug a real woman?"

"If I tell you, I might have to kill you because you may start feeling yourself," he laughed, still scoping her out from head to toe.

"Well, I don't want you to kill me." She chuckled as she patted his face. "Because you won't look so fly in prison. But on the real tip, you are a sweet person with a good heart. I know you are my boy and I am your girl.

but all bullshit aside, I would love to be your girl, but our friendship is more important, and I would not want to mess that up for nothing in the world."

Well, damn! he thought. She had just made what he thought was going to be a hard task very easy. *Don't let me find out she's been feening for me all of this time as well, and we've been wasting time bullshitting.*

Cane listened as she continued. "And to see that Kasha hurt you makes me sick to my stomach. But like I said, you can have anybody you want. You see them pretty little ladies over there already checking you out, and don't forget what stands before you," she said shyly.

He was thinking, *ain't no need in your ass acting shy now. You done already put it out there.*

Cane looked into the direction Shelia had nodded. He shook his head. "Auh, that's Tina and Tonya. Tina is Kasha's baby sister and cool as fuck. Even though me and Kasha don't kick it, Tina will always be my li'l sister."

"Oh, word? That's what's up, but on some real shit, that's cool and all that you see her as a little sister, but I've watched her watch you. Be careful because someone may just have a little crush," Shelia said, lifting her eyebrows.

"Naw, it's not like that," he said, playfully smacking Shelia softly on the face. "Tina is just a cool chick. She reminds me a lot of you. And as quiet as it's kept, although her and Kasha really don't get along, that's still her sister. She nor I would ever cross that line," he said to assure her.

"If you say so, but think about what I said. I will holler at you later. Let me go holler at Calvin and see if he has this paper before class starts." She reached up and kissed his cheek.

Chapter 4

Tina (1998)

She had her eyes glued on Cane, wondering who the beautiful female was who was smothering him. Her heart started racing when he began to walk in her direction. "Ah, shoot, here he comes with his sexy ass. That's going to be my man one day!"

"Girl, please. That fool is still in love with your sister. Besides, he's like a legend around here. He doesn't want your wet-behind-the-ears ass." Tonya laughed out, thinking Tina had lost her everlasting mind.

"Shut up, fool." Tina laughed, not paying Tonya any mind. She knew that Cane was going to be her man one day—maybe not today, but one day. She had seen the way that he looked at her, and she was going to be the queen who sat on his throne. Her sister proved to her, by leaving him for that lame-ass Ricky simply because Ricky had a car and money, that she was as stupid as Tina had always thought her to be. Ricky would never have the swag that Cane had, no matter how much he tried. That was some shit you just had to be born with. As he got closer, she felt a sensation travel through her entire body, a sensation she had never felt before.

"Ladies, what's up?"

"Hey, Cane!" Tina spoke up first, followed by Tonya. "What's up, Mr. CMB himself? I knew you were a legend in the hood but had no idea you had all these groupies in the school on your jock as well," Tina teased.

"Whatever, girl, stop playing," he said, unable to contain a bashful smile. "But on the real, my boy Calvin wants to holler—"

Tina cut him off. "Uhm, tell your boy I have a boyfriend," Tina said, not wanting to talk to his boy and lose her future chances of hooking up with him.

Cane looked at her like she was crazy and said, "Since when?"

"You know I don't, but I am not interested in your boy, so tell him that I have a boyfriend." Tina laughed.

"Well, great because it's not you he wants to hook up with. He wants to meet Tonya."

"Really? What in the hell is wrong with me?" Tina asked with an attitude.

"Nothing is wrong with you. I just told him that you had a boyfriend," Cane laughed.

"Why would you do that?" Tina asked.

"Because he is too advanced for your ass. You ain't ready," Cane said playfully.

"Whatever, nigga," Tina laughed, relieved.

"Doesn't he mess around with Meka?" Tonya asked.

"Look, you've got to ask him the fifty questions. I'm just the messenger," Cane said.

"Well, since you are so good at carrying messages, go and ask him why he didn't come ask me himself. He's scared or something?"

"Nah, that nigga ain't scared. He just didn't want to come on too hard and scare you off."

"Wow, did he tell you that?" Tonya said, writing down her number and giving it to Cane.

"Fifty questions," Cane said, smiling as he walked off, heading toward Calvin.

"Don't even say it, girl." Tonya was showing all her pearly whites.

"Say what?" Tina said, patting her on her back. "That you're trying to play hard to get? Girl, you already know you are soft as cotton. You see how fast you wrote that number down."

"You're so stupid!" Tonya said, giggling. "But Calvin is a cutie pie. I pray that he calls me."

Tina knew that Tonya didn't have to worry about Calvin calling. All summer long, all she heard was Kasha talking about CMB, and out of all the guys in the crew, Kasha couldn't stand Calvin. She said that he was a player.

"Don't worry. He will call you, trust me. You're fresh meat," she said, sucking her teeth.

"I smell hateration in the air. Don't hate me, hate the game. You get rid of that good girl image, buttoning your damn shirts all the way to the top, and maybe you can pull someone."

She's sounding more and more like Kasha, Tina thought, brushing Tonya's arrogant comment off.

They were walking to their next period class, which happened to be across the hall from each other, when they felt fingers tap their shoulders.

"Yo, do y'all shorties have a nigga? If not, me and my man would like to get them digits."

"Nah, we're both single." Tonya spoke up, trying to keep a straight face because Tina was looking at the guy as if he were an alien. Tina really needed to loosen up. She was a beautiful girl, but she always kept this no-nonsense expression on her face, and it made guys intimidated to approach her at times. Tonya gave the guy her number and then looked at Tina and pressed her lips together, raising her eyebrows as if to say, "Okay, you're up next."

Tina sucked her teeth and said, "Can I at least get a name before you come asking for my number?"

"My bad, shorty. I'm Raymond, but everybody calls me Ray-Ray for short, and this is my cousin, Chris."

"Nice to meet you, Chris and Raymond," Tina said, extending her hand.

"It's Ray-Ray," Raymond said, shaking her hand.

"I like Raymond," Tina said. "Ray-Ray sounds like the man selling CDs at the corner store or stealing lawn mowers." They all shared a laugh.

"Oh, she's going to be a piece of work, I see," said Chris. "But I'm up for the challenge," he said, rubbing his chin while looking Tina up and down seductively, as if he wanted her himself.

"Yeah, we will see about that," Tina said as she wrote her number down. "But just so you know, come correct or don't come at all," she said matter-of-factly.

"I gotcha, baby girl," Chris said, taking the number and kissing the paper before putting it into his pocket.

As soon as they walked off, Tonya bragged about being on a roll. Tina was still feeling some type of way with Tonya and the stunt she pulled. She couldn't care less about Chris and Ray-Ray. As far as she was concerned, there was only one man in this school for her—Cane. A few guys walked by, making hissing sounds. One guy even labeled them as Beyoncé and Monica. They both laughed.

The second period warning bell rang, so she hugged Tonya goodbye and then went to her math class. Mr. Robinson had already started roll call, so she sat in the nearest seat, listening for her name. When she heard Chris Bacon's name called, she prayed it wasn't the same pickle-faced Chris she had given her number to earlier. Mr. Robinson walked past her desk, stopping inches away from her. He was so close she could smell the Polo Sport cologne he wore.

"Mr. Bacon, I hope that you pass my class this year," he said as he wiped sweat away from his forehead. "Because I don't want to see you in my classroom again next year," he said to Chris and then proceeded to do his roll call.

Chris, unbothered by Mr. Robinson calling him out, leaned up to Tina and said, "I'm glad that we have class together so we can get better acquainted."

When he rubbed her back, she wanted to scream out, "If you don't get your nasty, rusty, crusty hands off of me . . ." But she didn't have to say anything because Mr. Robinson took three steps back and asked if he was bothering her.

As soon as the bell rang, she hopped up, feeling relieved to get away from Chris's annoying ass. She wasn't paying any attention when she bumped into Tonya. *Good thing it's Tonya.* She didn't want any beef with anyone. Tonya gave her the rundown on Ray-Ray and his beef with Cane. Tina tried to take in as much information as she could. She kept looking over her shoulders for Chris.

"Girl, I don't know what we got ourselves into. That nigga, Chris, is a bag of rocks! I can't believe I let you convince me to give him my number."

Tonya burst out laughing. "Heifer, don't blame me for your mishaps. You did that of your own will."

"By the look you gave me, you might as well have told me to."

"Well, that's on you, boo-boo. Just think of something so he won't call you."

"So, what do you think about Calvin?" Tina asked, changing the subject.

"Word is he doesn't talk to Meka anymore." Tonya giggled. "And I think he's a lot cuter than Ray-Ray, but I don't know. I might like them both," she said, holding her forefinger to her lips to tell Tina to keep it quiet.

"Just don't get caught slipping! And I'm not hating on you either," Tina added, smiling because she could tell by the expression that Tonya had made that she was about to accuse Tina of hating on her. "But if you don't want Ray-Ray, don't play with his feelings either," she said, thinking of how Kasha had played Cane for Ricky. Tina hoped that Tonya didn't take the same route Kasha had taken because karma was hell to pay. Tina's thoughts were interrupted by the same girl who was all up in Cane's face.

"Excuse me, I hate to bother you," the girl was saying.

Oh, Lord, here comes the drama, Tina thought. She didn't have time for any drama, and she certainly didn't want to break a nail. She looked at the girl with an attitude.

"I'm Shelia. I just wanted to introduce myself because Cane told me that you were Kasha's baby sister. You look just like your sister. Cane speaks very highly of you. Anyway, whoever is cool with Cane is cool with me, and if you need me, I've got your back."

"Thank you," Tina said, shaking Shelia's hand. "Oh, this is Tonya, my bestie."

Shelia extended her hand to Tonya and said, "Hi, I've seen you around, but nice to meet you. Well, I'm not going to hold y'all up. Just remember one thing: stay sucker and crab free, and last but not least, please stay away from these no-good-ass niggas around here. The majority of them are not hitting on shit," Shelia said as she walked off to meet up with her friends, who had been standing there, waiting.

"She seems nice enough," Tina said to Tonya.

"Yeah, she's pretty cool, but her girlfriends are a lot of drama. I had an encounter with one of them last year, but Shelia never seems to be in their drama. She is a lot more mature than they are. She is more like the mother goat," she laughed.

Chapter 5

Calvin

Damn, word travels fast! Calvin thought as he listened as Meka drilled him about Tonya. She had him by his collar, stretching the hell out of his new Polo shirt.

"Don't believe everything you hear. You know how these trifling hoes around here are always trying to break up a good thing. Stop being so damn insecure!"

"Well, you stop giving me a reason to feel insecure! I am not going to put up with the bullshit with you this year. If you want one of these bitches, just say the word because I am not trying to be a fucking leech, and I mean that shit!"

"You know this school is filled with nothing but hating-ass bitches. You gotta stop feeding into everything you hear. And let go of my damn collar before your ass be kicking out sixty-five bucks!"

She released him, seeing that he was really mad. Seeing the water that was filling her eyes, he pulled her to him and gave her a kiss. "Baby, you do know that I love you, right?"

"I want to believe," she started, but he shushed her.

"I don't want to hear about what you want to believe. I am only interested in what you know. Do you or do you not know that I love you?" he asked again.

Meka nodded her head yes. She placed her hands on his chest. "I'm sorry, boo. Please forgive me for not trusting you." She kissed the side of his face. "Baby, I swear I won't let these sluts come between us again. It's the first week of school, and they have already started trying to bring nonsense. I love you."

"Yelp! Well, let's get to class. We don't need to be late. Love you, girl," he said as he gripped her tight ass as they separated.

He knew that he had better tighten up his game because, here it was, the first day of school, and he already had to defend himself. These motormouth girls in this school couldn't wait to carry news. He spread his hands across his face, reminiscing about his first run-in with Meka.

Last year, in English class, he was leaning back in his chair with his mind on what the coach had just told him about him not being eligible to play ball until he got his grades right. He needed a tutor, and Meka volunteered since he was popular and cliqued up with CMB. She was from the west side, so they met on neutral grounds—the county library. They were isolated in the video room, watching a film on William Shakespeare. Meka had on a short miniskirt, which had his full attention. Midway through the film, he had placed his hands on her thighs. He felt his stomach do somersaults while rubbing up and down her thighs. Meka pushed his hands farther up between her legs. He felt the moistness seeping through her panties. He worked his fingers around her panties and into her slit. Her body tensed, but she didn't stop him from finger fucking her. Her moans had his manhood on a rise as she slid her fingers down his pants, stroking his tool up and down. The twisting from the doorknob distracted them, but from that day forward, he knew he had to have her. It did not scare him that she was the aggressor. There was something about Meka that told him that she was just a woman who knew what she wanted, and he liked it and the fact that she wanted him.

When he got into class, he sat in the rear of the room, still thinking about all that he and Meka had gone through. They had some great times and some not-so-great times. He had done a lot of things to hurt her but not because he didn't love her. He was just a nice-looking, young boy who had women coming at him from everywhere. Although, he went after most of them first. However, Meka hadn't been a saint either during the course of their relationship. Her motto was, "If you can play, so can I!" Calvin had been with plenty of women, but Meka had him pussy whipped, and her "take no prisoners" attitude had his nose wide open. She had been rumored to have been messing around with this guy named Chris who seemed to want to fuck everybody he knew Calvin was fucking, so he and Calvin had beef.

Last summer, Calvin was at home, horny as hell, and although he never went to the west side where Meka lived without an entourage, because he beefed with the majority of those west side niggas, his hormones got the best of him. He pulled out his bike and rode over to her house. He knew he was playing a dangerous game by being on the west side alone. When he got close to Meka's house, he saw that nigga, Chris, walking out. Not wanting to be seen by Chris, he slowed down and waited until Chris had gone up the street before he proceeded to her house. Not that he was scared of Chris, because he would beat the shit out of him, but he knew that Chris would come back with the rest of his posse, and he would be outnumbered.

"What was Chris doing here?"

"He was here seeing my brother," she said as she lifted herself up to reach his lips.

"Your brother? Ain't your brother like thirty?"

"Yes, but he looks up to my brother for some reason, and they are always talking about sports and stuff," she said, leading him to her bedroom to get what he had risked his life to come and get.

"So, your brother is here, and you're taking me to your bedroom?" he whispered.

"No, he just left out the back door to go to work. You know he keeps his car parked in the backyard, trying to hide from his women."

She had his mind so twisted, and eyes blinded by her sex, that all he wanted was to feel her wetness on his tool. He didn't question the fact that he didn't see a car leave out of the driveway as he walked around to the back to enter the house.

Once he relieved his pressure, he quickly got dressed and left because he knew he did not want to be caught in this area, especially at night. As he came from around Meka's house, and was riding out of the driveway on his bike, he saw Ray-Ray and his clique sitting on the porch next door, smoking and drinking. They locked eyes and all froze for a second before they all realized what needed to be done. Calvin jumped off his bike and ran back to Meka's house, straight through the back door. Ray-Ray and his crew approached the door just as he was slamming it shut and locking it. They were beating and kicking on the door, trying to get in.

"Y'all better get away from my house!" Meka screamed. "I am about to call the police. What the fuck y'all think this is?" Meka was heated.

"Tell that pussy-ass nigga to man up and come outside then," someone hollered.

"Only a fool would do that knowing y'all are going to gang them. Get off my fucking porch before my mom or the police get here!" Meka screamed at them. She was

not scared of them because they knew not to fuck with her, but they didn't give a damn about Calvin.

Calvin called Cane and was telling him what had just gone down. "Man, get your uncle and y'all come and get me."

"Man, you're a stupid-ass nigga! Thought you weren't fucking with that trick no more." Cane was upset that he was on the west side by himself and especially over at Meka's house, whom he hated with a passion.

"Man, I'll explain later. Y'all mo'fos just come on before her mom gets here," he said, knowing he had no intentions of explaining why he was at Meka's.

About twenty minutes later, Jack's mint green Lexus LX 470 pulled up at Meka's house. He knew he could always count on Cane and his uncle Jack, who was just eight years older than them, to have his back. He ran and hopped into the back seat of Jack's car. He hadn't even closed the door well, and Jack was already giving him hell for being over at Meka's house alone. Cane didn't make it any better by accusing him of being pussy whipped by a trifling-ass broad. "Man, you know she's sneaking around with that damn Chris behind your back. You saw a damn text where he said he needed to feel her. How much more evidence do you need? What, you need to actually see him on top of her before you believe it?" boomed Cane.

There was no way that Calvin would ever tell them that he caught Chris coming out of her house today. He thought that he didn't know what he was really doing there, but one thing he did know was that the pussy was tight and wet as hell for him, so either Chris wasn't packing shit like he bragged to be, or she was not sleeping with him. Fuck that shit Cane was talking.

Jack pulled right up to Ray-Ray's house. They didn't know who it was in the Lexus sitting on chrome. Ray-

Ray got up and walked toward the SUV, thinking it was one of the girls he fooled around with named Charlotte in her dad's car. It didn't dawn on him that this SUV was more mint green than her dad's money green one until it was too late. Chris and Timbo were still on the porch.

"Damn fools," Jack said, shaking his head as Ray-Ray got closer to the car. Jack rolled down the window and grabbed Ray-Ray by the collar, pulling his head into the car and sticking his Sig P226 9 mm down his throat, and he said, "If you or any of your goons call yourself lynching my people, you will pay with your life. If you fight, you better make sure it's one-on-one 'cause you don't want these problems."

Ray-Ray pissed on himself. Calvin watched as his bitch ass stood there, crying in front of his boys. Calvin knew that Jack was straight gangsta, but from that day forward, Calvin had the upmost respect for Jack.

The warning bell rang, pulling him out of his thoughts as he rushed down the hall so as not to be late for his next class. As he was turning the corner, he thought his eyes were playing tricks when he saw Meka and Chris walking together. He was ready to flip the fuck out, but he kept his cool and walked into class.

What he had just witnessed had him fucked up. Meka knew how he felt about that nigga, and she was supposed to be his girl. Everyone in the school knew that the two of them had beef, so for her to be openly in the hallway walking with him made Calvin look like the fool. As good as the pussy was, he knew that it was time to let her go. Cane and the other guys already gave him a hard time about Meka. Yep, it was time to move on. His mind quickly went to the fresh number that he had just gotten this morning. The best way for him to get over one piece of meat was by replacing it with another. Tonya was fresh, sexy, and seemed cool as hell. She didn't seem anything like Meka. Just the thought of Tonya made him feel good because he was digging her sexy, petite body. He took a deep breath. "I hope your head is on straight and level and your personality is as fine as your body," he spoke to himself about Tonya.

"What's up, Calvin?" Kim said, catching him off guard and bringing him from his thoughts of replacing Meka.

"What's up, Kim?" He smiled at Meka's so-called best friend, who he was fucking on the side. He saw her lustful look and knew she wanted a piece of him, but he knew he had to cut her ass off before he got himself caught up in more of a shitty situation. If he was going to break it off with Meka once and for all, he knew that meant breaking it off with Kim as well because he didn't want her thinking that she was going to be moving in as the replacement.

"We need to talk when you get a minute. A lot of bullshit is going on, and I need to make sure we are on the same page about some things."

"What's wrong?" Kim asked, alarmed.

"People talking, and you know how the rumor mill flows around here with the he-say-she-say bullshit."

"And?" she asked, not understanding exactly where he was going with this.

"Well, I heard that someone was trying to put a bug in Meka's ear that you and I are fucking," he said, lying. "I think we need to chill out for a minute until this shit dies down."

"What? Meka hadn't asked me nor mentioned anything about that to me," Kim stated nervously.

"Because she was sworn to secrecy. Supposedly, she is just supposed to be watching to see for herself is what I was told. So, just to keep the bullshit down, we are going to have to chill."

"If she calls herself my friend and can't be woman enough to come and talk to me about what she heard, then I say fuck Meka. And let her watch. I am always two steps ahead of her silly ass. And that trick doesn't deserve you anyway. Everything about her is phony and fake, and she's fu . . ." Kim cut herself off, realizing all eyes were on her.

"She's what?" He wanted to know what she was talking about. "Don't stop now!" He saw Timbo eyeing him. he wanted to walk over and slap his silly ass. "Are you going to tell me or what?"

"Only if you promise not to cut me off. I am in love with you, and truth be told, I need you right now." She wanted him in any way possible. "We can go to the bathroom now if you want to! I'll tell you everything."

Chapter 6

Calvin

He was lying in bed, chilling and watching "Project Pat" on BET's *Rap City* with The Basement freestyling in the booth with Big Tigger when the ringing phone got his attention.

"What's up, my nigga?" he said after reading the caller ID, seeing it was Cane.

"Shit, you!" Cane replied, laughing. "Man, your name was everywhere today. School hasn't even taken in good yet, and your ass is already getting caught up in shit. Them bitches was all over your dick, but anyway, have you talked to Tonya yet?"

"Man, go to hell," Calvin laughed. "Naw, I'll give her a call later after I clear my fucking mind. There's so much bullshit going on with Meka. Shit about to make a nigga's head spin off."

"You're the one that chose to deal with Meka and all the shit that comes with her."

"Man, it's just that I needed grounds for breaking it off with her, but she always seems to come out clean as a whistle."

Cane listened as Calvin made excuses for why he stayed with Meka as he ranted about wanting to leave her. Cane hated to be the one to drop the news on Calvin, but he knew that he had no choice. Calvin was his boy, and he needed to know that Meka was foul.

"I know you are really feeling Meka, but Meka is not what you need. Word in school today was that the entire Poison Clan banged her and Kim this summer. And, dude, they say that they were clowning you the entire time it was going on, saying shit like, 'Tell that nigga Calvin that next time he wants some, this is Poison Clans' pussy.' And they say that she and Chris have been fucking all summer."

The phone went quiet. Cane knew that Calvin was still there because he could hear him breathing. He didn't know what to say to his boy because he knew this was a hard pill to swallow. So what if Meka had been drunk when it happened? That was no excuse. She shouldn't have been fucking with them niggas anyway as Calvin had asked her so many times not to do because of their beef.

"Man, I know this must be killing you, but you've got to get over her. She is making you look like a fool, dude, on the real."

Calvin slung the remote control, sending it crashing against the wall. He threw it with so much force that it broke up into pieces and made a noise so loud that his grandmother came running into the room with his cousin in tow.

"What the fuck is wrong with you?" his grandmother screamed.

She stood in the door, just looking at him, waiting on an answer that was not about to come. She saw that his temper was on the rise, and he was almost at the point of no return.

"What is wrong with you, boy?" she demanded again.

"Nothing!" Calvin replied.

"Don't tell me nothing when you're in here throwing shit against the wall and breaking up shit."

"Just leave me alone for a minute, please!"

"Oh, hell no. You don't tell me to leave you alone for a minute while you break up my shit. Give me that damn phone," his feisty grandma demanded.

"Okay, I'm sorry. Let me wrap this up real quick. Is that okay?"

His grandma just looked at him with questioning eyes, but she said, "Hurry up because I need to call in my prescription before the pharmacy closes," as she pulled the door shut, still looking at him suspiciously.

"Look, man, because this is coming from you, I have to believe it to be true because you are my boy and we look out for one another. But this shit hurts me to my heart. I ain't even going to front. But I know I have to let that bitch go, so good looking out. Fuck Meka. I've been fucking Kim anyway."

"Yeah, I knew there was some chemistry going on between you two, but I had no idea that she would actually fuck with you, knowing you were with her best friend. She really is a trifling-ass ho."

"Man, you don't know the half of it," Calvin said.

"Well, you now have your grounds to let Meka go once and for all, so get your shit together and stop messing with these trifling-ass hoes. Get you a decent girl next time because I'm tired of always being the bearer of bad news because you make the wrong decisions for your dick," Cane teased.

"Man, fuck you." Calvin tried to laugh it off, but his heart was pierced. Although he knew that he had to let Meka go, his heart was still heavy. He had let her into a place that he never should have because he knew that she was shiesty when he first started messing with her, but as months went by, she seemed more and more into him, and he had let his guard down. That was all water under the bridge now—a bridge that he was determined to burn because his ass surely wouldn't be swimming back across because he couldn't swim.

"Man, don't let her bring you down," Cane said as if he had been reading his mind. "You can try to bring the gutter bitch to the throne, but sometimes, that gutter had them too drenched to sit up high, and they have to go back to where they are comfortable. So, let that bitch stay in the drenches and find you a woman fitting for the throne. Hey, have you reached out to Tonya yet?" he asked again.

"Nah, not yet. I can't play myself to be desperate, you know. Give it a few days before I pounce on her."

"Man, you know her and Tina are besties, so don't fuck up. I don't need to be caught up in your bullshit," Cane said, having second thoughts about giving Calvin Tonya's number.

"Cane, I need to use the phone," his grandma said as she interrupted their conversation. Calvin was glad he didn't have to go through sharing the phone with anyone, since he had his own line. "I need it now!" his grandmother said two minutes later after picking up the phone again.

"All right," Cane shouted, "Yo, let me hit you back later."

Once Calvin hung up the phone, he called Kim and got straight to the point with her, holding nothing back. He was tired of her and her games. She was trying to explain the drunken state they were in when all of that bullshit happened, but it didn't even matter to Calvin at this point. He was angry that Kim and Meka would play themselves and let the entire Poison Clan do that to them. He was even more angry that they had him being the laughingstock around town because everyone knew that Meka was his girl, yet she had been fucked by the entire crew. Now, it made sense to him as to why everybody was looking at him sideways. The joke was on him.

Pain aching from his heart sent shockwaves throughout his body. "I'm done with you. There won't be any 'let this rumor mill blow over.' I expected more from you than for you to let a damn army have their way with you. I can't forgive you for that shit."

"Calvin, I am so sorry, baby. I swear it was not to humiliate you. Hell, no one even knew that you and I were sleeping together. We were drunk, and I was so embarrassed the next day when I realized what had happened. They swore nothing would be said and that we would take it to our graves with us," she cried as if that made it right.

Disgusted, he hung up the phone and started master planning how he was going to get revenge on Meka's ass and yet save his own face. He put the broken remote back together, hoping the television would help uncloud his mind.

His mind drifted to Tonya. *Damn, she is fine and sexy as hell. Yeah, I need a woman of her caliber. Tonya would be the perfect candidate to take Meka's place.* Ignoring his "at least three days" rule, he dialed her number.

"Hello?" she asked into the receiver with a voice that was so sexy he felt his manhood stiffen.

"Hey, Tonya. This is Cane's homeboy, Calvin."

"Hey. What's up with you?"

"Nothing much. Just hoping to get to know you," he said, not beating around the bush.

"Oh, is that so?" she asked.

"Yeah, it's so. You have a problem with me getting to know you better or something?" he asked, joking with her.

"Nah, I don't have any problems. I'm single, but you, on the other hand, have your hands full from what I hear," she said sarcastically.

"No, no, no, I don't know where you're getting your news from because I am single too."

"Oh, really!" she blurted out, thinking he was full of shit. "Look, Calvin, your chances with me would have been better if you had left all of the lies and bullshit at the door before you called me. I know you are dating Meka. Hell, I saw you with her today even."

"I'm telling you the truth. I don't rock with Meka no more. As of today, it's a wrap with her. She is not the girl for me."

"Oh, really? What happened? This morning, you two seemed all in love."

"You happened," he said, messing with her. "Ever since I laid eyes on you, I knew I had to have you."

"Spare me with the bullshit," she laughed. "I may be a freshman, but believe me, I am not stupid or wet behind the ears. I may have been born at night, but it was not last night. I know your kind."

"Believe me, I am not trying to play you to be wet behind the ears. I am a lot smoother than those lame lines I just spit on you. I was just trying to make you laugh, and it worked. Real shit, I am feeling you, no games."

"I'm sure that you were really feeling Meka at one point, so what is this to you? A game where you get what you want and kick it with them until the next piece comes along that you want to feel?" she asked.

"Nah, man, Meka did some foul shit that I can't forgive her for. I've been kicking it with her for over a year now, so do you think that I haven't seen anyone that looks better than her in a year? If I flow with you, I roll with you. I'm not the cat you make me out to be."

"Well, I've heard differently. And if you and Meka were kicking it for so long, what could have possibly happened between me seeing you two all lovey-dovey this morning to now breaking up before the end of the school day?"

"Man, I found out today that, over the summer, her and her friend let some dudes run a train on them. I like a freak and all, but that's some slutty shit that I can't deal with." He went on to tell Tonya everything that had been happening with Meka and about all of the things that he had been suspecting. He told her how he felt that she and Ricky were creeping, but he thought it was just the two of them. He never would have thought that she would stoop as low as she did.

"What the hell! Are you serious right now? Who does that?" Tonya asked in shock.

"Apparently, they do," Calvin said, laughing, but in reality, his heart was ready to escape from his chest. He felt sharp needles poking at his heart every time he thought of Meka. He was ready to change the subject. Meka was nothing to him anymore.

"Man, I know that has to hurt you. You don't have to play the big boy like nothing bothers you with me," Tonya said.

"I'm good. I really do feel a lot better since I'm talking about it with you. Thank you for listening. I can feel that you and I are going to have something special one day. I think you are what I need in my life. I like your spirit."

"Really? You barely know me, Calvin."

"I know enough, just by talking to you, to know that you have a good head on your shoulders, and I enjoy talking to you. So, what's the deal?"

"What do you mean?"

"I know as sexy as you are that you gotta peel niggas off of you like a banana." He could hear her giggle through the phone. He knew he was breaking her down, and soon, he would have her where he wanted her, trapped in his spider web.

"I'm more than just a pretty face and nice body, Calvin. Yes, I have a lot of guys coming after me, but they don't have the mind frame to get me. You can't get me just by buying me a kid's meal. you have to challenge my mind.

Yeah, I said it. I'm beauty and brains. A deadly combination," she laughed.

"Word. I like that because I don't like clueless females."

"You were with Meka for over a year, so I beg to differ," she kidded.

"I didn't say that I wouldn't fuck one." They both laughed.

"Calvin, this is Tina beeping in on the other end. Let me call you back after I talk to her. We need to get our assignment done for Mrs. Farmer real quick."

Calvin wasn't used to any female telling him to let them call him back so that they could talk to someone else. He was the one that always ended the conversations.

"Make sure you call me back," he said, not ready to end their conversation.

"I will," she said.

"Don't play with me. Call me back!" he said, losing all of his cool points. She relaxed him and helped keep his mind off of Meka.

"I will." She laughed as she clicked back over.

About two minutes after he had hung up from Tonya, his phone rang. Hoping it was Tonya, he answered in his deep, Barry White voice, real sexy, "Hello."

"Hey, baby!"

When he heard Meka's voice, his entire attitude changed. "Baby?" He forgot that she had yet to get the memo that it was over. "What's up, Meka?" He wanted to sling the phone into the wall.

"What's wrong with you?" she snapped.

"Why don't you tell me what is wrong with me? Start with thinking of the worst thing that could ever get back to me. Something you most likely wanted to take to your grave."

"What in the hell are you talking about? I don't do anything that I'm ashamed of, so entertain me please," she said, having no clue that he knew her darkest secret.

"Oh, so you're not ashamed that everyone is talking about how you and Kim let the entire Poison Clan run a train on y'all asses?" he said coolly.

She was speechless. He continued to blast her ass, calling her every name in the book.

"I'm sorry, Calvin!" she cried out. "I was drunk. I didn't mean to hurt you,"

He cut her off. "Nah, no need for apologies. It's a wrap. You do know that, right? Lose my digits because yours are already lost to me," he said as he hung up the phone and turned off the ringer, just in case she called back. "It's over now." He felt liberated as he sang a new tune.

Chapter 7

Tina

Two Months Later

Tina dug the fact that Calvin seemed to be digging Tonya just as much as she was him. Calvin and Tonya complemented one another well. There was no questioning that Calvin was a street guy, and although Tonya was a good girl, she was what you would call conservative ghetto. She worked on being that good proper and conservative girl, but there was a thin line between all she worked for and who she really was. If you pushed her buttons the wrong way, she would set the bitch off with no questions asked. So, she and Calvin were a perfect fit, and she needed someone who cared for her because her love life had sucked. She always attracted bustas. Tina had originally thought that Calvin was no different from the rest of the bustas, but it had been a few months since he had started seeing Tonya, and so far, he had proven her wrong. He seemed to be all into Tonya, and she certainly was all into his ass. Tina just hoped that Calvin was being sincere because rumor had it that he had a few honeys, and she didn't want to see her friend get hurt. A part of her wanted to warn Tonya to keep her guard up, but she didn't want her to think that she was hating on their relationship. Since she had no concrete evidence and Tonya seemed happy, she decided to keep her thoughts to herself.

"What's up with you and Chris?" Tonya asked.

"Nothing is up with us!" she snapped. "And there will never be anything up with us."

"I just asked a question. You didn't have to get an attitude, trick."

"Who are you calling a trick, trick? You've got me confused with Meka's nasty ass." They both laughed simultaneously. "Chris is more interested in my sister than he is me. Makes me think that he is trying to use me to get her attention."

"Why would you think that?"

"Because anytime we talk, he finds a way to ease Kasha's name into our conversation. I have been feeling him out, just to see what his aim is. I think he is crushing on my sister and using me to get to her. I hate that I even let Chris have my number. Guys are so stupid, always going after the hoes and dogging the good girls. Kasha is not faithful to no one but herself. Hell, she's fooling around with a west side nigga and not just any west side nigga, but a fake, pretty-boy, wannabe motherfucker." Tina was so mad and into her rant that she didn't hear Kasha walk into her room.

"Am I the most interesting person in your and Tonya's little simple lives or something? Don't be jealous of me because I have it going on and you don't," Kasha said.

Tina turned around, shocked and embarrassed that her sister had walked in on her talking about her, but hey, it was what it was. She wasn't lying.

"Bitch, please, you don't have shit going on. Don't let that celebrity look-alike mess that Ricky done put into your head fool your ass!"

Tonya, still on the other end of the phone, burst out laughing. "Girl, you're so hilarious," she said to Tina.

"I'm telling the truth. Like they say, if it walks like a duck, quacks like a duck, nine times out of ten, it is a duck. And this chick here needs to get her quacking butt out of my room," Tina said.

"Make me," Kasha said, standing there with her arms crossed and tapping her foot as if she was waiting.

"Kasha, you are a joke. You further prove what everyone has always said, that the prettier girls are the biggest whores. You go from one guy to another, but you are only playing yourself, and everyone will soon see that you are nothing but a Mya look-alike trick. Everyone gets a turn."

Kasha picked up a bottle of Tina's perfume from her dresser and hurled it at her. "Bitch, I'll kick your little ass!" she said as she went charging at Tina.

Tina stood up and got in a stance, getting ready to wear her butt out if she got too close to her. Tina was not at all scared of Kasha, and every time they had gotten into a fight, she always came out on top, so she didn't understand why Kasha kept trying her.

"Hey, y'all, cut that mess out." Their mother walked into the room just as Tina picked Kasha up and slammed her onto the bed. Tina had gotten on top of Kasha and was mugging her face. Although she had every opportunity to punch her, she could not do it. This was her sister, and she really didn't want to hurt her. Their mother pulled Tina off of Kasha while fussing at them both.

"Y'all in here acting like you ain't got anybody's damn sense. What the hell is wrong with y'all? Kasha, get to your room!"

"She started—" Kasha was trying to say, but their mom stopped her.

"I don't want to hear it," their mom said sternly. "Get out of here, and neither of you come back out of your rooms tonight. I am going to tell your dad when he gets here!"

"But, Mama, she started it!" Kasha's crybaby butt said.

"I don't care who started it, and didn't I tell your ass that I didn't want to hear it? Now, go to your room as I said," their mother demanded, pointing her fingers. Kasha tried to plead her case, but her mother wasn't hearing it. She walked out, mumbling under her breath and slamming her door shut.

As soon as their mother finished her rant and left Tina's room, Tina picked the phone up from the floor and laughed when she heard Tonya saying, "Girl, I know that's your sister, but I swear I wanna slap the taste out of Kasha's mouth sometimes. She thinks everyone is jealous of her slutty ass. She don't want to start no beef with me because I am not the one," Tonya said.

Although Tina was mad at her sister, she still did not like the fact that Tonya was talking about her.

"Look, Tonya, that is my sister, so don't talk about her to me, a'ight?"

"Hell, I ain't said nothing that you ain't said yourself about her," Tonya said defensively.

"Yes, but that is my sister. I can say what I want to about her, but no one else can talk about her to me. You talk about your mom, but would you like for me to talk about your mom to you?"

"You are right, and I am sorry. You know I've got a whole new respect for you. That is your blood, and regardless of what goes on with the two of you, you will always be sisters."

"Well, at this moment, I would trade her ass for a Jack Russell. She makes me sick," Tina said.

"Girl, you're crazy," Tonya laughed.

"Well, let me catch up on some homework before I go to bed. I'll catch up with you tomorrow." Tina hung up the phone and got up and walked into Kasha's room.

"I'm going to call Mama if you don't get out of my room!" Kasha said, looking alarmed.

"I just came to call a truce. I don't want to fight or argue with you," Tina said.

"But you will sit on the phone and talk about me to your friends?"

"Look, Kasha, I am going to be honest with you. I don't like Ricky or none of his friends. They all are bad news. Plus, I don't want you to get caught slipping like Traci and have a child before you finish school." She was hoping to get through Kasha's thick, hard head. "A lot has changed, but you are my big sister, and you are supposed to be the one that I learn from. You are the one that should be setting an example for me, but thank goodness that I can see that the company that you keep is riffraff. You are so much better than those bustas you seek love from," Tina said matter-of-factly.

"First of all, Tina!" Kasha said, getting up from her bed. "You're not supposed to like Ricky. As long as I like him, that's all that matters. Secondly, I'm grown, and I know how to handle mine! And trust, I won't get caught up like Traci. Third, Ricky loves me, and I love him. Fourth and foremost, I know you are still upset about the Cane situation, but you are my sister, and you are supposed to be with me and not against me."

"We may not be on the same page, but I'll never be against you. I've got mad love for you—" Kasha cut her off.

"I can't tell you're not against me. What has Ricky ever done to you besides try and be nice to you and make you like him? Ricky is cool and at least he has time for me. Cane never had time for me. He wanted everything on his time."

"I'll never like him as long as he hangs around with them disrespectful wannabe thugs. You saw yourself before he got you in his fold how he acted. You even had your nose turned up at them at one point. Now, it's all love? Ughh, you need to start thinking. Ricky is a dog, and everyone knows it, including you, so why you want to play yourself like this, I don't know."

"Men will only do you the way you allow them to, and I would never allow him to disrespect me. You should know that. I do think for myself, and I do what makes Kasha happy. Ricky makes me happy, so get over it because he is here to stay. He loves me, and I love him, so fuck what you think, and excuse yourself from my room, please," she said as she turned her back on Tina to go back to her computer.

"That's your problem. Can't nobody tell you anything because you think you know it all and have it all figured out. When this shit comes back and takes a chunk out of your pretty ass, don't say I didn't tell you so!" Tina said as she turned to leave.

Tina walked back to her room, frustrated as hell. She started to call Tonya back, but Tonya was so opinionated, and she didn't need to hear her opinions. She just wanted to vent, so she called Shelia instead. As soon as Shelia answered, she didn't hesitate in telling her about everything that was going on.

She took heed when Shelia told her to stay away from all the Poison Clan members, not fool around with them knuckleheads from school, and wait patiently for "Mr. Do Right" to sweep her off her feet. She said that the only thing that could be done for Kasha at this point, besides keeping her in her prayers, was to let her learn on her own. "You and Kasha have been sheltered for so long. Thank goodness that only one of you is buck wild." Shelia gave her credit for being levelheaded. "I never understood why your parents made you go to private school all of those years, but you were still in the hood, experiencing everything that they all did."

Chapter 8

Kasha

She was admiring herself in the mirror, in awe of her figure. The Baby Phat jeans Ricky had bought her hugged her backside tightly. Although she and Ricky had now been dating for a little over three months, this was going to be their first official date. She was thankful that he came into her life, blessed with his own car and money. Ricky had been buying her things that her parents couldn't afford. Yes, both of her parents were in the home, but they lived paycheck to paycheck, and when they had both girls in the private school, that paycheck didn't even stretch from week to week. Despite how much their father threatened to enroll them back into private school when he got upset with them, they both knew that the extra money was a relief, and it was not going to happen.

Kasha was beside herself with excitement. She was actually going to be in the car alone with Ricky. No Tina and no parents dropping them off as Cane's uncle used to do when they were dating because Cane had no license or a car. She could deal with him not having a car because, after all, they were still in school, and you couldn't expect for everyone's parents to buy them cars, but at least have your license, so you could have access to driving.

She tried to stay put in her room until Ricky got there, but her dad summoned her out. Walking toward the living room, she knew her daddy was going to give her another lecture about this date and Ricky. He never gave her "down the road" when she was dating Cane as much as he did now that she was seeing Ricky, but Cane was a thug too. She did not know what it was about Ricky that everyone smelled but her. She didn't understand. She held her breath as she stepped into the living room.

Her daddy looked her up and down before asking, "Where did those jeans come from?"

"Uhm, I bought them with money I had saved," she lied.

"Well, you couldn't have bought them any looser?" he asked in disgust.

"Whatever," she mumbled under her breath.

"Well, where are you two going again?"

"Just to the movies and to pick up a bite to eat."

"Well, your sister is tagging along. Let her get out of the house also on this Saturday night."

"Daddy, no, let her get her own boyfriend to get her out of the house," Kasha whined. "Why can't you trust me to go out by myself? I'm almost old enough to buy cigarettes. Tina doesn't need to chaperone me everywhere I go!"

"Oh, did you think that I was asking your permission for her to tag along? Let me make myself clear. Your sister is going with you and Slick Rick tonight."

"Daddy, that is not fair. You are such a hypocrite! One minute, you say you trust me—"

"It's not you I don't trust," her dad said. "And you are not grown until you are doing grown-folk things like living on your own, having a job, paying some bills," he added, closing his newspaper. "As long as you're under my roof, I can tell you where to go, who's going with you, and what time to be home." He looked directly into her eyes without blinking to make sure that he was making himself clear.

"You are not being fair. I am tired of you always trying to be controlling. This is my life. Let me live!"

He removed his glasses and said, "Since you want to be so damn grown, you can move out and pay your own bills! You've been smelling your ass for a minute now. I have been noticing it, and that is why I am so strict on you because I am trying to protect you from ending up like a lot of these young ladies out here, pregnant and running the streets behind a no-good boy!" He put his glasses back on. "Open your eyes. You'll always be my daughter, and I'll be damned if you are going to be just another statistic."

Their mother walked into the room, wiping her hands with a dish towel, asking what all of the hollering was about. Kasha went crying to her mom, telling her that her dad was going to make Tina tag along with her on her date.

"George, you are doing too much. We have raised these girls the best way we could have. You have to believe that the morals we instilled into them count for something. You can't shelter them their whole lives."

Kasha was shocked to see her mother speak up for her. "That's what I was trying to tell him. I am not stupid!"

Unmoved by his wife or Kasha, he folded his paper and placed it under his arm as he stood up and said, "Like I said, young lady, you're not going anywhere without Tina! I don't want to hear anything else on the matter because you can very well stay at home," and then he walked off into the bedroom.

"Mama," she whined.

"I'm sorry, baby, but you know how your dad is when his mind is made up."

Frustrated, she sat on the couch, pouting, as she waited for Ricky. *One more year*, she thought. She couldn't wait to finish school and leave home.

"Tina, are you even ready? Ricky will be here any minute," Kasha hollered behind her sister.

"Look, don't rush me because I got as much of a notice as you did that I was going to be tagging along!" Tina hollered back. Although Tina did not like the idea of hanging out with Ricky and Kasha, she couldn't wait to see *The Players Club*. She heard the girls at school talking about how good it was.

"Come on, Tina. He's here!" Kasha yelled, getting ready to walk out the door until her dad stopped her.

"Where do you think you are going, young lady?" her dad asked sternly.

"Daddy, what is wrong with you? You know we are going to the movies. We are not going to leave Tina. I was just going to wait for her in the car and let Ricky know that she was coming," Kasha said with much attitude.

"Did he knock on the door?"

"No, sir. He just pulled up."

"Well, sit your ass down then. Any decent young man would come and knock, not just pull up like he's picking up a whore and she comes running out the door," her daddy said.

"He is," Tina said under her breath as she walked into the room.

"What did you say, Tina?" her dad asked.

"Oh, nothing, sir." Tina looked at Kasha and asked, "Where is Ricky?"

Kasha rolled her eyes at Tina and asked her dad, "Well, can I at least go and tell him to come in then?"

"Hell no. He will come in when he gets tired of sitting out there or leave," her dad said.

Kasha let out an exasperated sigh. The horn blowing sent them all running to the door—their dad to give Ricky a piece of his mind and Kasha and Tina to try to make sure their dad didn't hurt him.

"Who in the hell are you blowing for, boy? This is a young lady. I don't know what kind of women you are used to dealing with, but don't you ever come to my house to get my daughter and not come to the door ever again. As a matter-of-fact, Kasha and Tina, take y'all asses back in the house. You want her to go out with you tonight, you pick her up like a gentleman should."

Kasha was so embarrassed. She hated that her parents were older and not young like her friends' parents were. Her parents were so fucking lame to her. Kasha and Tina followed their dad back into the house. Kasha looked back, praying that Ricky would do as he was told and not just pull off without her. Even though Tina had to tag along, Kasha needed to get away from her parents for a while and was eager to hang out with Ricky.

The doorbell rang, and their father went to the door after motioning for Kasha to sit back down. He opened the door and stood eyeball to eyeball with Ricky. You could tell that Ricky was nervous as he spoke.

"Hey, Mr. Davis. How are you this evening?"

"I'm good," Mr. Davis responded.

"Sir, I am here to take Kasha out to the movies. Is she ready?"

"Yes, her and Tina are ready," their dad said, alerting Ricky for the first time that they were going to have a tagalong.

Ricky looked at Kasha with shock for a brief moment before collecting himself.

"Is there a problem with Tina going with y'all?" their dad said.

"No, no, sir!" Ricky said.

"Great then," said their dad. "Girls, let's go," their dad demanded without once inviting Ricky into the house.

Kasha and Tina hurried out of the house, both hoping that their dad was done. Kasha shook her head as she walked past her dad and out the door, glad to be getting away from him finally, but as luck would have it, their father trailed behind them.

"Make sure you have my girls back home by eleven o'clock."

"But, Daddy, the movie starts at nine o'clock. It probably won't be over until eleven."

"George!" their mother screamed, finally having enough of his over-the-top attitude. "Let them kids go. Y'all enjoy yourselves and just get home as soon as the movie is over," their mom said matter-of-factly, letting them know to ignore his eleven o'clock curfew.

DMX's "Slippin'" was playing, and Kasha was rocking her head from side to side, feeling DMX's rugged style. She looked through the rearview mirror at Tina, who was in the back. "Tina, you don't gotta be alone. We can go get Chris."

"Nah, I'm good, but if y'all want to get rid of me, just take me to Tonya's house."

Kasha wanted to hug her little sister. Dropping her off at Tonya's was the best thing that ever came from her mouth. They called Tonya to get the okay for her to come over.

"You better not tell Daddy on me," Kasha said as they pulled up at Tonya's house.

"Trust me, I can't tell. Dad knows that I am not scared of you and that my personality is a lot stronger than yours, so therefore, you can't force me to do anything," Tina kidded but was serious as well. Tina got out, closed the door, and jogged to Tonya's front porch while they waited for her to enter the house.

Ricky was happy to see Tina leave. He pulled out a blunt, fired it up, and started chiefing like a Navaho

Indian. Kasha's mouth was watering. She snatched the blunt out of his hands and puffed away. This time, she felt more mellowed out. The smoke didn't make her eyes watery.

She was glad to be alone with Ricky for the first time. He started rubbing on her thighs, and she enjoyed his touch as she closed her eyes. "Shit!" she moaned. She was lying back with her eyes closed, enjoying what the weed and Ricky's hands were doing to her. Suddenly, she jumped up, opened her eyes, and pushed Ricky's hands off her thighs. Ricky gave her a confused look.

"My daddy, did you see him?" she asked, alarmed.

"Girl, we are miles away from your daddy. That damn weed got you paranoid as a motherfucker." He laughed.

When they got to the theater, they sat in the car for forty minutes until the movie began to let her high come down. She felt so comfortable with Ricky. They walked into the movie theater, hand in hand, and he held on to her tight as they walked through the crowd in the lobby.

The movie was just starting when they walked in. The theater was dark and quiet. Kasha was mesmerized at how sexy LisaRaye's body was, and the funny thing was that her father kicked her out, pregnant, almost sounding like something her own father would do.

"Damn, babe!" Ricky muttered, nearly slobbering on himself. Kasha felt jealous as she took his hand and placed it on her thigh. He had his eyes glued on the gorgeous LisaRaye. She felt somewhat disrespected. "You can't do this to LisaRaye," she said, placing his hands between her legs. She now had his full attention. When he unzipped her jeans, her heart started pounding hard. *What the hell have I gotten myself into?* she thought as his hand dug into her panties.

"Oh, my God," she moaned when his fingers entered her wet walls. Her groans grew louder as he worked his fingers in and out of her nectar. "Oh God, Ricky, it feels so good," she moaned. She felt her juices flowing as her eyes rolled to the back of her head. She felt like she was in paradise, floating on cloud nine.

He pulled his hands out of her pants and licked his fingers, tasting her sweetness. "Damn, babe, you taste as good as you look." He was horny as hell, ready to get his rocks off. "Come on, babe. Let's leave this joint because I want to taste you tonight."

The way her body felt, she wanted to feel that sensation again and again for the rest of her life. "Let's go." Her body had never felt so good. The movie was the last thing on her mind. She loved the way Ricky took control of her mind and body.

He got the cheapest motel he could find off I-85. He parked his car in the back so no one would see it. From the time they entered the room, they didn't waste any time. They were kissing and sucking on their necks. "Don't put a hickey on my neck," she exhaled, feeling relaxed in his arms. He was trying to take off her shirt. She stepped back, taking off her own shirt, stripping down to her bra.

Her sexiness did not go unnoticed as Ricky quickly scanned over her beautiful body. When her pants hit the floor, his manhood was ready and as hard as steel. She stood in her black lace thong panties. he was ready to fuck the shit out of her. He dropped his pants in 2.3 seconds. He helped her out of her panties, still in awe of how beautiful her body was. He picked her up and laid her on the bed. Her pink nectar was calling his name. He went headfirst, straight downtown, and tongued her out, making love to her love box with his tongue.

Her body trembled as she reached a climax. She had never before experienced anything like this, and she wanted more. She lay in bed, feeling complete but thinking, *what in the world just happened?* Her body was weak as Ricky turned her onto her stomach. He placed soft kisses on her ass, and each kiss sent chills down her spine. "Damn, baby, you're so sexy. Mya or LisaRaye don't have shit on you." He worked his tool into her tight, virgin nectar. Her body tensed up as his mushroom slowly entered her.

Flashes of her father entered her mind. "Hold up, Ricky!" she moaned, trying to lift her body up. "Put on a condom. My daddy will kill me if I get pregnant."

He wanted to bust the pussy up raw, but he placed on a condom and gently eased himself back into her love box. He thrust hard, giving her his all. She was screaming in pain, biting down on a pillow, but he still penetrated harder and faster until he came.

He couldn't believe how good her pussy was. He was mad at himself for coming so fast. He had never had any female, especially a virgin, who made him come so fast. He rolled her over to her back. The look on her face turned him on just that much more. His tool was still hard as a rock. He tossed the condom to the side and entered back into her goodies. They both were mind, body, and soul into making love to one another. She had his mind all on her and making sure that he pleased her as he softly stroked her and nibbled on her neck. After they were done, she got up to go to the bathroom for a warm rag and screamed when she noticed the huge hickey that he had unknowingly placed on her neck and face.

"Shit, Ricky, what in the hell am I going to do?" she panicked.

"Damn, baby, I am sorry. Your shit was so good it just had me out of my mind. I wasn't thinking. Can you put some makeup on it?"

Kasha went to her purse to retrieve her makeup to see if it would conceal it when she glanced at the clock.

"Shit, it's twenty minutes to one! Come on, Ricky, let's get the hell outta here." He was lying across the bed, smoking a blunt.

She was looking a hot mess. Her hair was all over her head. Her lipstick was smeared over her face. She looked like she had been in a bull fight. She had to think of something quick, fast, and in a hurry. She didn't want to hear her father's mouth. "Let down your top, Ricky, so my hair can blow." She was desperate to do anything at this point as she packed the powder on the hickey. She prayed that her dad would be asleep when they got home, but she knew that was a long shot. She just hoped to get by him without him noticing the hickeys.

Tina was waiting on Tonya's front porch. "Thought y'all would never get here. You know it's one o'clock!" she said as she got into the back seat. "Why you have all of that powder on your cheek?" she asked.

"Oh gosh, is it that noticeable?" Kasha asked in a panic while pulling down the visor so that she could look in the mirror.

"You have a hickey on your face?" Tina asked, unbelieving. "You know Daddy is going to kill you!"

Ricky suddenly got nervous as hell. Her father was a force that he wanted no part of. In the passion of the moment, he hadn't been thinking about her daddy. His main concern was on how good the pussy was and to put a stamp on Kasha to let people know he was tapping that ass. He gave Tina $50 to keep her mouth closed.

"I wasn't going to say anything anyway," Tina said, putting the money in her pocket. "But thanks!"

Kasha rubbed the spot on her neck that was burning. She knew that once her daddy saw the hickey, her relationship with Ricky was going to be over.

She got her thoughts together, telling Tina bits and pieces about the movie, just in case their father questioned her. Ricky was so scared that he didn't even pull up to the front of their house. He dropped them off two houses away from their house. As soon as they walked into the house, he hauled ass.

Kasha hurried past her parents' shut bedroom door and right into her room to gather her things and shower. Her coochie was sore. It seemed as if she could still feel Ricky's dick inside of her. She couldn't believe that she was no longer a virgin, but she felt like Ricky deserved her cookies because he had been patient with her and never had he put pressure on her about sex since they had been together.

After getting out of the tub, she looked at the huge passion mark on her neck. "Damn, I'm going to kill Ricky," she mumbled, applying makeup on it, praying that it would dissolve a little by morning, so she could better conceal it, and her parents wouldn't notice it. She decided that she would just worry about that tomorrow. As of right now, she just wanted to get into bed and relive her great night with Ricky. She was in love with him.

Chapter 9

Trapp

Trapp was furious and irritated. Being broke was no joke. Although the clique was shining and looking like a million dollars, in reality, no one was eating, and they didn't have a pot to piss in or a window to throw it out of.

"I'm fucking tired of being broke," he shouted with anger. "Cane, you've got your uncle who takes care of you. I know that you've got to be tired of that shit!"

He looked at his clique, making sure he had their full attention. "Man, I'm telling y'all we need to make a power move because Ray-Ray and 'em outshining us and flossing hard with the money, cars, and jewelry. Those bitches are all over the Poison Clan dicks hard."

"Yeah, I'm tired of taking handouts. You know I'm down with it, but what do you have in mind?" Cane asked.

"Let's hit the mom-and-pop store up the street," Trapp said, getting amped, pumping his fist.

"Hell nah, nigga, that's too close to home!" Cane knew they would be identified as soon as they stepped into the store.

Trapp punched the table, getting more frustrated. "You scared, nigga?" He was all up in Cane's face. "Why in the fuck you think they make ski masks? For niggas like us! To hit a lick!" he said, answering his own question. "Nigga, it's CMB. We all we got." He saw the look in

Cane's eyes, which said that he wasn't with this shit, but he wasn't going to let him off the hook.

He had been planning the robbery for over three months, staking out the store every night. He was on top of his game. He knew how many people went in and out of the store, and he also knew that they didn't have cameras. He wanted to hit the lick himself, but he needed the clique to look out for him.

As he stared Cane in his eyes, he could see the fear in them. "You know, ever since Kasha broke up with you, you have been different. Nigga, you are Cane, and you don't let no bitch-ass female get your self-esteem on a low. You used to be down for whatever, but now it's as if you just want to fly under the radar at all times, and it is bringing CMB down!" Trapp said angrily.

"Am I my brother's keeper?" Cane hit them with the Nino Brown accent. "Nigga, I am down for whatever, whenever, and however!"

"Say no more then." Trapp gave Cane dap. "Y'all don't worry. I've got everything under control. We're going to use my mother's stockings for masks, and I bought some fake guns from the same store we're robbing." Trapp laughed.

"Oh, hell nah, nigga. I'm not wearing ya mama's panties on my head," Shi said as everyone burst out laughing.

"All right, let's get serious, fellas!" Trapp said with a straight face. "No one will recognize us with them on our faces." He already had them pre-cut, just in case everyone agreed on robbing the store. "Everything is going to work out just perfect." He tossed Calvin one, then Cane's, and Shi's last.

"Nigga, your mama is going to kill you once she finds out you cut up all her pantyhose," Calvin said as he placed his over his head and face. "Can y'all see me?"

"Hell yeah, bighead motherfucker," Shi said as Cane and Trapp burst out laughing.

"Ha-ha, real funny motherfucker," Calvin said, looking at them like they were some real clowns.

Trapp got up from the floor and went into a brown paper bag, retrieving the fake cap guns with orange tips. The look in everyone's eyes didn't startle him. He knew they were going to give him hell. "Y'all just give me a chance to explain." He pleaded his case by pulling out a black marker and painting the orange at the tip of the barrel black.

"Damn, that looks real as fuck," Calvin said.

"Told y'all niggas not to doubt me! Shit, I know what the fuck I'm doing! Shit, I can handle mine."

Everyone was looking at Trapp sideways while he continued to pump up his own ego.

"Look, nigga, the next time you plan something that involves us, make sure that you include us in your plans first, before you think to involve us in carrying out your mission. If we're going to do this shit together, we all need to be in on the plans," Cane said.

Trapp's bad temper wouldn't allow him to hold back, and he snapped out, "It won't be no motherfucking next time because, next time, I'm doing the shit by my fucking self—"

Cane cut him off before he let his mouth overload his ass. "Well, do the shit your fucking self this time, smartass! You're taking the shit the wrong way. All I'm saying is we're CMB. We all we got. We are all brothers and stick together for each other, but if you're going to have that attitude, then you can carry out this mission by yourself as well. You don't need us, Mr. I Got This!"

"My bad, fellas. I'm starving like a motherfucker. I got ahead of myself, been thinking about a come-up and how to get it." He shook his head. "I'm tired of them west side niggas outshining us. They are coming through in their rides, stealing our girls, and flaunting them in our face and shit!"

Silence filled the room. Cane was sure everyone was thinking about the latest episode which involved Ricky and Kasha pulling up at the stop sign in his ride while they stood at the bus stop, waiting on the bus. Although CMB was well respected, it was still all a fluke because they didn't have shit. Cane broke the ice. "So, when we going to make this shit go down?"

"Tonight!" Trapp said with a smile plastered on his face. "It's going down fifteen minutes before the store closes. Shi, Calvin, and Cane, y'all are going to go in and rob the store, and I'll be the lookout."

"This mutha'fucka—" Cane started, but Shi cut him off.

"Oh, hell to the motherfucking no," Shi barked out. "It's your idea, so you running your ass into the store. I'll be the lookout."

Trapp, not wanting his boys to know that he was scared, said, "No problem, nigga. Me, you, and Cane will run up in the store, and Calvin can be the lookout. Shi, you put the gun to the clerk's head while Cane empties the register and safe, and I will keep the door to make sure no one comes in or get a signal from Calvin."

"Nigga, this is your robbery, so your ass going to be in the heat of the action with us. Hell, who you think we are? We get a robbery charge, and you go down just as an accomplice. Hell nah, nigga!" Cane said. "Your ass is going to be the one holding the gun."

"Whatever, nigga, no problem. I was just thinking that I would be better making sure that no one snuck in on us. I don't want to get caught. Going to jail is not an option, so whoever the lookout is going to be, you better be on your game!" He agreed to hold the gun to the clerk's head while Cane took the money from the register. Cane was still looking at him sideways but agreed.

They all agreed to meet up at the old tree house once the robbery was over. Trapp went over the plans once again before everyone departed, going their separate ways.

Once everybody left, Trapp rehearsed over and over in the mirror with his gun and ski mask on. He was ready to get paid in a major way.

He continued to look at the clock, getting more anxious by the second. He could picture himself shining on them Poison Clan niggas once the robbery was over with. The Poison Clan had his mind messed up. They were all he thought about these days, especially after the episode of Ricky stopping at the stop sign, dropping his hood on his convertible, stunting on Cane and the entire gang. Although Kasha had never been his girl, Cane was his man, and he hated her for bringing those west side niggas to the hood like that. He felt even worse for Cane.

Cane was the leader of the clique, and he had sold them on making mad moves when it started, but nothing was happening but them perpetrating and fucking the hunnies. Yeah, they had the females because they were all a good-looking group of men and had a reputation, but the west side crew had the same and the money and rides to go with it. He was considering asking Cane to step down and let him lead the clique since he felt like he was a better leader. He was ready to test Cane's heart to see if it pumped blood or Kool-Aid.

They all stood at the stop sign. Trapp made sure that Shi knew his role on signaling Calvin if he saw anything strange. Everybody was in place. Shi flicked his light, giving them the green light to go in.

The coast was clear as they entered into the store. Trapp's adrenaline was pumping hard as he almost knocked Cane over, which would have created a bad situation because it would have given the clerk time to pull out a weapon.

"Bitch, open up the fuckin' register, and give my man all the fuckin' money!" he shouted as he put the gun to her head.

The elderly woman panicked and dropped the money onto the floor. "Lord, please don't take my life!" she prayed. "Lord, don't let them kill me."

"Bitch, shut the fuck up before I blow your fuckin' brains out!" Trapp shouted into her eardrum. "I told your stupid ass to put all the money in the bag." He started picking up the money, placing it into the bag.

Calvin saw Shi flick the lighter and noticed that a car had pulled up. "Let's roll out. A car just pulled into the parking lot."

"Hold up, man. I think this bitch got some more money," Trapp said.

"Nigga, are you stuck on stupid or something? A car just pulled up, and we need to roll out now!" Cane said.

"See, that's why I didn't want to bring your scary ass along." Trapp was fuming. Calvin was still looking out the window as he said, "You bitches hurry up and let's get out of here before he gets to the door!"

"Man, just chill the fuck out. When he comes in, subdue him, and we will tie him up. And, bitch, you better not scream, or your brains will be scattered all over the store," Trapp said, trying to keep his cool as he watched Cane and Calvin finish bagging thc loot.

"What's going on?" Cane asked Calvin.

"He's sitting in the car on his cell phone." When Calvin looked around the corner again, he locked eyes with the driver who was now looking through the window. Realizing that a robbery was going on because of Calvin's mask, the driver, who happened to be an off-duty cop, pulled out his .38 Special and aimed it at the window while shouting, "Freeze. Police!"

Calvin jumped back into the corner, dropping his gun that scattered into pieces when it hit the floor. The cop recognized that it was a toy gun and charged into the store. Calvin attempted to run out the back door of the store, but blue lights were swarming everywhere.

Everything happened so fast as more backup cops entered the store. They were placed in handcuffs and escorted out of the store. "Officer Fernandez, could you take this one, and I'll take these two with me," one of the officers said.

Trapp was cuffed to Cane while Calvin rode in the other squad car. "Dispatch, this is Officer Carson. I have two juveniles detained. I'm bringing them into Q-50, repeat Q-50," he radioed with a smirk on his face.

Cane didn't have a clue what Q-50 meant. He peeped over at Trapp, who looked lost and was in another world. He took a deep breath and then exhaled, praying that Shi would get in touch with Jack instead of his grandmother.

When they pulled up to the building, Cane noticed that Trapp had sweat beads on his forehead and looked pale. Officer Carson and Officer Fernandez helped them out of the car and walked them inside the building. Trapp was shaking badly when they sat down inside.

"Man, are you going to be okay?" Cane asked, concerned.

Trapp was nervous and on the verge of tears, but he knew he had to pull it together. He didn't want Calvin and Cane to see the water in his eyes.

"What do we have here? Three juvenile delinquents!" Carson was smiling from ear to ear. "Three fucking pieces of shit in my ass." He raised his voice since Fernandez was gone to prepare the identification kit. As soon as she walked back in, he backed off so she could process them.

"Listen, and listen carefully, because I'm not going to repeat myself." Her voice was strict and direct. "One at a time, name, address, and phone number." She stared at Cane's name for two seconds. "Curtis Griffin, are you related to a Mr. Jack Griffin?" He didn't respond, so she moved on. "Travis Shiggs, never heard of you before." She looked at Calvin and then shook her head. "The youngest of the bunch, Calvin Brown."

Carson winked his eye at Officer Fernandez before taking over the show. "I'm going to be straight up with y'all, so don't give me no bullshit, and I won't bullshit y'all." He stared in each of their eyes. "I don't want to take y'all to jail, so help me so I can help y'all."

Trapp wanted to spit in his face, "That's bullshit." He tried to whisper to Cane and Calvin, hoping they wouldn't fall for Officer Carson's "let's snitch" game.

"No, what's bullshit is you and your little thug buddies robbing that store and scaring the hell out of that old lady. She is on her way to the hospital as we speak with heart complications, and y'all asses better pray that she doesn't die," Officer Fernandez said matter-of-factly.

"My one and only day off this week and all I wanted was a beer, but I walked in on y'all's bullshit. Now, I am here having to fill out paperwork! All I wanted was a beer, so before y'all shitheads piss me the fuck off, you better start talking!" said Carson.

"Yeah, y'all better help yourself because twenty-five years in prison is a long-ass time," Fernandez said, adding fuel to the fire.

Trapp saw the seriousness in both officers' faces while his hands and lips continued to tremble. He couldn't hold it in anymore and broke down in tears. He was so scared of going to prison that he no longer cared if Cane and Calvin were in the room. He didn't want to spend the rest of his life in prison. Tears continued to fall from his face when Fernandez yelled that she was tired of their bullshit, tired of playing games with them, and they were going to jail.

Both officers sensed that Trapp was the weak link, so they escorted him into a separate room. Fernandez stood over him with her gun in his face, playing Russian roulette. She spun the cylinder as Trapp's eyes became the size of golf balls.

"All right, Shi was the lookout man, and Cane and Calvin put me up to robbing the store. I swear I wanted nothing to do with it," he said, wiping his runny nose with the back of his sleeve. Both officers laughed in his face. All he could do was shake his head, realizing they played him like a fool.

They gave Trapp a few minutes to clean himself up before they escorted them to the detention center. It didn't take the officers long to process their information and then place them into a holding cell.

Trapp, noticing how Cane and Calvin were staring at him, asked, "What?"

"What did they ask you when they took you into the back?" Cane asked.

Trapp dropped his arms to his side. He thought they knew he squealed like a pig. "Shit, nigga, they tried to make me snitch on y'all." He felt his ego coming back. "I told them doughnut-eating motherfuckers to go fuck themselves. I guess it pissed them off, and that's why we are sitting in the county jail."

"Damn, I knew this wasn't a good day to try to pull that shit off. It was ill planned. We should have planned this shit out better," Cane said.

"So, you trying to say that all of this is my motherfuckin' fault!" Trapp snapped.

"You may as well put one to our head." Calvin stood up, pointing his finger in Trapp's face.

"Nah, it's not his fault," Cane interjected. "It's all our faults, and we're family. We can't fall apart now. We've got to stick together and figure a way out of this mess."

"Today is y'all's lucky night. The judge won't be in tonight, but I got y'all a bond set at three thousand dollars apiece. Once we finish the paperwork, y'all can make a phone call to let someone know where y'all are." Carson said what he had to and then walked off.

Hours later, the guys sat talking about how they were going to get out and who they knew to make their bond. Trapp knew his mother was going to kill him once she found out he was in jail. He was stressed knowing he couldn't come up with three grand to get out. "I can't spend the weekend in jail!" he cried out, beating on the wall.

"Shit, nigga, we're broke as a joke. We don't have a choice except to stay the weekend," Calvin said, adding in his two cents.

"You should've thought about that before you planned on robbing that store," Cane blurted out.

"I'm tired of your smartass mouth." Trapp balled up his fist. "You're going to make me—"

He was cut off when Officer Carson yelled out, "Calvin Brown and Curtis Griffin, pack up. Y'all made bond."

"What about me?"

"What about you?" he replied with a smirk on his face.

Trapp couldn't believe he was about to be left behind. "This isn't fair. We all robbed the store, and I'm still stuck in here." Cane hated to leave him behind, but Carson rushed them out.

He went to make his phone call, but his mother didn't answer. He thought about calling his father, but instead, he hung up the phone, thinking Shi had most likely told his mother what happened, and they were on their way to pick him up.

He stretched out on the concrete floor since there weren't any beds, thinking back over how his perfect plot had gone wrong so fast.

It was the next morning before Officer Fernandez came back around. He hopped up real cocky like and said, "It's about time you came to get me!"

"Well, Mr. Shiggs, I hate to burst your bubble, but no one has posted your bond yet. But look at the bright side. You're getting a roommate."

"You've got to be kidding me. Please tell me that my mother is out there?"

She looked from side to side. "Nope, not your mother but a roommate."

Damn, she's not playing, he thought. His heart about jumped out of his chest when he saw his archenemy, Ray-Ray, step into the cell, carrying a blanket and pillow. From the look on Ray-Ray's face, you could tell that he was just as shocked to see Trapp. Neither of them spoke. Ray-Ray walked to his corner and started setting up his bed. The room was quiet for an hour before Trapp broke the ice, asking him what he was in jail for.

"Shit, Poison Clan, you know how we get down. I was trying to steal some rims off a nigga's whip and shit." He rubbed his hands together and then licked his lips. "Shit, what you in for?"

"CMB, nigga, you know how we do it," Trapp said with his chest out. "We robbed a store, but my niggas made bond yesterday, just waiting on them to come back to get me." He tried to match Ray-Ray's intensity, letting him know that his clique didn't have bitch in them either.

"Man, weren't y'all in this together, so how in the hell they leave you here? Y'all making the money, right?" Ray-Ray said.

"Yeah, man, we got it," Trapp said, perpetrating, but all along wondering why his boys hadn't scrapped up the money to come for him.

"Ahh, shit, nigga, them niggas probably snitched on you to get out."

Ray-Ray's words should not have moved Trapp, but they did. He understood that Cane's uncle most likely was the one to foot his bond, but what about Calvin's? Hell, they were broker than he was, and his mom would not have moved from her front porch to go looking for bail money. She always said that if he made his bed, he would lie in it.

Ray-Ray continued to pour gasoline on the fire that Cane was a snitch.

"I know that's your boy and all, but I don't trust that damn Cane. The way he sang on Jeremy last year in school when that laptop got missing. No real G would have done something like that," Ray-Ray said. "And didn't I hear that he was the one that told O that you were fucking Leslie behind his back?"

"Yeah, because O and his boys had come to Cane's house, thinking it was Cane who was doing her."

"So, that made it okay for him to get his boy fucked up and not even tell you? See, Poison Clan, we don't get down like that. If a mu-fa comes to me about their girl, and I know it's my boy they have me mistaken for, either I play clueless or I tell them nothing."

Ray-Ray had gotten into Trapp's weak head. Trapp started thinking back over all of the things that had happened over the years where Cane sold him out or did not side with him. Truth was that Trapp did a lot of things that were pure nonsense. Cane's attitude was "I am not going down over no stupid shit," but it had been nothing major.

"Fuck, Cane! Yeah, he's a little snitch bitch. Yeah, he told Kasha about me running a train on these chicks, and then when Kasha broke up with his ass, she told it."

"Damn, speaking of Kasha, that's a sexy-ass bitch. My nigga Ricky got her head fucked up." He continued to tell Trapp about the time she was smoking a blunt and got high as hell, and Ricky left the blinds open so they could watch him fuck her. "Damn, ever since then, I wanted some of that pussy."

"For real!" Trapp pictured her naked. Just that thought caused an erection.

"Hell yeah, Ricky got about six whores. He don't give a fuck about them bitches. He was the one who turned Meka out, and your weak-ass homeboy was in love with that slut bucket."

Ray-Ray had his full attention. He thought that Ray-Ray was cool as hell. "My nigga, if you want to make some real cheddar, holla at cha boy, and leave them lame-ass niggas alone. You know I can use a real nigga like you on my team."

Trapp was in deep thought. He'd been down with Cane since elementary school, and he didn't want to turn his back on his friends, yet they were making no major moves.

"Travis Shiggs, pack up. You made bond!" Officer Fernandez yelled out, breaking his concentration. He stood up and gave Ray-Ray some dap before leaving. "Somebody posted your bond in a weird way, but you are free," Officer Fernandez said.

He didn't care who got him out. He was just happy to be getting out.

Chapter 10

Cane

Cane wanted to tell Jack what Officer Carson had said, but Jack was raising so much hell about them getting locked up he couldn't get a word in. "Shi told me everything. How could y'all let stupid-ass Trapp get y'all into this bullshit?" He couldn't believe this. A single tear escaped his eye.

"You know if Mama finds out she's going to kick your ass. And if your daddy was still living, he would've killed you."

"It wasn't all Trapp's fault." He tried to defend his best friend, hoping Jack would ease up off of him. "Besides, I'm tired of always having to depend on you. I want my own money!"

"Well, make your own damn keep, but it ain't your mutha'fuckin' money if you're robbing people of theirs, li'l nigga! I swear, the more I try to teach your ass, the dumber you get! I don't know what plans you have about making your own money, but you better scratch that dumbass one that just got your ass locked up. But, in the meantime, y'all going to pay me back by working around my house, helping the contractors. I promise you that!" Jack had a huge house and was getting some renovations done to it.

"No problem," Cane and Calvin said.

"I know it's not going to be a problem," Jack boomed.

"We can get Shi and Trapp and get it knocked out quick."

"Fuck Trapp. He's the reason why y'all got into this trouble in the first place. Keep his roguish ass away from my house. Trust me, that nigga is going to be your downfall if you keep fucking with him. Just because you've known him forever doesn't make him your friend. Hell, you can meet someone tomorrow that will be more loyal," Jack said, trying to shed light into his eyes.

"You don't understand, Unc. Trapp is good people. He just doesn't have anyone to look out for him but us. You know his family is messed up. I just want to get him out, and then we can all talk and come up with other ways of making sure that we all are fed. But he's sitting there, and no one cares but his crew, and we're broke as hell," Cane said.

"Don't worry. He'll be out in a few hours. I just wanted him to sit in there and think about the shit he did," Uncle Jack said.

Cane smiled so hard he could feel his cheek bones burning.

Jack continued fussing, and they had to listen as he told the story again of how he made his money when he was younger by cutting grass, washing cars, babysitting, and walking people's dogs. When Jack mentioned them being a spoiled generation who only wanted handouts, that one thing got under Cane's skin.

"Well, Unc, if you worked so hard, why did Grandma kick you out of the house? She always tells me I'm going to end up like you and my father."

"She didn't put me out. I left on my own free will." Jack didn't want to have this conversation with Cane, but he knew that he had to tell him the truth about his lifestyle one day. "Mama doesn't want you to be like us. I know it seems like I got everything in life: a house, nice cars, and money. Just know that everything that glitters isn't gold. I worked hard to take care of the family, but that nickel-and-dime stuff wasn't cutting it, so yeah, I stepped into the streets for the quick money. You already know that Mama doesn't like the way I make my money, but once I got to a certain age, there was nothing she could do. Yeah, she gave me options, either I get an honest job or I leave her house. I chose to leave her house and never went back other than to visit. Been on my own ever since."

"Unc, trust me, I'm going to be all right. You have always been my role model, and one day, I am going to be just like you, but better. You have done a lot for me all of my life, and one day, I will be able to pay you all your money back."

Jack laughed out loud. "Nah, nephew, this game isn't for you, and having nice things comes with a price to pay. You can pay me back by listening to my advice and do better than me by getting your education and making an honest living." He loved Cane and knew that he had to take care of him since Cane's father had looked out for him and taught him everything he knew.

Cane glanced over at Calvin who was in deep thought. "What's up, bruh?"

"Shit, man, thinking about you having the best uncle in the world."

Jack lived on the outskirts of Greenville in Fountain Inn. His house had seven bedrooms, three Jacuzzis, an in-ground swimming pool, and a full basketball court. He didn't have any children but dated plenty of women with kids.

"Mama said to tell you that some girl name Kasha called for you and said for you to call her," Jack said, relaying the message. "She said that it was important."

Cane's heart dropped to his stomach when he heard her name. It had been eight months since he'd spoken to her. Even though she had a boyfriend, his feelings were still strong for her.

"What the fuck does she want with me?" he spat out, trying to play hard as if he didn't want to talk to her.

"Man, don't call that trick!" Calvin muttered.

Jack, noticing that Cane was only playing hard but was happy to hear that the girl had reached out to him, said, "Man, let me find out you're pussy whipped. That's what's wrong with y'all jitterbugs. Never let a woman know that you're pussy whipped."

Calvin cut him off by telling him that Cane couldn't be pussy whipped because he hadn't gotten any pussy yet.

"Shut up!" Cane fired back. "You don't know what I've got. Just because I don't go around bragging on my dick like you stupid niggas," Cane said.

"Don't get mad, nigga. The truth is the truth."

"Boy, your last name is Griffin. I paved the way for you. Them bitches supposed to be throwing pussy at you," Uncle Jack said.

Cane just sat there and listened to his uncle and Calvin talk about all the pussy he was supposed to be getting. He did not confirm nor deny that he was still a virgin. His boys speculated but weren't sure if he was a virgin or not because Cane had always been private about his relationships and what he and the girl did behind closed doors.

"Fuck y'all!" He laughed as his uncle and Calvin continued on about him not ever getting his dick wet. "Don't worry about my dick. It's good. And if you niggas would stop making everything about sex, maybe you can have a meaningful relationship. Sex is not everything. It's the inside that counts," Cane said, trying to save face.

"Is that what you did with Kasha?" Calvin joked. He and Jack had a good laugh.

Jack didn't know the history of this Kasha girl, but he knew she had to have been something special to his nephew because just hearing her name managed to change his entire mood. Seeing that Cane did not appreciate Calvin's latest joke of Kasha, Jack said, "Calvin, it's in the Griffin bloodline to get into them women's heads and fuck them up. Nephew, I'm proud of you boy."

"Man, whatever! Y'all Griffins don't have shit on the Browns." Calvin started clapping his hands. "I'm telling you, Jack. It's a new breed coming up, and y'all old school dudes are played out."

"Boy, I've been pimping since you were in diapers," Jack laughed out. "Little nigga, just because you're getting your dick wet, you think you're doing something. I'll put a bitch in your face that will freeze your ass in two seconds flat!"

"Oh, hell no I won't. Shit, I'll put this wood on her ass, and I promise you she'll never fuck with an old dude again."

Jack liked Calvin. His player ways reminded him of himself when he was young and chasing panties. But Cane, on the other hand, was the complete opposite, more laid-back, cool, calm, and collected.

"Okay, I got something for both of y'all since y'all big-time players. Promise me y'all won't tell nobody!"

"We won't," they both said with excitement in their eyes.

He thought about it, realizing they were supposed to be getting punished for what they did. "Nah, I'm supposed to be teaching y'all a lesson, so call Trapp and let him know I'll be over to pick him up in the morning because y'all got an ass of work to do."

Cane looked outside and swallowed hard. Jack's house seemed larger than ever. Calvin, as always, was walking around mesmerized, looking around the inside. "Damn, Jack, I'll move in with you. Shit, with all of this shit you've got in here, you need a house sitter to make sure no one tries to run up in here on ya. I'll hold it down for you."

"Trust me, I am good," Jack said, pulling out his chrome .357 Magnum. "If somebody ever tried to rob me, I promise they won't live long enough to talk about it. Those locks on those doors are for their safety, not mine," he laughed.

"I told him that he needed to get him a watch dog at least, a pit or German shepherd," Cane chimed in.

"Ain't having no dog shitting all over my place," Jack said. "This here gun is my best protection."

Cane, shaking his head, let it go and walked off with the phone to get some privacy while he called to see what Kasha needed with him that was so urgent.

"Hey, what's up, babe?" Cane asked all nonchalantly when Kasha answered on her end.

"I am not your babe. I belong to Ricky now," Kasha said very directly.

"Yeah, so you're letting his lame ass take ownership of you now? Wow, all this time I thought you were your own person."

"I am my own person, but I am his lady. And who are you calling lame, Mr. Scared to Fuck? Nothing is lame about Ricky, believe that!" Kasha said, throwing salt on him for not wanting to have sex with her when she advanced on him one night at her house. It wasn't that he didn't want to have sex. It was the fact that her dad was in the other room, and there was no way he was going to chance being walked in on by that gorilla.

"Whatever, Kasha. So, because I respected your ass that makes me lame? You're so used to niggas coming after you for your body that you don't recognize a real gentleman that wants to be with you for you. But that's your loss. Keep playing yourself. I'm good on my end, about to make some major moves."

"Well, good for you because I am good on my end too. Do you, and don't worry about me. Can you handle that?" she asked.

Before Cane could answer, Tina had snatched the phone from Kasha's hand and said, "Don't pay her any attention!"

He could hear Kasha in the background, telling Tina to tell him to move on with his life because she had moved on with hers. She was steadily talking trash as her voice continued to fade as Tina walked from her room.

"Like I said, Cane, don't pay her no mind. She's been smelling herself and acting crazy ever since Ricky came along. That dude got her head twisted."

"Forget her and Ricky, I am done with it," Cane said as reality kicked in that Kasha was not the one for him. "I was just calling because she left a message with my grandma for me to call, saying that it was urgent." He didn't want to talk about Ricky or Kasha. To him, they both were dead in his world. He was ready to move on with his life, for real this time.

"Yeah, your boy, Trapp, pulled up over here in a cab. He asked for her to call and tell you that he needed for someone to come through because his aunt wasn't home and he had nowhere to go," Tina said. "But he's gone now. That was a few hours ago."

"Cool. I have been with my uncle all day. Glad he is out and okay. I will call him later," Cane said as he heard Calvin calling him to come and play the video game. "Thanks for looking out, and I will holla at you later," he said, ending the call with Tina.

He tried to get into the game to get his mind off of all the stuff that Kasha had said. That girl was going to drown in her own bullshit if she didn't wake up. He picked up the phone and called Trapp to see if he was home. Trapp answered with an attitude, asking what in the hell was going on and why he had to stay overnight in jail when they had made bail. Cane told him that Jack was mad at them all, especially him, and said that he needed a reality check to see what the consequences could be if they decided to stay on this robbing track.

"Yeah, man, whatever, that's bullshit! We all were in this together, so why didn't he figure that we all deserved the same damn lesson?"

"Man, you have to take that up with Jack. I didn't have anything to do with his decision. I was just glad when the next morning came so he could pay your bond and get you out of that joint."

"Man, fuck Jack. I am going to give him every dime back because I don't want no muthafuckas that don't want to help me saying I owe them shit!"

"Trapp, what in the hell are you talking about? Jack looks at you like a nephew too. Hell, he don't owe you shit. He didn't have to come and get you. He could have left you to wait on your family to come," Cane said angrily.

"See, this that bullshit I am talking about. You know my mom ain't got no money, and neither would she have tried to get up any to get my black ass. So, that's a side jab you're throwing. But I swear if it takes my last breath, I will give Jack every penny back as soon as I can."

"Well, since you're so hell-bent on paying back your debt, you won't have a problem doing some yard work." Cane told him what Jack had said about them working around his house, and Trapp flipped the fuck out.

"I don't clean my own yard, so why in the hell am I going to clean up his shit? I didn't tell him to get me out! He could've left my ass in there."

"Man, you just finished saying that you wanted to pay him back ASAP, didn't you, nigga?"

"I'll pay him back, but I ain't being his servant to do it, and don't harass me about that shit either. Shit, what he think this is?"

"Man, you need to man up. You dug your grave, so don't be afraid to lie in it. We all owe him, and unless you have another solution to coming up with the money, we're going to be doing what he needs us to do around his house to pay off our debt," Cane said. "You got this mean talk, but when someone gives you the opportunity, your ass punks down."

He was tired of hearing Cane's lecture, like he was a real boss. "My nigga, I've been taking up for your pussy ass since first grade. So, don't play me like no punk. I handle mine. So, tell Jack he will get his ends when I get them!"

"Nigga, what is wrong with you? You act like somebody owes your 'Mayberry' ass something. Jack don't owe you, me, or Calvin a damn thing, so for you to be sitting here talking shit about what you ain't going to do is foul. If you handle yours so well, then you won't have a problem with paying up now," Cane said, glad that Trapp wasn't in his face because he would have knocked the shit out of him.

"I'm tired of you and your fuck-ass uncle acting like y'all better than everybody, so fuck both of y'all!" He hung up the phone in Cane's face, leaving him looking dumbfounded and furious.

He was pissed the fuck off. He tried to call Trapp back to give him a piece of his mind, but he only got a busy signal. What was wrong with Trapp? Jack had been nothing but good to him. "Fuck!" he yelled into the phone, startling Calvin, who was lost in the video game.

He told Calvin about Trapp flipping out. The only thing Calvin said was that he'd be all right once he got some rest. He hoped that Calvin was right. He tried to lie down to get some rest himself to ease his mind, but he was so mad at Trapp that he couldn't relax.

His heart started racing fast when a loud pound came from the door. He looked around to see who was going to answer the door. "Damn," he mumbled under his breath, going to the door. "Who is it?"

"Terry."

"Who's at the door?" Jack hollered.

"Someone named Terry," Cane answered as Jack came around the corner to the door, opening it.

"Come in, T-Lov." Jack and the young man dapped one another up. "This is Brenda's son," Jack said to Cane. "Brenda must be tripping because that's the only time he comes over," he laughed.

"Damn right," T-Lov laughed. "I had to get the hell up out of there. She mad because the lawnmower tore up and she told me to get the scissors because she wanted the grass around her flower bed cut today!" They all laughed.

"That damn Brenda is crazy. I know that much," Jack laughed. "T-Lov, this is my nephew, Cane, that I've been telling you about. But I was about to bounce, so you know the routine. I'll see y'all in the morning," Jack said as he walked out the door.

T-Lov came in and got comfortable like he was at home. They sat around, shooting the breeze about who all they knew in common. Cane was surprised when he brought up his father's name. T-Lov kept talking about how Cane's father, Big Curt, had been a real G. He had looked out for everybody. T-Lov was talking his head off, so Cane pretended to be sleepy and pulled the cover up over his head, hoping that T-Lov would get the picture and be quiet.

***

It seemed as if he hadn't been asleep but a few hours when he felt the kiss of the sun burning against his skin from the huge bay window. Stretching, he called out to his uncle before he moved. He lay there for another ten minutes before he decided that he needed to get up and get ready to knock some of this work out because he wasn't planning on spending his entire afternoon working. He had shit he wanted to do today. He got up, freshened up, and then made his way into the kitchen. *Just what the doctor ordered,* he thought after reading the note that Jack had left on the refrigerator. He didn't waste any time demolishing the eggs, bacon, and waffles his uncle left in the microwave.

After he ate, he went into the living room to see that T-Lov had met his partner in crime. Calvin had a weird smirk on his face that said, "This dude don't even know what he's gotten himself into." All Cane could do was shake his head, knowing that Calvin had tricked T-Lov into playing the game with him, pretending to be an amateur and was about to take all of his money.

"I hate to ruin y'all's game, but we've got work to do before Jack comes back home." They both ignored him and kept playing the game. Cane unplugged the game. "Let's go now!" he said, raising his voice.

"Lucky I fuck with you," Calvin said as he stood up. "Or you would have got fucked up for that stunt." Cane brushed him off, putting on his work face.

Jack had two riding lawnmowers and three weed eaters and tree blowers. After Cane was able to get Calvin and T-Lov to get serious and quit clowning around, they all went straight to work. Within two hours, they had knocked the whole yard out. After they finished, they all jumped right into the pool fully clothed to cool down until Jack walked up, looking at them as if they had lost their minds.

"Shit, y'all aren't finished yet, so y'all may as well get your asses out of that water. The cars are filthy as hell."

"Come on, Jack, man. We've cut, trimmed, and blown. You didn't say anything about any cars on today's to-do list," Calvin said, getting out of the pool and drying himself off.

"Nah, he didn't expect for us to finish so quickly. That's what it was," T-Lov chimed in as he picked up the basketball and shot from the fence, making the basket.

Calvin rebounded the ball and dunked it. "You don't want none," he said to T-Lov.

"Man, you don't even want these problems," T-Lov responded. "I am a beast on the court."

"Y'all niggas ain't getting ready to do nothing but wash them damn cars," Jack said, taking the ball from T-Lov, who had rebounded it.

Calvin took the ball out of Jack's hand and did a jumper while saying, "You just don't want me to embarrass your boy. That's all."

T-Lov and Calvin started arguing back and forth until Jack intervened with a solution. "I tell you two knuckleheads what. If Calvin can beat T-Lov, Cane and I will wash the cars, but if T-Lov wins, Cane and Calvin have to wash all the cars."

"What the hell?" Cane chimed in. "So, you're saying, either way, I am going to be washing cars? Hell, I want in the game too!"

"Yo' punk ass can't play no hoops. Just do what you always do and sit in the corner, be the pretty boy that you are, and watch the pro do his thang," a cocky Calvin said.

"Whatever, nigga. I hope T-Lov beats your ass," Cane said, tossing T-Lov the ball.

"Nah, we flipping a coin to see who gets possession of the ball first," Calvin said.

"We ain't got to flip no coin," T-Lov stated. "I will give you the ball first because you won't be getting it much after," he laughed.

To T-Lov's surprise, Calvin hit five jumpers in a row. T-Lov knew that he had to step up his game or he was about to lose to this cocky runt. They were both tied at eleven. Calvin had the ball. Jack screamed out to T-Lov, "I'll give you five hundred dollars to stop him!"

"You should have bet on me," Calvin said to Jack as he shot another basket. "I'm hot!" Calvin hit T-Lov with an Allen Iverson crossover, which caused him to fall. After laying up the ball, Calvin stood over him and said, "Game over!"

Jack couldn't believe what he had just witnessed. He used to mentor Calvin on the game, but he hadn't seen him play in forever. This kid was the truth! He could be the next Kevin Garnett, who was a native of Greenville, South Carolina, who went straight to the pros from high school. Calvin nodded his head, pointing to the car, and said, "Don't forget the soap. Lather her up real good."

Jack pushed Calvin into the pool as he told Cane, "Come on, let's get started on these damn cars."

"Man, this some bullshit," Cane said, upset because, no matter who won the game, he was still stuck washing the cars, and Calvin and T-Lov had been bullshitting around all morning. It had been he who made them get to work.

They all laughed at him while he pouted as he struggled washing his uncle's Benz.

Two and a half hours later, Jack and Cane had washed all four cars. Jack had pulled the boat out and started polishing it for his fishing trip the next day when a black limousine caught their attention. "Hold this down for me," Jack said, handing Cane the towel that he was using for the boat and making his way to the limo. He was in the limo for a few minutes before he exited with two suitcases. Before he could get into the door, Cane rushed up on him. "Who's in the limo?"

"An old friend of your father's. You don't know him though."

"Who, Tony Santana?"

Jack eyes lit up. "Yep. you remember Tony?"

"Somewhat, that's the dude that named me. He was my pop's partner. I thought he was dead, since no one talks about him."

Jack filled Cane in on Tony and said that he and Tony had been partners ever since his father died. "Tony always keeps tabs on you through me and tries to give me ends for you, but I told him you were straight, trying to teach you how to be a man and stand on your own two feet. You are only seventeen, so I will help you out for now, but soon you're going to have to find your own way."

Cane didn't have a clue as to what Jack was talking about. Jack was good to him and made sure that he had pocket change, clothes, and shoes, but he made him work for what he gave him, so he felt as if he was making his own way. Shoot, he cut the grass, washed the cars, took out trash, worked in the flower beds, and walked back and forth to the store for his grandmother. These were all things that his Uncle Jack expected him to do for his compensation.

"Take this and go shopping," Jack said, handing him a wad of money. "I've got to go and handle some business, and make sure you split it up with the fellas."

Cane looked down at the wad of money in his hands and thought that he could quit school and be straight. While Jack always gave him money, it had never been this kind of money. He would give him $50 here and $100 there, but this was at least a grand. Cane started counting the $100 bills. He divided everything down the middle, breaking T-Lov and Calvin with $500 apiece.

They couldn't believe that Jack freely gave them some money without a clause to it, but they weren't going to give him time to come up with something to do or realize that he had given them the wrong stash. They loaded up in T-Lov's '85 Honda Accord and bounced.

"This car is a piece of shit!" Cane said as the car sputtered along the highway. He turned his head as they stopped at the red light to turn onto Haywood Road beside a car full of girls so as not to be seen. He prayed that the car did not cut off right there at the big intersection as it was threatening to do. To Cane's surprise, they made it to Haywood Mall in one piece. "Jack should've let us drive one of his cars. You sure we're going to be able to make it back home?" Cane asked as they were looking for a parking space. As soon as he spoke it, the car started smoking and backfiring, just as they had found a parking spot and parked. He now understood the power of having money. As soon as he got his papers right, he told T-Lov he was going to buy him a car.

"Buy yourself one first," T-Lov fired back, laughing. "At least I'm rolling."

"I'd rather catch the bus," Calvin said from the back seat.

"You see that bus stop right there?" T-Lov said, pointing at the shed with the bench in it. "You can take it back home when we leave here, muthafucka," T-Lov said.

"Nigga, open the door and let me out of this death trap," Calvin kidded.

They walked into the mall, styling and profiling with all of the young and older women alike looking at the handsome threesome. They were looking, smelling, and feeling good. They had a pocketful of money and were ready to get their gear right for tonight's party they were talking about going to. Looking around the stores at the things that he liked, Cane thought that he had the taste of a huge sirloin steak, but his income was that of a cubed steak. This further confirmed to him that he needed to get serious about getting his paper right and not depending on Jack for the rest of his life. He picked up an application from every store that they entered.

T-Lov was digging Cane's grind and applauded him for his efforts. They had met just the day before, but they vibed like lifelong friends, and he knew that they would have a long friendship just from his ambition of trying to be his own man.

They were laughing, talking, and cutting up with one another, walking through the mall, but as soon as they got into Foot Locker, T-Lov noticed as Cane's entire facial expression changed. T-Lov looked into the direction that Cane was looking and noticed Ricky standing there in the store uniform, placing shoes on the rack.

"Can't stand that nigga," T-Lov said. "That nigga fucks with this chick that lives up the street from my house. Be riding on the set like he Mr. T with all them damn gold chains on with his top dropped."

Cane gave T-Lov a confused look because last night he had said that he lived in Kennedy Park and Kasha stayed by Lakeside Park. *Don't tell me that nigga is creeping on butter cakes.* Cane chuckled to himself.

"Fuck that nigga. I'm about to work his ass." He walked up to Ricky and asked for a nine and nine and a half in a pair of Jordans. He grabbed Shi a pair. He couldn't leave his boy out.

As soon as Ricky came back with the shoes, Calvin asked for sizes ten, ten and a half, and eleven. Ricky looked at him as if to say, "Why didn't you ask for this shit when you heard him ask for them?" Calvin looked at him and nodded his head to the side, motioning for him to go get the damn shoes, knowing that he wasn't going to buy all three pairs of them.

"Now, that's working his ass." Cane laughed as T-Lov asked for a size two shoe once he came back out. Ricky's face was beet red.

Cane burst out laughing when Ricky went back to the backroom to fetch the size two shoe. "Man, you stupid as hell. I thought I was going to laugh in the man's face when you asked for a child's two. What in the hell?"

T-Lov laughed with Cane but explained that he had a son.

"Word?" Cane asked. "Oh, I thought you were just being funny," he laughed.

"I was, but I still want the shoe," T-Lov laughed.

"You and your baby mama still together?" Calvin asked.

"Nah, man, she was just someone I was doing and slipped up. But gots to take care of my seed," T-Lov said. "She be on flip mode the majority of the time because a brother don't want her ass anymore."

"Does your baby mama go to Carolina too?" Cane asked.

"Nah, she goes to Southside."

"Southside? Who is she?" Cane asked, curious because he went to Southside.

"Her name is Traci Westmoreland," T-Lov said. "Y'all know her?"

"Hell yeah, I know Traci. Her and that girl I was telling you about last night are best friends."

"Who?" T-Lov asked.

"Her name is Kasha, but she dates that punk-ass Ricky now," Cane said, nodding his head toward the backroom where Ricky was fetching shoes.

"Oh, snap! Hell yeah, I know Kasha. That broad is sexy as hell," T-Lov said. "Damn, Jack must have paid her to go out with you," he said, pretending to be wiping his mouth and at the same time understanding why Cane didn't like Ricky.

"So, you're the one that Ricky was easing in on that Traci was telling me about," T-Lov said.

"Huh?" asked a confused Cane.

"Yeah, you know me and Traci are cool as fuck when she's not tripping. One night, she was mad at Kasha and called me venting about how much of a whore that Kasha was. She said that her boyfriend had just left, and then Ricky came over right behind him. I'll beat that nigga's ass right now if you want me to," T-Lov said.

"Nah, they're not worth it. I'm done entertaining those two," Cane said as Ricky brought out the next pair of shoes that Cane had requested.

"I'll take all of these," Cane said to Ricky, letting him know that his pockets were deep. Deep down, Cane did not want to drop 300 bones in this one store alone, but it was about saving face and letting this muthafucka know.

Chapter 11

Trapp

Three Months Later

Trapp wasn't down with CMB any longer. His attitude these days was "Fuck them" now that he was hanging out with Ray-Ray, who he felt was more on his level. Just because he and CMB went way back didn't mean that they hadn't outgrown one another. He needed people more like-minded in his corner, people not afraid to go after that dime at any cost. Ray-Ray had proven to be a "down for whatever" type of nigga when it came to making money.

Trapp thought that his and Ray-Ray's paths crossing in the manner in which they did was a sign. After his mother found out about the store robbery attempt, she threatened to send him to his father. She was embarrassed and mad as hell! He pleaded with her because going to his dad's was not an option as far as he was concerned. He had never cared two fucks about him, so why would he want to stay with him? Trapp couldn't believe that Jack had told his mom what had happened. His mom told him that he had better thank his lucky stars that Jack had got him out of jail because she didn't have the money, and neither would she have gone into debt trying to scrape up the money for him making a stupid decision to rob somebody.

People at school were looking at him sideways because he was no longer rolling with CMB, and rumors were floating around about him being the mastermind behind the attempted robbery. Ray-Ray had told him that Cane was the one spreading the rumors. He wanted to approach Cane and knock the hell out of him, but he knew that, if he did that, Cane was not the one to be played with, and they would have to fight. Plus, he had nowhere else to go if his mom kept her promise and shipped him off to live with his alcoholic dad if he got into any more trouble.

Trapp still held a major grudge against his dad, not just for cheating on his mom, but for leaving her and not bothering to help her take care of him and his siblings. He still remembered the heart-wrenching cries of his mom after his dad had left. For some odd reason, it reminded him of Cane. Although Cane didn't literally shed tears in his presence over Kasha, they all could tell by the change in him after their breakup that he was hurting very bad. He still didn't understand how Cane had let Kasha get into his head space the way she had. They all knew she was an opportunist and so did he. Cane was just a sucker for love. He believed in all of that happily-ever-after shit, but Trapp had vowed to himself and his boys that no girl was going to have him that way.

Kasha was fine as hell, but Cane knew what came with those types of girls, and Kasha was no exception. That didn't change the fact that Trapp wanted to fuck her. And when Ray-Ray had put that vision in his head of her naked, it only made him want her even more. He couldn't even front. Every time he saw Ricky, jealousy rose from his heart. There had been plenty of times when he wanted to throw a brick through his windshield himself.

The bell jolted him back to reality. He gathered his books to move on to the next class. When he stepped into the hall, Cane was in front of him, looking dapper in some brand-new kicks with the matching Adidas joggers and T-shirt. *He's a wannabe,* he thought as he walked behind him. *Look at him thinking he's all of that because he's got his uncle holding him down. Got all these people up in here thinking he's got it going on. Fake ass.* Cane had stopped and was talking to this cute chick named Alissa, so Trapp bumped him, causing his book that he was palming with one hand to the side to drop from his hand.

Cane reached down to pick up the book as he looked Trapp square in the eyes.

"Excuse you, nigga," Cane said angrily.

"Pardon me, but did you think I was apologizing?"

"You stupid, Trapp. Get out of my face because you don't want these problems, believe that," Cane said, stepping closer to Trapp.

Trapp did not want, neither could he afford, to get into a fight at this point, so he was happy when Tina walked up and stepped between the two of them.

"Both of y'all niggas need to chill out. It's bad enough that you guys have let rumors come between your brotherhood, and now you're about to fight over some foolish stuff. Y'all been friends too long for some petty stuff like this to come between you."

"Fuck that fake-ass nigga! You know where I be. Anytime you want to put up, holla at me," Trapp said as he walked off to join Ray-Ray who had just walked up.

Tina pulled Cane away, telling him he was not worth it. "Trapp's just going through something right now, and he is not thinking rationally, but don't let him get into your head and make you miserable because he is."

"Man, forget Trapp. He's trying to play hard around his new crew, but he knows that I will beat the shit out of him if he comes at me sideways," Cane said.

As Trapp and Ray-Ray were walking off, Ray-Ray dapped up Trapp and said, "You straight blasted that nigga." Ray-Ray and Trapp talked about the incident that had just gone down all the way to class. They walked to the back of the room and had just taken a seat when that trifling-ass Meka walked up and stood in front of them with her hands on her hips, demanding to know when they got so close.

"Over the summer, about the same time we became good friends with you and your girl," Ray-Ray blurted out.

"I can't stand your ass, with your smartass mouth." She rolled her eyes, turning her attention back to Trapp. "You need to talk to Cane and stop with this foolishness you are doing. Those guys have been down for you like four flat tires since you were kids."

"Bitch, be gone," he said. "Just because we grew up together doesn't mean we are to grow old together. They are two-faced snitches, and I don't need fake people in my life, so get the fuck outta here with that mess," he said, hoping to impress Ray-Ray.

"Trapp, I know that you ain't trying to trip or call nobody fake. You are the fake one. You're running around with this nigga now, who you hated just last week, turned your back on your day-one boys, and you're going to call them fake? You are a joke," she snapped. "You think you're doing something because you're hanging with this fool," she said, pointing at Ray-Ray. "Like I said, you are a joke. You ain't loyal. Fuck you and fuck you," she said to both of them and turned to walk away.

"I already have fucked you and your friend at the same damn time," Ray-Ray hollered at her back.

Meka turned around, looked at him, and said, "Nigga, that pencil dick you got was swimming in me. You were the smallest one out of the group, so don't think you can brag about something because I didn't feel a thing from you at all. If you can prove me wrong, pull it out and do it!"

Ray-Ray was hot! He stood up and walked over to Meka, towering over her by three feet, and said, "You've got me mixed up with one of those other three dicks you had in your mouth that night." Everyone in the class started laughing as Meka ran out of the classroom, crying.

The more Ray-Ray continued to tell about her, Trapp realized that Meka really was the real-life freak that he had thought her to be. Meka was messing with his boy Calvin at the time, but she was still trying to get on his dick. But since he and Calvin were no longer cool, shoot, he might get on that now to see if she was as good as the rumors going around were claiming her to be.

"I've got something for you, my nigga!" Ray-Ray said, winking his eye. "Meet me in the bathroom in five minutes." He got up and got a pass to the restroom.

He waited anxiously, counting down the seconds, then he too asked for a restroom pass. While walking down the hallway, he saw Meka coming his way. He kind of felt bad for her. Ray-Ray had gone overboard, but she had brought it on herself.

"You aren't shit, Trapp. I don't know what's gotten into you. You used to be so cool when you hung out with Cane and them. Now, I don't know who you are anymore. The new you isn't cute at all," she said with puffy eyes.

"I'm still the same person, Meka. I'm sorry for tripping on you like that. So much has been going on in my life, and if I could take back my bad words, I would." He reached out to give her a hug. "Sorry, babes."

"Thanks, I needed that."

"What I need, I can't get," he whispered into her ear, trying to set up a come-up with her.

She pulled herself from him, sucking her teeth. "Don't even go there with me." She pointed her finger in his face. "Just because I got drunk and them nasty-ass niggas took advantage of me doesn't make me a whore. So, what is this, you want to experience it for yourself now? You don't want me. You just think that I am an easy fuck," she said on the verge of tears.

"No, no, no, Meka. I'm talking about your phone number! I know what I said in the classroom. Please forgive me."

"Why would you want my number with the reputation I have now because of what those stupid niggas done? Come on, Trapp. I am not stupid. I can smell foul, and your ass is stinking badly."

"Nah, Meka, I am not that dude. I have always liked you, but you were rocking with Calvin, and I knew I couldn't cross that line. But now that Calvin and I are no longer cool, I'm like fuck it. I don't care what them niggas are talking about they did to you. I know you were drunk and out of your head because those are not the things that the Meka I know would do, so fuck them. I just want the digits, and we will take it from there. Real talk," Trapp said, pleading with his eyes.

Meka wrote down her number and placed it in his hand. "If what you say is true, I have a new respect for you," she said, looking at him doubtfully.

"I can show you better than I can tell you," he said, placing the number into his pocket. "Look, I will holla at you later. I've got to go handle some business with the john real fast," he said, speaking of the toilet.

When he walked into the bathroom, Ray-Ray asked what took him so long. Ray-Ray pulled out a fat blunt. From the look on his face, he could tell that Trapp was either uncomfortable or had never smoked weed before.

"This that good shit. It will have the women dropping their panties faster than an African running a marathon," Ray-Ray said.

At the sound of panties, Trapp's mouth got watery. "Fire up that shit," he said, looking at the blunt. Ray-Ray did just that, took three pulls, and then passed it to him. He didn't hesitate, putting it to his lips and smoking it like it was a cigarette, causing him to break out into a fit of coughs.

Ray-Ray, laughing, said, "I told you, my nigga, that's that fire. Give me that shit before you kill yourself."

"Hold up, fool, let me hit this shit one mo' time." He held the blunt and puffed it like a champ. With Ray-Ray pumping him up, they smoked another blunt, getting fucked up.

Smoke clouded the restroom and seeped out into the hallway.

"Who's in here?" came a deep voice.

Trapp quickly put out the blunt and stuck it into his sock as he ran into one of the stalls and pretended to be taking a shit, just as Mr. Coolly, the janitor, rounded the corner with a broom in one hand and talking into the radio with the other.

"Come on, Mr. Coolly, man. Why didn't you give us a chance to explain that this smell was in here when we came in before you started calling administration? We both were saying how someone had been smoking when we came in here. All we were doing was using the bathroom," Trapp said, trying to convince him that they were innocent.

"Well, son, I don't have anything to do with that. You have to take that up with Principal Dixon. I'm just doing my job."

"Your fucking job is sweeping the fucking floors and not snitching, you rat bastard," Ray-Ray snapped.

Trapp tried to calm Ray-Ray down so he could try to handle the situation, but Ray-Ray was mad and trying to charge at Mr. Coolly when Principal Dixon walked in. Shaking his head as he walked into the bathroom, Principal Dixon said, "Just the two I'm looking for. Your teacher called in a MIA on you two. She said you have been gone for over thirty minutes. Y'all come with me." He patted Mr. Coolly on the back as they were exiting. "I will call you in a little while because I am going to need a statement from you."

"That's what is wrong with your black ass now, always kissing the white man's ass," Ray-Ray hissed to Mr. Coolly as they were passing him. "These crackers don't give a shit about your black ass."

Principal Dixon did not hear what Ray-Ray said, but he knew that it wasn't anything pleasant by the look on Mr. Coolly's face. "I advise you not to say another word until I ask you to," Mr. Dixon said. "Did he threaten you, Mr. Coolly?" he asked the janitor.

"Fuck, I don't make threats. I make promises," Ray-Ray boomed.

"No, sir," answered Mr. Coolly, still looking as if he wanted to punch Ray-Ray in the nose.

Trapp was shocked to see how Ray-Ray was talking to Mr. Dixon. He was mad also, but he knew that he was in enough hot water with his mother, so he wanted Mr. Dixon to at least be able to say that he was cooperative and not loose at the mouth.

"Travis, Travis, Travis, why am I not so surprised to see you? As a matter of fact, don't even answer that," Mr. Lewis, the grade-level principal, said when they were escorted into his office. "A student just left my office in tears, saying that you and Ray were the culprits who embarrassed her in front of the entire class. So how ironic is it that the same two troublemakers would both be caught in the bathroom at the same time in a room reeking of smoke?"

Trapp tried explaining the same story to Mr. Lewis as he had Mr. Coolly, saying that the smoke was already there when they walked into the bathroom and that Meka cracking on Ray-Ray was why he started cracking on her.

Mr. Lewis didn't buy that for a minute, but since he could not prove that they were the two smoking, he suspended them for cutting class and causing a distraction because the teacher had reported what had happened in class, also backing up Meka's story.

"This some bullshit, and you know it," ranted Ray-Ray. "You're just trying to find anything to get us up out of here."

"Watch your mouth, young man!" Mr. Lewis said, standing up from his chair. "I could push this thing further and have my resource officer come in, search the both of you, and get your butts out of here for the rest of the year. Yeah, why don't I do that?" Mr. Lewis said, picking up his phone.

"Hold up, I saw Curtis Griffin exiting the restroom before we walked in," Trapp said. "He is a known weed head, so you better call him and have him searched too, then, because I ain't going down behind something I didn't do!"

Principal Lewis asked a few questions and then called Cane to his office. He asked Trapp and Ray-Ray to wait in the waiting room while he spoke with Cane. Cane came into the office just as they were exiting. Trapp had a smirk on his face the entire time as he stared him down.

Although they were in the waiting room that was adjacent to Mr. Lewis's office, they could still hear the round of questions that he was asking Cane. When Cane told him that he never left the classroom and Mr. Duncan could confirm that for him, Trapp's smirk faded quickly.

He heard as Mr. Lewis called down to Mr. Duncan for confirmation, and he also heard as Mr. Lewis told Cane that he apologized and he appreciated him for always being a respectful young man anytime he talked to him. He said, "Make sure you steer clear of some folks." Trapp couldn't see into his office, but he could imagine Mr. Lewis nodding his head toward the waiting room toward him and Ray-Ray.

When Mr. Lewis appeared in the door of the waiting room, there was no doubting that he was angry about Trapp's accusation of Cane. He gave Ray-Ray his three-day suspension referral and sent him on to class but asked Trapp to step into his office.

"Mr. Shiggs, you just dug your own grave." He paused, tapping the pen on the side of his face. "Actually, you've fallen into the grave. I'm suspending you for ten days, and you can't come back until I have a conference with your parents."

Mr. Lewis didn't want to hear shit he had to say. He charged out of the office, pissed the fuck off. How was he going to hide from his mom that he was suspended? When he was cool with CMB, he would have stayed at one of their houses until school was out. He knew that he had better figure out something or his black ass would be up the river without a paddle. Ray-Ray stopped him to see what happened. he told him that the redneck suspended him for two weeks because Cane snitched on him.

"I knew he was a snitch, punk ass," Ray-Ray said. "Look, I'll holla at you later. I have to go. My mom is already here in the office."

"Man, that was fast."

"Nah, man, supposedly she had come up to get a paper filled out for her caseworker, and they told her that I was in the office and what had happened. Man, I wasn't even going to tell her about the suspension."

"Man, that sucks. Well, holla at me when you get a chance. Let me get into this class because he already told her that I was on my way back to class and to let him know if I was ten seconds late." Trapp laughed as he and Ray-Ray dapped one another up.

Trapp walked into class just as the bell rang. He scoped out the area to make sure that Cane and the CMB crew weren't lurking before he continued down the hall. He spotted Ray-Ray with his mother escorting him from the office. Ray-Ray winked his eye at him, but Trapp wasn't in the mood to fuck with Ray-Ray. His mind was on the bus ride home with the CMB crew. This was going to be his first time riding the bus since he and Ray-Ray had started hanging because he normally rode with Ray-Ray.

He tossed his hood over his head, eased behind the bus driver, and slid down into the seat.

Once the other students were on the bus, he was pushed over to the window because two girls sat in the seat with him, and that was fine with him because they camouflaged his body. He stayed slid down and never once looked back. When the bus came to a halt and all the students had gotten off of the bus, he peeped out the window and saw that Cane, Calvin, and Shi hadn't even been on the bus. They were getting out of a blue Honda with a brown-skinned dude. He eased up out of the seat and flipped his hood back on as he exited the bus and walked in a fast pace to his own house.

After dinner, Trapp went to his room to call Meka to see what she was really about. They hadn't been talking a good three minutes before she brought Calvin's name into the conversation. *Here we go with that Calvin bullshit,* he thought. But she actually had him tripping as she talked about how he thought he was dogging her, but she already had the scoop on his game, and that was why she had the "I don't care" attitude with him. She went on talking about how fake Traci and Kasha were also.

Meka was enjoying the conversation she was having with Trapp. He was cool as hell. The longer they talked, she could feel herself being caught up in his smoothness.

Once Trapp explained why he decided to cut ties with CMB, Meka understood. Although, he didn't tell her the whole truth.

"So, you are down with the Poison Clan now?"

"Hell no, I am riding solo. I'm just doing me from here on out."

"Cool. I noticed that you and Ray-Ray have gotten pretty close, so I was just wondering."

"Ray-Ray is cool as fuck. I know you hate him, and I can't blame you for being mad about what he did today because that was foul, but you pushed his buttons too, Meka."

"Forget Ray-Ray. if he never said another thing to me in life, I would be good," she said, getting mad all over again about the day's events.

He looked at the clock, realizing he'd been on the phone with Meka for over three hours. He decided that he had better wrap the call up. After telling her he would talk to her tomorrow, they hung up.

"What's up, my nigga?" At first, Ray-Ray didn't recognize Trapp's voice. It took him a few seconds to pick up on it.

"What's up, nigga? I've been waiting for you to call me all day. Heard you got suspended for ten days, but hell, they're trying to expel me from being able to go to any school in Greenville County because I went off on Mr. Dixon's ass today. I've got to go before the school board for some hearing, but fuck that shit."

"Word? That is some bullshit for real. They're always complaining about the black man not being educated but always want to kick him out of school over some stupid shit," Trapp said.

"Have you talked to anyone today from school? What are they saying about that bullshit?" Ray-Ray asked.

Trapp didn't want to tell him that Meka was the only person he had talked to, so he said no and listened to Ray-Ray rant about snitches. Ray-Ray was a loose cannon, ready to explode at any second. He went on about how they thought they were hurting him by kicking him out of school, but he was about to be on some real gangsta shit. Being suspended with a recommendation for expulsion was going to be beneficial for him. He started telling his plans of jacking a few cornball-ass niggas from his hood.

"Now, this is what I'm talking about," Trapp said, getting amped up as Ray-Ray told him about how he had robbed the same niggas for two grand and a gun just last week.

"What about Chris and Timbo? They down with this?" Trapp asked.

"Fuck them niggas. It's just me and you, my nigga. We can split everything fifty-fifty!" Ray-Ray thought for a second, realizing it was his lick, and said, "Scratch that. I am the mastermind. We can split it sixty-forty!" He laughed.

Trapp peeped out the window when he saw a high-beam light flash across his blinds as a car pulled into Kasha's yard, which was two doors up from his house, but by his room window facing their house, every time a car pulled in, the lights bounced off of his blinds and wall.

"There goes your boy, Ricky, dropping off Kasha. I can't believe she fucks with that nigga," Trapp said to Ray-Ray.

"That nigga got so many bitches on his dick, she's just temporary. But I enjoy the shows he gives us when he is fucking her though. That bitch is fire to watch. But on the real, let them mofos have those bitches. We about to be about our money. The bitches will still be there after we hit this lick, even more so. They will really be sweating us hard when we're rolling in that dough, you feel me?"

"Yeah, man, I'm with you," Trapp said. "Well, look, I will get up with you tomorrow. Let me get my clothes and stuff together so I can pretend to be going to school for the next couple of days. I'll call you in the morning before I head out to catch the city bus over to the west side."

After hanging up from Ray-Ray, he closed the window, singing Tupac's "Picture Me Rollin'" in his head. He went into the kitchen and got the ironing board out, all for his mom's benefit, to make her believe he was getting his things together for school. After he finished ironing, he took a hot shower and had just gotten back in his room, slipping on some sweats, when his phone rang. He picked up the phone and said, "What's up?"

"Man, what did I tell you? Ricky just pulled up with a dime breezy thick-ass red bone."

"Damn, that nigga moves fast as hell," he said as he looked out his window to see if Kasha's room light was on, masterminding his plan to get into her panties.

"Look, just called to tell you that. But check it, my nigga, Ricky, just gave me the signal. It's *Showtime at the Apollo*. I can't miss this shit. I'll see you tomorrow." Ray-Ray laughed.

Trapp hated Ricky. *He is always taking the fine girls and making them the laughingstock of the school. You would think these girls would learn from the ones before them not to trust his ass. Everyone I want to fuck Ricky has already recorded or let his boys watch through a window fucking. Damn!* He pulled out the half of a blunt he had stashed in his sock from earlier. He made sure that his mother was asleep before he stepped outside and fired it up. He could feel the weed taking over his body, relaxing him. Kasha's room light going off drew his attention to her bedroom window. he was contemplating going to knock on it before she went to sleep.

The bud told him that he could do anything. He got up and looked over at Cane's house to make sure the coast was clear and then jumped off his porch, walked behind the house that divided his from Kasha's, and went to her window. His adrenaline was pumping as he softly knocked on her window.

"What are you doing at my window?"

"I need to talk to you about something."

"Really, Trapp, now?"

"Well, I saw that you were still up, and I just heard the news, so . . ."

"If it's about Cane, you can save it. I don't want to hear anything else about Cane," she snapped.

"Fuck Cane's snitch ass. It's about that faggot-ass nigga Ricky you call yourself dating."

"What about Ricky?" she asked, pushing the window up farther. He could tell that he now had her undivided attention. "Come in, because you know Mrs. Rose is nosy and sees everything. Don't need her telling my parents that I had a boy at my window," she said as she helped pull Trapp through the window.

"Shhh," she said when he tripped over one of her shoes. "We don't want to wake anyone. What's going on? What do you know about Ricky?" she whispered. She was sitting on her bed in a Strawberry Shortcake gown that was so thin that he could see her erect nipples standing at attention. She was all ears as her heart slowly crumbled to pieces as Trapp told her all the things that he had heard. But knowing that it was merely hearsay, she told Trapp, "You of all people know how people gossip when they see a good thing. Ricky is good to me and has never given me a reason to think he was seeing anyone else."

"Okay, so that makes it okay that he allowed his boys to watch him fuck you or to show them video of you sucking him dry?"

"Merely hearsay," Kasha said stubbornly, but in the back of her mind, she believed him and was furious with Ricky.

"Hell, I just got a call that he has just pulled up at his house with another shawty in the car with him. Didn't he just bring you home? Damn, that nigga has got a mean sex drive!"

Curiosity got the best of her as she picked up the phone and dialed his number. As expected, he did not answer. She was ten seconds away from stealing her mom's car keys and heading over there to see for herself when her phone rang back.

"What's up, baby? I thought you were asleep," Ricky said really low as if he had been asleep.

"Well, I tried to sleep, but you were on my mind," Kasha said. "What are you doing?"

There was silence, but Kasha thought that she heard breathing. *Did he just fall asleep on me?* "Ricky!"

"Shit, Kasha, baby, that feels so good!" he moaned out in a low, sexual tone.

"Did you just call me Kasha?" came a female's voice. "Hell to the fucking no. I'm down here, giving you head, and you call me by another bitch's name."

Kasha could hear licks being passed, and she knew it was the female attacking Ricky.

Kasha had heard enough. She hung up the phone with tears rolling down her cheeks. She fell into Trapp's arms, hiding her face into his chest to muffle her cries.

"Why does this keep happening to me?" she cried.

"Because you keep fucking with these lames that don't give two fucks, that's why. A real man doesn't brag on his dick. Just like I said when Cane told us that he had fucked you and how he had turned you out. That was foul. If that's your girl, the shit you and her do should be private," Trapp said, lying on Cane.

"He said what? He's actually telling people that? Oh, gosh, everyone must think that I am a slut bucket. I can't believe this shit is happening to me. Why me?" she cried out.

Trapp embraced her. "Don't worry about them clowns." Knowing that she smoked, he pulled out the remainder of the blunt and asked her if it was okay. She said yes as she placed a towel under her door to keep the smell from seeping out. She needed a hit of that blunt to relax her nerves. Trapp fired it up. Kasha took it and pulled on it as if she was trying to hurry and get an instant high.

She and Trapp sat there and continued to talk about everything. He told her everything Ray-Ray told him, even about the hickeys that she had put on Ricky's ass.

Heavy tears continued to escape her eyes as she leaned over into Trapp's arms. "Just hold me please," she begged. She felt lost and betrayed.

Her body felt so warm. He felt a chilling sensation travel through his body. *Now or never*. "Don't worry about them. I've got you," he said.

She looked up at him, and he kissed her on the nose. She was breathing heavily as she lifted her head so that her lips were close to his. He kissed them softly first, and then it turned very passionate.

She voluntarily lay back on her own as she invited him on top of her. "Hold up. Let me turn the radio on so we don't wake my parents." As soon as she hit the power button, he was taking off his shirt. He wasn't going to waste any time in case she changed her mind. He slid his hands up her gown, feeling her wetness soaking through her panties. His manhood was hard as a brick as he took off his pants.

He couldn't believe how tight her love box was, but at the same time, he couldn't believe that he was filling up her insides. "Turn over." She didn't protest and did as she was asked. She arched up her ass and then put her head under the pillow as he mounted her. She couldn't believe that Trapp was packing like he was. His dick was bigger than any she had ever had.

She bit down on the pillow to try to muffle her groans. "Hold up," she said, removing the pillow. "We can't be doing this. we're supposed to be homies."

"We are homies. We are now homies with benefits," he moaned in ecstasy.

"No, seriously, we've got to stop," Kasha moaned. This was feeling too good to her.

"Hold on, Kasha. This shit feels so good. Besides, you know that you love it."

"Stop, Trapp, for real. This ain't right," she said, trying to free herself from him, but his grip overpowered her. The more she resisted, the harder he penetrated her. She gave up the fight and flopped onto her stomach and cried for him to stop.

After he came, he wiped himself off with her gown. "Damn, Ray-Ray was right. Mya don't have shit on you. You've got some fire-ass pussy."

Hearing Trapp's statement set her off, and she knew that he had used her to see if she was all that she was rumored to be. "Trapp, get the hell out of my house!" she screamed in a whisper. She was mad as hell.

He chuckled out, "Why you tripping? You weren't saying that when I was piping you down."

"Now!" she demanded, picking up the clock, threatening to hit him with it. "Da—" She started to scream, but he held his hand over her mouth. He pulled up his pants and then jumped out the window with his shirt in his hands.

He ignored the screen that he tripped on that was lying on the ground. When he got in front of Cane's house, he could have sworn that he saw the curtain move, but then again, he knew that the weed still had him tripping. *Yeah, nigga, I got that ass. Something you didn't get, and you were dating her,* he thought as he passed Cane's house.

He walked back into his house and went straight to the bathroom, smelling Kasha's scent on his dick. He couldn't wait to tell Ray-Ray how he put it down on Kasha's ass. He didn't wash her off of him. Instead, he lay on the couch until he fell to sleep.

"Travis! Travis Shiggs, if you don't get your ass off my sofa, I'ma—"

"Hold up, Mama," he said, cutting her off as he stretched while trying to adjust his tired eyes.

"Why didn't you tell me about this mess that you have gotten yourself into? The school called and left a message on the answering machine saying that you have been suspended for two weeks. So, where in the hell have you been going for the past four days?" she demanded to know with fire in her eyes. "I don't know who in the hell you are anymore. You're running around, trying to rob stores, and now suspended from school for getting high in a damn bathroom. You have lost your mind! Get your ass up now!" she screamed.

He got up and walked slumped from being so tired to his room, ignoring his mother. When he got to his room, he rubbed his eyes, making sure that they weren't playing tricks on him. His mother had packed all of his clothes.

"Why you got my stuff packed up?" he turned and asked her.

"Because I can't do anything with you anymore, so you are going to have to leave my house. I will not have a child in my house who I can't control."

"Where am I supposed to go?" he asked in desperation just as the doorbell rang.

When he heard his father's voice in the living room, he got angry at his mother immediately. How could a woman send her child away like this? He couldn't believe that she was serious this time. She was shipping his black ass out.

Chapter 12

Cane

Cane was chilling and waiting on the mailman to run. He'd been expecting a letter from his mother. He prayed that once she got out of prison she would get her shit together and they could live like a real family should. He felt as if he needed her now more than ever. Although his mom messed up a lot, she was always an ear to vent to, and he knew that she would never judge him and loved him unconditionally. He had his grandma and Uncle Jack, who he knew loved him, but it was different. He knew that if he made them mad enough, they would cut him off with the quickness, but his mom would never leave him.

The telephone ringing startled him. He looked at the caller ID and noticed Jack's number. "What's up, Unc?"

"I took care of y'all's charges, but you and Calvin got to go to pretrial intervention so they can clear y'all's records."

"Good looking out, Unc. I owe you my life." He paused for a moment as he thought about Trapp. "What about Trapp?"

"I'm sure Trapp can handle his own since he's so damn grown. I have tried to help that boy, but nobody is going to disrespect me and I still try to help them. But anyway, I talked to T-Lov, and he's going to take y'all since I'll be out of town."

"That's cool because we're supposed to play ball later on anyway, so we can kill two birds with one stone."

"Cane, listen, you're not the only one that lives in this house. There's other people trying to use the phone!" his grandmother yelled as she stepped onto the porch. Gina was hiding behind her, silently laughing her ass off so that Grandma didn't see her.

He knew that Gina had something to do with his grandma wanting the phone. "I'm talking to Uncle Jack," Cane said, knowing that she would not argue with him about that.

"It's cool. I just called to tell you that. Plus, Tony just walked in. Tell Mama I said hello, and I'll holla at you later on," Jack said.

"I know, man," Cane said into the phone, as if he and Jack were talking about them demanding the phone. "Okay, I'll holla at you later," he said, disconnecting the call.

"You didn't have to hang up from Jack," Grandma said, feeling crazy for coming out there with the attitude that she had. Jack was the breadwinner in her household.

"Nah, it's fine. He said for me to just give Gina the phone. He will call me back later," Cane said, making them both feel stupid.

"Why did he say give Gina the phone?" Gina demanded to know.

"Because he knows how you and Grandma do. Every time Grandma demands the phone, you are always in the shadow."

Gina snatched the phone away, furious with him for making her uncle think she was the villain. She always played innocent around him. Cane, pleased with the way he had handled their interruption, jumped down from the porch to meet the mailman when he spotted him coming down the street.

As he was flipping through the mail, looking for his letter from his mom, he caught a glimpse of Kasha out of the side of his eye in her sweatpants and bedroom shoes, checking their mailbox.

"Cane, can you come here? I need to ask you something," she called out to him.

Wondering what she could possibly want with him, he started crossing the street to head over to see.

"Sorry to hear about your mom getting locked up. My mom was telling me about it a few weeks ago, but you know, I hadn't seen you, but I hope she will get herself together this time. I know how much you love her," she said.

"Thanks," Cane said, digging his hands into his pockets. "She promises this time that she is going to get into a treatment center. Only time will tell, but she seems to have opened her eyes since she got sent away. I hope so."

"Cool. But let me ask you something."

"What's up?"

"Why are you going around telling people that you fucked me?" she asked, clearly upset.

"I ain't told nobody no shit like that."

"Well, if it's a lie, your boy, Trapp, told it," she said.

"You know what, Kasha? I don't put anything past Trapp these days. It seems as if all he is doing lately is going around, telling lies on me, trying to ruin my character, so you can believe what you want to believe, but all I can tell you is that I ain't said nothing like that to nobody. I'm still a virgin and proud of it," he stated with authority, not being ashamed.

"I don't understand why he would make up something like that," she said.

"When did he tell you all of this bullshit?"

"Last night," she responded.

"Last night? Oh, so you two cozy like that now that you talk other than in school? Shoot, you barely even spoke to him in school, and now you talk to him after hours? Wow," Cane said, realizing that it was indeed Trapp he thought he had seen coming out of Kasha's bedroom window last night.

"Kasha, telephone! Ricky wants to talk to you!" Tina yelled out as she held the phone in her hand.

"Tell him I'm not home," she said as she rolled her eyes, turning her attention back to Cane.

"If that's what you want me to do, I'll do it," Tina said as she headed back into the house.

"Ugh, I can't stand that cheating bastard! And Trapp . . ." She broke down crying. "He raped me last night!" She leaned against Cane's chest for support. "I tried to fight him off, but . . ."

Cane was furious. He held on to her tightly, trying to calm her down. He was having flashbacks of his mother when she used to cry. "It's going to be all right, Kasha. I'm here for you." A few tears escaped his eyes. He rocked with her back and forth as she cried as he was thinking about how to handle this. "Pull it together. I'm going to handle Trapp. What you need to do in the meantime is call the police and tell them what happened."

"They might not believe me because I did let him into my room through the bedroom window in the middle of the night," she cried.

"Speaking of, why did you do that anyway?"

"Because he had some information to tell me about you and Ricky. It was late, and you know Mrs. Rose is nosy. I didn't want her to see him at my bedroom window and tell my parents. I didn't ask for this to happen to me!"

He was mad as hell, but all he could do was comfort her and let her know that they would get through this. She backed away as she thought about the fact that her crying in Trapp's arms was how she got caught up in the moment with Trapp. But it dawned on her that she was tripping because Cane and Trapp were cut from two different cloths. Cane had a heart of gold. She walked back to him and hugged him, thanking him for being such a good friend even when she was being a straight ass toward him. She kissed him on the cheek.

Ricky's Mustang came around the corner so fast that neither Cane nor Kasha had an opportunity to break their embrace, even if they cared to.

"Bitch, I should beat your ass! How you going to be out here in the public, disrespecting me with this punk-ass nigga?" Ricky said, leaving his car in the middle of the street when he jumped out. "This what you want? This muhfucker here?"

"Pussy muthafucker. Maybe if you were giving her the attention you're giving the other hoes," Cane snapped, walking toward Ricky, "your woman wouldn't need my shoulder to cry on."

"This is between us, Ricky," Kasha said as she quickly got between the two of them. "We wouldn't be going through this if you weren't so messy with your secret affairs and news getting back to me!"

"Man, I told you that was a fuck flick that was in the VCR that I was masturbating to," Ricky said in a final attempt of trying to defend himself.

"Ricky, just leave and go back to continue to fuck yourself to your fuck flick, you lying bastard. It was one of your friends, your boys," she said, putting up the air quotes with her fingers, "that called and told me that you had just rolled on set with another female. You had just dropped me off and moved on to the next that fast, huh?"

"Who told you that bullshit? I want to know because, if someone in my camp is hating on me and lying like that, they don't need to be in my circle!" he demanded.

When Kasha refused to tell who the informant was, he started accusing her by saying that since she was trying so hard to protect them, she must care more about that person than she did him. Therefore, she must be sleeping with whoever it was.

"Nah, nigga. I'm not trying to hear your ass, so talk to the hands because the face doesn't want to hear it."

"I'm not going anywhere until you hear me out." He grabbed her by the arms, but she snatched away and started backing away from him.

"Come on, baby. Don't do this to me!" Ricky said, as if he really cared.

Cane, growing tired of Ricky's excuses and his begging, shook his head and said, "Nigga, you're acting like a bitch with all of this pleading. Thought you were supposed to be a G. You heard her, so ride out."

"Nigga, go fuck yourself," Ricky spat out, "before I kick your ass up and down this street."

"Nigga, I'm good over here. According to you, you are the one that has been feeling yourself, and I can tell that's true if you really think you can kick my ass anywhere. Don't let your fuck flick and you feeling yourself get you fucked up," Cane said with authority as he walked right up to Ricky's face, where the bridges of their noses were almost touching.

Kasha, again, tried to intervene, but Cane moved her out of the way. As Cane looked off to move Kasha, Ricky stole on him, catching him with a right hook. He stumbled backward as Ricky charged him, swinging wild punches. Ricky was on top of him, pounding his head into the ground. Kasha jumped on his back, trying to pry Ricky off of him. When Kasha bit into Ricky's shoulder, he backhanded her, knocking her onto the ground.

After Ricky had gotten Kasha off of him, he drew his arm back with his fist balled up to punch Cane in the face when he felt a hard blow to his head that caused him to lose balance. He was dizzy as he drunkenly stumbled around, trying to regain his vision and focus on his target. Just as he regained his vision, he felt his body being lifted into the air and driven into the ground. Cane and T-Lov were stomping the shit out of him.

Mr. Davis, who was just pulling into his yard, saw the commotion and his daughter screaming. He ran over to make sure that she was all right. Mrs. Davis, who had come to the porch to greet her husband, ran and grabbed the phone and was yelling to everyone that the cops were on the way.

Ricky, finally being able to break free, jumped to his feet, running to his car, hollering, "It's not over, motherfuckers!"

Cane jumped into T-Lov's car, and they too left the scene. T-Lov teased him about Ricky kicking his ass and, at the same time, gave him credit for standing up to Ricky.

Once Shi and Calvin were in the car, they filled them in on what had gone down with Ricky as they rode over to the west side to play basketball. Cane, Calvin, and Shi didn't like being on the west side because, although they were cool with a lot of the cats there, they still had many more enemies, and this was enemy territory, but T-Lov convinced them that it was cool because that was his hood, and no one would gang them while they were with him because he had mad stripes in the hood.

They walked into the gym, confident as ever, and started balling. Calvin and T-Lov turned the game into something personal. Cane and Shi sat down and let them go at it one-on-one. Little kids were clapping as they watched them play. After the game was over, all of the animosity that T-Lov and Calvin had shown on the court was left on there, and they were boys again.

Chapter 13

Trapp

As much as Trapp hated to leave his home and his mom, he could not help but to smile to himself when he saw the West Greenville sign, knowing that Ray-Ray stayed a block away. Now, since he had been kicking it with Ray-Ray and his crew, he was no longer intimidated with the west side, and staying with his dad would make it a lot easier to get together with his boys.

Before his dad even put the car in gear, he started laying down rules. "Son, let me lay down my house rules so that there are no misunderstandings. There will be no late-night phone calls, because I work, and I am not going to have no phone ringing, waking me up all night long. Your ass will be in the house at night before I turn in for bed, and since you're suspended from school, your curfew is eight p.m."

"Dad, you can't be serious. I am seventeen years old, and you want me in the house before the streetlights come on?"

"The streetlights come on at six," his dad said sarcastically. "Son, your mom and I are only hard on you because we don't want you to end up as another statistic, in prison, or dead."

Trapp couldn't care less about his father's rules. *Why do you all of a sudden want to play dad?* Trapp wanted to ask. Yes, he paid child support, but he had not been a father. He dropped in occasionally, which was maybe once a month, unless his mom called him about something that Trapp had done and demanded he come over to set him straight. Trapp just bit his tongue and tried to stay calm because, unlike his mother who would only rant and rave, he knew his father would go to the extent of beating him if he dared to talk back.

Once in the house, his father followed him to what would now be his permanent bedroom, continuing to lay down his wack rules. After what seemed like an eternity, he finally left him alone. After putting away his things, Trapp grabbed the telephone and called Ray-Ray, telling him what all had gone down.

"Damn, bro, your mom wasn't bullshitting, was she? Well, welcome to the hood where the player's play," Ray-Ray laughed. "Man, there is plenty of pu-nanny over here. These little tricks are nothing like the other side. You can buy them a candy bar and a soda pop, and they think you're doing something and they're special," Ray-Ray laughed. "But that girl that stays two houses up the street from you—"

"Who? Kasha?" Trapp asked.

"Yeah. Now, that is fire there. You will need five candy bars for her," Ray-Ray said, cracking himself up.

"Man, I hit that without even giving her half of a bar," Trapp said, boasting, ready to tell all.

"Man, shut the fuck up. You ain't hit that."

"Man, all I can do is give you the facts. Whether you choose to believe them is totally up to you," Trapp said in a no-bullshit tone.

"Well, I ain't believing that. How in the hell you pull that off?"

"One thing led to another is all I can say. I was at her house, talking to her the other night about her punk-ass boyfriend, Ricky, and what had gone down. You know she's been feeling me anyway on the low, so I just took advantage of the opportunity," Trapp said, shrugging his shoulder as if Ray-Ray could see him.

"Man, I knew pretty boy Ricky couldn't have been putting it down enough to satisfy that," Ray-Ray said in disbelief of what he had just heard. "Man, I've got to give you your props on that one. Shoot, wish it had been me tapping Kasha's ass."

With his high on Kasha finally coming down, Trapp was ready to talk business. Shoot, he had been broke long enough. He was ready to talk money.

"Since I stay with my pops now, you can show me all the ropes that you've been boasting about. A nigga is hungry as hell and starving like a motherfucker."

"Yeah, my nigga. Things are about to get better for the both of us. It's going to just be you and me, no dividing up the earnings four and five ways anymore. Fuck that, we robbing every nigga in this hood. Hell, we even going to rob the robbers," Ray-Ray laughed while rubbing his hands together, "Check this, we're going to hit our first lick on Tuesday morning."

"Preach then, nigga. You know that I need the dough, so we can go and hit it now for all I care," Trapp said, getting amped up.

"Dang, you really are hungry, huh?" Ray-Ray laughed. "Nigga, calm your ass down, and come on over and blaze up."

Trapp grabbed his wallet off the dresser and went out the front door. His dad rushed behind him.

"Where in the hell do you think you're going with all them damn bags on the floor?"

Trapp didn't say anything back as he turned around and climbed the steps two at a time, brushing past his father as he headed back to his bedroom to put up the clothes. He was so anxious to talk to Ray-Ray that he didn't think about cleaning up his room. He could hear the weed calling his name, and the way his mind was set up at the moment, he needed to answer it quickly. He shoved the bags into his closet.

After he finished setting up his room, he rushed out the door and jogged down the street, trying to get out of earshot in case his dad had a change of mind and called him back.

As he rounded the corner, he almost hit a shocked Meka head-on as she was heading to her house that sat on the corner. She looked at him as if she had seen a ghost.

"What the hell are you doing here?" she asked.

"Don't be surprised!" He held back his laughter. "I'm here to see you and make sure you're all right."

"Why?" she asked, confused.

"Because I care about you, and the way things went down between us just wasn't cool."

"Boy, stop playing." She chuckled while blushing.

"I'm for real. I moved in with my pops, so I hope we can at least be civil since we are practically neighbors now. Who knows what tomorrow may bring, so don't laugh too hard," he said as he walked closer to her and hugged her. He then kissed her on her lips.

"What was that about?" she asked.

"For you being such a strong woman and overcoming all the suffering and pains Ray-Ray and them clowns put you through. I promise you that I will never stand by and watch them try to humiliate you again. I'm sorry for my part in that whole mess." He could see from her eyes that he had her hypnotized. "But, baby, I'm about to go and talk to Ray-Ray and tell him that he needs to back off."

"No, Trapp, just stay here with me. I am over it, so let's just let it go."

"I'm just going to talk to him, that's all. No trouble, and anything pertaining to you is worth it." He fought hard to keep a straight face. "I'll call you later." He gave her a goodbye hug.

Ray-Ray started fussing as soon as he saw Trapp round the corner about how long he had been waiting to fire the blunt up waiting on his slow ass.

"Man, my pops was tripping. He's on his wanting to play the good dad role and was giving me a list of dos and don'ts," Trapp laughed. "Then, I ran into Meka on the way over."

Ray-Ray ignored his excuses, lit up the blunt, and took a hard pull before he passed the blunt to Trapp. They had it looking like a chimney was on the porch. An hour later, Trapp was feeling good, and his only worry in the world at that moment was his stomach growling. "What do you have to munch on?"

"Shit, my nigga, every fucking thing. It's the first of the month, and our refrig' is swole." Ray-Ray laughed as he opened the screen door to go into the house.

Trapp followed Ray-Ray into the kitchen, grabbing everything in sight from cookies to chips. Ray-Ray's mother's boyfriend came into the kitchen, and he was cool as shit. He told Ray-Ray to give him a blunt. He sat at the kitchen table and smoked it with them as they demolished the chips and cookies.

Ray-Ray's mom walked through the kitchen, just as Ray-Ray passed the blunt to Trapp, who tried to hide it under the table. His heart was beating a mile a minute at the thought that they had just gotten busted, and his dad was going to kill him.

"Man, what the hell you doing?" asked Ray-Ray's mom's boyfriend. "Pass the blunt!"

"Y'all take that shit on the back porch! Having my house smelling like marijuana," his mom said as she grabbed a soda and walked back out of the kitchen.

"Man, she don't care about you smoking weed?" Trapp asked in disbelief as he passed the joint.

"Man, as long as I have my share of the rent money, she don't give a damn," Ray-Ray said.

Trapp wished like hell his mother was that cool. Now, he knew why Ray- Ray had the "I don't give a fuck" attitude. His mother let him get away with murder. Shoot, Trapp was thinking about asking if he could move in with them. They were too cool.

A loud banging at the door startled all of them as they quickly put the blunt out, and Ray-Ray grabbed a can of air-freshener that immediately neutralized the marijuana smell.

"Why the hell are you banging on my door like you're the damn police?" Ray-Ray asked a stunned Ricky when he snatched open the door.

Ricky was at the door, looking a mess. "Damn, nigga, which one of your bitches beat the shit out of you?" Ray-Ray laughed in his face, shaking his head.

"Nigga, I got jumped, and it's your fault," Ricky said angrily as he stepped into his face. "You're running around here, dropping salt on me, telling motherfuckers my business and shit." He looked over Ray-Ray's shoulders, noticing Trapp. "What in the hell is he doing here?"

"That's my dawg. He's cooler than a motherfucker. What'cha mean you got jumped? By who?" Ray-Ray asked, ready to go and handle some business.

Trapp walked up and stood next to Ray-Ray, giving him dap. Ricky looked at them both sideways, trying to make sense of the situation. He balled up his fist, mad as hell. "You told this fuck nigga my business? Is that how everyone on the other side knows what I'm doing?"

"Ain't told nobody a damn thing!" Ray-Ray said.

"Well, somebody's been talking because she ain't just grabbed this shit from the air. And now, seeing how cozy you are with this nigga, I see where the leak in the camp is coming from. You're trusting this nigga, and he ain't even loyal to his own camp! Fuck both of y'all punk-ass niggas," Ricky charged.

"Nigga, you don't know a damn thing about me. All of your animosity is coming from the fact that you are mad because I fucked your bitch and left my nut on her ass beside the hickey you left," Trapp said.

Ricky, without a word, rushed him. Trapp, not expecting for Ricky to attack him, fell over the table, shattering the glass. Ricky had the best of him since he had caught him off guard, and he was beating the hell out of him. Ray-Ray, mad at Ricky's accusations, jumped into the fight to help Trapp. Trapp got to his feet and grabbed the broom that was leaning against the wall and beat Ricky, who was now on top of Ray-Ray, until he was unconscious.

Ray-Ray's mom and stepdad came running into the kitchen. "What in the hell are y'all doing?" she yelled.

"He came in here and charged at us," Ray-Ray explained.

"Is he dead?" she asked in a panic.

"Nah, he's just knocked out," his stepdad said calmly as he rose up from checking on Ricky.

"Well, who's going to get him woke up?" she asked, clearly upset.

Ray-Ray's stepdad turned her to walk her out of the kitchen. "Y'all get him woke," he said as he walked out with Ray-Ray's mom.

Trapp went through his pockets, taking the $6,017 that Ricky had. "Yeah, my nigga, we won't have any problems buying the sticky-icky now!" he shouted with joy, feeling on top of the world. "Here's to our first lick together and many more to come," he laughed as he handed Ray-Ray half of the money that he had taken from Ricky.

"Damn right," Ray-Ray said. "More money means more power. We in it to win it, and bump anyone that tries to get in our way!"

They dragged Ricky to his car, laying him on the back seat. Ray-Ray drove him home and parked his car in the backyard.

"My nigga, you're a fucking fool. That's why I fuck with you," Ray-Ray said to Trapp.

"I feel so good right now. Shit, nigga, I'm ready to hit a lick right fucking now."

"Calm down, my nigga. We gotta be patient and do it as planned. We're not in this shit to be getting caught because we didn't do as planned. Why masterplan if you're not going to follow what you mastered?" Ray-Ray saw in Trapp's eyes that he was hungry, and he liked that. "But we can go and buy a dime to bait the suckers. You know, let them get comfortable with us."

"Well, let's do it," Trapp said.

When they got to their destination, Trapp knocked on the door three times as planned. A slim Chris Rock–looking motherfucker came to the door. "Who sent you?"

"Pretty Ricky. Man, I just want a dime bag!"

"Come on in and have a seat." He walked into the back bedroom to retrieve a dime bag. "What's your name, player?"

"Cane," answered Trapp, not daring to make eye contact with Ray-Ray, who was looking at him with a smirk.

"Well, Cane, they call me Black, and since you and Ricky are friends, that makes us friends." He gave him a fat-ass dime.

"I hope it's fire. If so, I'm coming to buy a half pound tomorrow. Shit, I know I can make a killing off this shit."

Trapp went into his pockets, flashing a few big-face hundreds. He pulled a $10 bill out of the middle and paid Black. "I'll be back Tuesday, right before I go to school, only if it's that fire."

"Trust me, it's that fire, so I'll see you Tuesday," Black said, confident in his product. He was ready to make a deal now, and he didn't want to let any buyer escape his house.

"Like I said, if it's correct, I'll see you on Tuesday," Trapp said as he walked out.

He and Ray-Ray didn't utter a word until they got to the corner. "This is going to be a piece of cake," he said to Ray-Ray as they split the weed.

"Are you going to be all right walking home by yourself?"

"Hell yeah, fuck that nigga, Ricky," Trapp said, looking over Ray-Ray's shoulders. "I'm good, nigga, and I'll call you when I get home."

On his way home, he saw Meka sitting on her front porch. She hopped up and ran to the road. "What happened to you?"

"Just a little scuffle with that punk-ass Ricky. He came over to Ray-Ray's, trying to talk shit." He held his head up high, looking into her concerned eyes.

"You're already suspended from school and getting into fights is only going to cause more beef. I told you not to get into any trouble." She touched the bruise under his right eye. "I played a part in you getting suspended from school, so to make it up to you, I'm going to skip school tomorrow so I can be with you," she said as she kissed his soft lips, closing her eyes, mesmerized by how soft they were.

He pulled away as he started feeling a bulge form in his pants. "Don't start anything you can't finish."

"Oh, I can finish it," she said seductively, grabbing him by his hands, leading him into her house. "Don't worry, my mother won't be home for a while." She turned around, showing off her oiled legs. "If you want me, I'm yours." She stripped down into her bra and panties.

He unbuttoned his pants and pulled down his boxers. Meka lay across the bed, arching up her ass. "Just stick it in me!" she begged, wanting to feel his hardness thrusting against her walls.

Without any foreplay, he slid into her from behind, pounding her hard. He was shocked about how fat her love box was. "Damn, girl, I didn't know that you were this good!" He pulled out, wiping himself off. "We should've been did the damn thing."

"There's a lot of things about me that you don't know," she said, taking him into her mouth, sucking him until he dropped to his knees. He lay on the floor, trying to figure out what had just happened. He felt like an overnight superstar.

Chapter 14

Ricky

The sunbeams crept in, waking him up. He rubbed his eyes, trying to adjust them to the light, feeling light-headed. He looked around, delusional, not knowing where he was. After a few minutes, he realized he was at home. He was finally able to pull himself together enough to stumble into his house, dragging himself into the bathroom. He nearly lost his breath after seeing his reflection in the mirror.

Everything came rushing back to him in that instant of the previous night's activities. He quickly grabbed the phone and called to curse Kasha out for being the bitch she was. She denied everything, even having sex with Trapp, but he knew her ass was lying, and he was tired of listening to her lies. He told her that she was a tramp, and he was glad that he hadn't let himself fall in love with her. He threw the phone onto the floor, hoping to rupture her eardrums by doing so.

Retaliation was the first thing that crossed his mind. He grabbed his baseball bat and jumped into his car. He burned rubber on every corner until he got to his friends Face and Slim's house.

He knew they were always at home since they didn't want to miss a sale.

"What in the hell happened to you?" Face asked.

"One of them bitches fucked your ass up?" Slim said, holding his mouth to keep from laughing.

Ricky punched the steering wheel, frustrated as hell. "Ray-Ray and this little fuck nigga named Trapp jumped me from behind!" He wiped away snot, using the back of his hand. "Those motherfuckers robbed me for six grand." Slim and Face shook their heads in disbelief.

"What are y'all going to do, stand there or what?" asked an angry Ricky.

"Say no more, nigga," they both replied simultaneously, hopping into the car. Ricky pulled off, burning rubber and leaving a cloud of smoke in the air.

He crept by Ray-Ray's house slowly. He noticed that his stepdad's car was in the driveway. That made him hesitant about running up in there because Big Willie was a stone-cold killer who had just come home from doing a state bid. They rode on past. None of them wanted to feel the wrath of Big Willie.

Ricky circled the block a few times, praying that Ray-Ray or Trapp would magically appear. His heart started beating fast when he spotted T-Lov's Honda at the recreation center. He stopped abruptly and jumped out with his bat. Slim and Face followed him into the gym.

"Yeah, motherfuckers, I got y'all bitch-ass niggas now!" Ricky ran up to T-Lov's face, ready for war.

"Hold the fuck up, Ricky!" Slim said, looking at him like he was crazy. "These Jack's peeps." He took a deep breath. "Shit, nigga, you gotta squash this beef."

Ricky cocked his bat into the air. "Fuck whoever Jack is!" His nostrils were flaring as his arms trembled.

"It's your funeral, but Jack is cool as fuck, and he supplies a lot of work on our end," Slim said, patting him on the back. "You're on your own." Slim had mad respect for Jack, and he sure wasn't going to get on Jack's bad side behind Ricky's bullshit. Ricky was hotheaded and never thought about the consequences when he was mad, so Slim thought he'd enlighten him as to who he was dealing with.

Ricky lowered his bat. "See what your homeboy, Trapp, did to me?"

Cane stared at the knots on his head. "Shit, we don't fuck with that nigga. He's been on some other shit since he started hanging with Ray-Ray. He's become a loose cannon. Trapp has turned into an insane monster. His stupid ass even raped Kasha the other day."

"He did what?" Ricky asked as the bat slid from his hands.

"Yeah, you heard me correctly. That's what me and her were talking about when you pulled up, raising hell."

Ricky followed suit, dropping down next to his bat. He was traumatized after hearing that Kasha was raped. "I'ma kill that fuck nigga!" he spat out, picking up the bat. He gathered himself and apologized to Cane. They stood there talking for over an hour, squashing all the beef.

"Man, anytime you are in West Greenville, look me up," he said, extending his hand. Before he left, he gave them an ounce of weed to let them know there were no hard feelings.

Ricky was so mad that he ignored Slim's advice for him to not go to Kasha's house. He sped down the highway, not even caring about the fact that he was riding dirty. Kasha consumed his mind.

When they pulled in front of her house, he jumped out and headed to the door.

"What the fuck do you want?" Kasha snapped as she opened the door.

"Calm down, baby. I just want to apologize. I am sorry for everything I said out of anger. I'm sorry, Kasha. I love you, and I just want to make it right." He tried to grab her hand, but she snatched away as a single tear escaped her eye.

"Baby, let's start over. We were doing so good. I just don't understand how things went wrong for us so fast," he pleaded.

"Are you really that stupid?" she asked, stepping up into his face. "We went wrong when you had that bitch sucking your little-ass dick! It's not like you have that damn much to be sharing!" she snapped.

Ricky heard Slim and Face giggling behind him, and he was glad they couldn't see his face because he was beet red with embarrassment. "Chill out, babe. Let's go to the backyard and talk. I don't want your parents or these fools all in our conversation."

She reluctantly turned to walk to the backyard. "I heard about Trapp raping you." He pulled up his shirt to show her his heat that he had tucked into the waist of his pants. "He's going to pay for what he did to you and for jumping me. I'm going to blast his ass."

"Put that gun up before you hurt somebody or yourself!" she cried out. "Trapp is going to get what's coming to him. Traci is on her way over here to pick me up, and I am going to take a warrant out on him."

She thought about all the pain she'd endured over the past three days, from Ricky cutting their date short to go and get with another girl, to Trapp not accepting no for an answer. She was tired of being handled by these men and was ready to take control of her life. Love only got her hurt over and over again.

"I can't accept your apology. You played me." She punched him in the chest. "You let your boys watch through your window while we had sex, and then I hear that you got two other females pregnant. What in the hell is wrong with you, Ricky?" she cried.

"Baby, those girls aren't pregnant by me. I always used a condom!"

She slapped the shit out of him. "You're a nasty, dirty dog! I can't believe that I gave my heart and soul to you and you do this to me!"

He tried his best to take everything back, but she wasn't trying to hear shit he had to say.

"I don't want to hear it, Ricky. You need to take your weak ass away from here. I am done with you and all of your bullshit!" she said as she turned to walk away.

Ricky grabbed her arm. She tried to pull away, but he pulled her closer to him and said through clenched teeth, "I'm tired of your smartass mouth. You will listen to me!"

"Get the fuck off of my property!" her father yelled as he opened the back door.

Ricky let go of Kasha and ran to his car. Slim and Face stared at him, wondering what happened because of how fast Ricky came running from behind the house and jumped into the car, speeding off.

"Everything good? You didn't do anything stupid, did you?" Face asked, looking concerned while wondering if they were all going to be charged for whatever Ricky's dumb ass had done.

"Hell fucking no, Slim!" He pulled the gun out and handed it back to Face, its owner. "Her dad came out while we were arguing, holding a damn bat. He thought I was trying to handle Kasha, which I wasn't."

Ricky was so messed up that he had to pull over on the side of the road once they got back to their hood.

"Man, what is wrong with you? You never acted this way over losing a girl before," Face argued.

"Man, I love Kasha. I don't want to lose her over no bullshit. When I find out who in my camp is talking, it's going to be a wrap!" Ricky said as he hit the steering wheel.

"Look, nigga, get your damn nuts back. You're letting a bitch handle you like this, and your ass is tripping. She don't want you, so get over your damn self and move on!" Slim said.

Ricky grabbed the gun and put the gun to his head. "I can't take this shit anymore. My entire life is just fucked up!" Although Ricky was tripping, Slim didn't think it was funny and took the gun from Ricky.

Ricky and Face started laughing as Slim said, "Ain't no pussy that good in the world."

Chapter 15

Trapp

He was enjoying Meka's company. She had been playing hooky from school since he had been suspended, and they had been lying up in his father's bedroom, having sex every day, all day.

"Baby, you've got to go to school today," he said as he exhaled the smoke.

"Yeah, I was thinking the same thing, but I really don't want to leave you alone. Trapp, I love you so much," she said, massaging his nuts before leaning down to kiss his mushroom-shaped man tool.

"Auh, shit, girl, you're trying to turn out a nigga," he groaned, nearly choking on the smoke. He put out the blunt as she started deep throating him, taking him all in.

"Damn. Damn. Yeah, girl." His moans grew louder as she bobbed up and down his pole.

"You like that?" she asked as she straddled herself on top of him. "What about this?" She ground slow on top of his head and then dropped it all the way down. She wanted to give him all of her.

Trapp had to catch his breath as Meka sat on top of him, rubbing his chest. He loved the way her insides felt. "Damn, baby, that felt so good, but you know that we need to start using protection." He wasn't ready to have kids yet.

"I'd love to have your child, Trapp. You're such an awesome man, and I love everything about you, from your smell to your strong arms." She kissed his lips softly. "I just want you forever and ever." She kissed down to his navel. "Let's do it one more time?"

"Nah, girl, you've got to get ready for school. Plus, I promised my mother that I'd come over and rake her yard this morning," he lied, hoping she would leave before Ray-Ray showed up.

"All right, I guess I'll go to school today and cuss out Cane." She got up and started getting dressed. "I'll call Kim before she goes to school and see if her mother can come scoop me up."

"Fuck Cane," he snapped, pulling out the chrome .357 Magnum Ray-Ray gave him for the robbery. "I'ma get his ass before it's said and done," he said, kissing the barrel.

"Put that thing up, Trapp," she whined. "You're not a thug. You're a lover." She put her hand on top of his, holding the gun down. She tongued him down, feeling her panties get wet again. It took all she had to pull herself away from him before she ended up skipping school again.

"Let me go home and freshen up so I can go get my education." She kissed him again before leaving.

He hopped into the shower, washing her scent and the smell of sex off of him. A knock at the door made him cut his shower short. He wrapped a towel around his waist and headed to the door.

Ray-Ray was standing there with a puzzled look on his face. "Nigga, I'm not trying to get all up in your business, but why was Meka leaving your house?"

Trapp laughed out loud. "Shit, that bitch just wanted me to tap that ass," he said as he turned and walked down the hallway to his bedroom to get dressed. "I had to bust that pussy up. I didn't want her to think I was a fruitcake."

Ray-Ray sucked his teeth. "Shit, my nigga, you had to do what you had to do. Just don't fall in love with the skeezer," Ray-Ray said, feeling a little jealousy growing. "And remember, you can't turn a whore into a housewife."

"I'm not in love with her. She's just an easy screw," he said to convince Ray-Ray, but the truth was he was really feeling Meka and didn't like the fact that Ray-Ray was trashing her. He walked back into the living room dressed in blue jeans and a black hoodie, ready for war, waving the pistol.

He was somewhat disappointed that Ray-Ray had on a red hoodie, smoking on a blunt like everything was cool. "Nigga, what's up with that hoodie? You need to change that shit."

Ray-Ray was so high from smoking weed with his mother's boyfriend that he thought he had on a black hoodie. His stomach was growling. He walked into the kitchen and fixed a ham sandwich.

Trapp rushed Ray-Ray to eat because he was ready to hit the lick and get paid. On their way over to Ray-Ray's house, he spotted Meka standing next to Kim's mother's car. She waved him over and warned him about being with Ray-Ray. She felt like he ditched her for Ray-Ray, whom he supposedly hated, and she was totally confused about his real motives. After finally getting her calmed down, he gave her this bogus story about how he went over to deal with Ray-Ray, and they talked and squashed the beef.

"I thought you were supposed to be raking your mom's yard?"

"I am. Ray-Ray is going to help me so I can finish early. So, I should be back in the hood with his help before you even get home from school." He kissed her goodbye and whispered, "I love you," into her ear.

When the car pulled off, he hated the fact that Ray-Ray had witnessed the scene between him and Meka, and Ray-Ray didn't hesitate in telling him that he was in love with a ho. He told Ray-Ray that he couldn't help that his dick game was like crack—one hit and it would have a bitch feening for more. Ray-Ray was mad, but he laughed and played it off so Trapp couldn't see the jealousy seeping through his pores.

He was jonesing for another blunt after smoking their last one. All the smoking had him paranoid as hell. He thought he saw Ricky's Mustang creeping up and dove under the table.

"What in the hell are you doing?" asked an amused Ray-Ray. "Who in the hell are you hiding from?"

"Shit, I dropped something."

"What the hell ever," Ray-Ray said, pulling his hoodie over his head and passing Trapp the heat. "It's time to make a move. You ready or not?" he asked.

"I hope you are right because this shit ain't for the weak. You've got to be built for this type of shit. It's got to be a part of your nature," Ray-Ray said, looking at Trapp sideways.

When they got to Black's house, Ray-Ray hid on the blind side, quickly pulling his ski mask over his face. Trapp's heart was about to jump out of his chest as he knocked on the door. He was nervous as hell, but he couldn't let Ray-Ray see the fear in him.

"What's up, Cane? I was beginning to think that you didn't like my fire," Black said as he opened the door.

Trapp had to calm his nerves before he blew his cover. "What's up, Black? You said you would look out for me if I came back. I've got three hundred fifty dollars."

"Damn, Cane, them things go for four to five hundred a half, but shit, you're a new customer, so I'll settle for a loss," Black said with a smirk and shaking his head. "Come on in. We can't do business out here on the porch. This block is hotter than a motherfucker."

Trapp tried to sit as if he were comfortable as to not alarm Black that something was up, but he was sweating bullets on the inside.

"Did you hear about what happened to Ricky?" Black asked, eyeing him suspiciously before shaking his head.

Trapp got nervous, thinking that his cover had been blown, and was ready to pull out on him but decided to wait a minute and see what Black really knew. If Black said anything that gave any hint that he knew who Trapp really was, he was right by the door and would make a dash for it.

"Nah, what happened?" he asked, hoping his voice didn't give away his nervousness.

"Ray-Ray and some nigga named Trapp robbed him. Shit don't make sense. We raised li'l Ray-Ray, and he goes and bites the hands that fed him." Black's whole demeanor had changed from tripping to angry in a matter of seconds. "But them niggas better hope they become invisible because when we find them . . ." Black shook his head as he pounded his fist into the other hand. "If we don't kill them, they are going to wish we had." Black went to the back room to retrieve the weed.

As soon as he disappeared, Trapp unlocked the door to let Ray-Ray in. Trapp sat back down as if he never moved while Ray-Ray hugged his body against the wall. Black walked back into the living room with a pound in his hand.

"Since you fuck with Ricky, I'm going to front you the other half. When you finish running it off, I'll hit you off again." From his peripheral vision, Black saw something coming at him from behind. He dropped the weed, but it was too late. He was staring down a barrel.

"Nigga, this is a fucking robbery. I want everything you got!" Ray-Ray barked out from behind the mask.

"Cane, you set me up? I'ma kill your motherfucking ass."

Trapp slapped him with the pistol. "I've got the gun, muthafucka, so you are in no position to make threats! Now, tell me where the shit is at!" Trapp said, slapping him again with the gun.

"It's in the back room," Black cried out in fear. He didn't want to die over some bullshit homegrown weed.

"The shit better be back there. If not, tell God I said hello, and I'll see you in the next lifetime." Trapp tied him up with the phone cord while Ray-Ray held the gun to his head.

His adrenaline was pumping as he walked into the bedroom. Black's girlfriend was lying naked with her eyes closed across the bed. "Baby, come on and keep me warm," she said in a seductive tone. The hard, cold steel on her face made her open her eyes. She screamed when she saw the strange man.

"Bitch, don't yell or say a word unless you're telling me where the money is."

She continued screaming, so he struck her in the head. "Shut the fuck up before I kill your ass." She muffled her cries and pointed to the area where Black kept his money.

"Don't you move!" he demanded as he grabbed the paper bag filled with weed. He stuffed his hoodie with the six stacks of dead presidents that were on the dresser and grabbed the cocaine that was already packaged in the Ziploc bags. He stuffed it into his back pockets. He was loaded down, ready to get the hell out of dodge. As he was leaving, he glanced back at Black's girlfriend, who was very sexy and reminded him of Nia Long. He walked back to the bed, setting the bag down.

"Bitch, turn your ass over on your stomach!"

"Noooo!" she cried.

"I'm not fucking playing with you!" he yelled, sticking the gun barrel down her throat. She did as she was told. Trapp pulled his pants down to his knees and started pounding her from behind. She was crying for him to stop, but her cries only turned him on. Before he knew it, he was cumming inside of her.

"Hurry the fuck up, nigga!" he heard Ray-Ray yell, but he ignored him and continued until he was completely dry.

Ray-Ray, who had grown impatient, walked into the bedroom. "Man, you're sick," he laughed as he saw Trapp pulling up his pants and the naked girl, lying on her stomach and crying. "Come on, and let's get the fuck outta here before somebody comes," he said as he grabbed the weed.

Trapp told the Nia Long look-alike, as he started tying her up, that she was as good as she looked and he'd hate to slit her throat but he would if she moved. He and Ray-Ray made their departure, leaving both Black and his girl bound.

After Trapp made it home, he went to the bathroom to wash Nia off of his tool before he pulled the money out of his hoodie. He noticed a stack was missing, and he knew he had it before he left Ray-Ray's house, so he had to have dropped it along the way. He hid the five grand in the vent and put on his clothes to go retrace his steps. After not finding it in the house, he hit the front door. As soon as he was on the sidewalk, he noticed the stack of money two houses damn. *Damn, my luck is good.* As soon as he picked up the money and was turning to run back to the house, he bumped into Ricky.

"Yeah, nigga, I got your pussy ass now. Let's see how bad you are without your boys to help you," he said, punching Trapp in the face, not giving him a chance to respond.

Trapp was on the ground with Ricky on top of him, pounding the shit out of his face. He was trying to reach for his gun that was tucked in his waist. Ricky got up off of Trapp and started pouncing around like the boxer he was and said, "Get your pussy ass up and take this ass whipping like a man."

Trapp, finally able to retrieve his gun, pointed it at Ricky from the ground.

"What's up now, nigga?" Trapp said, pointing a shining chrome .357 Magnum in his face. He got up from the ground and was walking up to Ricky when he saw a police cruiser coming their way. He dropped his gun.

"Pussy-ass nigga, I knew you didn't have no heart," Ricky said as he reached into his waistline and pulled out his burner, pointing it to Trapp's head, about to pull the trigger.

"Drop your weapon!"

Ricky, not wanting to drop his gun and it be some of Trapp's goons, asked, "Are you Five-O?"

"Yes, police! Drop your weapon!"

Ricky let his gun drop to the ground as he slowly turned around. They both were forced to kick their guns away and lie flat on their stomachs as the officers cuffed them.

Trapp tried to resist as the officer got him up to his feet. When he looked up, Officer Carson was smiling. Trapp held his head down, thinking, *why in the hell does it have to be Carson's redneck ass?*

"Mr. Shiggs, you just made our job a lot easier. We were on our way to pick you up."

"Pick me up for what?" Trapp asked, tempted to spit in Officer Carson's face. "Man, y'all got the wrong man!" he said as he spat on the ground. "Y'all saw that motherfucker pointing that gun at my head!"

"What? You didn't think we saw your gun?" Officer Carson asked.

"Man, I was just trying to defend myself. You can't take me to jail for that."

"Watch me," Officer Carson said with a smirk on his face. "And while you are there, we are also going to book you for sexual assault."

Trapp was embarrassed that he had been caught and that Ricky heard that he had sexually assaulted someone.

No man who was getting money would sexually assault a female because pussy would be plentiful to them, so this would further prove to Ricky that Trapp was broke and perpetrating.

Dang, how did they figure out that it was me that fast? He was placed into the back seat of the cruiser and was headed to the detention center. He wished he could turn back the hands of time. He would have taken the weed and money and kept going as he had planned, but Black's girl lying naked was too enticing, and he couldn't resist her sexiness.

"Mr. Shiggs, if you knew how to keep your dick in your pants, you wouldn't have to go through this. The young lady that came into our office was traumatized. Most women that this happens to are too scared or embarrassed to come forward. I'm proud that she is not afraid of you and placed a warrant for your sorry ass."

Trapp tried to tell him that the sex was consensual, but Carson wasn't trying to hear it and told him that he would have a chance to plead his case before a judge, and hopefully, he would be indicted. Once the car pulled into the detention center, Officer Carson escorted him and patted him down. To his surprise, he found a wad of money and three ounces of cocaine. "Whoa, son, you've got enough drugs on you to bury you under the jail cell."

"That's not my shit!" Trapp screamed out, forgetting about the coke in his back pockets. Carson processed him and then took him into general population.

He made a phone call to Ray-Ray, telling him what happened before they had to be locked down. He took Ray-Ray's word that he wouldn't be in there long. Just the thought of being on lockdown for twenty-two hours a day, two of which to shower and use the phone, was making him sick to his stomach. He lay on the cot, thinking about spending the rest of his life in prison.

Two days passed, and he was on the edge, contemplating killing himself. He was stressed out, not able to reach anyone to know what was going on or if anything was going on to get him out. When he got a special visit from his state-appointed lawyer, Frank Benz, alone with Officer Carson, he thought his life was over. Carson let them know he was no longer on the case. He was being promoted to homicide next week. Trapp felt somewhat relieved, but his lawyer wanted him to meet a good friend of his from the DEA, Jack Jackson.

Jackson entered the room and, wasting no time, got to the point. He told him that he would get all his charges dropped, from robbing the store, to the gun and drug charge and his pending rape charges, only if he helped himself.

He didn't hesitate telling him where Black stayed and how much drugs he had at his house. He let Jackson know that he broke into Black's house and stole his stash. Jackson told him that if his story was true and checked out and they made a bust, he would be released immediately.

Jackson stared at him while flipping through his records. "Mr. Shiggs, I see that you hang out with the Griffins?"

Trapp cut him off. "Yeah, I hang with Cane." He was more than ready to drop salt on Cane.

"Who's Cane? I'm talking about the infamous Jack Griffin. Now, if you can tell us about his drug involvement, we'll give you two thousand dollars cash." However, Trapp knew nothing about Jack's drug relations.

He was anxious to get back home to Meka. He had received two letters from her today. As far as Ray-Ray went, he just hoped that he was a man of his word and had his money when he got out.

Chapter 16

Cane

After Kasha told Traci how T-Lov had whipped Ricky's ass, Traci had been turned on by him more and more. It seemed every time that he came around now, he seemed more together and stronger. They had been talking a lot, and she was even considering taking him off of child support. She wanted to see if they could make a go for it again since he claimed that the only reason that he couldn't fuck with her was because she had put the boys on him to take care of his child.

T-Lov was ecstatic when Traci called him, asking him if he wouldn't mind keeping little Terry Jr. for her today. Although she did not stop him from seeing their child, she would never let him keep him or take him off. His visits were limited to her house with her present because he had once left the baby with a girl that he was dating and Traci hated. T-Lov couldn't wait to pick up Terry Jr. and take him with him to hang out at the mall. T-Lov was so happy about Traci's attitude change and the way she talked civilized with him for a change that he was even thinking about seeing what she was really about. He shared his thoughts with Cane, who looked at him like he was crazy as hell.

"Man, think about it. Traci and Kasha are girls. You and I are boys, man, and we would have some fun together hanging out."

"Shitting me!" Cane said. "You follow your heart, and I'll follow mine. And mine is telling me to have no dealings with Kasha. She's done too much for me lately. Nah, man, you can have that."

T-Lov laughed at Cane and said, "Well, look, I'll hook up with you guys later, but I do need to talk to you about something when I get back."

"Okay, cool. Hit me when you're back," Cane said.

Cane had been in deep thought, thinking about Trapp and how their relationship used to be. Ever since he started hanging with Ray-Ray, he had been different, and once he moved to the west side, he became even worse. Cane had heard that he was into everything, diving in headfirst without asking any questions. Cane shook his head as the realization sank in that his childhood friend was now the enemy, and they could never be cool again because he could not be trusted. Cane knew that he had to wash his hands of Trapp for good.

He called Calvin to make sure everything was still on for tonight. Calvin gave him confirmation that it was on and popping for the night, and he had a girl for T-Lov, too. Cane didn't care who he hooked up with as long as she was a female he could chill with.

"Man, did you hear about Trapp and Ricky?" Calvin asked.

"Nah, man, ain't heard nothing about them jokesters and don't care to," Cane said, stopping Calvin from dishing the scoop. "Where you at?"

"At the movies with this cute shawty," Calvin answered.

"Don't make Tonya beat that ass!" Cane joked. "She's going to kill you if someone sees your stupid ass and goes back and tells her that you were at the movies with another female."

"Man, she is not my girl. We're just fucking, I'm my own man, and last time I checked, it was a free world, I am a free man, and I can do whatever I want and whenever I want to," he laughed.

"A'ight, don't come running to me when she gets on that ass, like you did that time at Lakeside Park when Shi took your basketball." Cane laughed.

"Damn, low blow, nigga. I was six or seven years old." Calvin laughed. "Let Shi try that shit now. And get out the past, nigga, and back to the future."

"Speaking of the future, if you are serious about going into the military after we graduate, you may want to lay off the pot because the way your ass was smoking last night, you are on your way to becoming the number one draft pick to the Greenville Pot Heads."

Calvin laughed out, "Whatever, man. Just because you're a square, don't try to shape me. I love my circle, and you need to loosen up a little and smell the coffee. Don't let the world pass you by because the world has a lot to offer."

Cane shook off Calvin's comment because he knew that he was not a square. He just didn't condone some of the stupid shit that they did. "You talked to Shi yet?" he asked, changing the subject.

"Yeah, I got him hooked up for tonight too. Just be patient. I've got a major surprise for y'all. All we have to do is show up for the big dance, so be on point and ready for the festivities. Hell, y'all may meet your Miss Do Right tonight," he laughed.

There was a knock at Cane's door, and he told Calvin, "Hold on, someone's knocking. It may be Miss Do Right." Cane opened the door and said, "Man, this what you sent to me? A dark-skinned, six-foot-tall, shiny, bald Amazon!"

"What the hell you talking about?" asked a confused Calvin.

"It's ugly-ass T-Lov," Cane answered. "I'll hit you back later."

"Nigga, y'all asses be on time," Cane heard Calvin saying as he hung up.

He stepped outside to talk with T-Lov because his grandma was very nosy. He watched as T-Lov paced the porch and his hand movement, as if he wasn't sure what to say or how to say it before he finally blurted out, "Man, we need to bring CMB to life."

Cane thought, *here this fool goes with the Trapp syndrome.*

"If Ricky can sell weed, we can sell it. I've got a spot, and all we need is the product," T-Lov said, licking his chapped lips. "I know Jack looks out for us. Don't get me wrong. I appreciate Jack, but I'm twenty-two with a son. I can't keep looking for handouts."

He saw the hunger in T-Lov's eyes. His eyes screamed what was on his mind and that was that he was ready to start getting paid. He knew extra money would help out his grandmother tremendously. First things first, he wanted to put her in a new house with a big garden. All he had to do was convince Jack that he was ready to be his own man.

"Man, I understand what you are saying. But right now, I'm getting ready to call Jack and ask for some funds for tonight," Cane laughed.

He called Jack to let him know he needed some money for the movies. Jack started teasing him about going to the movies with the "Alone Gang," as he called Cane, Calvin, Shi, and T-Lov because they were never with women, at least none that Jack ever saw. Cane never found Jack's jokes about them not having a woman amusing, and he didn't now either. He just overlooked him and said, "Whatever, man, I am on my way over."

On the way over to Jack's house, T-Lov's car started sputtering, as if it was going to cut off. "See, this the bullshit I'm talking about," T-Lov said, frustrated. "I can't let my son ride around like this. Man, we gotta make some money soon. I need a big truck so me and Terry Jr. can chill in style, sitting on them chrome things."

"You sound just like Jack, always looking to stunt. But I'm going to keep it plain and simple when I get my wheels so that these hating-ass niggas won't do me in and put the police on me."

"Nah, man, you need to represent! Balling, stunting, and riding phat-ass whips is what CMB is going to be about."

As soon as they pulled into Jack's driveway, Cane spotted Tony's limo exiting through the east entrance.

"That's who we need to be talking to," T-Lov expressed.

"Yeah, but we've got to make sure the timing is right. We can't step to him without a good presentation," Cane said, looking at the back of the limo as it exited through the gates.

When they got into Jack's living room, T-Lov stopped dead in his tracks when he saw three sexy Latinas relaxing in Jack's Jacuzzi.

"That's what I'm talking about, Jack! Put a nigga down and don't come with that mama shit because I'm a grown-ass man," T-Lov said while undressing the Jennifer Lopez–looking one with his eyes. He was mesmerized with how beautiful and sexy she was. Seeing how Jack had these beauties jocking him made him all the more hungry to make money.

"Nah, T-Lov, you already have baby mama drama. I'm not going to get blamed for bringing more drama into your life," Jack said while looking at Cane, who was damn near drooling at Maria lustfully.

"You don't have to stare, nephew. Pick you out one and show her how the Griffins put it down!" Jack nodded at Maria, and she got out of the hot tub and walked over to Cane, grabbing his hand, escorting him into the bedroom.

Cane looked back at his Uncle Jack, unsure on what to do. He did not want to tell Jack that he was scared, but he did not want to seem amateur in front of the lady either. Jack nodded his head with a huge grin on his face. He could tell that Cane was scared.

"Take it easy on him, Maria," Jack hollered out, still grinning, damn near about to burst out laughing.

"I got him, *papi,*" Maria assured.

Cane could hear T-Lov begging Jack to put him down as they closed the bedroom door. Maria didn't waste any time doing her job. She was rubbing his man tool, trying to get an erection. "What's wrong, *papi?*" She squeezed his dead knob, hoping to get some life in it.

He was nervous as hell. "I'm not ready for this yet," he said, being straight up and honest.

"Aww, how sweet, *papi,* you're still a virgin." She removed her hands from his manhood. "I wish I was still a virgin, but being an adult entertainer has a lot of benefits. Jack is a huge client of mine, and at seven hundred dollars an hour, we gotta do something."

That's a lot of money, Cane thought, thinking he should get into the entertainment business.

Not wanting to look like a square in front of Jack and T-Lov for not having sex with the beautiful, sexy Maria, he came up with a plan.

"Oh, *papi!*" she moaned in her sexy accent. "Yes, it feels so good, *papi!*" she groaned out loud enough so Jack could hear her. She made it seem as if Cane were really laying it down without him even touching her. He looked like a king, and she got paid. After their supposed sexcapade, they lay in the bed, talking, with Maria giving him sound and solid advice.

"You know, Cane, you are a great guy. I love the fact that you followed your heart in here. Never let what others think be the factor in you doing something that you are not ready for. When you decide to have sex with that special person, I hope she feels the same way about you and she knows how lucky she is." She loved the fact that he had respect for women.

A whole hour had passed before they walked back into the living room. Jack and T-Lov were smiling from ear to ear. "Bye, *papi*." Maria kissed him on his face, winked her eye, and walked off, strutting like she was walking down a runway, shaking everything God blessed her with.

"That's what the fuck I'm talking about, nephew," Jack said, giving him a high five. "T-Lov, you see how us Griffins get down? My nephew is packing an elephant trunk down there," Jack continued, laughing proudly.

"We need to talk, Unc!" Cane said with a straight face.

"The way you laid pipe, we can talk about anything."

He didn't bite his tongue. "I need some weed, and I know how to get rid of it."

Jack's eyes grew big as hell. "Hell, fuck no, don't ever ask me for no shit like that again. You know if something went wrong, Mom would kill me for it!"

"Come on, Unc. I need to make my own money!" he begged. "I promise I won't let you down."

"I give you money."

"Jack, I get tired of asking you for your money. I want to stand on my own and make my own."

Jack thought back to when he was a young teen. Big Curt introduced him to the dope game, showed him the way to success, and bailed him out of trouble. He gave Big Curt his word that Cane wouldn't have to want for nothing. Jack knew that the day would come that Cane would have to stand on his own, but he had hoped that it would be after he had graduated high school, gone on to college, and had a respectable career. He shook his head, thinking of the conversation that he had just had with Tony about Cane making his own money.

"Unc, I'm not stupid." He nodded for T-Lov to step out of the room. "The limo that left with Tony Santana in it was my father's best friend. I was there when him and my pops were sniffing cocaine. I saw him pass out onto the floor face-first. My mother called out his name, but he didn't respond. After she saw me sitting on the stairs, she made me go back to my room." He paused to get his mind right. "I was there, Jack, and I remember it all. I have been around this game my entire life, and although I may act oblivious and naive, I'm far from it. I'm smarter than you think that I am."

Jack's eyes watered up as he walked over to a portrait of Big Curt hanging on the wall. He removed it, pulling out two pounds. "Cane, I know you are smart, and that is why I never wanted you in this dope game." He wiped his eyes. "This is my personal smoke stash," he joked. "But real talk, grind out this shit, and the money is yours. You don't owe me nothing in return. But check this," Jack said as he threw his arms over Cane's shoulders and talked to him about the ins and outs of the dope game. Of all the things that Jack said, the one thing that really stood out to Cane was him saying, "If you can't trust your crew, always trust your instinct. Most can't even talk until they get caught, and then they learn to sing like a mockingbird."

"I got this, Unc. It's in my blood to be a made nigga. And don't worry about me. I won't slip. I'm that dude that was made for this shit."

"Never get too confident and comfortable in this game, nephew. And please don't leave shit in the house for Mama to find. As a matter of fact, don't even take that shit in Mama's house because if the police run up there, they're taking everybody!"

Jack proceeded to tell him the story of the time that he had left weed in his back pocket, and his mom found it while doing the laundry.

"Like I said, Unc, don't worry. I got this," Cane said, assuring him that it was okay.

Cane put the dope in a shoebox and placed the box into his gym bag. As soon as he got into T-Lov's car, the first thing he asked about was Maria.

"Was she as good as she looked?" T-Lov asked.

"Man, get out my business," Cane replied, not wanting to lie on his dick.

Cane was paranoid as hell and wanted to get the hell out of dodge. He told T-Lov to not do anything to cause them to get pulled over.

"What's up? Did Jack hit you off?" T-Lov asked, excited.

"Turn that shit up, nigga," Cane said, ignoring T-Lov's question when The Notorious B.I.G.'s "Big Poppa" came on the radio. He sang along with the song, waving his hands in the air, aggravating T-Lov by refusing to answer him until the song ended.

"And, nigga, Biggie needs to rise from the dead and kick your ass for messing up his lyrics," he said when the radio went to commercial. "Did Jack hit ya off or what?"

Cane nodded yeah. T-Lov hit the steering wheel happily as he started bobbing his head. Cane joined in, knowing there was money to be made, and they were about to make it.

"Man, forget them hoes tonight and that bull that Calvin has planned. We need to put our heads together and make this money," T-Lov said.

Chapter 17

Kasha

Ricky had been locked up for a few weeks. Kasha really wanted to see him, but she was unsure as to whether he would want to see her because so much had happened over the past few weeks.

She had written to him several times, but he had yet to reply. After tossing and turning all night, she decided to just go and take her chances. After telling her dad that she was going to the mall with Traci, and being able to ditch her sister, Tina, at her girlfriend's house because her dad had demanded that Tina tag along with Kasha, she then went to the detention center.

Kasha was already sitting at the window when the door opened and Ricky walked in, dressed in an orange jumpsuit. Something about his rugged look was very sexy to her. He looked unsure when he saw her but took his seat on the opposite side of the window and just stared at her for a few seconds before he picked up the phone to speak with her.

"What's up?" he asked. "You were the last person I expected to see here."

"Why?"

"Because the last time we spoke, you were cursing me out and your dad was running me off of y'all's property."

"Ricky, I was hurt. I am still hurt, but that doesn't change the fact that I loved you, and I am still in love with you. I have been worried sick about you."

"Word?" he asked with a raised eyebrow.

"How are you holding up in here? Have they been mistreating you?" She couldn't hold back her tears and frustration. "Damn, Ricky, I hate that you're up in this hellhole. I hope they let you out soon."

"I'm holding up, but it's looking bad for me, Kasha. I may never get outta here, since the Feds went into Black's house, finding over thirty grand in cash, one brick of coke, and four loaded guns." His eyes watered up. "Black thought I had him set up to be robbed, so he told the DEA agents we were partners." He wiped his eyes before a tear could fall. "He's dropping on everyone. Man, it's some crazy shit. He even dropped on Cane, saying that Cane raped his girl. I don't get down with Cane like that, but that just doesn't sound like Cane to me."

"That's crazy as hell. That's not Cane's style. You sure he said Cane?"

"I'm not deaf. I hear well. He also said the other dude that was with Cane had on a mask, but it sounded like Ray-Ray, which makes no sense because Cane and Ray-Ray don't get down at all."

After he went on to finish telling her all that he knew, the puzzle came together for Kasha clearly.

"Are you serious?" she asked.

"Yes, very."

"Think about it, Ricky, Black said that the other guy was masked, but he recognized the voice as that of Ray-Ray. Ray-Ray and Trapp are suddenly the best of friends since he no longer fools with Cane and them, so does it not make sense to you that Trapp would tell Black that his name is Cane since Black and Cane obviously don't know one another?"

"I be damned!" Ricky said after carefully thinking about Kasha's logic of it all. "And to think about it, I heard through the vine today that Trapp had been released with all of his charges dropped!" Ricky exclaimed.

Kasha raised her eyebrows as if to say, "Well, there you have it. Trapp has set everyone up."

"I really do miss you a lot," she cried, "It's so lonely without you."

Ricky was looking at Kasha as if something was really bothering him, and he did not know how to approach her with it.

"Why are you looking at me like that?" Kasha asked with a shy grin on her face, misinterpreting the look he had as him wanting her.

"Look, let me ask you something, and you be totally truthful with me because this shit is tearing at me," he said as he wiped down his face with his hands.

"What is it?" Kasha asked nervously.

"Did you let Trapp into your bedroom willingly, or did he break in on you? Because he is saying that you let him in and the sex was consensual until you had an epiphany."

Kasha just stared at him blankly before she looked away. Tears immediately filled her eyes. "Let me explain."

Ricky flipped out, not wanting to hear her explanation. He punched the glass window. "It's your fault I'm in this predicament, protecting your trifling ass!"

She snapped back. "Hold up, nigga, don't blame me for your mishaps. True indeed, I messed up by letting Trapp in my house, but the shit he said about you was on point!" she said, standing up so that she was eyeball to eyeball with him since he was now standing also.

"You know what, Kasha? You are a low-down, dirty whore! People warned me to stay away from your ass. I'm in all of this bullshit because of your ass! Because I made a mistake of trying to protect you!"

"No, nigga, you're in this bullshit because you made a choice of trying to play a badass as always! I didn't tell you to go and do anything. You are not a child. You made a decision! Just like you made the decision to drop me off and go get with another girl. That's where all of this shit started from because someone saw your ass! So, blame your little dick for your choices, not me!" she charged.

"Well, if you knew how to suck my little dick, I wouldn't have to have other bitches do it for me!"

"I can't believe you," she said, looking at him, wishing that she could get through the glass at him. She slammed the phone down, hoping to burst his eardrums, and stormed off, leaving him beating on the window, calling her everything but the child of God.

She was so upset and blinded by tears that she collided into another person. "Oops, I'm sorry," she stuttered, looking at the familiar-looking girl.

"Hey, Kasha," the girl said.

Kasha was trying to recollect how she knew the girl. She was very pretty, rocking a short Halle Berry naturally curly hairstyle with a thick, high-yellow figure and juicy, luscious red lips.

"You go to Southside, right?"

"Yes, I am Tyla," she replied with a handshake.

"Yeah, that's it. I'm sorry for colliding into you."

"Honey, no problem. But are you going to be okay?" Tyla asked, looking into Kasha's red eyes.

"Yes, I will be," Kasha said, looking away because she knew she must look a mess. She was sure that her mascara was probably mixed in with the tears and had stained her face.

"Word of advice?" Tyla asked Kasha.

"Sure," said Kasha.

"Don't let Ricky stress you out. He's not worth the headache and pain. We've got to learn to treat niggas just as they treat us. Have fun while you're together, but do not get emotionally attached because they will certainly go after the next thing that they think looks good to them in a heartbeat. Girl, men come a dime a dozen, and the more changes you go through with one, you make better choices in choosing the next, so eventually, you will land the right one." Tyla laughed, lifting her hand to give Kasha a high five.

Kasha took a step back and looked at Tyla as everything started making sense to her. *Why is Tyla here? Isn't she the same girl who was all over Ricky's jock at the beginning of the school year? And that voice. I can't swear on a Bible, but that sounded a lot like the voice that I heard the night that I called Ricky and he had another female with him. Did this heifer actually have the audacity to sit and talk to me about my man she was fucking on the low? What in the hell?*

"You nasty, trifling, dick-sucking bitch! I know you are not this bold to step to me, trying to give me advice about my man that you were seeing behind my back. It's bitches like you that fucks it up for women like me."

Tyla cut her off by stepping into her face and pointing her finger at her. "If you were doing your job, your man wouldn't have had to call on me to pick up where you slacked," she hissed. "I don't see what he sees in you anyway. Hell, he should've been dropped your young ass like a bad habit."

"How can I please him when it's bitches like you roaming around, fucking and sucking everything in sight?" Kasha's body was trembling she was so mad. She wanted to attack Tyla right then and there, but she knew that they would only walk her the few steps to the women's part of the jailhouse. "You know what? You can have his ass."

"I already have him, so you are not giving me anything, doll," Tyla said with an evil smirk on her face.

Kasha stared her down before finally turning to leave. When she hit the door, she ran to Traci's car in tears. Again, she found herself being humiliated. Traci was half asleep when Kasha opened the door. After seeing her crying, she assumed Ricky had said or done some fucked-up shit.

"I told your ass not to come and see him. He wasn't responding to your letters, so that should have told you that he was on some other shit," Traci said.

"Girl, it wasn't even the fact that he blames me for his situation and called me a whore. That girl, Tyla, from school also came in to see him, talking shit."

"What? She is in there visiting with him now?"

"Yes," Kasha cried uncontrollably.

"Oh, hell no! We're waiting on that bitch to come out. I already owe her two ass whippings, so I'm whipping that ass today," Traci said, putting the car back into park and killing the ignition.

"We can't fight that girl here. We are already at the jailhouse. They will only march our butts on in," Kasha said, trying to convince Traci to leave. "As a matter of fact, forget Tyla and Ricky. Neither are worth me getting in trouble over. As she told me, move on. Men come a dime a dozen."

"She told you that? Wow!" Traci said as she backed out of the parking space. "Well, her rotating ass should know. But who wants a dozen men? That bitch's luck has helped her once again, but I am going to get her eventually for calling my niece ugly," Traci said.

Kasha sat over in the passenger seat, quietly whimpering. She was mad at herself for not being able to control her tears in front of Traci and for loving Ricky and letting her guard down because she had been warned not to.

Traci tried consoling her the best way she could while driving by softly patting her leg and telling her that it would be okay.

Traci made a stop at the Spinx gas station because Kasha wanted to get a drink. Traci decided that she wanted a piece of their chicken because it was the best in the world to her. Kasha cleaned up her face before getting out of the car because this was a hood Spinx, and everyone stopped in there.

After Traci got her chicken, she told Kasha, who was talking to some dude, that she was going to the car. As Traci was heading out the door, she saw Tyla pull up. *This is my lucky day,* Traci thought as she watched Tyla park on the side of the building because there were no parking spaces in the front. "Thank you, God," she said to herself. "She is parked out of view, so no one will see me kick that ass!"

Traci stood behind Tyla's car and waited for her to get out. Tyla, oblivious to what was going on around her because she was digging in her purse, finally opened the door and got out of the car. Traci walked up, jumped in front of her, and slapped the shit out of her, knocking her to the ground. Tyla got up and jumped back into her car, locking all the doors. Traci started kicking on her car door, putting dents in the door.

"Get out the car, bitch! You so full of shit talking, so let's see you back it up. We both agreed no police would be called, so let's fight it out. Here is our chance!" Traci shouted as Kasha walked up and pulled her back. Traci pried herself loose from Kasha, picked up a brick, and threw it through Tyla's windshield.

"Are you fucking crazy?" Kasha screamed at Traci. "Come on before the cops come out here and arrest your crazy ass. You've got a child at home that needs you. You can't be going to jail over this ho!" Kasha pulled her to the car. "Girl, I can't believe you just did that."

"That bitch had it coming. I'm not done with her yet because I didn't get her the way I really wanted to. Talking about my niece and shit about me having a child while in high school. And then for her to approach you today, trying to give you advice and she was there to see your man, girl, she ain't got half of what I have in store for her," Traci said.

"I hope your son doesn't grow up and be as crazy as his mother." Kasha laughed, still in shock at how Traci showed her ass. "What if she presses charges against you?"

"Let her, I am good. I have never been in any trouble before, and I have money saved. So, it will be money well spent for kicking that ass," Traci said, laughing.

"Yes, you may have money saved, but why throw it away on someone like her? That money can be spent on your child. Forget Tyla."

"You just don't know how much I want that girl," Traci said. "But speaking of my son, we have to run by and pick him up real quick because my mom is going out."

"Cool, I want to see my li'l man anyway with his bad ass," Kasha said.

"Bad is not the word for that boy, and I don't think there is one strong enough to fit him," Traci said of her son. "I thank God that my mother watches him for me, giving me a break, because he is nonstop from the time he gets up until he lies down at night. But that's my li'l stank butt," she said proudly.

"Why don't you let his dad keep him sometimes then?" Kasha asked.

"I actually let him take him for a few hours this past weekend. But I am not comfortable with him staying overnight with him because T messes with a lot of skanks, and I don't trust everyone around my son. Too much shit happening these days. When he dated that girl that did not like me, she constantly talked shit about my child, and then he had the nerve to leave him with her while he went and played basketball with his boys, and it was a wrap for him taking my child off. Thank goodness she did nothing to my child, but you never know what could have happened as much as she hated me and was jealous because T and I had a child together. So, he made his own bed by making that decision to leave her with my child," Traci said, seemingly getting mad all over again as if it had just happened.

"I feel you," said Kasha.

"Yeah, that nigga was calling me in the middle of the night, calling us punk asses and hanging up the phone." T-Lov laughed at Calvin's humor from them not showing for the gathering with the honeys he had hooked them up with last weekend.

"Yeah, he done me the same way," Cane laughed. "Calvin is crazy as hell. I think it's time that we introduce the clique to the game. You know, if one eats, we all got to eat. You're talking about CMB. Let's make it do what it do!"

"I told you that you were the man," T-Lov said.

Cane had hated not telling his boys what was going on, but he had to make sure his plans were going to work first, so it was for a good cause. Shi was outside waiting on them. As soon as he hopped into the car, he mumbled, "I hope Calvin hasn't hooked us up with any scalawags as payback for us not showing last weekend."

"If he did, at least it will be dark, so can't nobody see who you're with," T-Lov said, laughing.

"Fuck that shit, nigga. I don't care if it's Grace Jones. I'm ready to get this shit over with," Cane spat out, feeling his pager vibrating in his pockets.

"Man, hush with the lies, Mr. She's Not Thick Enough. I know you won't settle for anything," Shi said as he looked at Cane like he was crazy.

"Whatever, nigga," Cane said.

"I wouldn't let you go out like that," T-Lov blurted out. "I'll tell Jack to call Maria first before you ever think about considering Grace Jones."

Cane gave T-Lov the eye that was saying, "Shut the fuck up," but T-Lov didn't see it.

"Who is Maria?" Shi questioned.

"Man, Jack," T-Lov started, but Cane cut him off.

"Nobody important. Just someone Uncle Jack knows," Cane said and left it at that. T-Lov picked up on it and

Chapter 18

Cane

Cane hopped in T-Lov's car, counting dead president He'd been pumping weed like a motherfucker. "I'm abou to run out. This shit is that fire," he said, rising up h rear to stick his money in his back pockets.

"Man, your pager is on fire," T-Lov said to Cane whe he got back into the car. "It seemed like it went off eve five seconds."

Cane picked up the pager, looking at its log. "Man, i Calvin. He done paged me four times."

"Nah, that pager went off about fifty times. Let me fi out you done turned that fine-ass Maria out, and sh blowing you up like that," T-Lov teased.

"Nah, man, nothing like that," Cane said, still look through his log. "Man, I can't believe the money I h made this week. Shit, soon, I'll be getting me my whip

"Boy, you're on top of your game. My shit is mov slow right now, but I know it'll be all gone by tomorr T-Lov couldn't believe Cane's hustle. It had only bee week since Jack had given Cane the product, and alre Cane had gone back twice to purchase more. He had b pushing the weed hard.

"Man, we need to scoop up Shi and get to Calvi cause he will kill us if we don't come tonight. He's talking shit all week about us reneging last week Cane laughed.

changed the subject as they saw Calvin standing outside, waiting.

"Look at this pretty motherfucker here," T-Lov said as he stopped in front of Calvin.

"Fellas! Fellas! Fellas, what's up?" Calvin spoke as he got into the back seat.

"Don't 'what's up' us, nigga. Tell us about these females we're going to meet. I hope it's not any hood rats because I've already got a crazy-ass baby mother, and I don't want any more drama."

"Trust me, nigga. they're far from hood rats. Just wait until y'all see what I have in store for your country asses!"

Cane wasn't really feeling going to sit up in a movie with some chick he was sure he probably wouldn't even like when he could be making his money, but he knew that he had to show or Calvin was going to act a fool. Growing tired of their petty conversation about the girls, he interrupted with, "Well, fellas, enough with the bullshit. It's all about CMB." He pulled out two ounces of weed. "Am I my brother's keeper?" He hit them with his Nino Brown accent.

Calvin's eyes glowed. "Shit, nigga, fire it up."

"Hell nah, fool! We in the game. This is your supply, and we can't get high on our own supply!" He tossed Calvin and Shi an ounce a piece. "This is what's going to make CMB official and put us on the map." He felt like a leader for the first time.

"What? This is ours? Legit?" an amazed Calvin asked.

"Yep, that's yours. You sell it and bring me back my part, and the rest is yours," Cane said, proud that he was able to put his boys on.

"Shut the shit up!" Shi said in disbelief. "Where you get this?"

"Man, don't worry about all of that. Just do your thing," Cane said.

"Fuck the movies and these bitches. Take me back home! Shit, I've got money to make," Shi said, excited.

Cane was with Shi, but he didn't get a chance to say, "Let's do the darn thing then," because Calvin said, "I be damned if your ass is not going to the movies. Y'all asses already made me look bad last week. Hell, I want to make my money too, but this is my girl, and I really like her. So y'all asses not going to have her friends mad at her for standing them up two weekends in a row!" he said with authority.

"Man, chill," Cane said instead. "We've got tomorrow and the rest of our lives to make this money. Tonight, we're just going to have a good time with the honeys because, after this night, we're making mad moves." Cane gave them the same talk that his Uncle Jack had given to him.

"This shit is that fire!" T-Lov said as he pulled out a blunt and passed it to Calvin so he could fire it up. Cane didn't agree with T-Lov's method of sampling the weed. He didn't want to witness another tragedy gone wrong since his father's death and his mother's drug addiction.

T-Lov and Calvin smoked the blunt to the head. Calvin tried to convince Cane and Shi that weed relaxed your mind, so they should try it. They both declined the offer. Cane's pager was blowing up. He got anxious seeing how many people were calling for weed and how much money he could be making right now. He wished like hell that he had played sick and not come out with them tonight.

T-Lov told them that he was about to stop smoking weed.

"Yeah, right!" said Shi.

"Man, on the real, I've got to. Traci finally allowed me to get li'l man and take him off again without her supervision last week, and I was feening like hell to light up a blunt. I didn't because he has asthma, and if Traci somehow found out that I had been smoking around him, she would be on trip mode again. Plus, I just need to stop anyway because I am going to have to eventually find a job," T-Lov admitted.

"That's real shit there," Cane said. "Check it, guys, we're going to be smart with what we do. If we play our cards right, we're going to be rolling big in a minute, and you know what comes with money," Cane said, turning to look at each of them eye to eye. "The gold diggers are coming, and we are not going to let them be the cause of us slipping up. Trust no one," Cane said again, giving them the rest of the speech that his Uncle Jack had given to him.

"Cane's right, fellas. Think with the right head because the wrong head will get you fucked up. Y'all are young and have no responsibilities other than to yourself, unlike me. I've got a child that I have to worry about and make sure is straight. If I was a deadbeat, I would have been threw in the towel with the hell that Traci puts me through in order to see him, but I am not that dude. I love my seed. So, once the money starts rolling in, protect your seeds with a condom and make sure you don't end up sharing them with a girl you wouldn't have chosen to be the mother of your children. Don't get me wrong because Traci is a damn good mom to Terry Jr., but if I could have chosen, it wouldn't have been her mean ass. And I think she's fucking girls now."

"Shut the hell up," Shi said, laughing. "Aren't her and Kasha like best friends?"

"Hell, they may be fucking because they sho' real cozy," T-Lov laughed. "At least that's word on the streets."

The guys took in everything that T- Lov was saying. They listened attentively as he told them about catching an STD. They were in shock as he told of how he had picked up a random big-booty chick while driving Jack's

Mercedes-Benz. She didn't waste any time giving up her goods because she thought he was a baller.

"Damn, you're nasty as hell," Calvin said once T-Lov told them about the green-yellowish puss discharging from his penis and the doctor sticking a Q-tip down his man tool to see what type of infection he had.

"And the moral of this story is weed makes you horny as hell, even though it mellows you out. At the end of the day, it kills your brain cells." T-Lov laughed as he tossed the blunt out the window.

They walked into the movie theater, looking for the four females who were supposed to be standing at the front entrance.

"They said they were going to be here," Calvin said, scanning the room. He looked at the fellas and said, "I hope they didn't stand us up as payback for y'all niggas not showing last week."

"Well, they are not here, so let's bounce," Cane said, ready to get back to chasing the paper.

"Come on, let's check and see if they're upstairs first," Calvin said.

As soon as they got upstairs, Cane spotted Tonya, just as a Stacey Dash look-alike approached Calvin, asking him what took him so long to get there.

"Yo, dawg, four o'clock," Cane said to Calvin, their code that a bust or a punch was about to come.

Calvin, hearing Cane's warning, stepped away from the Stacey Dash look-alike and stepped to Cane while looking around to see where or who the threat was. He acted annoyed when he saw Tina. He asked Cane why he felt a need to warn him about Tina. "We aren't messing around, only flirting," he said, stepping back to Stacey Dash.

Calvin was about to start talking to the Stacey look-alike again because he wasn't worried about Tina. Hell, they didn't date, and she was not putting out. But as soon as he stepped to Stacey, Tonya stepped between the two of them. Calvin, caught by surprise, quickly stepped back to Cane and said out loud, "Your girl is a trip. She said you come and ask her."

Cane looked at Calvin as if he was stupid, which he was if he thought that Cane was going to risk getting hooked up with Tonya's friend if they thought he already had a girl. Cane was thankful that he did not have to throw his boy under the bus because the Stacey Dash look-alike spoke up and said, "Calvin, baby, what is going on?"

"Baby? Are you calling Calvin your baby?" Tonya asked.

"Yes," the girl said with attitude as she shifted her weight to her left side and placed her hand on her waist.

"Tell me this," Tonya said to the girl. "Do you know that he has a girlfriend?"

"Who has a girlfriend?" she asked.

"The guy whose face you were all in!"

"Chill out, Tonya. It's not even like that!" Cane said, trying to help out with the situation before it got ugly.

"Cane, he has his own mouth, so don't speak up for him," Tonya snapped out with her arms crossed, waiting on Calvin to speak.

"Come on, baby, calm down. Don't start anything in here," Calvin cooed, attempting to hug her, but she shoved his arms away.

Shelia walked up and said, "Tonya and Tina, do y'all have a problem with this bitch?"

Cane couldn't believe this shit. T-Lov was lost while Shi and Calvin looked on blankly.

"Shelia, you're better than this. Please don't start no shit!" Cane said.

“Go to hell, Cane, because I am going to handle this bitch!” Shelia said as she balled up her fist.

“Nah, Shelia, it is not her that we are going to handle. It’s Calvin’s cheating ass. It’s not the girl’s fault because it’s not her responsibility to keep my man straight. Hold my purse,” Tonya said, passing her purse to Shelia. “I’m about to kick his ass.”

Before Cane could object, Tonya took a wild swing that ended up around Calvin’s neck as they stood there and passionately kissed.

“What the hell?” Shi said in disbelief.

The girls, including Stacey Dash, and Calvin cracked up, laughing.

“Boo, we fooled the hell out of them.” Tonya couldn’t stop laughing.

“Y’all full of shit,” Cane said, relieved.

After Tonya introduced her cousin, Trevia, to everyone and hooked each of the guys up with her friends, Cane was cool with hanging with the girls they were already cool with, but he felt gypped that they had put him with Tina because he couldn’t push up on her because she was like a sister to him.

Cane felt like a fourth wheel because all of the other guys had girls they could really kick it with.

Chapter 19

Trapp

Trapp couldn't wait to catch up with Ray-Ray because they hadn't spoken since he had gotten arrested. Trapp had been out of jail for a full day, but all three times, he went to the center or to Ray-Ray's house, looking for him. He was never home. He had a strange feeling, for some unknown reason, that Ray-Ray had been dodging him.

Trapp had just gotten to Ray-Ray's house and climbed the porch when he noticed that his shoe was untied. He sat down in the chair that was on the porch to tie his shoe when the front door opened. He looked up and he could tell that Ray-Ray was shocked to see him there. If Trapp didn't know any better, he would have sworn that Ray-Ray looked as if he wanted to run at first.

"Damn, nigga, you're hard to get in touch with!"

"Man, things have been crazy as hell around here," Ray-Ray said, all fidgety, not looking him in his eyes.

"The Feds came and got Black, and the block has been hotter than a motherfucker. I stashed our shit in the woods, but somebody must have followed me because the shit was gone the next day," Ray-Ray said, talking to him but looking past him, still avoiding eye contact.

He had split the weed up with his boys, Chris and Timbo, and then they had smoked the rest.

"Come on, nigga, you mean to tell me we did that shit for nothing?" Trapp asked.

"Nah, I got a little something for you," Ray-Ray said as he flashed a few twenties. "Shit, my nigga, I'ma take you shopping and buy you some fresh gear for holding it down in there."

"That's why I fuck with you," Trapp said as if he were all right with it, but he knew something wasn't right with that story.

"I told you, my nigga, I'm the realest nigga alive." Ray-Ray nodded his head up and down. He felt like he'd won Trapp back over. He continued to feed Trapp bullshit as to why he couldn't bail him out of jail. Trapp looked over him since he held out on the five grand he'd stashed plus the two grand Agent Jackson gave him for snitching on Jack.

He followed Ray-Ray to his room. "Shit, nigga, I'm ready to hit another lick!" Since he already had money stashed, he wanted more. "I'm hungry as hell. My pockets are on E. The police took my gun. I can't survive like this!"

"Yeah, I'm ready to bust another move myself. I gotta give it to you, my nigga. Your ass got plenty of heart. I don't know what to say about Chris and Timbo. If I had two more niggas like you on my team, we'd be unstoppable," Ray-Ray said as he gave Trapp $600.

"That's what I'm talking about, nigga." He put the money in his pockets. "Shit, let's go to the mall and ball out."

"Nah, I can't right now. I've got some business to handle with this shorty. You feel me? But maybe we can hook up later on and hit a lick."

"That's what's up, nigga. Don't let me hold you." He gave Ray-Ray dap and got a light.

***

Trapp was smoking on a blunt while walking to Meka's house, feeling good as a motherfucker. She was sitting on the porch. *Right on time,* he thought as he walked onto her porch, puffing away.

"Damn, boo, a nigga missed you like hell! Thanks for holding it down for me. You're the realest woman alive!" Trapp blew smoke in her face, giving her contact. "I don't know what to say about that fuck nigga, Ray-Ray—"

She cut him off. "If you said that was some fucked-up shit he did, that would be sufficient." She smiled, giving him a hug. "I can't believe he put drugs in your pockets and ran off, leaving his gun behind when the police came." She kissed his lips.

"As I was saying, fuck that nigga and this chump-ass six hundred dollars he gave me." He pulled it out of his pockets. "You want this chump change? Your ass gotta put in some work for it!" he said, smiling.

"Well, show me to my station," she said, provocatively taking his hand. He followed her to the living room. She told him to wait there while she changed clothes. He pulled out a few $5 and $10 bills. She entered back into the living room wearing a white tennis skirt with a matching white sports bra, showing off her pecan tan complexion and cut abdomen. He stood up and placed a $10 bill into her bra, letting her know there was plenty more where that came from.

She shoved him playfully as his body flopped back onto the couch. She threw her mother's Bible onto the floor, along with the junk mail, and hit the power button on the remote. Usher's "Nice & Slow" serenaded the room as she danced exotically on top of the table in rhythm, lip-synching to the song.

Trapp was mesmerized by her sexy lips that poked out from under her skirt. His shaft started rising. He stood back up, throwing a few $5 bills onto her back. He ground on her while she was on all fours, making it clap. "Come on, baby. Let me hit it," he begged, taking off his shorts.

"Noooo!" she cooed. "I'm not finished yet." She slowly removed her bra. He lightly kissed and nibbled on her nipples until they became hard. Meka playfully pushed him back onto the couch as she pulled off his shirt, and he kicked off his shoes. She kissed all over his nude body, teasing him by avoiding his stiffness as she licked on his thighs. She continued to dick tease him by grinding her ass on his Mandingo.

She was driving Trapp insane. "Come on, baby, let me have it!" He tried to ease inside her wetness. She pulled away, pushing his chest so that his back was against the couch.

She kissed around his copperhead-shaped tool. "You want me to suck it?" she moaned while wrapping her tongue around his tool. He dropped every bill he had in his hands on the floor. "Not until you do me!" She stood up on the couch, putting her coochie in his face, close to his mouth. She ground on his mouth, giving him an introduction to her sweet mango. "You like the way I taste?" He was speechless as he dug his tongue deeper into her nectar, savoring her wetness.

Trapp slid down as they got into the sixty-nine position. Meka was sucking and pulling with all her might until he came into her mouth. His mind was blown as she sat on top of his shaft and rode it until the wheels fell off. After cumming inside of her, he wrapped his arms around her and threatened to take her life if she ever gave his pussy to another man.

"Boy, you know that this pussy belongs to you and only you!" She lay on top of his chest, thinking about what she was going to do with the money she had just made. *If money was this easy to be made, I should've been doing this shit.* She laughed to herself as they discussed their future together.

Meka was awakened by a car door slamming. She looked up at Trapp, who was sound asleep.

"Oh, shit!" She woke Trapp up. "You gotta get the hell out. My mama is coming in."

Trapp panicked as he searched for his boxers. He put his pants on and ran out the back door with his shoes and shorts in his hands. He stopped at the corner to put on his clothes and shoes.

When Trapp rose from tying his shoes, he noticed that a black 1970 Chevy Impala was sitting there at the stop sign, and the driver was eyeballing him. Trapp didn't recognize him, so he continued on his way. All of a sudden, he heard the passenger's voice cry out, "Yeah, Slim, I'm sure that's him. That's the motherfucker that raped me and robbed Black."

Running was the first thing that came to his mind, but he was stopped before he could run. Slim had a Glock 9 pointed at his head. "Yeah, destiny finally caught up with your ass. I'm going to beat your ass and then put one in your head for what you did to my sister. You fucked with the wrong one," Slim said as he landed a punch on Trapp with every word he said with the pistol.

"Man, I never saw your sister in my life!" Trapp cried out as he spat blood from his mouth.

"So, you're calling her a liar?" Slim fired the first shot, hitting him in the leg.

"Ray-Ray made me do it!" he cried out in pain, trying to make the bleeding stop.

"Nigga, Ray-Ray isn't here, so you gotta wear this hot steel!"

Trapp closed his eyes and cried out for mercy, begging Slim not to take his life. The only thing Trapp heard was Slim's sister crying out, "That's enough. He's not worth you going to jail, and I've pressed charges." But Slim fired more shots, leaving Trapp in the street to bleed to death.

Chapter 20

Calvin

"Today is a good day!" Calvin bragged to Cane since Tonya's parents weren't going to be at home at all that day. "T-Lov needs to hurry his ass up. I've got business to handle," he said, getting impatient as he paced the floor.

"All you think about is sex. Damn, nigga, there's money to be made, and you need to be getting your paper up so you can buy your own ride and won't have to be waiting on T-Lov," Cane said, irritated. Calvin's money had been coming up short since they started hustling. "Just give me the rest of the work you have. I'll get rid of it for you 'cause I need to get another supply, and your money is what's holding me up."

Calvin knew that he needed to pull himself together. Cane, T-Lov, and Shi were stacking their chips, but he had been smoking up his profit and coming up a little short with what he owed Cane for his supply. This week, he didn't have any of Cane's money and had been dodging Cane all week. Cane had been calling him for the past two days, wanting his money. Calvin finally borrowed it all but $100 from his sister, promising to pay her back next week. He vowed that he was going to get himself together.

"I've got the money, except one hundred dollars, but, bruh, you have to trust in me and let me get rid of the shit myself." His pager went off. "You hear that? That's that money calling my name right now, so let me hit you back in a second."

"You heard about Trapp?"

"Yeah, man, I heard about that shit. Scary that no one saw anything, and he's in a coma."

"Man, Trapp needs to watch the company he keeps. That shit is crazy! His mom came screaming out the house when she found out about it. Her cries were heart-wrenching. I feel bad for her," Cane said.

"Man, that shit is wild," Calvin said. But Trapp had done so much crazy shit against his boys that he couldn't help but think he got what he deserved. He hoped he pulled through and realized his wayward ways to come back to the ones who were loyal to him. Speaking of loyalty, Calvin hated to lie to Cane, but he didn't want him all in his personal space. He called Kim to let her know that he would be over there in about thirty minutes. Then, he paged T-Lov, putting 911-911, hoping he would speed up his pace.

T-Lov was beating on the door as soon as Calvin had finished paging him.

"You don't have to blow up my shit, nigga. I told you I was on my way over," T-Lov said.

"My bad, nigga, calm the fuck down, but anyway, I gotta get my rocks off. I'm tired of Tonya playing with a nigga's head. Don't tell anyone, but I'm going to see Kim. And please don't tell Cane because I told him that I was going to go and get rid of this stuff, but shit, her parents are out for a while, so I've got to take advantage of this."

"Take advantage of what? Hell, y'all already fucking on the regular. When Tonya finds out . . ." T-Lov laughed.

"See, you're missing the big picture. Her parents are gone for the night, so this gives me more time with her. She's going to be out them panties all night." Calvin was joking, but he was hoping things went his way. He was fed up with Tonya. He wanted some nookie, and she wasn't ready yet. Kim was always ready and willing, and he had taken a liking to her.

"Just be patient with Tonya. She'll come around when she's ready. Respect her decision and don't seduce her because she will hate you for it afterward, especially if she really wasn't ready."

"Look who's talking. Didn't Traci tell you that she wanted to wait until she was married to have sex, and you stayed on her about it until she finally gave in?"

"And that's why I'm telling your stupid ass that when a girl says she wants to wait, don't coax her. I learned from Traci the hard way. She still holds that against me because not only did I take her virginity prematurely, but I impregnated her also."

"But that's still no reason for her to keep acting like she has toward you because you do take care of your seed," Calvin said.

"I know, right? She is the reason I started seeing Trevia. I was going to stick with Traci, especially after finding out that she was pregnant, but she decided that she wasn't giving up the booty anymore, so what was a nigga to do?" T-Lov asked.

"What a nigga done," Calvin laughed. "I mean, come on, she really expected a sexually active man to just stop having sex? She pushed you into Trevia's arms."

"Damn skippy!" T-Lov said. "And as quiet as it was kept, as long as I was breaking her off on the regular, Trevia was cool with me and her doing our thing on the low and I stay with Traci and my son, but when Traci found out, whew!" T-Lov said, shaking his head at how Traci's wrath was on him. "Of course, because of all of that, she hates Trevia and does not want Terry Jr. around her. So she wouldn't allow me to be the father I wanted to be because she wouldn't let me take him off alone as long as I was with Trevia. Boy, I tell ya, it's been hell!"

"Yeah, before I even knew who you were, I used to hear Traci talking about you and your girl, but she acted like you were a deadbeat or something. She forgot to tell us that she was holding the baby away from you because she couldn't deal with the fact that you were seeing someone else."

"Yeah, they always forget that small part," T-Lov agreed.

Calvin pulled out a blunt and rubbed it against T-Lov's nose, letting him inhale the aroma of good-smelling weed. T-Lov couldn't resist the sweet smell that brushed against his nose. He snatched the blunt from Calvin and fired it up.

"You must be psychic or something. You read my mind." He took two pulls and then passed it back to Calvin. "And don't worry, I won't tell nobody I dropped you off at Kim's house."

He told T-Lov to come back early in the a.m. to pick him up. Kim was on the front porch, pacing back and forth. "We need to talk," she snapped with an attitude, walking into her house. He trailed behind her, rubbing her ass.

"The only thing we need to talk about is you coming out them panties."

"That's all you think about is sex? I should be more than a sex symbol to you. I'm tired of being your side piece. You are going to have to choose because you can't continue to have your cake and eat it, too. I love you. I have put my life on hold for you, and it's not fair that you don't expect for me to see anyone else but you have a girlfriend."

"Baby, stop tripping. You know I love you." He palmed her ass like a basketball and then kissed her on the neck.

"I'm not playing with you, Calvin. It's ether me or Tonya!" She jerked her body away from him.

"Say no more then." He picked up her phone and paged T-Lov, putting in his code to come and scoop him up. "I can't believe I wasted my time coming over here. Hell, I could've stayed at home and made some money."

She snatched the phone from him. "You fake, Big Willie–wannabe gangster. I don't know why I got caught up fucking with your no-good ass." She rolled her eyes, hanging up the phone.

"You got caught up because you are a trifling, money-hungry bitch who thought you were going to get a free ride by fucking with me!"

"I got your trifling bitch. Punk!" She picked up a vase and threw it at him, missing his head by an inch. He rushed her, tossing her onto the couch. "Get your fucking hands off of me. That's why I'm going to tell Tonya that we're still fucking! I'll show you trifling!" she snapped. "And I'm going to get my brother to kick your ass!"

Calvin felt his temper rise. "Fuck your bother!" He slapped the hell out of her, almost knocking her down. "I'll beat both of y'all asses!"

She caught her balance and picked up another vase. She threw it with all her might. The vase shattered after connecting with his head. Calvin felt dizzy as he lost his balance. He sat there rubbing the knot on his head, trying to gain his consciousness back. He zeroed in on her as she was charging his way like a brahma bull with a butcher knife in her hand. He pulled himself up and ran out the door like a bat out of hell. After feeling the knot on his head, he wished he would've punched out her lights.

Calvin was really angry when he realized that he was unarmed in enemy territory, alone and walking past the enemy Ray-Ray's house. "Just my fucking luck," he muttered under his breath when Chris and Timbo came from the side of the house.

"Lookie what we got here," Chris said.

"Fellas, I'm not trying to start shit with y'all today," Calvin said cowardly when he saw the death look they were giving him.

"Oh, so you're bitching up, huh? You know we were about to kick that ass. Well, I tell you what, since we have bigger fish to fry at this moment, we're going to let you slide today," Chris said with a smirk on his face.

"Go on before we change our minds," Timbo added.

Calvin was walking off as fast as he could when he felt a hard blow to his head, which caused his knees to buckle, and he fell face-first to the ground. "Nigga, you couldn't possibly believe we were going to let you slide," Chris said as they started stomping a mud hole in him. "I've been waiting on this moment forever," Chris bragged out. "Fuck CMB. They're not here to save your ass now!"

All Calvin could do was take the punishment. He covered up the best way he could, trying to protect his face.

"Get the fuck off him!" a deep voice yelled.

"Slim!" they both said simultaneously, looking like a deer caught in headlights.

"In the flesh," he added with his pistol pointed at them. "Where's Ray-Ray?"

"We don't know! We haven't seen him in weeks," Chris said cowardly.

Calvin said a quick prayer, thanking God for rescuing him. He remembered Slim from the center, rolling with Ricky.

"What's up, Calvin? You all right?" Slim spoke. "Give me a good reason why I shouldn't smoke these niggas."

"It's not worth it. Besides, you can't get any credit for killing two cornball-ass niggas."

"It's easy for you to say." Slim slapped Timbo with the butt of the gun. "It's little pussy-ass niggas like this that's fucking up the hood." He turned to Chris, sticking the barrel down his throat. "Give me a reason why I shouldn't kill your ass." Chris tried to talk, but he gagged on the barrel as he cried tears, pleading for his life.

"Come on, Slim! If you are going to prison, go for something more serious than these clowns," his sister said. "Let's go!"

He took his sister's advice to get the hell out of dodge. Calvin was skeptical about riding with Slim, but what choice did he have? He hopped into the back seat. Slim introduced him to his sister, Starr.

He couldn't believe how flawless her beauty was. If he didn't know any better, he could've sworn she was Nia Long's twin sister. His pager went off.

"So, what was that all about?" Slim asked Calvin.

"Man, you know these west side niggas don't fuck with us CMB niggas. They hate on us."

"Oh, so you're in a gang also?" Slim's sister cut in. "Guys like you are why us women don't have much of a choice to choose from because all of the nice-looking guys are either gang bangers, in jail, or dead because of gang-banging. Everybody wants to be a hustler or gangster," she said, frustrated. "Why do y'all need a gang to validate who you are?"

"Man, she's wet behind the ears. She don't know what it is like to be a black man in these here streets, in these here neighborhoods. Don't pay her any attention," Slim said.

"Shitting me!" she said. "Don't tell me what I don't know because I was raised in these same streets you were. I've gone through just as much as you have. I've dated the gangsters and the guys you call lame. But I tell you one thing for certain, I never got a gun put to my head or raped while I was dating the so-called lame," she said, using her fingers for quotation marks.

"Not downplaying what happened to you, little sis, but that could have happened even if your boyfriend hadn't been a dope dealer," Slim said.

"True, but you are missing my point. What I'm trying to say is that this drug world will only land you in prison or buried six feet deep. Look at Black. My baby may never get out again after this bullshit," she said, shaking her head. "So, what choice do I have? I love that man."

Calvin could tell that whatever she had gone through played heavy on her heart. She was fine as hell. He watched the way her ass bounced when she got out of the car.

"Nigga, that's my little sister. You better keep your eyes in your mothafuckin' head before I do you like I did Trapp," Slim said, waving the gun in his face.

Calvin swallowed his spit. "Nah, big homie, it's not like that. I'll never check out your sister like that."

Calvin wrote down Slim's number and then paged T-Lov. A minute later, T-Lov called back. He was happy to hear T-Lov's voice. He was ready to get the hell away from Slim's crazy ass. *And what did he mean, the way he done Trapp?*

T-Lov wanted to know what happened at Kim's house because she cursed him out as soon as he pulled up at her house. Calvin told him he'd fill him in on what happened as soon as he picked him up.

Starr walked into the kitchen as Calvin was hanging up the phone to get something from the refrigerator. She bent down to get something from the bottom shelf, exposing a pink thong from her white low-rider short shorts. Calvin's eyes were glued to her body.

"Is there something wrong with your eyes?" she asked with an attitude.

"Nah, my eyes are straight," he said, embarrassed.

"Yeah, I hear you," she said, knowing that he was lying.

"Do I look stupid? I'm not trying to give your crazy-ass brother no reason to kill me."

"You don't look stupid. You are actually very nice looking and intelligent, but your involvement in a gang tells me otherwise," she laughed.

Ignoring her gang remark, Calvin dug his hands into his pockets and asked, "So, you think I'm cute, huh?" Calvin was elated that she was actually flirting with him.

"You are," she said, giving him a shy grin. "You are definitely someone I could see myself dating if circumstances were different."

"See, that's why shit happens to your fast ass!" Slim said, walking into the kitchen, breaking up the flirt party that was going on between the two. "Man, what I tell you about my sister? You thought I was playing?" Slim asked.

"Man, nothing was going on. I was just telling her that I had a girl that I was—"

She cut him off. "Just because I said you were cute doesn't mean I want you. I've got a man. You may be cute, but you're not even on my level, little boy." She strutted off, leaving him looking stupid.

Calvin felt like a sucker. He was glad when Slim told him T-Lov was outside. He gave T-Lov the rundown on what Kim did and what Slim did to Chris and Timbo. He was happy to get out of the west side. Shit was real over here.

Chapter 21

Cane

Cane thought for the hundredth time that buying the pager was the best investment he had ever made, because before the pager, people had a hard time getting in touch with him if they needed weed and he wasn't home. He always kept it on vibrate so his grandma or cousins wouldn't hear it. He kept his weed in a chest that he kept hidden under the bed, secured with a super heavy-duty padlock. He had five pounds left and only owed Jack two grand. After tucking half a pound under his sweatshirt and securing it with a belt, he was ready to go and make some quick money.

He walked past his grandma, telling her he'd be back shortly. It was easy to get past her these days since she thought that he had a job cutting people's grass, and he was dropping her a few ends. Although he would have liked to give his grandmother a lot more, he knew that he would risk her finding out about his extracurricular activities if he did. He was on a grass cutter's salary, so he made her believe that he gave her half of his entire day's earnings. *Jack had to be a fool to let Grandma catch him,* Cane thought as he packed the weed into a trash can and sat on the swing, waiting for Slick.

At the rate he was going, he knew that by the end of the week he should profit over three grand. And once Shi paid him, he was going to send his mother some ends for her books so that she could buy from the canteen and the personal hygiene products that she had been complaining of needing. Cane felt good being able to help his grandmother out and making sure that his mother, who had finally let her activities catch up with her, was straight while in prison. Jack gave her money but not that often because he was always so busy that it would slip his mind, and Cane did not want to keep bugging him about sending it once he had already delivered his mother's messages to Jack.

He was in deep thought when he heard a raspy voice telling him to give up everything he had on him. At first, Cane thought Slick was playing a joke on him until he felt a hard, steel object on his rib cage. Hollering out in pain, he said, "Come on, Slick, man, why are you doing this? I looks out for you!"

"Nigga, the only way you can look out for me is to give me all your weed and money," he snarled. "Fuck it, I want the pager also!" he added.

Tears fell down his face. He couldn't believe Slick was robbing him. He thought about how he had worked his butt off grinding in these streets, trying to get his money up, and this nigga was about to just take it. He got angry instead of scared as his boiling blood started flowing through his body. He balled up his fist and stared Slick dead in the eyes. "I ain't got shit to give you, nigga! So you might as well pull the trigger!"

Slick stepped back, laughing, and said, "Youngblood, you've got heart. I was just fucking with you. I came to give you some damn money, not take yours," he said, pulling out $450. "I'm fifty dollars short, so I was going to pawn you this gun until I get it," he said, handing over the gun to Cane.

Cane was pissed, and his adrenaline was still pumping hard. He took the gun and stuck it to Slick's head. His fingers were trembling as he applied pressure. He saw the look of fear in Slick's eyes. "Nigga, I'll kill you if you ever try to rob me!"

"Youngblood, we're like family. I practically raised you. I'll never hurt you. I'm trying to show you that you've got to always be prepared for whatever. These streets are dangerous out here, especially when you're a child playing a grown man's game." They looked each other in the eyes without blinking. Slick saw a warrior transform right before his own eyes.

Cane eased the gun away from his head, feeling a little at ease. He told Slick the weed was in the trash can. Slick gave him credit for being on top of his game and not having the weed in his possession. He slid the gun into his waistline and then counted the money to make sure Slick wasn't living up to his name. After the incident with Slick, Cane just wanted to go home because, although it was a joke, he was still shook from it. He decided to call it a night. After all, he had made $450 in less than thirty minutes off of Slick.

As soon as he got into his yard, Kasha was calling his name. He didn't have time to put up his money or the gun. "Be straight up with me," she said, placing her hands on her hips. "What's going on with T-Lov and Trevia? And don't feed me any bullshit!"

He smiled. "I don't know what's going on with them. All I can say is mind your own business and stay in your own lane."

She was shocked to see Cane talk to her like that. She couldn't quite put her finger on it, but there was something totally different about him. "I'm not trying to be nosy. I'm just concerned about Traci, that's all. I just don't want her to get hurt since T-Lov is trying to act like he wants her and him to give it another go. Traci is my girl, and I don't want him to hurt her. Then, he's giving her all of this money all of a sudden, talking about saving for a place for them."

"Understandable, but Traci has a mind of her own. What they do is not your business. That's his baby mama, and he's supposed to look out for her!"

"It is my business if my girl is going to be hurt at the end of the day. If T-Lov knows he is just playing games, then he needs to leave Traci alone if Trevia is who he wants!"

"He and Trevia are just friends, that's all. Damn, get off the boy's jock!"

"Well, if he really wants Traci back, that is one friend that he needs to drop because he knows her and Trevia do not like one another."

"What? You want him to stop being friends with someone just because he and Traci are trying to get together? You don't just flip on someone that's been there for you because you've got a jealous girl. Unlike yourself, some people are more loyal to those that they know care about them," Cane said, throwing shade on Kasha.

"Don't go there with me, Cane! I've told you I was sorry. I made mistakes, but no one is perfect except for God." Although she said it, she could not help but to think that maybe all of this was coming back on her for what she did to Cane. It seemed like everyone was against her, even the police. They had told her that there was not enough evidence to bring charges against Trapp after hearing her true story. Plus, she had drugs in her system. She could see her life falling apart, and she couldn't trust anyone except for Traci. She closed her eyes, wishing she could undo the evil she'd caused, but unfortunately, it had been done, and there was nothing that she could do about it but try to do better.

"Kasha, Mama wants you!" Tina yelled out. "Hey, Cane."

"What's up, Tina?"

"Nothing," she said, reaching up to give him a hug. He met her to return the love.

Shi walked from around the corner and saw Cane talking to Kasha, trying to be a mack daddy.

"Man, I've been paging you for the past two hours, and you're out here, trying to mack and ignoring my calls? Man, I need to re-up. There is money to be made, and you're fucking up my money!" Shi said.

"Damn, my shit is dead," Cane said, checking his pager.

"That goes to show that your butt don't need no pager," Kasha said, laughing.

"I know that's right," said Tina. "Walking around here, trying to look like a little thug. You know you're not about that life," she continued, laughing with her sister.

"Forget the both of y'all," Cane laughed.

Shi pulled Cane away from the girls and said, "Money rules over everything. If you weren't so preoccupied with these girls, you would have realized that your pager was low or dead."

The gun fell from his waist, hitting the concrete. Kasha, Tina, and Shi stared in disbelief at the gun lying on the concrete.

Ms. Shiggs came onto her porch, and Cane froze. He had a flashback of when Trapp had gotten shot, and he could still hear Ms. Shiggs's cries. "My son. Oh, Lord, my son has been shot! God, I have been a good mother and a good wife. I refuse to let the devil steal my joy. Please Lord, don't take my baby from me!" she had cried.

Kasha picked up the gun and was asking him why he had it, but Cane's mind was still listening as Ms. Shiggs cried out for her son.

"Cane! Where did you get this gun?" Tina asked, but he was still zoned out on Ms. Shiggs. He watched as she sat on her porch to smoke a cigarette, which made him feel even worse for her. He thought about all of the bad luck she had endured, just this year alone, and the cigarettes had come after she caught her husband in bed with their preacher's wife.

"Cane?" Kasha jabbed him in his shoulder to get his attention.

"What?" he asked, snapping out of his trance.

"What are you doing with this gun?"

Neither of them noticed that Ms. Shiggs had gotten into her car until she called for him.

"Curtis," Ms. Shiggs called out as she rolled down her window. He told Kasha to hold the gun while he went to talk to Ms. Shiggs.

"I'm glad that Travis had you by his side. You were truly a blessing to him. I can't speak on them hoodlums he engages with now, but thanks so much for being like a son to me," she said as she took another pull on her cigarette.

He reached through the window and grabbed her hand. "I'll always have love for Trapp, no matter what. He just started hanging with the wrong kind of dudes, but we pray that he will see the light after all of this is over. And I'll always love you like a mother."

"Curtis, I just can't take much more. I feel like it's all my fault. If only I hadn't forced him to move in with his father, none of this would've happened." She started crying. "God, please let my baby make it."

"You sent him there to try to save him because he was getting into so much trouble here," Cane said, trying to comfort her.

"But look at what's happened to him," she cried. "At least here he wasn't getting shot up."

Cane tried to calm her down the best way he could. He opened up her door and hugged her tight, letting her know that God was in control of Trapp's situation, and she needed to stop blaming herself for the mishap. She fed off of his wisdom and thanked him again for being such a wise young man.

After she left, he walked back over to Kasha to retrieve his gun. They all stared at him as if he'd lost his ever-loving mind.

"It's for protection. You see what happened to Trapp. He's fighting for his life." He tucked it back into his waistline.

"Well, Trapp shouldn't have done what he did. Karma is a bitch. Thank your lucky stars that you quit fucking with him. Trapp is a bad seed. I feel bad for his situation, but he just got a taste of his own medicine. I just pray that if he comes out of this, he gets right," Kasha spat with anger.

Cane thought that she was truly one cold chick, but he also knew her situation and why she spoke with so much hatred for Trapp, so he didn't argue with her. He turned his attention to Shi because there was still money to be made.

"Let's roll, dawg."

"Cane, please tell me you're not trying to get revenge on who shot Trapp," Tina said, sensing a weird vibe from him.

"He's my brother. Somebody has to pay," he replied, walking off.

"Cane, you gots to be kidding me," Kasha spat out. "Trapp doesn't give two shits about you!"

"Man, she is right. That nigga turned his back on us," Shi said, still looking at him as if he were crazy. "Plus, word on the street is that he used your name to rob people. Real friends don't do shit like that." Shi couldn't have cared less if Trapp lived or died because of the way he had flipped on them. The only true friend that he had was already dead to him. He got what he deserved.

Cane couldn't speak for the next man, but he was going to stay by Trapp's side no matter what. He didn't respond to Shi. He walked into his house to put the money up and to get some more weed.

When he got outside, T-Lov had come through and was talking to Shi. Cane gave Shi his weed so he could make his moves.

"Cane, I need a huge favor," T-Lov said, looking him straight in his eyes. "I need to borrow a few dollars until I can see better."

"Shit, nigga, what happened to your money you bragged about having earlier?" he asked, already knowing that Traci was milking him dry. He had heard from a friend of his who worked at the Michael Kors outlet that she and T-Lov had come through there yesterday, and he had dropped a grand buying her three of the summer collections.

"I'm a grown-ass man. I don't have to explain to you about my money. At least I'm not letting motherfuckers take my shit . . ." T-Lov cut himself off, realizing he was letting his emotions do the talking.

"Shit, nigga, don't get all hype with me because you're letting that girl milk your ass. And hell, you are the grown-ass man asking me for a favor, not the other way around, so don't get it twisted," Cane shot back.

T-Lov looked at Cane in shock at how he had come off on him. Cane was always the more mellow of the three, but he also knew that Cane had a side of him that was borderline crazy. But nonetheless, Cane was right. He was the one asking for a favor, so he had no right to come off on him that way either.

"Man, I'm just stretched to the limits these days. My mom needs help, my sister's no-good baby daddy didn't pay for the field trip to New York, so I had to drop her four hundred twenty-five dollars, and of course, there's

Traci and my seed that I had to make sure was straight. So, this week, they just tore my pockets to shreds," T-Lov confessed.

To Cane, those were poor excuses because they had been on this money trip for a minute now, so his chips should have been stacked. He knew that T-Lov was fronting in the streets like he had more than he had. He had heard about him losing $1,500 gambling last week and how he was dropping all these designer bags on these hoes. But as long as his money was good, he couldn't check T-Lov on what he did with his.

"I was just fucking with you." Cane embraced him. "I'ma give you a pound to get on your feet. That's how much love I have for you. But make it do what it do, and stop letting people drain you for your chips. Help your family, but you've got to be smart and put something back for you," he said before he went back into the house through the back door, dodging his grandma from questioning him about the back-and-forth traffic.

Chapter 22

Cane

Cane had been worried about Trapp's condition. He wanted to go to the hospital, but with the bad blood that had been boiling, he knew to stay clear of it. He had gone over to Ms. Shiggs's house several times, and even left messages, but she had not called to fill him in on what was going on with Trapp. He sensed something was wrong. One day, he saw her getting into her car, so he walked to the edge of the road to stop her once she backed out, but she didn't even look at him as she went in the opposite direction. Against his better judgment, he made up his mind that he was going to get T-Lov to take him to the hospital as soon as he got to his house.

His grandma was sitting in her favorite chair when he walked into the living room. "Cane!" she called out, stopping him in his tracks. "Sherry called me last night and told me about what happened to Travis. Why didn't you tell me that you boys fell out?"

"Grandma, Trapp is on some other stuff these days. I don't even know how all of this came about. We've been boys since day one," Cane said.

"Well, you can't control how one will act, but you can control how you react to it. You are a warrior, and you are a leader, so don't let that boy bring you down the wrong tracks with him. You have a heart of gold, and it's going to take you a long way in life. Just remember to always put God first in your life."

He already knew where she was going with the story. Every time she felt the devil lurking around the house, she thought that trouble was coming via his way.

"Grandma, I'm going to make it in life. You don't have to worry about me running the streets and hanging with the wrong crowd. I know that the angels are watching over me, and they have Trapp. I won't let the devil steal my joy."

"Amen to that." She stood up and embraced him. "You can't let what happened to Travis dictate your life. Just be your own man and do things decent and in order, and you will be okay."

T-Lov's horn got their attention. "Grandma, I'm about to ride out with T for a minute," he said, digging into his pockets, pulling out some money to give her. He placed the money into her hands, kissed her on the cheek, and ran out the door before she could question him.

"It's about time you got here," he said to T-Lov as he hopped into the car. "My grandma was bugging out with the religion stuff. Don't get me wrong, I love her, and I know she means well. But . . ." He cut himself off, noticing T-Lov's "I don't want to hear it" look. "What's wrong with you, nigga?" Cane asked.

"Man, it's been a day. I just want to give you your money, re-up, and go somewhere and get drunk," he said, pulling out a Crown Royal bag from under his seat and passing it to Cane. "That's the grand I owe you."

Cane didn't want to go back into the house and have to face his grandma, but he didn't want to hold T-Lov up from getting paid. He crept through the door, letting out a sigh of relief when he didn't see his grandma in the living room. He stayed as quiet as possible, sliding his chest from under the bed.

After unlocking it, he reached under his shirt, feeling nothing but the bottom. He had to see Jack ASAP! *Dang, we've been moving like that?* He loved the fact that he had been making his own moves and owed his uncle Jack nothing because he paid in full up front.

When he heard his grandmother calling out his name, he stuffed the money into a sock and shoved it into the drawer. He vanished before she could reach his room. He hopped into T-Lov's car and told him to mash out before his grandma came outside. He started feeling in his pockets, searching for his pager. He thought for a second, realizing he left it on his bed. T-Lov told him that he would take him back to get it, but Cane told him it would be all right since it was on vibrate.

Cane was still unable to shake Trapp from his mind as they listened to Bone-Thugs-n-Harmony's "1st of tha Month." They both sang along.

"Man, let's ride over to the hospital and check on Trapp," Cane said to T-Lov.

"You mean pull the damn plug?" T-Lov said.

"Nah, man," Cane laughed out. "I just want to check in on him. I just need to see for myself that he is good because, although I can't fuck with him anymore, I still see him as a brother. And that song was right on time," Cane said, amped up. "'Cause we're getting paid on the first." He laughed out, letting T-Lov know that he had over ten grand saved up.

T-Lov couldn't believe how fast Cane was blowing up. "Yeah, man, I've been saving a little something, but these bills be killing a nigga." Cane was waiting for T-Lov to open up the door, so he could go in on him about his wayward ways of handling his money.

"Nigga, you need to stop paying for pussy! Don't get me wrong, Traci is cool, but she doesn't have anything on Trevia. Trevia at least tries to meet you halfway. All

Traci does is milk you bone dry. How many times has Trevia asked you to take her shopping and to these expensive-ass restaurants? Trevia loves you for you, not what you can give her. I'm telling you, Traci may love you, but let the funds stop."

"Yeah, you're right," T-Lov said, pondering what Cane had just said. "But, man, Traci sucks dick so good though!" he said, grinning. "I can't get enough of them sexy, juicy lips on my shaft. That's why she gets all my money." He stopped grinning and got serious. "But real talk, Trevia really does love me and treats my son like he's hers. I know I gotta get my shit together before I lose her."

Cane insisted that he follow his heart instead of his dick, since his dick might get him into something he couldn't get out of. As they rode past the store, he thought about getting his mother a $200 money order. He told T-Lov to stop at the next store they came across.

"Damn, that's some real shit," T-Lov said, giving him dap. "Even though your mother abandoned you, you still show her love."

"My mother didn't abandon me. She was just fucked up on them drugs, so my grandma raised me. And no matter how bad my mom was, my grandmother raised me to always love and respect my mother, no matter what. Don't get it twisted. My mom loved me. She just was messed up, but when she was around me, it was always about me."

Cane spotted Ms. Shiggs's car in the hospital parking lot. T-Lov maneuvered his car around, parking next to her car. They went straight to the gift shop and bought Trapp a fruit basket, a sympathy card, and three "Get Well Soon" balloons. He bought Ms. Shiggs a white teddy bear that sang "World's Best Mom."

"Go on, see your peeps," T-Lov said, rubbing his stomach. "I'll be down in the café, getting my grub on."

He rode the elevator to the floor that the intensive care unit was on. As he got off of the elevator, he met Mr. Shiggs and his mistress. He nodded his head and walked on past them when Mr. Shiggs said, "Cane, my boy!" Unable to shake how dirty he had done Mrs. Shiggs, and then to have the nerve to bring his tramp to the hospital knowing that Mrs. Shiggs was sitting here daily holding rituals, he was glad that he didn't have his gun in his waist because he wanted to shoot the both of them. Mrs. Shiggs was sitting next to Trapp, holding his hands, when he walked in.

"Hey, beautiful, this is for you," he said as he gave her the teddy bear.

"Aww, baby, thanks so much." She hugged him, nearly squeezing the air out of him. "It's so beautiful." She pressed the button and listened to the song. She set Trapp's balloons and card on the table and then got up and said to walk with her. She walked Cane out of the room.

Once they got into the waiting area, she rolled her eyes at her ex-husband, who was sitting there with his ho. Cane could see the agony in her eyes. Mrs. Shiggs got her thoughts together and then asked Cane why he wasn't in school.

"They are doing EOC testing today, and I am exempt from them," he replied.

"What is EOC?" she asked.

"End of course testing. You know we do that at the end of each semester. My grades are high enough that I had the choice whether to take it," he said, not lying. While Cane was a thug, he was smart as hell. He always made all A's in all of his classes. That was why his uncle stayed on him about going to college.

She broke down crying. "You know, Cane, you were always the special one. Although you hung out with all of the neighborhood knuckleheads, you were always respectful and never in a whole lot of mess." She continued crying and blaming herself for Trapp's decisions. Cane held her and let her cry on his shoulder until she couldn't shed another tear.

Mrs. Shiggs gave him permission to go in and see Trapp. She walked him to the room and then said, "I'll leave you alone with him. Talk to him and let him know that you are here," she instructed before leaving.

He walked up to the bedside and said, "Trapp." Trapp lay there, not making a sound or an attempt to move. Cane looked at all of the tubes that were running through Trapp and broke down in tears. He tried to conceal his whimpers, but Mrs. Shiggs, who had been standing outside of the door, heard him and came in the room.

"What's wrong with him?" Cane cried.

"He's in a coma, Cane. I thought you knew."

It was Cane's turn to cry on Mrs. Shiggs's shoulders. He cried out to God to heal his friend and give him another chance at life.

After staying by Trapp's bedside, talking to him for about twenty more minutes after Mrs. Shiggs had told him that the doctors said to talk to him because people had been known to hear while comatose, he finally hugged Mrs. Shiggs goodbye. He walked to the elevator, ignoring a waving Mr. Shiggs, and got on the elevator. His timing couldn't have been more perfect because T-Lov was standing in the lobby, checking his pager.

T-Lov dropped him off at school so that he could take his eighth period EOC because, while he had an A in that class, it was a low A, and he didn't want it to turn to a B because he exempted the test. He prided himself on having all A's. He shook his head after T-Lov's shitty car burned rubber as he pulled out in a rush to pick up TJ from Traci's mother's house. After turning in his tardy pass, he was approached by Kim. She didn't sugarcoat anything about Calvin smoking up his weed and then making false allegations about Chris and Timbo robbing him.

He thanked her for the information and gave her $20. He couldn't believe that T-Lov lied and went along with Calvin's story about being robbed.

"What are you doing, talking to that slut bucket?" Tina asked, coming from his blind side.

What now? "Hey, sis!"

"That bitch, Kim. That's what up." She rolled her eyes. "What, are you fucking the slut, too?"

He was confused as to why Tina was flexing on him. "Look, Tina, I don't know what your problem is, but whatever you have with Kim is between you and her, not me. Last I checked, I could talk to whomever I wished," he said, becoming annoyed.

"My bad, but be careful of the company you keep is all I'm saying," she said, embarrassed at how Cane had come off on her. "I just try to look out for my boys, and sometimes I let my feelings get in the way. You're right. You can talk to who you want. I mean, why should you be any different? All of your boys are doing the same thing, so . . ."

"What the hell is that supposed to mean?" Cane demanded.

"Because Calvin is fucking around on Tonya with that ho, and we all know how she gets down. I'm concerned about my friend's welfare. You need to talk to that dog-ass friend of yours because Tonya is about to be done with his cheating ass."

"Let me go holler at him," he said, giving her a hug. He went straight to Calvin's hangout spot—the back staircase.

"Man, don't believe everything you hear!" Calvin said, reading Cane's facial expression before he could say anything.

"What about Kim?"

"Like I said, don't believe everything that you hear! That bitch is jealous of me since I'm getting my papers up."

"Word?" Cane put his hand under his chin. "So, none of the shit she said is true?"

Calvin put his head down, not wanting to look Cane in his eyes. He felt bad because he'd been fucking up and blaming everybody else for his mistakes.

"Well, I just came to let you know that T-Lov was coming to pick us up after school." He was going to give Calvin some space to get himself together. He had too much of his own bullshit going on to get caught up in Calvin's foolishness, so he walked off to class.

After the bell rang, Cane met up with the clique at the front of the school. They spotted T-Lov's smoking car coming their way. "I'm going to have to buy him a car myself!" Cane said, shaking his head, embarrassed as the other drivers rolled up their windows to keep T-Lov's smoke out.

As soon as they got into the car, T-Lov told Cane he'd been paging him until it dawned on him that he had left his pager at home. Cane felt uneasy as he thought about his pager being home, but he decided to stop worrying about it because, after all, it was on vibrate, and no one should be in his bedroom anyway. He looked at T-Lov and Calvin in a stern way, wanting to confront them about the weed, but he bit his tongue and decided now was not the time.

"Stop by Takina's Flower Shop," Cane said, pointing to the shop that T-Lov was about to pass.

"Let me find out you're a Keith Sweat begging-ass nigga," T-Lov laughed out, pulling into the parking lot.

"Yeah, let me find out," Shi added, nearly choking from laughing so hard.

They all walked into the shop, and to Cane's surprise, them fools went running into the flower section after they had tried to clown him. *Caking-ass niggas*. He bought two dozen red roses and two cards. He whispered to the beautiful clerk what message he wanted on the card so that Shi and T-Lov didn't hear him. The clerk could barely hear him, so he was leaning over, whispering the message to her again when they came up, trying to peep over his shoulder to see who he was buying the roses for.

"Y'all mofos get outta my space!" Cane said as he quickly took the cards and shoved them in the envelopes and then tucked them in his back pocket. T-Lov mashed the pedal to the metal as they headed to Tonya's house.

When they pulled into her driveway, Cane felt butterflies churning in his stomach. "We're all we've got," he mumbled, pumping up his ego as he knocked lightly on the door. As soon as Tonya's mother opened the door, he introduced himself as a classmate who was concerned about her illness. She escorted him to Tonya's room and then walked back into the living room.

"What are you doing here? If it has anything to do with Calvin, I can tell you now to save your breath," she said.

"Just give me five," he said, pleading with his eyes. He hated to lie, but he was ready to take one for the team.

"First off, Kim is a compulsive liar. Meka was using her to break you guys up so that she could get back with Calvin," he lied. Calvin had bet him good money that he couldn't win Tonya back over for him.

"But Calvin just got a pager, and if he had stopped talking to Meka when he told me he had, then why did she have his pager number?" Tonya asked.

"Because you know that Meka is a weed head, and when it comes to money, forget a personal relationship. Calvin is about his money."

"What does her being a weed head have to do with Calvin?"

"Duh, Calvin sells weed, so of course she's going to call him for it when she or someone wants it."

"Calvin's selling drugs?" Tonya asked in disbelief.

"Calvin sells weed," Cane said as if that made it better.

Cane explained to her their activities over the past few months and that was why they had all been so busy. She was shocked that they were all selling drugs. She felt even worse that Chris and Timbo had robbed and beaten up Calvin. She wanted to talk to him and asked Cane to go outside to get him.

"Yo, man, don't go in there and fuck up what I just put together," Cane said to Calvin, explaining what he had told Tonya.

He shook his head as Calvin nearly broke his neck getting out of the car. Calvin was moving so fast that he forgot about her roses and card.

"Nigga, who you buy the roses and card for? Your mama?" Cane hollered out to him.

Calvin skipped back to the car to retrieve the roses. "Thanks, man. If you got my baby back for me, I owe you my life," Calvin said.

"Fuck that, you owe me five hundred dollars!" Cane said, reminding him of their deal.

An hour later, they were finally headed home. They had paged Calvin's ass three times before he finally came out.

After Shi had dropped off his roses, the guys asked who the other dozen was for that Cane had. They knew one was for his date tonight with Trevia. Cane told them that he had got them for his grandmother.

After T-Lov dropped Calvin and Shi off, Cane told T-Lov to drop him off at Kasha's house because he did not want to be seen walking down the street with the roses in his hands.

"I knew it!" T-Lov boasted. "You sneaky dog, still got a thing for Kasha."

"Nah, player, it's not even like that," Cane said, embarrassed.

"Shitting me!" T-Lov said, jabbing him in the arm. "You might as well holler at her since you're balling now."

"Nah, player. Her and Tina are just my girls, and I am trying to stay in their good graces because you know when you have two strong-willed girls on your team, they will look out for you."

"You think you have all the sense, but that's the craziest shit I've ever heard. But I'll get with you later on," T-Lov said as he pulled up to Kasha's house.

Cane knocked on their door and waited. Their parents loved him, so he knew it wouldn't be a problem with him popping up. After the second knock, Kasha opened the door. He was mesmerized by her beauty every time that he saw her. She was wearing a tight body dress, and all he could do was pull the roses out from his back.

"Aww, for me? They are so beautiful!" she said, taking the flowers from his hand.

Tina walked into the living room to see what all the commotion was about, followed by their mother. "And these are for you," he said, giving Tina her roses.

"Cane, you are so thoughtful!" Tina said, taking the roses and giving him a bear hug.

"See, this is what I'm talking about," Mrs. Davis said, smiling. "You are so sweet. This is the kind of man you need, Kasha, a gentleman that is thoughtful on days other than a holiday. I don't know what you saw in that Ricky fella anyway. You need to wake up because good men are hard to find," she said, walking back to her room.

"Come on, let's go to my room so we can talk. Alone!" Kasha said, giving Tina a "leave us alone" glance. Tina still trailed behind, but Kasha slammed the door in her face.

"Me and Traci have been talking, and she told me how you have been making money. Cane, be careful because I don't want you to end up like Trapp and Ricky. In spite of everything that has happened, I do care about you."

She walked back to him, rubbing his legs, working her way between his thighs. She felt his hardness through his pants. "My mama was right. Good men are hard to find." He slid his hands up her dress, gripping her ass. "Oh, Cane, that feels so good," she moaned. "I'm yours. Take me. I've always wished that you could've been my first."

A loud knock came from the door, startling the both of them. "Kasha! Mama wants you," Tina yelled through the door.

"Ughh, I swear she gets on my freaking nerves," she huffed, pulling her dress down. She rubbed his hardness before she exited the room.

He was thinking that he had been saved by the bell since they were interrupted. He was gathering his things to leave before she returned because, as bad as he wanted Kasha, he wanted it to be right when they experienced one another. Tina stepped into the room as he was about to leave. She stared at his hardness as he tried to pull his shirt over it, but the bulge was still noticeable. "You don't have to leave."

"I need to get home so my grandmother won't be worried."

"Well, give me a hug before you leave," she said, motioning him to her.

When he hugged Tina, he felt embarrassed because his man tool poked her in the stomach. He quickly released her and walked toward the living room. Kasha tried to call him back, but he rushed out the door, adjusting his clothes.

Later that evening, he sat on the front porch, looking down the road at Kasha's house. He wanted to feel her so bad and had come to the conclusion that he was going to call her and see if he could come over once everybody went to sleep. Forget this waiting to have sex mess. He was a teenager. He was supposed to experience this stuff, he convinced himself. He was good-looking, blessed with money, and he wanted Kasha.

He got up and walked into the house. Jack and his grandma were sitting at the table.

"I didn't know you were in here. Where's your car?" he asked Uncle Jack as he looked out the back window and saw that the car was parked back there. He turned around to ask him why he was parked in the back when his heart nearly stopped. The room started to suffocate him as he noticed that his money, weed, pager, and gun were displayed on the table, as if it were an auction. His lips felt heavy as they dropped to his chin.

"What has gotten into you, Cane?" his grandmother snapped. "You done lost your freaking mind by bringing this stuff into my Christian home. Where did you get this stuff from? I need to call them to come and get it. If I didn't think that you owed someone money for this stuff, I would have flushed it. But I don't want someone coming after you because you owe them money!" she said, thinking this was something bigger than what it was. "Where did you get this stuff from?" she demanded.

Cane looked at Uncle Jack, not to tell on him but for help. Jack just looked at him, letting him know that he was on his own.

"I didn't raise you like this, Cane! You or your uncle here," she snapped, fanning herself as if she was about to faint. "I'm telling you, this is not permissible at my house." She paused, standing up and shaking her head. "I can't believe you. You're lucky your uncle is over here. If not, I would beat the black off your ass!"

Jack shoved him into the corner. "I'll take care of him, Mama!" He had Cane by his collar, cursing him out. He then dragged him outside, away from his mother.

"Boy, what's wrong with you, leaving your shit on the bed? I swear, Cane, it's over with us. You are careless, and I can't risk you fucking me up because you're not thinking smart. Hell, the next time there's no telling who will catch you. I can't afford to have heat at my house."

Cane closed his eyes, wishing he could wake up from this nightmare.

Chapter 23

Kasha (1999)

She checked her calendar, looking to see when the last time was that she had a visit from her monthly friend and noticing that it was going on three months. She was hoping that the weakness and vomiting that she had been experiencing this week was from the virus that everyone around school was reporting.

"Girl, look at that booty," Traci teased her, wondering how she got into her jeans without them busting.

She wasn't in a joking mood. She felt a sticky, nasty film in her mouth that sent her running out of study hall and to the restroom to throw up.

"Girl, you all right? You scared the hell outta me," Traci, who had run behind her, said.

"No," she groaned. "It feels like I'm going to die." She washed her hands and then filled her palms with water to rinse her mouth out. "I have this nasty taste in my mouth, and it makes me feel nauseated."

"Girl, I hate to tell you this, but I think you are pregnant!"

"No, I can't be pregnant," Kasha said.

"Why can't you be? You're having sex, aren't you? Let's go to the health department and get a pregnancy test. We can be back before fifth period."

"No, I can't go right now." She felt like throwing up again. "I have a math test to take. I can't afford to miss any more classes."

"You're not going to do well on the test feeling the way you feel," Traci said, convincing her to go be tested.

"Don't you throw up in my car, bitch," Traci teased.

Kasha felt so bad that she didn't even put on her seat belt because she didn't want anything touching her stomach. She let the window down just in case she had to vomit again.

Traci's driving made her feel even worse. Not that she was driving fast, but just the car motion was making her sick. She closed her eyes and prayed to God that this was just a bug. A single tear rolled down her face.

"Girl, I know how you are feeling." Traci held her hand. "I remember throwing up three to four times a day when I was pregnant with Terry Jr.—"

Kasha cut her off. "Please stop with the pregnant nonsense because I'm not pregnant. I've been having protected sex anyway," she said, still convinced that she had the same stomach virus that had been going around school.

Traci raised her eyebrow and looked at Kasha sideways. "So, what's up with Cane? Did he give you money for the party this weekend?"

"Yeah, he's going to give it to me before the week is out," she said, not in the mood for small talk.

"Like I said, don't get your feelings caught all up in him because he is making money now and is going to be feeling himself. Get what you can get and give as little of yourself as possible while getting it. Hell, that's what they do," Traci said.

"I did what you told me to do. Girl, he even came by the house and brought me flowers. I played with his dick a little. I got his head fucked all the way up." Kasha giggled.

"Are you sure that's all you did? You don't have to lie to me. It's okay if you gave him a little taste to reel him on in," Traci laughed.

"I promise that's all I did besides let him feel on my goodies. I was going to give him some, but Tina's cock-blocking ass interrupted."

"Girl, you know they're all buddies and they are all doing the same thing, but little do they know that the final laugh will be on them. I love T-Lov, but for him to go and get with Trevia, knowing our history, that was a low blow," Traci said.

"But look where he is now. He's trying to make it right with you and his child. Just as I said, Trevia was a temporary ho because you dropped him," Kasha said with her eyes closed.

"It's hard for me to let it go though. I can't believe that he let that girl tear us apart. And then to think that he even bought her a ring really makes me envious."

"You mean to tell me you're jealous of Trevia because T-Lov bought her a ring?"

"Hell yeah, girl. That's supposed to be my fucking ring!" she yelled out, getting frustrated. "I'm the one who had been sucking and fucking him for pennies when he had nothing!"

Kasha wanted to throw up again. Every time Traci mentioned sucking dick, it made her sick to her stomach.

"Pull over. I am about to throw up," Kasha said, opening the door.

"Hold up, girl. We're here."

Kasha threw up right outside of the car door. After she was done throwing up, Traci decided to move the car into another parking spot so they wouldn't have to look at it when they came back out. They went into the health department and got signed in. Kasha took a number and waited in the lobby. Traci held her hands, letting her know that everything was going to be all right.

"I'm straight. I was thinking about that Blow Pop sucking you were talking about. You're just nasty as hell."

Traci fell out laughing. "Girl, you better get with the program if you want to step up your game."

"Oh, hell to the fucking no!" Kasha waved her hands in the air.

"Honey, if you want to keep a man, or at least keep him happy, you better get them jaws ready. Because what you don't do, trust and believe, there will always be somebody willing to do it."

"I know that's right," the girl sitting in front of them turned around to say. "Oh, shit, Kasha. What are you doing here?"

The same reason you're here, trick, she wanted to say to Meka's trifling ass. Instead, she said, "Just got that virus that's been going around the school. And you?"

"I just found out that I am pregnant," she said. "Waiting on them to get a caseworker to talk to me and get me signed up for this prenatal stuff."

"Oh, shit," Kasha said. "Who are you pregnant by?"

"She don't know," Traci mumbled under her breath.

"Trapp," Meka said with pride.

"Trapp?" Kasha turned up her nose. "Isn't he half dead?"

"What the fuck did you just say?" Meka asked, standing up.

"Oh, my bad," Kasha said sarcastically. "I hope his ass dies! He raped me, and I have no love for his perverted ass. And you shouldn't be proud to be carrying his baby. He is sick!"

"Hold the fuck up!" Meka said, getting into Kasha's face. "I'm not about to let y'all bitches talk about my man! Your trifling ass should stop going after men because you think they've got some money for you to get and keep your damn legs closed. Then, when you don't get what you want, you want to holler rape! Going around, making false allegations about my man taking your goodies. Why would he take anything when he's got all of this?" Meka said, displaying her knockout figure.

"You stupid little bitch! Trapp ain't got no money, so why would I go after him for something that his ass don't have? You're just mad because your man wanted me so bad that he took what he wanted because it didn't want him!" Kasha retaliated. "And you are the trifling one. You are the one out here sucking every penis you can find!"

"Yep! But you best believe that if I am sucking, then they are eating as well. And with that being said, your boy, Ricky, ate all of this, slurping like it was his last meal. Then your ass called him while he was in the middle of his dinner, saying you needed to be knocked off, and he finished me up and came to you. So, that night when you kissed him, you were eating my pussy too!" Meka said with a sly grin on her face.

Kasha's fist collided with her face. *Just who all is Ricky fucking?* Meka stumbled back a few steps with her vision impaired from the impact. She thought she saw four Kashas and six Tracis coming her way. She balled up her fist and started throwing wild punches into the air.

"Hey, hey, y'all break it up!" one of the counselors said as she ran over and grabbed Meka, who was still throwing wild punches into the air. Traci and Kasha were just standing there, looking at her as if she were crazy. She had to be disoriented because she was nowhere close to either of them.

The lady took Meka to the back as the other lady came to them and said, "Take a seat before one of the white workers come out because they will call security and have you thrown out or jailed. I'm trying to look out for you girls, so sit down and behave," she demanded. As soon as the lady said what she had to say and turned to go back to her desk, a short man came to the door and called Kasha's name. He noticed Traci sitting there.

"Hey, Traci. Don't tell me you're here because you think that you are pregnant again," he said, adjusting his glasses.

"No, not this time," she laughed, embarrassed. "I'm here with my friend," she said, pointing to Kasha.

"Well, come on back," he said to Kasha.

When she got into his office, he asked her how long it had been since she had her last menstrual cycle. He explained to her what he was about to do and then gave her a small white cup and sent her to the bathroom so he could get a urine sample. When she came back into the room, she hopped up onto the table and lay on her back with her eyes closed, praying that she wasn't pregnant.

After what seemed like an eternity, the doctor finally came back into the room with a sullen look on his face.

"Well, Ms. Davis, I have your test results back, and you are indeed pregnant."

The doctor was talking, but Kasha did not hear anything he said because the room began swirling around her really fast, causing her to pass out. When she came to, she could not stop the tears as her body shook as she cried, "No, this can't be true. I can't be pregnant. My parents are going to kill me."

"Well, dear, when you have unprotected sex, it is bound to happen. You need to go home and talk to your parents, and you together can decide on how to carry on from here. We have counselors here also that I would like to get you with, and they can help you get signed up for some classes and prenatal vitamins as well."

"No, I can't tell my parents. I can't have this baby," she cried.

"Well, you appear to be about three months pregnant. I can't be totally sure until an ultrasound is done, but in our state, after the first trimester, you cannot have an abortion."

She was noticeably upset when she stormed from the office. Traci knew the outcome before she even broke the news to her. Traci consoled her friend the best way that she could as Kasha cried on her shoulder.

"I can't have this baby. The doctor said I was too far along to have an abortion though. What am I going to do?" she cried.

"There are places that will allow you to have an abortion after the first trimester in Georgia," Traci told her.

"Stop at the store. I need a cigarette," Kasha said to Traci's surprise.

"Are you going to tell Ricky?"

"Hell no. What he doesn't know won't hurt him."

"Fuck that shit." Traci looked at her like she was insane. "We're going to pay his so-called balling ass a visit. He can at least help you with the abortion."

They got to the detention center at the right time because visiting hours were just starting. Kasha was nervous as she waited to see him. His eyes lit up when he saw her because, after the last visit, he thought she was done with him.

"What's up, baby? I've been writing you. Why haven't you been writing me back?"

Her nervousness quickly went out the door. "I'm not even going to bother answering a question that you already know the answer to," she said, getting mad all over again. "You continue to play me for a fool and knowing these girls go to school with me."

"Baby, I told you that I was sorry!" He pleaded with his eyes. "But, baby, I need you. I know it may be hard for you to believe because of all of the fucked-up shit that I have done, but I do love you."

"You should know that I just had a run-in with that bitch Meka."

"Huh?" He looked like he wanted to disappear.

"Yeah, nigga, you heard me. She spilled her guts and wasted no time in telling me how you ate her pussy and then left her to come and sex me. Yeah, the bitch even said that you were kissing me, knowing you had just eaten her out! Fuck you, Ricky. I am done. Standing by your side is not the reason that I am here. Get that bitch to stand by you!" she said angrily.

"I don't want Meka. Fuck that shit she's talking. You've got to know that I care about you. I have never done as much for another female as I have you," he said.

"Nigga, please, the only thing you've done for me is get me pregnant," she said as she poked her fingers on the glass.

"You're pregnant?"

"You heard me! And I need eight hundred dollars so I can get an abortion!"

"Girl, do you really hate me that much?"

"Yes!" she screamed.

"Well, every time you look at that baby, I guess you're going to have to remember me because I'll be damned if I give you money to abort my child!" He leaned back in his chair with a smirk on his face.

"Ricky, you said yourself that you could be facing up to twenty-five years in prison. So, are you really that self-centered that you would leave me to raise a child all alone?"

"Baby, you know I'm trying to pay my lawyer. I really don't have it right now," he said, shaking his head.

"Fine! I'll ask Cane for it," she said, standing, knowing that she would strike a nerve.

"Fuck that nigga. It might be his fucking baby anyway. Don't think that I don't hear shit from the inside. Word is you're slinging pussy like you're selling crack rock on the corner."

"Fuck you, Ricky! I hate your sorry ass! I hope that these crackers give your ass a thousand years, you stupid son of a bitch," She hung up the phone, leaving him angrily pounding on the glass that separated them, wishing he could get to her.

Chapter 24

Kasha

She had to get away from home. She was stressing herself out trying to avoid her parents and Tina to hide her pregnancy. She thanked Traci for letting her stay over for the weekend. She knew she had to face her parents soon because her figure was beginning to spread.

"Have you talked to Cane yet?"

"Nah, I haven't heard from him. I believe he's gotten his pager number changed."

"Come on, girl, and get your shit. We're about to go to the mall and pay them Chinese folks a visit because you're stressing me the fuck out," Traci said as she helped her gather her things. "And don't worry, it's my treat because I tricked T-Lov out of a few dollars. Girl, I worked hard sucking his dick just to get this little chump change." She rolled her eyes playfully because she knew that when she talked about sucking dick it grossed Kasha out. "Come on, let's go to the mall before Derrick starts bitching about us using his car."

They stopped by the food court first because Kasha was craving a banana and strawberry smoothie.

"What's up, beautiful?" this fine guy said as he approached.

"Hey," Kasha said as she looked him over from head to toe.

"My name is Twon, but most people call me Tee-Tee," he said, extending out his hand to shake hers.

"I'm Kasha." She smiled as she shook his hand. "And this here is my friend, Traci." After shaking Traci's hand and saying it was nice to meet her, he directed his attention back to Kasha.

"So, what's up, baby? Do you have a man?"

She felt a bad vibe in the air. Something about him and his smoothness reminded her of Ricky. She wasn't built to deal with another player. "I'm sorry. You seem like a good guy, but I'm not interested at this moment. I just got out of a bad experience, and I'm not ready to jump back into anything," she said, looking him in the eyes.

Traci, overhearing the conversation, stepped to Twon and said, "Excuse me, whatever you said your name was, but my friend has had a rough day and is not thinking logically right now. So, give me your number, and I will make sure she calls you."

"Whatever," Kasha laughed.

"Girl, just let me handle this."

"Well, since you want to play mama, I'll meet you at Tokyo Nails," Kasha said as she walked off, leaving them standing there, slurping on her smoothie. As she passed Hollister, Ricky's favorite store, she reminisced about the good times she shared with him.

"Wait up, girl," Traci said, bringing her back from her stroll down memory lane. "Guess what, girl? That nigga got bank," she said, unfolding a $100 bill. "He's paying for you to get your shit done. Girl, he is cute, don't mind coming out the pocket, and tall. If you are not going to call him, I'll call his ass," she said, tucking the money into her bra.

She didn't want to get involved with anyone right now, but she thought, at the very least, he would be someone she could get to take her out every now and then.

Kasha finished her smoothie and craved another one. Traci had given her the money that Twon had given her, but she thought that she needed to be saving it if she was going to get this abortion. She didn't know how much money she was going to be able to wean off of Cane and a few others she talked to. Traci was looking at the new Phat Farm T-shirts. They both agreed that Terry Jr. would look good in it. Traci picked up five different polo-style shirts.

"Girl, exactly how much money did T-Lov give you?" Kasha asked, knowing that all of those shirts were at least $200 easy.

"We don't need any money," Traci said, waving her over to come closer. "Since you have on them baggy clothes, you can stuff them down your pants."

"Oh, hell nah, girl, I'm not trying to go to jail," she muttered, looking at Traci like she had lost her mind.

"Come on, Kasha, you can't be scary all your fucking life. Don't you want to raise some money for the abortion? We can do the shit our damn selves. We can sell this shit."

It didn't take Kasha long before she was headed to the dressing room and stuffing her pants with Ralph Lauren Polo, Ecko Unltd., and Tommy Hilfiger shirts. She walked into the dressing room to adjust the clothes. After coming out of the dressing room, she was paranoid as fuck and sped up her pace, feeling everyone was watching her. *Slow down, girl, and walk normally.* She thought she was hearing voices but realized it was her own inner voice, trying to calm down her nerves.

Once she was outside, she exhaled. Never in life had she ever been so scared. "I told you we could do it, but the next time, you have to keep your composure because being scary will get you busted. We should get three hundred and fifty dollars for all twelve shirts."

Kasha wanted to know why they couldn't stay at full price. Traci told her all street value was half-price. Traci pulled over to use the pay phone. She called T-Lov, knowing he would buy all the shirts, but he didn't answer. She automatically assumed that he was with his trick-ass bitch.

After three failed attempts, Kasha convinced Traci to drive to Shi's house. Hopefully, she could get in touch with Cane. Once they got to his house, Traci pulled out a few shirts from under her shirt. "Girl, if you hang around me, I'll turn you into a beast." She put two shirts up for Derrick for using his car.

"Shit, if I keep hanging around you, I'm going to end up like Ricky, facing twenty-five years in prison with our baby lost in the system," Kasha joked, shaking her head, praying this was going to be the last time she stole.

Shi came outside to check out all the shirts and bought them all. He was excited about the deal and told them that if they got some more, he'd buy them too. Kasha changed her mind about that being the last time once she saw the money.

"Girl, we gotta go back. That was too easy," she said to Traci.

"It's getting late, and Derrick has to go to work tonight. We will go back tomorrow if Derrick lets us get the car," Traci said.

When they got to Traci's house, Derrick was on the porch. "Where the fuck you been all day in my car?"

"You said you were going to sleep until around eight p.m., so I am back, and it's only seven thirty. I bought you something," she said, pulling out the two Polo shirts.

"Damn, these are sweet. Thank you," he said, hugging his sister. "What you got for me, Kasha?" he asked, looking at her seductively.

"Kiss my ass, Derrick," Kasha said, laughing as she walked past him. She and Derrick had tried messing around once, but it hadn't worked out well. However, it had led to her and Traci's great friendship, but he was still always flirting with her.

She walked to Traci's room and started playing with Terry Jr. She thought about how it would be to have a baby. Terry Jr. was her heart, but she knew that her father would be torn up if she had this baby. He always told her and Tina that he did not want them to be teen parents, that there was so much more to do with their life than raising a child when you were just a child yourself.

"Girl, snap out of it!" Traci interrupted her thoughts. "Tee-Tee is on his way over, and I know that you don't want him, but get that nigga's money."

"Who?" Kasha asked, forgetting for a minute the nickname of the guy they had met at the mall today. "Wait, why is he coming over? I didn't call him."

"I know. I did," Traci laughed.

"Shit, I don't need his money. I'll boost clothes before I ask him for shit."

"Girl, that's chump change. We're too beautiful to be stealing. Besides, you can have a baller taking good care of you." Traci licked her chapped lips. "I didn't tell you this, but that nigga had about five grand in his pockets. That's what caught my full attention, and we're not going to let him get away," she laughed.

"Since you're so into the motherfucker, why don't you holler at his ass?"

"All right, since you're acting all stupid and shit, I'll take his ass."

"Good, now we can change the subject because, frankly, I am getting tired of men."

"I know that shit is right. Men only give you a headache, and I have heard women give better head anyway," Traci laughed, playfully snatching her son away from Kasha.

"Whatever," Kasha said as she lay down, thinking about how she was going to get to Atlanta. Her eyelids became heavy, and she dozed off into a deep sleep.

Kasha was awakened by Terry Jr. crying his lungs out. She tried to calm him down, but his cries became screams. She didn't see Traci, so she walked him into the living room—still no sight of Traci.

"Come to Granny, baby! Kasha, go and get the Children's Tylenol out the refrigerator," Ms. James, Traci's mom, instructed.

After she came back with the Tylenol, Ms. James asked her where Traci's fast ass had gone. Kasha told her that she was asleep when Traci left. Ms. James told her to go back to bed, and she'd watch Terry Jr. She couldn't wait to have an abortion. There was no way she was going to have a child after the way Terry Jr. cried.

She tried to relax, but her mind was in overdrive as she lay there, trying to figure out solutions. She was still short $500. She crept to Derrick's room. He rolled over as soon as she walked in. "Hey, Derrick," she whispered, "I need to borrow five hundred dollars. I promise I will pay you back as soon as I boost some more clothes."

"Girl, you done bumped your motherfuckin' head," he snarled, rolling back over to his side.

"I'm serious, Derrick." She paused. "I need it for an abortion."

"Ah, shit, I knew you were fucking. That's why your ass is so thick." He rolled back over, facing her with a grin on his face. He reached into the dresser drawer and pulled out a wad of money and then started counting out a few twenties. "So, if I give you the money, what are you going to give me?"

"A few Polos and a few Sean John shirts," she said proudly.

"Fuck that! I don't want any damn shirts. I want some of that fucking pregnant pussy," he stated, being direct.

"Derrick, you are like a brother to me. I can't believe you!"

"Trust me, baby, I don't look at you like no damn sister." He started putting the money back into the dresser.

"All right, Derrick!" she said. "If this is what you want, then let's do it, but I need that money." She still liked Derrick anyway, but he was older, and he had cheated on her in the past. She pulled her pants down, then slid off her panties and strutted over to the bed where he was. She lay beside him on her back. He leaned over and kissed her passionately, and she rubbed the back of his head, getting in the mood with him.

"Damn, I've been wanting you for a long time," he said.

When he stuck his tool inside of her, she immediately tensed up. It had been months since the last time she had sex. Derrick was humping like a madman until he released his fluids into her womb.

"Damn, this is some good-ass pussy. I should've been hit this pussy a long time ago."

She made him lie on his back as she started kissing on his stomach. "Sucking a man's dick is the key to his heart," she could hear Traci's voice telling her. Seeing how slimy his tool was from her juices made her stomach churn, so she didn't go through with it.

"Where's my money at?" He gave her $100 and told her he would give her the rest tomorrow. "I didn't give you half of the sex today! So, I don't want half of my money. I want it all!"

"Hey, what can I say? You played yourself. You always get your money up front. I got you tomorrow for real."

Chapter 25

Cane

Cane was glad that Jack came to the conclusion that he should get his own apartment. Initially, the apartment had been for him to use to stash his shit so that he didn't get busted again by his grandmother. But lately, he had been living in it as well because his grandma had been coming down on him so hard prior to him leaving. One night, he got home after midnight, and she told him that he needed to go back where he came from because he was not going to be coming into her house at all times of the night. Gladly, he went back to his apartment and had been there ever since. He still dropped in on his grandma often, and she still stayed on him about how he was living. He never talked back to her. He only listened and then went home.

He'd really gotten his weight up since he had his own space. He bought a 1968 Chevy Impala to get around in. He made sure all his bills were paid ahead of time, even though he had to make every money order out to a Frank Vincent. It was killing him on the inside to ask Jack who that person was, but he knew the motto was to never ask questions, just handle your business.

Over the summer, he learned a lot about the dope game from Jack and Tony. And meeting Tony's father, Mr. Big, was like a theme from an old gangster movie.

Mr. Big lived in Miami in a mansion which was equipped with ten bedrooms, two full-sized basketball courts, a bowling alley, two in-ground swimming pools, and a movie theater.

When Cane visited for the first time and saw the thirty exclusive foreign cars parked outside, he knew this man was living as large as they came. He fell in love with the SL500 convertible Mercedes-Benz, but Mr. Big's favorite was his 1955 Lincoln Sportsman convertible. After the visit to Miami, he was ready to step up his game in order to live a lavish lifestyle.

Cane literally jumped out of his skin when Calvin tapped him on the shoulders, bringing him out of his thoughts. "I've been calling you for the past five minutes. Sherry is waiting on you." She was lying in the bed, butt-naked, when he walked into his room.

"Just give me a little bump, Cane. I promise I'll get your rocks off," she begged as she reached for his man tool. She wrapped her hands around his tool and then slowly started stroking him back and forth. "Come on!" she continued to beg, "Just give me a bump to wake me up, and then I'll suck this big, black, juicy dick. Oh, Cane, baby, my pussy is aching for you," she moaned, tugging on his tool.

Before she could wrap her mouth around his pipe, he jerked his body away and then gave her two cracks. He thought that he could go all the way, but thoughts of how many dicks she sucked a day came to mind. He left her in the room so she could do her thing.

Calvin had a grin plastered on his face as he walked into the living room. "She's got some blazing-ass head game and pussy. I know you tore that ass up."

"Hell nah, nigga, I couldn't stoop that low to fuck a dopehead."

"Nigga, you're scared of pussy. Fuck that, I'm going to get our money's worth out of her ass."

"Nigga, you're a sick motherfucker." He was shocked to see Calvin tricking with a crackhead. Now, he saw why Calvin was always coming short with his money. He sat back on the couch, thinking about the accomplishments his crew had achieved. T-Lov had bought himself a Ford F150 and Trevia a brand-new Honda Accord, and they were in the process of buying a new house.

Calvin walked back into the living room, sweating profusely, bragging about Sherry eating out his ass. Cane shook his head and wanted to ask him if he had ever heard of a sexually transmitted disease. Sherry exited the room, and stupid-ass Calvin walked up on her and kissed her in the mouth. Cane wanted to curse him the fuck out. All he could do was shake his head.

They all hopped in Cane's car. He let the top up because he didn't want to be seen riding around with Sherry in the car. Calvin was in the back seat, hugged up with her as if they were in a committed relationship. Cane turned up his radio because he was tired of hearing Sherry's lies about being in love with Calvin and how good his lollipop tasted. She had Calvin's head fucked up. He chased behind her and told Cane he'd get up with him tomorrow.

Business was slow today, so Cane decided to go and visit Trapp. As soon as he stepped on the elevator, Shi started blowing up his shit. He called him once he got into Trapp's room. Shi wanted ten pounds. Since Shelia lived close to the hospital, he told Shi that he would have it delivered to her house.

He realized he didn't do his weekly ritual, so he went back to the gift shop and bought Trapp a balloon and card. That was something he'd been doing every week for the past eight months since Trapp had been in a coma. Every day, he prayed that Trapp was going to wake up.

Chapter 26

Kasha

"I don't know how I got caught like this," Traci screamed out, feeling frustrated.

"Calm down, Traci. Everything is going to work itself out." Kasha exhaled. "I got caught up also and feel the same frustrations as you are. But believe me when I say that things do work themselves out."

Kasha closed her eyes and sat back on the bed. She was tired of talking about the abortion. She went all the way to Atlanta for an abortion, but she was two weeks too late. She hated the shit she had to go through in order to get to Atlanta. She sucked Derrick's dick. Just the thought of him cumming in her mouth made her sick. She hated the fact that she had to stay there and be close to him.

After her daddy found out she was pregnant, they got into a huge argument. She decided to leave. The more she thought about Derrick, the more she missed being at home. She never thought she would miss having arguments with Tina, but she realized how much she loved her sister. Occasionally, she'd call her to give her the rundown about boys and staying focused in school.

She was happy to have a sister instead of a brother. Derrick was a selfish asshole who only thought about himself. Whenever she asked to use his car to go stealing, he not only wanted clothes, but pussy, too!

As she lay on her back, she let out a sigh of relief. Luckily, she wasn't going to steal anymore. Her last encounter didn't go too well. The manager caught her stealing and let her go, seeing how hysterical she became. That taught her a lesson.

She sat up in the bed, looking Traci in her eyes. "I'm sorry, Traci."

"I can't blame anyone but myself. This is not my first rodeo. I should have known not to have unprotected sex, especially since I hadn't been on my pills." Traci sat down next to her. "I knew I should've made him wear a condom, but he insisted that if I got pregnant, he'd never leave. But as soon as I got pregnant, the motherfucker told me he was married!" She shook her head with disgust. "Girl, I knocked all his and his bitch's windows out of their cars."

Traci crossed her arms. "Girl, I can't wait to have this baby so I can put his ass on child support." She uncrossed her arms. "I hate the fact that I put T-Lov on child support, but if he can buy that bitch a house and a new car, he can do the same shit for me!"

Kasha was seeing how childish Traci was acting. She was the older person and was supposed to be setting an example for her. "You know you're wrong for that! T-Lov gives you one hundred dollars a week and takes good care of his son."

"I mean, a hundred dollars is all right, but after I get my nails and hair done, I don't have enough money to go shopping."

"That money is for li'l Terry and not for your extracurricular activities."

"I know, but I need money too." Tears began to roll down her face. Kasha embraced her to calm her down. She told her that she should've been the one in tears, since her child may never see his daddy in life.

They both sat there with tears flowing down their faces. This time, Traci wrapped her arms to comfort her friend. "We're both in a fucked-up situation. I don't know why we are being punished like this!" Traci wiped away Kasha's tears with a kiss. She felt a sensation throbbing inside of her body. She kissed Kasha on the lips. When Kasha didn't resist, Traci locked lips with her, reliving the moment, making sure she wasn't dreaming.

"I think we are made for each other, Kasha. I'm telling you, we've both been hurt, and I'm tired of feeling pain."

She didn't know what to do nor think about what had just occurred. For one second in her life, she felt loved. She touched Traci's face, feeling the smoothness of her skin. "Oh, shit, I think I'm ready!" she screamed, feeling wetness between her legs. Traci started rubbing on her erect nipples. "No, Traci, my water just broke!" she yelled out in pain, pushing her away.

Traci panicked and grabbed Derrick's car keys. She helped Kasha inside the car and mashed out. "I think it's coming. Oh, my God, please help me!" she cried.

"Just breathe in slow. We're almost at the hospital."

Traci stopped at the front entrance. She tried to get Kasha out of the car, but she was in so much pain that she didn't want to move. Two paramedics were close by and brought over a stretcher and wheeled Kasha inside the hospital. Her head was spinning. She felt like she couldn't breathe. There was so much light in her eyes that she thought she was dying and going to heaven.

Chapter 27

Trapp

When Cane saw Trapp's eyes open, he nearly fainted. He gathered himself and ran out of the room, looking for a doctor. Trapp looked around the room, trying to figure out where he was. He stared at the balloons and cards, and then he looked at the tubes running into his arms. His eyes lit up as he nearly went into shock.

"Trapp, it's me. Cane!"

The nurses, followed by the doctor, rushed into the room, stopping Trapp as he was trying to remove the tubes from his throat. They told Cane to leave until they got him settled back down. Trapp continued to try to call out for Cane.

"I'm here, Trapp. Just try to relax and calm down."

"What's going on with me, and why are all these people in here?" he asked in a deep, raspy voice.

"Man, you got shot nine months ago. You've been in a coma." Cane saw the worried look in his eyes.

"Where's my mom? I gotta get the hell outta here." His heart was beating off the charts. The machine was beeping loud. The doctors gave him a shot that knocked him out instantly so he wouldn't go into shock.

Trapp woke up and started pulling all the tubes out of his arms again. He tried to roll onto his side and balance himself. As soon as his foot touched the floor, his entire body collapsed. The nurses came to his aid, helping him back into bed. "Travis, you've got to get some rest. Your legs are not strong enough for you to walk yet."

Dr. Roll walked in and let him know that, if he got some rest, he could start rehabilitation in the morning. Once he explained everything to him, he informed him that he had some visitors.

His eyes studied the white Jim Carrey look-alike, who stood over him in his jet-black suit. "Do you remember me, Mr. Shiggs?"

"How could I forget about you?" he replied, remembering multiple dreams about Agent Jackson. "So, what happened to me?"

"I don't know what happened. That's what I'm trying to find out." After asking Trapp a few questions, he then pulled out a photo album, letting Trapp scan through it. He pointed at Slim, indicating he was the trigger man. "Samuel Solon, aka Slim, just as I thought," Jackson mumbled under his breath. "Thanks again, Travis, for your help. I promise that Samuel and Ricky will never see the streets again," he stated since he felt Ricky put a hit out on Trapp from the inside. "Please contact me once you get out the hospital. I've got a grand waiting on you." He smiled, closing his folder.

Trapp relived the vision over and over when Slim pulled the trigger. He was hoping that he got to him before Agent Jackson did. Agent Jackson gave him a stern look and informed him not to tell anyone about their new relationship of working together, to let it be their little secret. He gave Trapp a card and then disappeared out the door.

Trapp closed his eyes as memories of stashing money came to play. His vision was fading in and out. He finally opened up his eyes hours later and sat up in bed, reading his cards. He smiled, seeing that CMB had been visiting him on a regular, despite all that he had done to them. Cane had outdone everybody. He stopped reading all of the cards once he spotted Meka's card. He opened it, looking at her picture, noticing her stomach poking out tremendously.

He started reminiscing about spending time with Meka before he got shot. He rubbed the picture, wondering how she got pregnant. He picked up the phone, but he couldn't remember any numbers. He slung the phone on the floor and then started throwing fruit from the basket on the table next to him. All the commotion drew the nurses into the room, and they gave him a shot, which put him back to sleep.

Chapter 28

Trapp

He was walking around the hospital every day, building up his strength. The rehab helped him out a lot. His memory was coming back to him fast. The doctor told him that he was going to be released today. He still couldn't believe he was in a coma for nine months.

He called Meka's house but didn't get an answer, so he called Ray-Ray's house. When he heard his voice, he wanted to hang up the phone. He didn't recall anybody on the west side showing him love since he'd been gone.

"What's up, my nigga?"

"Who this?"

"Trapp!" he snapped, feeling some type of way, since Ray-Ray didn't recognize his voice.

"My motherfucking partner, Trapp? Damn, my nigga, they said you were dead. Slim's bitch ass has been running around town with teardrops tattooed on his face, like he's a fucking killer. I wanna murk that nigga so bad for what he did to you, but every time I see him, I'm the one that's not on point."

"My nigga, we're supposed to smoke his ass and leave him dead and stinking somewhere so the vultures can eat his ass."

"My nigga, I want to, but these streets are dangerous out here. So much shit has changed out here. I'm on the run now as we speak. You just don't understand, my nigga!"

Trapp snapped out, "Well, the only thing I do understand is that you've never been up here to visit me! Shit, Cane was up here about every day strong."

"Like I said, my nigga, I couldn't see you like that. But fuck what you're talking about. I've been taking care of Meka since you have been gone."

"Yeah, I can see that. No wonder she sent me a picture with her pregnant. Shit, she couldn't tell me in person that y'all been fucking around?" He tried not to show his emotional side. "Damn, nigga, you could've at least wore a condom."

Ray-Ray burst out laughing. "No, my nigga, I didn't get her pregnant. You did! Hell, her stomach is huge as hell. She looks like she's got two watermelons in her stomach," he joked. "But anyway, her ass is in the hospital."

He hung up the phone in Ray-Ray's face and then took off doing what he thought was running. He didn't know which way to start. He was anxious to find her. He went from room to room and eventually ended up running into Cane.

"I see that you're feeling good today!" Cane said, looking at the excitement in his eyes. "Your mother told me to come pick you up."

He told Cane that Meka was about to have his baby and he wasn't going anywhere until he found where she was in this hospital. They walked to the nurse's station and gave her Meka's information. He broke out to the elevator, leaving Cane behind. He was excited to become a father.

Cane finally caught up with him. As they walked into Meka's room, her eyes glowed when she saw him. Her bright, wide smile lit up the room. He walked up to her and then kissed her. Cane walked out of the room, feeling Meka's negative energy toward him.

"Why didn't you tell me you were pregnant?"

"I did while you were in the coma. I told you a lot of things. I knew God would hear my cries and wake you up." She let him know that she didn't like the fact that he was hanging out with Cane, and she didn't want him to leave until she had the baby. He told her that he hadn't planned to. She started dropping salt on Cane by letting Trapp know that he was spreading rumors that he raped Kasha, and her cousin shot him.

He told her that wasn't true and that Slim shot him.

She was curious as to how he found out that she was in the hospital. He told her Ray-Ray informed him. She sat up the best way she could, holding his hands. She let him know that Ray-Ray had been a big help and looked out for her with a baby crib and clothes. She didn't feel the need to tell him just yet how he had been pimping her out for sexual favors.

"That's my dawg. I love that nigga, and I owe him big time for taking care of you." He kissed her on the forehead.

Meka started having bad contractions and hit the emergency button. "I think he's coming!" she yelled out in pain. Nurses entered the room, telling her to breathe in and out slowly. Trapp saw the nastiest thing he ever witnessed after looking between her legs. Seeing all that blood, he passed out on the floor.

Chapter 29

Cane

He got off the phone just in time to catch his shirt from burning. He looked back at his phone, thinking about the time he almost caught his bedroom on fire by leaving the iron on. He'd never forget the ass whipping his grandma gave him for burning a hole into her carpet. He thought those days were over, but nothing much had changed. He had to be more careful.

He was making sure all his clothes were ironed for the week since school was starting back up. He was entering his senior year a baller, and he had to stay fly and continue to be the best dressed. His only competition was Shi.

"What's up, Cane? How long have I been asleep?" Trapp asked, looking around.

"Ever since you passed out before your son came out the womb! But anyway, Meka and your beautiful son are doing well." He walked up next to him, giving Trapp dap. "Your son looks just like you. Boy, you spit him out."

Trapp wanted to see his son, but Cane told him that his doctor said that he was not to get back up until tomorrow. He saw the look in Trapp's eyes that said he desperately wanted to go see his son.

Looking around Cane's apartment, Trapp said, "Damn, nigga, you're really balling now!"

"Yeah, man, it gets lonely when the fellas aren't here, but ain't shit changed. CMB for life, and the only difference is we're weather and we make it rain." Cane pulled out three grand, breaking off Trapp a stack. His bag of crack fell onto the floor. He tried to hurry and scoop it up, but Trapp had his eyes on it.

"Damn, nigga, y'all niggas are really balling now. Shit, nigga, put me on. You know I gotta take care of my son."

"Like you said years ago," Cane said, checking his pager, "bringing CMB to life." He called Shi back to see what he wanted.

"Shit, nigga, I'm CMB too! Put a nigga on?" He didn't want to hear Cane talking about being patient. Cane's wardrobe, apartment, and car were all fire. He needed to get back down with the clique if they were doing it like this.

Cane's pager went off again. He had forgotten that he needed to go by Jack's house before he left town. "Damn, I have to run by Jack's house. I know he'll be happy to see you. He told me that he doesn't see how I was making money, since I was always at the hospital with you."

"It's about time that nigga put you on." Trapp wanted to get down and fast so he could stack his chips up.

"Oh, it wasn't easy. Shit, nigga, I put in work to get where I'm at. I hate to give him ten grand, but that's a part of business when you're your own man."

Trapp's mouth got watery as he stared at the money. "Shit, I wouldn't pay that nigga shit. Just think what you can do with ten grand. You can make your car look like something out the *Rides* magazine."

"Yeah, it would be nice, but, nigga, I'm on a paper chase, and like Pookie says in *New Jack City,* this crack keeps calling, my man." He turned it into a joking matter. "Hell, I can't even keep up with Calvin anymore. That nigga loves to trick them dopeheads. I feel sorry for Tonya. That nigga better tighten up before he loses her."

"Hell yeah. I'll take her fine ass off his hands. That nigga's dick always makes him lose out on the best thing for him. He needs some sex therapy classes." Trapp laughed.

"Nah, nigga, you've already had your share of Calvin's leftovers. I see that you haven't changed yet."

"Man, fuck that, Meka chose me. She didn't really like Calvin anyway. She always wanted to hook up with me until Calvin started hating on me, throwing shade on my character."

"I don't know about all of that, but the bottom line is that we are boys, so we are not supposed to let no pussy come between us," Cane said, not wanting to get into a dispute because Trapp had been on some grimy shit.

Cane crept up on Jack while he was uncovering his 1966 Shelby GT 350 convertible Mustang that Mr. Big bought him for his birthday off the showroom floor. "What's up, Unc? I got stacks for you." He didn't respond as he looked over Cane's shoulder, spotting Trapp.

"What the fuck are you doing with that nigga at my house?" he snapped out. "Cane, you're really violating me now! You know that I don't get down with no shady-ass niggas, and neither should you! I understood your concern for him, but he is out of the woods now, and you better not trust him as far as you can throw him. That nigga is going to be your downfall. I can smell a snake a mile away, and that nigga is a rat bastard snitch," Jack hissed as he warned Cane. "You have a heart of gold, but remember gold can be melted by the right incinerator, and family doesn't mean shit to a snake!"

"Unc, I'm not as naive as you think I am. My bad for bringing him over. I thought you wouldn't mind and might want to see him with all—"

Jack cut him off. “You thought wrong. I have not been in this business for as long as I have by having a good heart. You have to know when to let people go that mean you no good.”

“My bad. Just let me get my stuff, and we will bounce. It won’t happen again,” Cane said, getting frustrated. He just wanted to get his weed so he could bounce. Jack wasn’t trying to give him shit as long as Trapp was around.

“Are you shitting me?” Cane asked.

“Do I look like I’m shitting you?” Jack said, giving him his best “get the fuck out of here” stare. “You bring that hothead to my house and think I am about to go down behind your snitching-ass friend? Get the fuck outta here. You’re stupid, Cane. You may need to rethink this game.”

“Fuck it!” Cane said, upset for wasting his time by driving thirty-five minutes out there only to get turned away. “You’re not the only supply man around.”

“Go ahead and find you another supplier and see just how much them muthafuckers give a shit about you. We’ll see how much they will have your back and how good of a deal they give your ass. Look at you. You’re just like your muthafuckin’ mama. If shit doesn’t go your way, you flip out.”

Knowing his uncle was right, Cane apologized for his actions. “It’s cool, but you better learn and fast,” Jack said as he pointed at a television. “I bought you a TV for your apartment. Make sure you read the instructions before you turn it on.”

He didn’t want no fucking television. He wanted his supply he had come for. He could buy his own damn television!

“Thanks, man,” Cane said as he embraced his uncle. After putting the TV in his truck, he hopped into the driver’s seat and peeled out.

"Damn, nigga, I though Jack would be happy to see me. That nigga acted like he saw a ghost or something," Trapp said as he threw Jack a peace sign.

"Don't worry about Jack. he's acting like an asshole."

Trapp insisted on Cane taking him to the mall. The stacks that Cane had given him were burning a hole in his pocket. Plus, he wanted to look like the man when he returned to the hospital to see his son, bearing name-brand gear for his boy. Cane finally agreed after Trapp's persistence that it would be fine. His mother wouldn't mind as long as she knew he was with him and not getting into anything. Jack's words came down on Cane as he studied Trapp's vibe. He was hoping that for once his uncle was wrong, that Trapp understood who was real to him and not bite the hands that fed him.

"What's up, family?" Shi said as he changed positions with Cane, taking over the driver's seat and sliding his gun underneath the seat. "I'm glad you survived the war, nigga. I kept you in my prayers daily," he said as he reached back to give Trapp dap before he put the car in drive, heading to Calvin's house.

Cane was proud to see the crew back together like the good old days. Calvin hopped into the back seat, acknowledging everyone except Trapp. He just stared at him with a disgusted expression on his face.

The entire vibe was sour. Cane could feel an altercation arising, so he decided to leap in before it was too late. "Yo, check this out, fellas. We're family. We have to let the past stay in the past. CMB is on some new shit. We're getting paid and laid in a major way. We can't be statistics and out here beefing when we can talk it out and fix it."

"But, Cane, this nigga ain't family no more. He betrayed us in the worst way. I can't believe he's riding around with us like nothing ever happened." Calvin didn't give a fuck if Trapp almost lost his life, and he most definitely didn't care about God giving him another chance to breathe again.

"Just hear me out, fellas. If God gave Trapp another chance, so should we! We grew up together, and we have all did some foul shit. We always said that we were our brother's keeper, so was that just a bunch of steam?"

"All right, Cane, you win. But this nigga flips out one more time," he said, looking at Trapp. "I'm going to be the one to do him in," Shi hissed. "If I'm wrong then my bad, my bad," he said, reaching out to dap up Trapp.

"That's what I'm talking about. We all we got, one big, happy family," Cane said, happy seeing his crew getting along.

They got to the mall, and all eyes were on them. Girls were following them around, giggling as if they were superstars. They were straight chilling, acting as if they were unbothered by all of the attention that they were receiving. They left the mall, and Shi wanted to go on the west side of town. They didn't feel funny about going since they had been playing ball at their center, but Cane didn't trust Ray-Ray for shit. That was why they all stayed strapped.

"Yo, pump that Pac, nigga. These motherfuckers can't relate to a real motherfucker." Cane nodded his head to the beat. "Can't nobody fuck with 2Pac, the realest rapper alive." He rapped along with Pac's lyrics as Shi turned down the wrong road, not paying attention to the street name.

"Damn, Shi, turn this motherfucker around. I just saw a bad-ass bitch back there," Calvin shouted, pointing in the direction of the female who was standing in front of the mailbox. "Just turn around so I can see what she's about."

They had their eyes glued to her thick pecan tan legs. When she turned around, Calvin smiled, recognizing her. "Starr?"

"Hey, Calvin," she said, smiling until she glanced into the back seat of the car. All of a sudden, her eyes stretched wide as if she had seen a ghost, and she took off like a cheetah, running for her house.

"Yo, Shi, pass me the fucking gun. That's the bitch whose brother shot me," Trapp said, trying to reach under the driver's side to get the gun.

"Hell fucking no!" Cane said. "You ain't bringing that heat here, and we're dirty."

"Nigga, they shot me, and y'all are going to let that shit ride? Let's put that bitch's lights out now!" Trapp insisted.

"Nigga, your ass raped her. What the hell did you expect for her brother to do?" Calvin said. "Slim's not even that cat unless you provoke him in some way. He saved my life."

"I thought y'all motherfuckers had changed. Y'all still the same old scared-ass pussies." Trapp was fuming, "Y'all let Cane call all the shots now? So, everything he says goes? Fuck CMB, we ain't all we got." Trapp punched the window. "That's why I fucked Kasha and Meka. Give me a week, and I'll be fucking Tonya!" Trapp had flipped out.

Calvin swung at Trapp, nearly knocking him out. Cane couldn't believe how Trapp had tripped nor the shit that came from his mouth. Uncle Jack's words were stinging his ears as he sat and watched Calvin beat his ass.

Chapter 30

Trapp (2000)

He never thought parenthood would be so stressful. With Meka bitching every second, and the baby crying all night long, his nerves were wrecked. He gave her a grand to go shopping to shut her up. After counting his money, he realized he'd been blowing more than he'd been making. He spent two stacks on weed and bought a Cadillac for $2,500. He was waiting on Agent Jackson to break him off with a few hundred more.

Jackson wanted him to make a buy from Jack, but Trapp knew it would be a problem since Jack didn't trust him. Jackson wanted Jack so bad that all Trapp had to do was sign statements that he received drugs from Jack, and he would be compensated once they made an arrest.

A couple of weeks passed by, and he still hadn't heard from Agent Jackson. He needed money bad as hell. He had bought his car, but he needed money to insure and pimp it out.

He got distracted by a loud noise coming from the kitchen. He charged into the kitchen with his pistol pointing at his victim. "Oh, I'm sorry, Ms. Taylor. I didn't know you were here." He slid the gun into his waist.

"What are you doing with that gun, Travis? Does your father know you've got that thing?" she asked. "You're gonna get yourself or someone hurt with that thing! I told your daddy you are a lost cause," she said with disgust as she started unloading the groceries.

"Like you hurt my mama by fucking my daddy!" Trapp got loud. "What kind of bitch are you? You were married to the preacher."

She was shocked at his outburst and didn't expect him to go off like he did. "How dare you talk to me like that? Have some respect for your elders."

"My elders I do respect, but not sluts! And in order to get respect, you have to give respect!" He stepped into her face, pulling his gun from his waist. He saw the fear in her eyes. She dropped her glass of orange juice and tried to run, slipping on the juice and falling to the floor, hitting her head hard.

Trapp panicked when she didn't move or respond. His mind was saying to call the police because it really wasn't his fault, but he panicked. He intended to drag her into the living room and leave her on the couch, but when he saw her solid, thick thighs, his mind went into the gutter. "This is for hurting my mama." He unbuttoned his pants, releasing his snake. He pried her mouth open and then slid it inside of her mouth. Once he got his whistle wet, he slid off her panties and then entered into her womanhood.

Before he got ready to cum, he pulled out and skeeted in her face, next to her mouth. "You stinking slut. I don't know why my father cheated with you. Your shit ain't no good." He spat in her face. She was still knocked out cold. He started to slide her gown back down, but instead, he left her lying half naked. He called his father at work, but there was no answer, so he left a message that Ms. Taylor was on drugs and she tried to rape him.

After cleaning up, he drove his car to Ray-Ray's, feeling it was safe since it was right down the street. "My nigga, I'm just in time to hit that shit," he said, taking the blunt from Ray-Ray's hand. "What the hell is this shit?" He felt an instant contact and his eyes watered as his vision became blurry.

"Nigga, that's that stank one, weed and coke mixed." Ray-Ray had a smile on his face as bright as the sun.

Trapp felt sweat beads forming on his forehead. Every few seconds, he ducked behind Ray-Ray, thinking Slim was coming at him with a gun. "I'm going to kill your pussy ass!" he shouted, pulling out his gun.

Ray-Ray grabbed him. "Calm the fuck down. This shit got your ass tripping."

"Fuck that. We need to find Slim's ass so I can sleep easy."

Ray-Ray gave a nod to Chris to get the minivan. Timbo was hanging out the window. "It's about time motherfuckers get some fuckin' heart around here. I've been ready to off that pussy motherfucker and save the police a job." Ray-Ray passed the blunt to Trapp, who smoked it all the way to the head. He was glad to be back with Ray-Ray. He felt comfortable and safe, like the world was his.

"Yeah, motherfucker, I'm back." Trapp raised his gun into the air. "It's a new me, and when I'm finished handling my business, I'm going to make the whole world bow down."

The cocaine had them all rattled up as they rode past Slim's house. Trapp was ready to pepper spray the house, but Ray-Ray told him to be patient. He sat back in frustration, thinking that Ray-Ray sounded like Cane. "Shit, Chris, you know the deal, puff-puff pass!" He looked at them all sideways.

Chris didn't pass him the blunt. "Shit, nigga, just because you did a little Jack move, it don't make you a superstar." Chris threw the blunt out the window.

Trapp put the gun next to Chris's temple. "What now, nigga? Say something fucked up and I'll make you famous!"

"What in the hell are you doing, Trapp?" Ray-Ray pulled out his gun, placing it to Trapp's head. "Get that shit off my cousin's head before it becomes a fucking bloodbath in this bitch."

"I'm just playing with this scary-ass nigga, trying to see where his heart is at." He sat back, keeping his eyes on him. He wanted to pull the trigger to let him know he wasn't a fuck nigga. Ray-Ray told him that Chris helped take care of Meka when he was in the hospital. He was fed up hearing about Meka and them taking care of her while he was gone.

They rode all over the neighborhood. There was no sign of Slim. They were heading to downtown Greenville when a female voice screamed out, "Hey, babies, let me catch a ride with y'all so I can show y'all what a real woman is made of."

"Hold up, Chris. Turn around so I can see what's up with them hoes."

"They hoes, just as you said, that's what's up with them! Come on, nigga, we don't have time to fuck with no prostitutes!" Ray-Ray saw the look of lust in his eyes. "Shit, we've got to find Slim and get this beef over with."

"Just back the fuck up so I can holla at the bitch," Trapp shouted as Chris backed up. "What's up with you?"

"Whatever y'all want to be up. Babydoll is down for whatever."

"Shit, a little head for me and the boys."

She looked inside, counting all the heads, letting them know that she would give them a group discount, $200 and an extra $200 for some pussy. Trapp studied her figure, already knowing what he was going to do with her. They dug into their pockets, trying to get the money up. Trapp already had a hard-on, ready to fuck something.

Suddenly, Chris stepped on the gas, burning rubber in Babydoll's face. "What the fuck you do that for? Shit, we were about to get some head and pussy." Trapp was mad as hell.

"Nigga, I just saw Slim's car go down the street. Y'all get ready," Chris said as he sped up, trying to catch up with him.

Trapp put a black bandana around his nose, covering his mouth. They spotted Slim's car parked at the store. He came up with a plan since Slim wanted him so bad. He told them to drop him off in front of the store and wait on him on the next road over.

As soon as Slim walked out of the store, he caught his attention by calling him a pussy-ass nigga and then took off running.

"I'm going to kill your ass." Slim gave chase. Trapp ran for his life. Running out of gas, he was thirty feet from the van. He wanted to stop, but he pushed it with all he had in the tank.

He stopped in front of the van and then turned around to face Slim. "Yeah, my sister told me you were still alive. I thought she was lying, but now it's time to meet your Maker!" Ray-Ray and the others hopped out of the van with their guns locked and loaded. Slim's lips hung low, eyes wide, as he realized he had just been set up.

"Yeah, motherfucker, you should've killed me," Trapp spat out as he opened fire on Slim. He stood over him, emptying his clip into his chest. He went through Slim's pockets, taking his keys and money. He wanted the rims off his car as well. They put his dead body in the van and drove to Ray-Ray's house.

They switched out the rims and system from Slim's car to Trapp's car, as if they did not have a dead body they needed to dispose of. Trapp was smiling as his car was sitting phat. He wanted the system hooked up, but

Ray-Ray told him that they had to get rid of Slim's body and car first. Trapp split up the money he took from Slim.

They all split up. Timbo and Chris drove Slim's car with his body in the trunk. Their plan was to dump his body into the river. Ray-Ray paid his mama's boyfriend to clean up the van and pick up Chris and Timbo.

Trapp and Ray-Ray were riding around, stunting on new chrome shoes. He pulled up on Babydoll and her friend, ready to get the party started. Ray-Ray called Chris to let him know to meet them at the Ramada Inn. Once they got back into town, Trapp was stunned that everyone had cell phones except for him. "Shit, my motherfucking papers are right. What y'all bitches wanna do?" Trapp pulled out a few twenties.

"That's what I'm talking about," Babydoll said as she stripped naked and then helped Trapp out of his clothes. He closed his eyes, savoring the moment, as she took him into her mouth, swallowing his juices. He was ready to do some freaky shit.

"Bend that ass over, bitch!" he demanded. She did as she was told as he tossed a few twenties on her back. He rammed his pipe into her rear end without protection. He loved the tight fit as he penetrated her brown eye. "Shit, Ray-Ray, come and get some of this action."

He did just that, letting Babydoll suck on his manhood. He rolled his eyes over toward Sunshine, who looked like Halle Berry on crack. "I don't know why you're sitting over there being bashful. Bring your ass over here and suck my ass." Trapp didn't like the fact that Ray-Ray was outdoing him. He paid Sunshine $200 to eat Babydoll's nectar while he fucked her in her rear end.

He was putting on a real freak show. After he came inside her, he told Ray-Ray to fire up a juice joint. He offered them a blast, but they declined. He told them to burn up the road since he didn't need them any longer.

Ray-Ray tried to convince him to let them stay until Chris and Timbo got there, but his motto was fuck them. It was about him and Ray-Ray.

He couldn't care less about Chris bragging about how he left Slim's car sinking in the river. He was more anxious about fucking the two prostitutes. Ray-Ray convinced him to go find the bitches since they were supposed to be a clique. They all loaded up in the van. Trapp protested because he wanted them all to ride in his pimped-out car, but they argued it would bring unwanted attention.

The van was smoked out while they rode down Pendleton Street, looking for prostitutes. Trapp couldn't get enough of the juice joint taste. He wanted to smoke every five minutes. "Fellas, I got an idea," he blurted out. Everyone looked at him as if he were crazy. He told them about Cane's uncle Jack and how he was a millionaire, living in this mansion with millions of valuables in it as well. Their eyes were glued to him as he continued to give them the rundown about Jack and why they needed the prostitutes. Everyone was down with the lick. Ray-Ray pulled up next to the prostitutes. Trapp hopped out of the car. "What's up, Babydoll?"

"Ugh, y'all again," she snapped out, rolling her eyes. "What do y'all want? We're about to call it a night!"

"Check it, since y'all put on a good show for me, I want y'all to put on the show for my uncle."

"Nah, not tonight because my dawgs are killing me, and y'all didn't make the situation any better by kicking us out."

He pulled out the two grand that Chris and Timbo gave him. "Maybe this will change your mind." The money caught their full attention, and they agreed to do it. Babydoll split the money up with Sunshine as they hopped into the van.

They pulled up in front of Jack's house. Everyone's lips were hanging under their chins, amazed at the size of the house. "Damn, look at the size of this shit," Sunshine cooed as she licked her chops, mesmerized over his phat-ass whips. "Yeah, girl, he's got to be a baller," she added, talking to Babydoll. She was trying to fix her makeup and straighten her hair out. She smelled money, and Babydoll was ready to get paid.

"Yeah, he's got plenty of bread, and if y'all want to eat, you better put on a good show." Trapp reminded them to make sure to tell him that his nephew, Cane, sent them. He let them know, since it was a surprise, they were going to hide on the side of the house.

As soon as the prostitutes got out of the van, Trapp looked at everybody. "Jack Boys, grab your ski masks, and Timbo, you keep the van running." He looked at everyone, making sure they were ready.

They were all in position as planned. Everything was going good until Sunshine asked why they were wearing ski masks.

Jack, knowing that something wasn't right, came to the door with his gun aimed and ready because he knew that Cane would never send anyone to his house without permission or calling ahead. Trapp started firing his gun at him as he fired back. Rapid bullets were flying everywhere. To his surprise, the hookers weren't screaming, but he heard Ray-Ray screaming out that Chris was hit. He looked into his direction as he stood in Chris's blood.

"I'm going to kill that son of a bitch!" Ray-Ray shouted as he walked straight through Jack's front door. He took off his mask so Jack could see him well. He was lying on the floor, gasping for air as blood seeped from his body. "Get your bitch ass up!" he said as he kicked him. "You thought you were going to get away with trying to play me small?"

Trapp walked up on him and removed his mask so Jack could see him. Ray-Ray opened fire on him. He added a few shots to the dome, making sure Jack wouldn't live through this shit. He took Jack's necklace off of his neck and then spat in his face.

Before they could search the house, Timbo was blowing the horn after he saw the neighbor's lights come on. Trapp and Ray-Ray ran out of the house empty handed. He was mad as hell that the plan got fucked up. He wanted to go back, but police sirens could be heard from miles away. "Dammit!" shouted Trapp.

Chapter 31

Cane (2001)

He couldn't believe it was his last year in school. The time had flown by faster than he could have imagined. Although he was ready to be out of school so that he could really do his thing without the distraction of having to make sure he was in at a decent hour, so he could rest and get to school, a part of him was nervous about actually being a grown up. Although, he had been on his own for a minute now. The one thing that kept him from dropping out of school was Uncle Jack's wish for him to finish school, go on to college, and make a legitimate name for himself playing football. After all that Jack had done for him, he felt he had to do that in his memory.

The prom was coming up, and he couldn't decide if he wanted to take Shell or Tangie.

"Well, fellas, we've been boys since childhood." He choked, feeling emotional. "It seems like yesterday we were running around with snotty noses, shoes untied, and hard-headed as hell. Without you guys, CMB wouldn't be possible. And with the prom coming up, we have to go all out." He rubbed his hands together. "How about we rent a stretch Navigator limo?" He watched as Calvin and Shi's eyes glowed with excitement.

"Boy, we're going to be stunting like a motherfucker." Calvin gave Shi some dap.

"Our ladies will be happy once they find out how we're rolling in style."

"Well, I'm going to get with my peeps to check out some fly-ass tuxedos. And let Tonya and Shelia know that I will pay for their dresses because I know their parents have a tough time," Cane said.

"That's why I always looked up to you as a real brother. No matter how many times I fuck up, you never cut me off. I love you, bro." Calvin hugged him with a brotherly hug.

"If it wasn't for you guys, there wouldn't be any me. You guys have saved my ass more times than not. So, with this prom thing, I don't want y'all to spend a dime. Like my uncle always said, you take care of family first."

Tina walked up, interrupting them, pulling Cane by his arm. They all looked down silently at the mention of Jack's name.

The first thing that came into his mind was that he was going to have to kick somebody's ass when he saw her red, puffy eyes.

"What's wrong, baby girl?" he asked, ready to go and handle business.

"I want to go to the prom," she blurted out.

He let out a sigh of relief as she continued.

"Twan had asked me to go, but then he tripped after I told him that I would not be going to a hotel with him once I found out that he and his boys were all getting hotel rooms after the prom for them and their dates. The other girls may be down with it, but he and I are not dating. We are only friends, so how would I look sleeping with him? I already have my dress and everything."

"Your ass don't need to be going to the prom with that loser anyway. What were you thinking?" Cane said. "Everyone knows what Twan is about, and that's getting ass. You should have known better."

"I know, but I didn't think that he would try that with me, knowing how I am. I only accepted because my girls, Shelia and Tonya, are going with your boys, and I wanted to be in on the festivities of getting glammed up and hanging with the crew."

"Okay, knucklehead," he said, jawing her playfully. "I don't have a date yet, so I'll let you tag along."

She let out a soft, "Yippee," and then hugged him and kissed him on the cheek. He watched her as she skipped back over to her friends, delighted, as he made his way back over to his boys, who were looking at him sideways with smirks on their faces.

"Y'all fools always keep y'all heads in the gutter. That's my li'l sister. Stop tripping. Her prom date backed out on her, and since I don't have a date anyway, I said she could go with me. It's because she's cool with your dates that she asked me so she can be with her girls," he said, blushing but thinking of how thick and sexy Tina was looking to himself.

"Bro, you need to open up your eyes," Calvin said. "Even Ray Charles can see that she has a thing for you."

"Yep!" Shi added.

"Y'all need to cut that shit out, but anyway, I'll holla at y'all later on after class."

When he got to class, his mind was cluttered with so many crazy thoughts. He had so much on his mind. He had always dreamed of going to college ever since he became a fan of Deion Sanders. He had the grades to go anywhere he wanted because, although he was a thug, he was a smart one, sitting on a 4.5 GPA in honor classes, but his test scores were low. He had anxiety when it came down to taking standardized tests. His counselor told him this was not unusual and that a lot of smart people had test anxieties. His boys always playfully clowned him on awards day when he was always called up for having several of the highest averages.

"Mr. Griffin, you need to pay attention in my class," Ms. Moore said, tapping her ruler on his desk, snapping him out of his zone.

"I'm sorry, Ms. Moore. Can I go and talk to Coach Eddie?" Graduating and college had him stressed. He knew that selling dope was not his retirement plan.

"Ah, go ahead." She smiled, giving him a pass. Being the teacher's pet had lots of perks. She allowed him to do whatever whenever he wanted to.

As soon as he stepped into the coach's office, Coach Eddie said, "I was about to page you, son." He took off his glasses. "I've got some good and bad news. Seeing that your SAT scores are low, I recommend you go to Greenville Tech for two years and then transfer to Florida State."

His knees nearly buckled. He didn't want to hear that mess. His sights had been set on Florida State. "Greenville Tech! Coach, I can't go to Tech. I will be slow as a turtle in two years if I sit out that long!"

"Son, we will make sure that you continue to train so that you stay in shape. I'll let Darryl know that you will be working out with him at least three days a week, if not every day, depending on you. Son, don't let this discourage you. You have to have faith in God, and He will guide you through all things." Coach talked to him and made several calls to ensure him that everything was going to work out fine. He embraced him like a son.

After leaving Coach's office, he felt somewhat better. He walked to his car, checking his voicemail. Mr. Big was a mystical person. He never knew how to contact him, except through Tony, who would magically pop up on him.

When he turned his ignition over, his woofers were thumping Jay-Z's "Izzo (H.O.V.A)." All eyes were on him as he cruised through the parking lot in his smoke gray

1996 Chevy Impala. His shit was sitting on twenty-two-inch chrome Giovanni rims with the interior decked out with red velvet leather seats trimmed in white. His shit was equipped with three TVs.

He pulled into his apartment complex and spotted a dark green Hummer in the parking lot. He pulled up next to it and cut his engine. Tony's mind frame was the bigger and classier the car, the bigger the star. While Cane could afford it, he knew that Greenville wasn't ready for any type of shit like that. The Feds would be knocking at his door, ready to throw a motherfucker under the jail.

When he got into the Hummer, he and Tony dapped up. He asked Cane what was wrong because he looked as if he had the entire world on his shoulders. Cane told him about his meeting with the coach and his suggestion that he go to Tech. Tony let him know off the top not to be worried about school because, in two years, he would be a millionaire at the rate he was going. He could still picture himself wearing the gold and garnet colors of Florida State.

Tony let him know that his shipment of twenty-five kilos of pure, uncut Colombian cocaine would be here Friday, packed inside the limo refrigerator. He was relieved that he didn't have to ride to Miami to get his work.

"Let me go and get the money," he said, acting like he was about to make his exit.

"Don't tell me that you have all of that money stashed up in your apartment. Didn't Jack used to warn you about that? I see that you haven't learned yet!" Tony shook his head, pointing his index finger at Cane. "What did I tell you about keeping that type of money in your apartment? Don't worry about the money. I'll get it when you're in Atlanta."

"Nah, man, I was just messing with you to see what you were going to say," Cane laughed. He knew not to keep that kind of money around since the Jack Boys were on their kick of robbing everything in sight. He kept all of his money at his grandmother's house, inside her old floor-model TV. He distractedly answered his phone. It was Calvin giving him everyone's dress sizes and the website to find them.

"Cool, gotcha, man," Cane said, telling Calvin that he would call him back in a few. He apologized to Tony for taking the call and told him it could have waited. It was just Calvin giving him some prom info.

"Shit, I remember my high school prom. I was a straight G!" Tony blushed, clearly strolling back down memory lane, nodding his head. "Man, I rocked an Armani tuxedo with white Stacy's. Man, you have to represent and kill the game," Tony said, reaching to his back seat to retrieve his computer.

Tony flipped open his laptop, letting him see different styles of tuxedos. He loved the Gucci tuxedos and the Gucci dresses. Tony ordered everybody's outfits. He felt blessed to have that type of money.

As he was getting out of the Hummer, Tony said, "Hold up. I almost forgot. Mr. Big sent you a gift." Cane didn't hesitate to open it. Inside was a platinum Presidential Rolex flooded with diamonds with the matching bracelet.

"Damn," Cane said in awe of the way it was blinging.

"Man, you're doing the damn thing. Mr. Big awards big," Tony said, prideful.

He walked into his apartment, feeling like the man. He couldn't wait to show everyone the printout of the dresses and tuxedos, but his watch and bracelet were going to be the showstopper. He knew he was going to be outshining everyone with his watch and bracelet.

He sat on the couch, contemplating what he was going to do with all of this money he had made. He had enough to retire if he wanted to right now, just stashed away, doing nothing. It was time that he made an investment. He was going to build his grandmother a house from the ground up, so she could have her own garden. His grandmother had been a hard worker her entire life, still worked hard, and didn't even own the house that she had occupied for over forty years. He knew he was going to have to get really creative in his approach to her as to how he got enough money to purchase her a house because she wouldn't take his money since she considered it as blood money. The only reason she used to take money from Jack was because he had the barbershops, and she thought he was rolling from that money, but little did she know. His own mother had been out of prison for a few months, but she just wasn't going to do right, and he refused to take care of someone who did not care enough about themselves to try to stay off of drugs. Plus, she had stolen from him. He was going to tell his grandma that she could not live in the new house that he was going to buy unless she agreed to go to rehab.

T-Lov walked in with his little protégé, Redd. Redd had grown on him since his uncle's untimely death, and he was around T-Lov twenty-four seven nowadays. He'd nearly forgotten about Terry Jr., it seemed, since Traci had full custody of him and wouldn't allow T-Lov to see him unless he paid her a grand a week. Cane told T-Lov that he should drag her into court, but with his priors, he didn't want to deal with the court system, so he saw him when she would allow. Cane applauded T-Lov for not flipping out as he was known to do. T-Lov was maturing a lot, and he showed that by dropping money off even though Traci would barely allow him five minutes with his child before she hollered he had to leave because she was about to go here or there. Traci and Kasha were running around, talking about they were engaged to be married and shit, but T-Lov held his head up high and seemed unbothered.

He spoke to them both and showed them his watch and bracelet. "CMB for life," Redd shouted after seeing the bling. They all chuckled. He could see Redd being the next up-and-coming big thing.

T-Lov placed a shoebox on top of the table filled with $50,000. He gave him a look, asking what he was doing. Shit had changed from back in the Jack days and how they used to handle business. "Check it, the white T-shirts are at the park in the woods in the old tree house," he said in code. He loved his boys, but he still had to be cautious.

Once T-Lov left, he called Gina to make sure his grandmother was gone. She was the only person to know where he kept his money. He paid her $500 to keep an eye on everything. He would never forget the incident when he left the bag with twenty grand on the table and his mother stole it while he was using the bathroom. He hopped into his car, heading to his grandmother's, pumping Dr. Dre's "Still D.R.E.," featuring Snoop Dogg.

Chapter 32

Cane

Three Weeks Later

The entire clique had just left District 25 Barbershop. They stopped by Greenville Florist to get corsages and then went to Haywood Mall. Cane purchased Tina a diamond bracelet from Shirin Jewelers. Since he was cool with the owner, he didn't have to pay for it. Being the man had its good and bad points.

Calvin tried to call Tonya, but Tina answered her phone, letting him know that she was still under the dryer. He knew how serious females could be when it came to getting their hair done. It was something he'd been dealing with every week since he'd been getting Tonya's hair done.

Cane opened up the sunroof, looking over cars, shouting out, "I'm on top of the world." He called for Calvin and Shi to join him. He loved the fact that his entire crew was doing championship good. Calvin had his own car, and Shi bought his parents a new car. Shelia was four months pregnant, and they were planning on buying a house.

They were all young, chilling, and enjoying the good life. Cane went down memory lane, reminding them about the times that they tried to rob the store and went to jail. Then they joked about T-Lov's raggedy-ass Honda that they used to ride around in, barely making it. They looked at each other, appreciating how far they had come along in life.

Cane popped open a bottle of Cristal that Tony left them. He was wilding out, pouring bubbly out the window. "What are you doing?" Calvin asked, shaking his head. "Save that shit so we can show them niggas how we ball."

"Fuck them niggas. We don't have shit to prove to anyone," he barked, "All we can do is worry about CMB."

Calvin sucked his teeth. "Man, I'm just trying to do me." He looked in the opposite direction. "I'm going to show out and show off as long as I'm living."

He hated Calvin's cocky, arrogant attitude sometimes. He hated to think that he was going to end up like Trapp, but he loved him and couldn't see any of his boys not getting paid. He sat back, thinking about the time Mr. Big invited them all to Miami for the Bulls versus Heat basketball game as a getaway after Jack was murdered. Calvin got to meet his idol, Michael Jordan. He'd been spoiling Calvin like a 2-year-old child. "You're right, Calvin. Shine on them niggas," he agreed to make him feel powerful.

T-Lov dropped everybody off at home and told them he'd be back to pick them up later. Cane needed a break so he could cook up five kilos and then go bury them in the woods so the traffic wouldn't be so heavy at his apartment. He was happy that his grinding crack for crack days were over with. Ever since Jack died, he was pushing major weight, stepping into his place, not missing a beat.

After cooking up the coke, he sat down and then turned on his television. BET's *106 and Park* was on. He was scoping out Free's thick ass, wondering if A.J. was tapping that ass. His eyes became heavy, so he closed them for a short nap.

He jumped up out of his sleep and looked at the clock, realizing he was running late. He took a shower and then put on his cologne. He got dressed and topped his gear off with his watch and bracelet. He did a double take as he looked at his reflection in the mirror. He was dressed to impress, looking like a million dollars, and couldn't anyone tell him any differently.

His timing couldn't have been any more perfect because, as soon as he thought about his crew, they were knocking on his door. He was mesmerized by how fly his boys looked. Calvin had a cubic link necklace with a cluster diamond "C" charm custom-made, and he had two large diamond stud earrings in his ears. Shi kept it plain and simple with a cross necklace. He gave everybody their props and then pulled up his sleeve to show off his ice.

"Damn, nigga, that shit is nice," Calvin blurted out in awe. "I thought I was the only one with a bag of tricks." He still had his eyes on Cane's watch. "I tried to outshine you for a change, but you still got the best of me."

"Nah, bro, we shine together," he replied with a hug. They all walked out, heading to the limo.

Chapter 33

Kasha

She hopped out of the shower and started freshening herself up. She was still mesmerized and at a loss for words over how flawless Traci's nude body was after having two kids. Her body was still tight. Traci slid her two fingers inside her own nectar and sucked on her own juices. "Come on, baby, let's get another round in. You know I love the way you taste," she moaned, sliding her fingers in and out of her mouth.

She loved when Traci made love to her. She felt a tingling sensation travel through her body. Ricky Jr. was beating on the door, calling her name. "Here I come, boy. Let Mama get dressed." She turned her attention back to Traci's luscious body and made her way to her, kissing on her nipples.

"Damn, baby, I hate to leave, but I've got to go over my parents' house to see my sister." She watched Traci play with a twelve-inch dildo, sliding it halfway into her wetness.

"Mommy!" Ricky yelled out, beating on the door.

"Ugh, I swear that boy gets on my nerves," she hissed out, sucking her teeth. "I'm coming, son." She wiped the wetness from between her legs and then changed her panties.

"Tell your sister and brother bye. We're going to see Aunt Tina." She loved her sister and knew Tina loved Ricky Jr. At times, she didn't know what she would do without her. To her astonishment, her parents even acted as if they couldn't live without Ricky Jr.. They loved him so much. Her sister, Tina, who was now taking cosmetology at the vocational school, always kept Kasha's hair on point.

She put on Ricky Jr.'s seat belt and kissed his cheeks. She loved him and wouldn't trade him for anything in the world, but the only thing she hated was naming him after Ricky. She had received a letter from his attorney, stating why he was no longer ordered to pay child support after the DNA test that she had insisted on having done to prove that his trifling ass was the father of her son came back 99.9 percent sure that he was not the father to Ricky Jr.

As a matter of fact, she was ordered to pay back child support that Ricky had paid. Luckily, Cane paid all her debt for her. She tried to hook up with him because he seemed to be the realest nigga in the streets these days, but he wanted nothing from her but friendship. No one but Traci knew that Trapp was the father to Ricky Jr. After the test results came back negative for Ricky being the father, she knew exactly who it was, and there was no way in hell that she was going to tell Trapp that he was her son's father, who had been born on the same day as his other son. He hadn't been there for his son nor paid his child support. She and Traci shared the secret, and she loved being one happy family with Traci.

She screamed out, "Look at your aunt, Ricky. She looks so beautiful!" She hopped out of the car to hug her. "Damn, sis, that dress is phat as hell. Cane must have spent a fortune on that shit."

"I'm not worried about how much money he spent. I'm just excited to be going to the prom with him." She fanned herself. "He's like the ghetto superstar—"

She cut her off. "Yeah, yeah, anyway, look at you, you've gotten so thick. I can't believe how beautiful you are."

"Girl, you need to raise up off my body. I don't get down like that," she joked. "Come on, Ricky Jr. Let me take a picture with my handsome little nephew."

She was shocked when she saw Tonya and Shelia in their dresses. "Ah, shit, look at the divas." She clapped her hands, ignoring her mother ranting about cursing in front of her son. "But, Mama, look at these fly-ass ladies! They look so glamorous. Oh, girl, that dress has got your ass looking bootylicious."

"All right, Kasha, just letting you know I'm strictly dickly," Tonya joked.

She was getting agitated with all the dike jokes. She kept her cool and ignored them. When the stretch limo turned the corner, she started acting a fool. She couldn't believe how blessed the girls were to be going to the prom in style. She wished like hell she would've stayed in school.

After Cane stepped out of the limo, she nearly drooled on herself. He looked so sexy. She felt the moistness seeping through her panties. She hugged him and thanked him for taking her sister to the prom.

When he gave Tina her bracelet, she felt somewhat jealous. She wished she had stayed with him. She never thought he would become the baller he was today. She didn't want to hold them up any longer, but she told him to treat Tina like a lady and have fun.

After the limo pulled off, she felt left out, and her mother didn't make the situation any better by asking her why she let such a good man like Cane get away. He was such a good young man. She knew she made a huge mistake back in the day, and she was feeling the wrath of it today. She wanted to cry, but instead, she hugged Ricky Jr. and said, "I have a good young man right here. That is my pride and joy."

Chapter 34

Cane

Three Years Later

As soon as he got into the limo, T-Lov handed him an envelope with Mr. Big's name scrawled on it, which contained information pertaining to the presidential suite at the Hyatt. Tina was pulling on his arm. He fought her not wanting to go to the room. The look in her eyes spoke volumes. She wasn't trying to go back home. They went to the room. Another card was on the table. He read the contents and walked to the window. His knees buckled as he stared at the 2004 Mercedes-Benz CLK with his name on it. He was so caught up in his own excitement that he didn't notice how the room was set up. Rose petals were on the bed. Tina walked up behind him wearing her sexy Victoria's Secret. He turned around, mesmerized by how thick her 36-24-36 frame was looking without clothes. He tried to turn away, but she grabbed him by his shoulders, spinning him around. Before he could say something, their lips locked. She unbuttoned his shirt as she softly sucked on his neck. He scooped her up and walked her to the bed. She pulled off his wife beater and teased him about having abs and a little chest. He continued kissing on her neck until he felt a bulge growing in his pants.

All he could keep hearing in his mind was T-Lov telling him how to eat pussy. He stripped off her lingerie. Her skin felt so soft. He saw her pink nectar staring at him, begging for his attention. He put a piece of ice into his mouth and then went SCUBA diving between her legs.

Her moans turned him on as he made love to her with his sharp tongue. All he could hear was her crying out his name in ecstasy. Her body shook tremendously after she released her fluids into his mouth. His manhood was so hard he thought it was going to burst out of its skin. He gently inserted it into her wetness. His eyes rolled into the back of his head from feeling her warmness around his tool. She held him tightly as he penetrated her. Her cries and groans made him speed up his pace. His body started locking down like a tractor trailer before he masturbated inside her.

"What's on your mind?" she asked as she rubbed his head, lightly snapping him out of his trance.

He didn't want to tell her that he was reminiscing about prom night, the night he fell in love with her—a night he relived over and over daily, cherishing the moments like it was yesterday. He stared at her beautiful naked body as she got up to head to the bathroom to shower. He knew that she had to go to work, but he wanted to make love to her over and over. He stood up, walking up on her backside. He started rubbing her shoulders and then started kissing her neck passionately.

"Oh, baby, baby, don't do this to me. You know I have to go to work." Her body trembled as he worked his way between her thighs. "Cane, you're going to make me late for work," she whined as she felt the moistness seeping between her legs.

He ignored her pants as his tool was ready to go to work. He kissed on the back of her neck, softly sending chills down her spine. He ran his tongue down the middle of her back until he reached her backside. He planted kisses on her soft, luscious, round ass before sliding his tongue between her crack.

"Ssssss, baby, come on now," she pleaded as she tried to pull her body away. He latched on to her, and before she knew it, she found herself bracing herself against the dresser with her ass arched up. "Ssssss, Cane, I love you so much," she groaned, backing her ass up in rhythm.

He grabbed her by the waist to keep his balance. He loved to watch her ass jiggle. It turned him on just that much more. Sweat was coming down his face as he ground into her womanhood. His eyes rolled into the back of his head as he released himself inside her womb.

"See what you've started," she said, backing him up onto the bed. She straddled him and rode him reverse-cowboy style until she reached her climax. "Cane, you are my first and my last. I'll always love you."

"You're my first and my last also, and I'll always love you too." He kissed her passionately, letting her know that all of him loved all of her.

They both hopped into the shower together and took turns washing each other's backs. He didn't want her to leave his side. He wanted to make passionate love to her all day, but he knew she loved to do hair, and he didn't want to hold her any longer from making money.

Chapter 35

Calvin (2004)

He was meditating about him and Tonya living together for three years strong. It seemed like yesterday they were in high school, in the gym, kicking it with each other. *Time really has flown by*. The only problem was that he did not own his freedom to come and go as he pleased. He went regardless of what Tonya had to say about it, but an argument always followed.

"I'm going out tonight, Tonya," he said.

"You're always going out. I've been working late nights, and I'm off tonight, so I thought that we could spend some quality time together," she said as she started massaging his shoulders.

"I don't go out all the fucking time," he snapped. "I be handling my business. How do you think the bills get paid? I don't ask you to pay shit. All you do is work four hours a day and hang out, having lunch with your friends every day. It's not like you're pulling eight and ten hours a day."

She removed her fingers from his shoulders. "I don't know what has gotten into you lately, but you are not the man I fell in love with!" She was pointing her finger in his face. "And if you stayed your ass at home, I wouldn't have to spend so much time with my friends." She was getting agitated with the same old shit. "Matter of fact, I don't have time for this shit. I'm not going to strain my voice arguing with you. I'll be at my parents' if you need me!"

He stood up, realizing he spoiled her and made her the way she was. "I'm sorry, baby," he said in his baby voice. "I've been stressing about Cane and T-Lov. They're like my brothers, and when they're stressing, I'm stressing." He knew he could win her over with their names, it never failed.

"Why didn't you just say that in the first place, instead of going bananas on me? But you know I'm here for you, so don't ever hold anything back from me."

They started kissing as he palmed her ass like he was holding a basketball, trying to pull her pants down. Before she could wiggle out of her jeans, his pager started beeping.

"Hold on, babe, let me get that."

"Can you go one damn day without answering that damn thing?" She blew her breath out in frustration, wishing he would throw the damn thing away since pagers were nearly obsolete.

"Shit, this is what pays the bills." He checked his shit and saw that it was Meka's code, 18*6, in his pager. He knew that code meant she was located at the old Motel 6 off Frontage Road, and he knew she wanted a half brick. "Baby, that's my boy from Spartanburg. I've got to get this lick before somebody else beats me to it." There was no way he was going to tell her that he had been seeing Meka and doing business with her for the past month. She would act a fool if she knew, but Meka was making him mad money, and he was not about to let Tonya's insecurities mess up his cash flow.

His pager went off again: 18*6*112. He was glad that she put the room number in. He couldn't believe that he was dealing with her again himself after the way things had gone down before, but he'd rather deal with her than Trapp, who he didn't fuck with period.

Tonya laid her head under the pillow, frustrated with him always putting his business ahead of her. He grabbed his work and then hit the door without saying bye.

The streets were quiet, and traffic was light. He didn't see any cops, but he wasn't going to take any chances on the back roads. He jumped straight on Interstate 85, heading south. When he pulled into the motel, he circled the parking lot twice to make sure no fishy shit was popping off. He always followed Cane's number one rule: check the parking lot to make sure there are no undercover cops and no strange niggas loitering.

He parked next to Meka's car, tucking the half brick under his shirt, making sure it was secured. Before he could knock on the door, she opened it. "Okay, I see that you're on top of your game."

"I have to stay on top of it," she chuckled out, "so I can be driving the big-body 500 SL Benz."

"All I can say is put in that work. You'll be driving one." He poked his chest out, feeling himself as he stepped inside her room, looking around.

"Anyway," she said as she sucked her teeth, "where's the shit?"

He tried to pick up on her vibe because she seemed a bit antsy. "What, you're the police now?"

She snapped out, "Do I look like the fucking police?" She couldn't believe his ass. "You can't be serious. We've been handling business over a few weeks now, and you come with the bullshit." To show him she wasn't Five-O, she started taking off her clothes, piece by piece, until she was naked.

"Damn, Meka, your body didn't look like that back in the day," he said as he checked out how thick she'd gotten. "Let's make up for old times' sake. I just wanna hit that ass from the back."

"Naw, my nigga, it's not that type of party. Business only," she said as she flipped through a stack of hundreds.

"Don't act like that. You know you used to be in love with me!"

"Yeah, key words: used to. Let's get down to business!" She put her clothes back on while he pulled out the coke. She stared at it and then complained it wasn't the same blow as last time. He cut open the bag so she could sample it. She sniffed the shit like a vacuum. He was shocked.

After she realized the coke was the same, she sat back on the bed, trying to unfreeze her brain from the brain freeze the coke had given her. It was good stuff. She gave him the money and called herself checking him about the police shit before she said that she would call him later in the week.

He didn't count the money. He just tucked it into his waistline, trusting her because she always came straight, and then he walked to his car. He circled the parking lot twice to make sure no one was following him. He threw the money into the back seat. After seeing Meka's nude body, he decided to go to the strip club since he had just made a quick thirteen stacks. He unrolled his personal stash and took a sniff of the coke out of the dollar bill.

The manager smiled when he saw him. "Big timer, your VIP table is waiting on you, and we have some new dancers in town for the night, so enjoy yourself."

He gave the manager $500 and then walked into the club.

Chapter 36

Cane

Cane reached over without opening his eyes, trying to locate his ringing phone. "Hello!" he answered with his eyes still closed. He couldn't quite hear Tonya, so he adjusted the phone to his ear so he could make out what she was saying.

"I really need to come over and see you. It's very important, and before you say it, it can't wait until the morning."

"All right."

"Let me grab my house coat, and I'll be on the way."

He tried to wake up his tired body. He didn't want to move. He was still tired from his Florida trip. He met with Mr. Big in South Beach at his favorite hotel, The Beacon, which was three minutes from the Gold Rush strip club, a spot where all the famous people hung out.

He got up and deactivated his alarm since Tonya was on her way. After disarming his alarm, he sat in his living room, turning on the television, flipping the channel to the local news. He fought his sleep while pondering and waiting on Tonya to see what was so urgent that it couldn't wait until morning.

His mind wandered back to the last time she and Calvin got into a huge fight. She called the police but didn't press charges. She told the cops he didn't touch her, but they still tried to charge him with domestic violence. She begged them not to charge him with a bogus charge. All she wanted was for him to leave until things cooled down. He packed his clothes and stayed with him for a few days.

He prayed that wasn't the case this time because he hated to see Calvin moping around with his lips dragging on the floor and nearly starving himself.

"This is News Center 4 on your side, the most watched neighborhood news. I'm Kay Fields, along with John Roundtree. We just got a special on a home invasion that took place in the west side community, which left one dead and two in critical condition."

His eyes popped open wide as he turned up the volume. The home invasion had his full attention.

"I'm going to turn it over to reporter Scott Smith, who's live on the scene. Go ahead, Scott."

"Thanks, Kay. I'm here live at the horrific crime scene that took place on the west side of town. If you can see just past me," he said and pointed at the house, "a robbery here ended with one dead and two others in critical condition."

His heart nearly fell out of his chest when he saw Redd's house in the background. All he could think about was T-Lov bragging about how he had just purchased Redd a new Lexus 470 and put twenty-four-inch chrome rims on it and then added five TVs.

Kay broke in, asking him if any victims had been identified and what the motive was.

"Well, Kay, I'm here with Investigator Carson, and he can fill us in with all the details."

"Thanks, Scott. Yes, I'm investigating this horrible crime scene. We identified the victim as sixteen-year-old Danny Jones, aka Redd. He was shot to death with two bullets, one in the knee area and the other to the skull. The surviving victims are twenty-year-old Felicia Jones and forty-year-old Netta Jones. And so far, witnesses say that they saw six masked men running from the home and entering a dark-colored van. So far, it appears to be a drug deal gone badly."

Off the top, he knew the Jack Boys were on a mission. He was prepared for them if they ever came his way. He wasn't going out without a bloodbath, which was the only reason he had his perimeter alarmed, just for intruders.

He had just picked up the phone to call his boy, T-Lov. He knew that he must be distraught, when a knock at his door startled him. He hopped off the couch, paranoid as he looked through the peephole. With the news of Redd, he had forgotten about Tonya coming over just that quickly. "What took you so long?"

"I'm sorry. I couldn't find anything to wear," she said as he let her in. He could tell that she had been crying.

He noticed that she was wearing a long black trench coat with a black hat on her head and house slippers. He told her what he had just heard on the news. She looked at him like she could not believe the fact that people would stoop that low and kill over money. He explained to her that women and money made the world go around, and niggas who lived by the gun would die by it.

"Give me a second, and let me check on T-Lov real quick." Cane went back to the phone to call T-Lov. Trevia answered the phone and said that T-Lov was in bed.

"Has he heard from Redd or anyone?" Cane asked, trying to figure out how much Trevia knew.

"If he has, it hasn't been in the past five hours because this man has been in bed, out like a light. You want me to wake him for you?" she asked.

"Yeah, please."

He didn't know how he was going to tell him that Redd was dead. His heart was beating a mile a minute.

"Yo?" T-Lov said into the phone groggily.

“Have you heard anything about Redd?” Cane asked.

“Nah, what’s up?” T-Lov said, clearly wide awake now.

“Man, he was shot tonight and killed. They just reported it on the news,” Cane sadly reported.

“Noooo!” T-Lov cried out, dropping the phone. “This can’t be true.”

Trevia got on the phone to see what had made T-Lov upset. Cane told her what happened. When Cane told her the news, she screamed out as well. After she calmed down, she said that they were headed to the hospital.

He wanted to be there for them both, but he saw the tears in Tonya’s eyes, and he wanted to know what was going on with her as well to bring her out at this time of the night, looking distraught.

After telling Trevia to tell T-Lov that he would catch up with him in a few, he then turned his attention to Tonya. “What’s up with you?” he asked her.

“I’m tired of Calvin’s shit. Cane, I don’t even know where to start,” she said as she wiped away tears. “He used to be so sweet. He was a gentleman and treated me like a woman, but now, all we do is argue and fight whenever he is home. He is so disrespectful to me and acts like he doesn’t give two shits about me anymore. He even forgot my birthday!” she cried out in disbelief. “Ever since he started sniffing coke and drinking heavy, it seems like he doesn’t care about anything anymore but himself.”

She stared him in his eyes. “Why can’t he be more like you? You treat Tina like a queen, and she doesn’t have to want for nothing. All she talks about is how good of a man you are.”

He felt a little uncomfortable with her question of why Calvin couldn’t be like him. He put a sincere smile on and said, “I know things look bad right now, and Calvin is going through something. You have to be patient with him. I am talking to him, and he is going to get it together. If you really love him and want him, maybe you should talk him into going into rehab also."

"I have asked him to go into rehab, but he insists that he doesn't have a problem and that he can stop when he wanted to. He doesn't take me out anymore or anything, but I'm always finding small clues that he is fucking someone else."

"I don't know anything about that," Cane said, lying. "But if he was fucking someone else, you are his heart. You are the one that he's taking care of," Cane said, trying to make her feel better.

"But, Cane, I'm his woman and deserve to be treated like a queen. I'm getting tired of his bullshit," she cried.

Tears rolled from her eyes. He embraced her and told her everything would work out. He hated to see women cry, and he told her just that.

"See, Cane, you're a real man, and you know how to make a woman feel like a queen. Your character makes you even more attractive," she whispered into his ear. She knew he was a special man. She wanted to feel loved, emotionally and physically. She wiped away her tears and leaned on his shoulder for support. "I'm glad that I can talk to you about anything without you judging me."

"Anytime, sis. You're like family, and that's what family is all about."

She hugged him and then kissed him on the cheek. "Thanks for being such a good friend." She turned to leave and then stopped at the door, reaching into her coat pockets, as if she was searching for her keys. She looked around on the floor and the couch area. She noticed Cane's attention going to the floor as if he was trying to see what she was looking for.

He heard her keys hit the floor. He looked down, and by the time he looked up, she was standing in front of him in her bra and panties. "Cane, I told you the only reason I was late was because I didn't have anything to wear. Tina's always bragging about how good you are in bed, and that made me want you just that much more," she said, walking toward him seductively.

His eyes were glued to her body like a magnet. He was mesmerized by how soft looking and flawless her skin was, and she was standing like a stallion, as sexy as she could be. "I've always wanted you, Cane. I'm so in love with your personality and the way you carry yourself. I want to fuck the hell out of you!" she stated, rubbing on her body sexually. "No one has to know. It will be our secret to the grave."

He was at a loss for words as she played with his ears. Her breasts were in his face. He jumped back, slightly pushing her away. "We can't do this! What do I look like fucking my girl's best friend and my boy's lady? Fucking me will neither solve your problems nor take away your pains. It'll only cause a bigger-ass problem."

"You ain't shit, you black scared-ass, pussy motherfucker!" she snapped, picking up her coat, embarrassed and feeling hurt because he had turned her down, and she walked out the door. He locked the door and turned on his alarm, feeling weird about what had just happened. With all the craziness going on, all he wanted to do was get back in his bed and hope that tomorrow this would all have been just a dream. He could not believe that Tonya had been having these hidden feelings for him all of this time, and he really thought of her as a sister. Calvin was his boy, and Tina was her girl. Why did she think he would ever do something so grimy when she claimed to know his character?

Chapter 37

Calvin

The club was hyped as DJ Tay-Tay shouted, "Yo, yo, yo, give it up again for Sparkle! Wasn't she hot? Now, gentlemen, get them dollars ready! Coming straight from the Nestle Quick Factory, give it up for Chocolate!"

Calvin stood at the front of the stage, waving $100 bills. He was lost in her thick chocolate brown legs, flat stomach, round breasts, and jet-black silky hair. He knew that he had to have her, no matter what it took. She was shaking her ass like a salt shaker, popping her ass up and down in his face. He tore a $100 bill in half and then told her that if she wanted the other to meet him in the VIP area. She responded with a smile and then started dancing again.

As he was walking off, the crowd was shouting for her to take it all off. She took off her top and then threw her top at him, causing it to land on his head. He smiled with a nod and then sat down, watching her juicy watermelons bounce and ass jiggle like a tidal wave.

"Hello, gorgeous." He felt some soft fingers rubbing across his neck. "My name is Honey, and I'm all about that money. What's your name, sweetie?"

"Calvin!" he replied, not paying her much attention as she sat next to him. His mind was on Chocolate. He wanted to see if she tasted like her name.

"That's a cute name. How about letting me give you a little table dance for twenty dollars a song?"

He pulled out $50. "What about this?" He smiled flirtatiously.

"A very good lap dance." She took his money and then started grinding her ass on him. He was comparing her to Chocolate. Her frame was more petite, her tits were small but perky, and she had more tattoos.

While she was dancing on him, she rubbed his waves and ran her fingers across his chest. She started whispering freaky shit into his ears. He was enjoying that shit as he choked down his beer. She continued grinding hard on him. "How much money do you have?" she whispered into his ear while kissing on his earlobe. "Do you want to go into the back room?"

He looked over her shoulders and caught a glimpse of Chocolate looking at him, sucking on her fingers. "Naw, baby, I've already made a promise to Chocolate that I'll take her to the back, but maybe next time, sugar." She stopped rolling on him instantly and looked at him as if he were crazy. She got up from him and rolled her eyes at Chocolate and then walked off with an attitude.

The beer had his kidneys about to explode as he rushed to the bathroom to relieve himself. As he was locked behind the stall, he pulled out his personal stash and sniffed the entire line. His eyes rolled into the back of his head. His brain felt like it was frozen as he received a huge rush. He licked the residue off the dollar and then flushed it down the toilet.

As he was walking back to his table, he noticed someone sitting at the table, wearing a long coat and cowboy hat. "Excuse me!" he said, walking up on them from the back side. "This table is already paid for."

"Okay, say no more. I guess I'll leave then."

"No! No! No, please don't do that. I didn't know it was you hiding behind that big hat," he said after he noticed it was Chocolate in disguise. She let him know that she wanted her other half of the $100 bill. She stood up, opening up her coat, letting him see her goodies. She closed his face inside her coat, letting him get a mouthful of her Milk Duds. She pushed his head off her chest and then turned around, lifting up her coat, revealing her thickness. She made each cheek clap so that his eyes were glued to her midgets dancing to the Ying Yang Twins' "Shake It Like a Salt Shaker" that was pounding out the speakers. He pulled out his money and started tipping her.

She peeped his stash and knew she had hit the jackpot. Her appetite was hungry for money, and she was striving to get into his pockets. "Do you want to know why they call me Chocolate?" She licked her lips seductively. He nodded as she led him into the private area.

He tipped the bouncer an extra $100. He didn't care how much money it cost him. He had to have her. He sat down in a recliner chair while she took off her coat. She walked back up on him and started rubbing and kissing his neck aggressively. She was so aggressive that she popped three buttons off of his shirt. "Hey, baby, this is Sean John. Be easy," he cooed. Although it didn't really matter to him as long as he got satisfied. She ignored him and ripped open his shirt, causing two more buttons to pop off, and started kissing down his stomach. She felt a bulge growing from his pants. She stood up with a naughty little girl look plastered on her face.

"Are you ready to see why they call me Chocolate?"

"Hell yeah," he replied, adjusting himself in the recliner.

She picked up her coat and reached into her pockets, pulling out a bottle of chocolate syrup. She pulled down his pants enough to pull out his man tool. She squeezed chocolate on the tip of his head and then licked it off slowly. His eyes rolled into the back of his head as her wet, warm mouth worked on his head.

"Ah, shit, baby," he moaned. With every pull, he felt like he was losing his breath. She didn't give up. She pulled and sucked harder until his milk exploded into her mouth. His high came down when his pager went off, and he noticed that it was Tonya. He looked down at his watch that read 2:33 a.m. He knew Tonya was probably worried about him. He gave her $500. He told her now he knew why they called her Chocolate and that they had to finish their business another time because he just got a page and had some business to take care of.

"When can I see you again? I only gave you a sample of this Chocolate. There's plenty more sweetness where that came from." She gave him her number and licked him on the inside of his ear.

He placed her number in his pocket and told her that he would call her real soon. He walked straight to his car, ignoring all of the advances from the other dancers as he left the club and peeled out. He knew Tonya was going to be tripping, and he didn't want to hear her bullshit. Instead of taking I-85, he hopped on the back road, hoping it would get him home faster. He was ten minutes from Cane's house. If push came to shove, he would stop by and tell him to call her and claim that he was at his house, crashed on the couch, drunk, just in case she was tripping. He was willing to do anything just not to hear her bickering.

His mind instantly went back to Chocolate. he wanted to fuck the shit out of her ass. His plans were to call her tomorrow so they could get up. He would get rid of Tonya for a few hours by giving her some money so she could hang out with Tina and Shelia.

As he was approaching Cane's house, he saw that Tonya's C230 Benz was parked in Cane's driveway. He could hear her now, complaining to Tina about not spending quality time together. He pushed the accelerator to the floor, trying to get home, so he could clean himself up before she got home.

"Home sweet home," he said as he hopped out of the car, jogging into the house. In his haste of getting undressed to hop into bed, so that he could pretend to have been home asleep all night, he left his clothes scattered everywhere and had to run back to pick them up and throw them into the hamper.

The water was steaming hot. He looked at his frame in the mirror, shaking his head at his flabby-looking arms and the six pack that he could no longer see. "Shit, fuck some abs. I'll buy me a fucking six pack." He laughed to himself, seeing that his man tool was big and fat. He stepped into the shower, quickly washing the rest of the chocolate residue from his body.

He got out of the shower and dried off, put on some cologne, trying to smell good just in case Chocolate's scent was still on him. He put on his silk boxers that Tonya bought him for Valentine's Day. He hopped into bed, ready to play sleep and give Tonya hell for being out so late, but he dozed off. When he woke up, Tonya's side of the bed was still empty, and the clock read 4:21 a.m. He was pacing back and forth as his pressure was building up. "Fuck this!" he muttered, picking up the phone to call Tina.

"Hey, sis, sorry to be calling you so late, but let Tonya know that she can come home now."

"I'm sorry, but I haven't seen her all day."

"Stop playing games. I know she's with you! Her car was there when I was headed home."

"No, really, she is not here. I don't know whose car you saw because I haven't been home all day. I have been in Atlanta with my sister and just got in around three a.m."

He hung up the phone, frustrated, because he could have sworn that he had seen her car at Cane's. Yes, Cane had lots of people at his house these days, so it could have easily been someone else's car. He hopped into the bed and replayed the scenery from Cane's house. He couldn't remember if he saw Tina's car in the yard. He heard a car door slam and then heard the front door open up. He closed his eyes, playing asleep when she entered the room. She tiptoed into the bedroom as he lay playing possum. He peeped and noticed that she was wearing a hot-ass leather trench coat. He saw as she peeped over at him to make sure that he was asleep and then grabbed her nightgown and headed for the bathroom. His eyes opened wide when she took off her coat as she was entering the bathroom. To make sure that there was no mistaking what he was seeing, he halfway sat up to get a better view. He was ready to explode because she was half naked!

Chapter 38

Tonya

It was eating her up on the inside how she humiliated herself last night. She tossed and turned all night long, not getting any sleep. Her mind was telling her to talk to Calvin and come clean as to what she had done because she wasn't sure if Cane would tell him, but she didn't know how to. A part of her told her that Cane most likely wouldn't mention it, so let it go and apologize to Cane later and blame it on the emotional roller coaster and alcohol that she had been on last night. She got out of the bed and started cleaning up to help ease her mind. She washed all the windows and scrubbed the stains out of the carpet. She gave her energy into trying to figure out how she could get his full attention because their relationship was going down the drain as fast as Drano, and she really loved him.

The phone was ringing as she walked out of the bathroom with the hamper in her hands. "Hello?" She nearly froze up when she heard Tina's voice.

"Girl, you and Calvin need to get y'all act together. That fool called me last night looking for you. He swears that your car was at Cane's place."

She took a deep breath, thinking she was about to be exposed for trying to fuck her man. "I thought you were at your man's house last night, so I stopped by, hoping to see you, but I ended up talking to Cane. Calvin had my head in a bad place last night, and I just needed to vent."

"Oh, I see. So Calvin did see your car. I thought he was tripping. I hope you guys worked everything out. Sorry I wasn't there for you. What are you doing now? Are you all right?"

"I'm doing Calvin's laundry right now, but yes, I'm all right." Her eyes became watery, and her nose started to run. She felt bad for coming on to Cane. Tina was her best friend and was loyal to her.

"Are you crying?" Tina asked, alarmed.

"I'm just fed up with his ass," she said as she separated his clothes. She shook her head after seeing the shit stains in his boxers. She looked harder at what looked like lipstick. She got curious and then smelled his boxers. "Oh, my God, Tina, this nigga has some chocolate and lipstick inside his boxers." She balled up her fist. "I know he's cheating on me. I'm going to kill that motherfucker."

"Girl, calm down and please don't do anything stupid! Maybe he didn't cheat on you, and that's shit in his boxers," she said, trying to turn the matter into a joking matter. "Just don't say anything to him about it. I'll get Cane to talk to him."

"No, Tina, I'm tired of you and Cane fighting my battles. It's time for me to handle my own shit. And this nigga is on some foul shit."

She didn't know what to say, but at the same time, she didn't want her to get into any trouble. "Tonya, don't do anything stupid. I'm pregnant, and my baby will need a godmother. We need you," she pleaded.

She thought that her ears were hearing things. "Did you just say that you were pregnant?"

"Yeah, that's what I said."

"Wowwww!" she cheered out. "Congratulations. We have to get with the girls and celebrate. I can't believe you're pregnant, girl."

"That's cool, but I'm scared."

"What in the hell are you scared for? You have a good man with a good heart and plenty of money to support you."

"I haven't told Cane yet. We had agreed no kids just yet since we're both in school and trying to achieve our goals." She started biting her nails.

"Well, shit happens. You just need to talk to him. And I know Cane loves you, so nothing will come between y'all. This child is going to be the joy of y'all's hearts. I know it. Trust me, he'll understand. That's the only person I can go to with my problems, and he always gives me good, logical advice, so I know he'll be excited."

"All right, I'll let him know before the week is out."

Tonya was proud of Tina. It seemed like she had everything positive going on in her life. Her own beauty salon, a real, genuine man, and a child on the way. What else could a woman ask for?

Tina told her that all she wanted was for Cane to come out of the streets. He had accomplished so much, and she didn't see anything else coming from his lifestyle but prison or death. If any of those things happened to him, she would be stuck raising their child all alone. She said all of this material stuff meant nothing to her. She'd rather have all of him, and she didn't want her child growing up in a drug-infested environment.

Tonya was caught up into the glamorous lifestyle, but Tina had her thinking that maybe she should get out and do something with her own life so she could make her own way. After seeing what happened to Redd and his family, it put everything else into perspective with her own life. She was really fed up with Calvin and his drug usage, partying, and running around in the streets with Lord knows who. And there was no way she was going to sleep with him until he showed his loyalty.

"Yeah, I feel you on that street life shit. All I want is a good man who loves me for me." She wanted to live Tina's fairytale lifestyle, but she knew God had a plan for her, and she was destined to find out what He had in store for her.

"Girl, you know you're that diva who everybody wants to be with. You remember the time we went shopping in New York, and all those people surrounded us, thinking you were Monica? You were giving those fools an autograph."

All she could do was laugh because that was one moment she'd love to recapture. "Hell yeah, child, I remember that shit like yesterday. That's why I admire you so much. You are the best, and I thank God for blessing me with a friend like you."

"Well, let's go out and do something fun because I need to get my mind right before I make this announcement to Cane about me being pregnant."

"Well, I do need to get some new lingerie. I'll come pick you up," Tonya said.

Chapter 39

Calvin

Calvin woke up with a slight headache from a hangover. His head was spinning like a set of twenty-four-inch Sprees that were on a car that suddenly stopped rolling at a hundred miles per hour. He rolled out of the bed and went to the bathroom to shower and clean his blinged-out grill.

He walked down the stairs, looking for Tonya, but she wasn't anywhere in sight. He checked outside and noticed that her car was gone. His stomach was growling. *What kind of woman is Tonya to leave and not fix me anything to eat first?* He entered the kitchen and grabbed the note off of the refrigerator.

Gone to the mall with Tina. I'll be right back.

His eye strolled toward the clock on the microwave. He didn't realize how long he had been asleep. He grabbed the largest bowl in sight and filled it to the rim with Cap'n Crunch, his favorite cereal. He flopped on the couch and flipped through some channels on the TV, landing on the Spanish channel. Understanding nothing of what the women were saying was a small price to pay in order to look at those fly amigas. He laughed to himself. The way they shook their asses made him want to learn the salsa dance.

Watching them Spanish hoes made him think about Chocolate. He jumped up, nearly breaking his neck trying to get upstairs to the bathroom. His heart dropped to his stomach after he didn't see his clothes in the hamper. He rushed downstairs to the laundry room. His jeans were on the floor. He was hoping that Tonya hadn't found Chocolate's number. He breathed a sigh of relief as he pulled out his money and Chocolate's phone number. He felt today had to be a lucky day because, normally, Tonya checked all of his clothes.

He paged Chocolate. There was no way he was about to call her from his house number. Tonya would act a fool if another bitch called his house besides his mother. While he was waiting on his cell phone to ring, he sniffed a line of coke. He sniffed so much coke at one time that he nearly clogged up the straw.

The blood went straight to his brain, which caused blood to rush out of his nose. He didn't give a fuck about his blood dripping on the couch. The coke had him feeling cocky as hell. He wished that Tonya was next to him so he could give her a piece of his mind.

He thought that his mind was playing tricks on him when he heard his cell phone ringing. After the fifth time the phone rang, he answered it.

"You paged me?"

"It depends on who me is!" he replied, being smart.

"Oh, what's up, Big Calvin? I didn't think that you were going to call so soon," she said, sounding excited.

"I would have called earlier, but eating chocolate can be sweet on the tooth early in the morning," he said, flirting.

"I see that besides your cute name, you have a cute sense of humor also," she chuckled.

"Well, you know a little chocolate will make any man hyper and excited."

"You're so silly, Calvin, but in a sexy way," she said.

He was tired of all the small talk. He wanted to know what was on her agenda for the day. She told him that she was going to Hot-lanta in a few hours. "A girl has to do what a girl has to do to keep the Chocolate Factory running," she laughed. He explained to her that was the reason that he was calling to see if he could get a sample of the chocolate. She asked him a few questions, just to see where his pockets really were because she didn't want any chump change. She wanted some real money, and so as not to make him think that she was just a gold digger, she asked him questions about his job. His answer that he worked in pharmaceuticals was music to her ears. But because a lot of knuckleheads she had met in the past had worked in pharmaceuticals as well, but were only cigarette rich, she asked him what kind of car he would be driving. When he said a 1986 Benz, she knew she had struck gold. "Oh, if you're pushing a whip like that, then I know you are going to set a sister up nicely for her birthday weekend in the A for allowing you to sample the chocolate," she said.

He convinced her that he'd pay like he weighed, told her to get a room, and to call when she got there. *Today is my lucky day,* she thought, because she was already at a room that was fifteen minutes away from his house, and he was going to reimburse her for it.

He threw on his Versace suit and gator boots. He was dressed to kill as he looked for his car keys. He was so wasted last night that he didn't know where he placed his keys. His pager started beeping. He answered the phone. It was Cane.

"Calvin, what's up, bro'man? I'm tired and had a hell of a trip. Tina called me, telling me that I need to have a talk with you. What's up?"

He had forgotten all about Cane's trip to Miami. "Yeah, nigga, it's about time you got back in town. But check this out, I'm kind of in a rush. We have to talk later on!" he said as he was still trying to find his keys.

"Well, I'm not going to hold you up from your business. Go get that cheddar before the rats get it!" Cane said, hanging up.

He looked down at his pager. It read: 72*6*112. His eyes lit up when he saw the numbers. Straight off the rip, he knew it was Meka and that she wanted two keys of cocaine and some sex. His thoughts went to making fifty grand or tapping Chocolate's fine ass.

Ten minutes passed, and he still hadn't found his keys. There was no way he was going to call Tonya for his extra set of keys and have her coming home, tripping. And he wasn't about to drive his 1972 piece of shit pickup truck either, especially not with his Versace suit on. He decided to kill two birds with one stone.

When he pulled the cover off of Cane's red Range Rover, a smile came across his face. It seemed cleaner today than ever. He made sure the dope was hidden well in the secret compartment. He thought that if Cane knew he had dope in his ride, he would be shitting all on himself. Cane didn't play anybody riding with drugs in his whips.

He loved the Rover. It seemed to him as if Cane didn't drive it much anymore since he had gotten the 2004 Rolls-Royce Corniche. Calvin was waiting on him to pass it down to him like he did everything else. Calvin was the one who drove it all the time anyway, so he felt like it was his.

His foot pressed harder on the pedal, speeding up just enough not to get pulled over. His pager was going off again. It read: 72*6*110*911. It was Meka. He called the hotel to let Chocolate know he was going to be late. She told him that she was leaving in a few hours for her trip, so he had better hurry. He wasn't about to miss out on Chocolate since she was about to leave town, so he told Meka that he was coming from out of town and he'd be back in town in an hour or two.

He parked the truck slanted in a corner space, so no one could see it from the highway. The room was at the right spot. He had a clear view of the truck. The door was cracked open as he knocked.

"Come on in," Chocolate said softly. He walked in and saw her bending over, wearing a housekeeper uniform. Her ass was looking soft like cotton as she made it gyrate. He wanted to fuck her in that position, right then and there.

"Damn, nigga, you must be a baller for real. You're rocking the hell out of that Versace suit," she said, seeing dollar signs.

"Yeah, baby, I told you I'm going to pay like I weigh, and that's phat, baby, not f-a-t but p-h-a-t. That's how I do it," he bragged, pulling out two large stacks of money.

The money made her hot as hell. She started fingering herself as she rolled on her fingers, fucking herself. She had his manhood at full attention.

"Damn, shawty, I like that," Calvin said, massaging his manhood, getting ready to pounce on her.

"Come and taste the chocolate, daddy," she cooed.

He started walking to her, moistening his lips, getting ready to take a lick of chocolate when he heard footsteps coming from behind him. Before he could turn around, he felt a pistol on the back of his head.

"Freeze. Put your hands in the air. You're under arrest!" a female voice hissed out.

"Bitch, what the fuck is this? You setting me up?" he said in a weak tone.

"Yeah, nigga, you got caught slipping. Now take off your clothes," Chocolate demanded.

"What the hell?" Calvin asked, wondering what in the hell was going on.

The nose of the gun was pressed hard on his head.

"You're a bad boy, Calvin, so me and my freaky police friend are going to have to frisk you and punish you," Chocolate said in a sluttish tone as she reached down his unzipped pants and started massaging his manhood.

Still shocked, but a little relieved, he turned around and noticed the woman with the police hat on wearing a star-shaped bra, a belt made out of stars, a thong, and a toy gun. "Damn, Chocolate, y'all had me fucked up for a second." He laughed out, still unnerved.

"Just a little extra surprise. This is my girl Starr," Chocolate proclaimed.

Once he got a good look at her, he knew exactly who she was. "You don't remember me, Starr?" he asked as she looked confused. "Calvin from back in the day with your brother, Slim. RIP, my nigga," he said.

"Oh, my gosh! Yeah, I remember you! Dang, you've grown up a lot and put on a few pounds," she replied. "The weight looks great on you."

"Yup, I've put on a few pounds since the last time we saw each other. I should say you look good as hell." He reminisced about the first time he saw her. He wanted to fuck her so bad. She reminded him of Tonya but much thicker. "Damn, I used to want you so bad, Starr," he admitted. "So, I'm really about to get this?" he asked with a crooked smile.

"You're not ready for what you are about to get yourself into!" she stated.

His eyes lit up with excitement as he shouted out, "Oh, I'm ready. I've been waiting on this moment for a long time! Fucking two dime pieces. You can't beat that."

"Calvin, this is your last chance to back out of this and go home to your girl because what we are about to lay on you will have her unable to do much more for you," Starr warned, but he wasn't trying to hear that shit.

He counted out two grand, sniffed a line of coke, and shouted out, "I'm ready for whatever."

He moaned when Chocolate started sucking his dick. "That's what I'm talking about!" He was trying to convince them to hit some powder. "Come on, Starr. Take off them panties because I'm about to bust a nut, and I've got to tap that ass. Matter of fact, I'm a bad boy. I've got two kilos of cocaine in my truck, so come on and arrest me."

"Be careful what you ask for, Calvin, because you might get something you don't want."

"I know what I want." He nodded his head. "I want some of that pussy, so quit tripping." He pulled out another grand. "Come on, Starr, arrest me! Look, I've got drug money. I'm being bad. Spank me, Ms. Freaky Policewoman! Take that big-ass belt off and whip my ass," he demanded.

"Nah, I can't spank you with this belt. It's one of a kind," she replied, pulling off her thong.

He busted all in Chocolate's mouth, making her suck him dry. "Oh, Calvin, I need to call you Mr. Chocolate as good as you taste. Come on, girl, and get this money. Let that nigga get some of that fire pecan pussy!" Chocolate said to Starr.

Starr was lying on her back with her legs open. He went over and penetrated her nectar. Chocolate was playing in his butthole, which to his amazement really turned him on and made him cum faster.

"That's all you got?" Starr laughed.

"Hell naw, Starr. I'm not finished yet!" he yelled out, trying to get his manhood back.

Starr reached for Chocolate, laid her down, and started eating her pussy. That shit turned Calvin on. He got his dick up and started pounding Starr from the back while she continued eating Chocolate's pussy. His second wind made his dick Ford tough. The cocaine and what was going on under him had him banging Starr from the back like it was going to be the last piece of pussy he would ever get. He fucked her for an hour straight, nonstop. After he finished, he smoked a blunt, asking Starr if they could hook up again. She told him her job was done. He didn't have a clue as to what she was talking about.

They were all knocked out in the bed until Calvin's pager woke them up. He looked at the pager and it read: 72*6*112*911111. He had totally forgotten all about Meka wanting two bricks. He hopped up, putting on his clothes. "Hey, ladies, thanks for a good time! I really enjoyed the costumes, especially yours, Starr! The whole police thing was sexy. That really turned me on. I want to go and fuck a real police officer now."

"Maybe you fucked a real police officer, but that's something you will never know until you get arrested for being a bad boy!" Starr said, being sassy.

"Well, I'm going to continue being bad as long as I can get arrested by you," Calvin said, grabbing his tool. "Well, ladies, I've got to go and handle some business for Cane. I need to set him up to spank you two dimes as a birthday gift from me."

"Don't have us hooking up with no scrub," Chocolate said. "We don't do broke niggas."

"Y'all see that red Range Rover out there that's sitting on them twenty-four-inch rims, right?" he said, pointing to the truck. "That's his. And that nigga has also got a Rolls-Royce sitting on chrome twenty-three-inch rims. That nigga has way more bread than me," he said, bragging on Cane.

"Well, we are about to head to Atlanta. I'll holla at you when we get back," Starr said.

"I'm jealous that you didn't give me some of that good dick. I wanted you to feel the inside of this Chocolate Factory," Chocolate said.

"I wish I could give you some of this dick now, but I've got shit to handle. I'll give you a call next week so that we can hook up and do the damn thing."

Meka was paging him so much his screen read page full. He didn't realize that he stayed at Chocolate's room for five hours. Her room was only five minutes away.

She came to the door naked and shouted, "It's about time your ass got here! Do you have the shit?" She looked him up and down. "How do I know that you're not wired?"

"Miss me with the bullshit. Don't even play me like that. Let me get my money."

"I'm not giving you shit unless you prove to me that you're not wired," she said with an attitude.

Calvin went ahead and unbuttoned his shirt and pulled down his pants to give Meka what she wanted. After all, he had done her the same way. The two bricks fell from his waistline as he took off his clothes.

"Is this the same shit as last time? You know that I want that fish scale."

"Damn, Meka, do we have to go through this today?"

"Yes, we do!" she replied, sucking her teeth.

He pulled out his personal sniff bag. He laced two lines on the table. He sniffed the first line. Meka snatched the bag from his hands and then sprinkled powder over his limped worm. She licked off the residue. He was tired, but he loved the way her moist tongue felt as it glided around his tool.

Everybody wants to suck on the jimmy today. His tool felt numb as Meka continued to shake residue on his tool. He was ready for action.

"Come on, nigga. You know that you want some of this pussy!"

"Shit, say no more." He jacked his tool, ready to fuck the shit out of her. "You got some condoms?" He had a flashback from back in the day when she let them clowns run a train on her.

"Nah, nigga. Besides, I'm clean anyway. I don't fuck around like that." She rolled her eyes.

"Girl, don't fuck me up," he warned.

"Come on with your scary ass and fuck this pussy!" she moaned. She was riding him reverse-cowboy style. She didn't feel anything, and she was getting tired of him ranting about her not having any walls. "Shit, nigga, it's not my fault that your shit is little. Just stick it in my ass and get the shit over with."

"Sounds like a plan to me." He primed himself up and then tried to ram it into her backside.

"Hold up, nigga, let me go and get some ice so I can numb my ass up."

He lay back on the bed, waiting for her to get back. Minutes passed as his shit went limp. "Damn, what's taking her ass so long?" he said to himself. He closed his eyes, thinking what he was going to tell Tonya once he got home. He pictured her bitching about him hanging out all day. He prayed that she didn't want to be made love to tonight.

He heard the door open up, so he closed his eyes tighter. "It's about time you made it back! Now, come over here and give me some head so I can get back right. I'm ready to fuck that phat ass." He stayed calm when he felt the hard steel on his face. "So, you want to play, Ms. Naughty?"

"I finally caught up with your pussy ass. CMB, we all we got." He opened up his eyes. His heartbeat sped up as Trapp, Ray-Ray, and Timbo stood over him with their pistols pointing at him.

All he could do was lay there defenseless while they took the dope, his money, jewelry, and clothes. Trapp let him know that if he moved, they would make him famous like Biggie and Pac.

He couldn't believe Meka set him up for the kill. As soon as they left, he eased off the bed and took off running to the Range Rover, butt-naked. He saw the truck leaning on its side due to two cut tires. He couldn't get into the truck because the keys were in his pants pockets. He ran back up into the room, and luckily, in his haste of fleeing, he had not closed the door, but they had taken all of his belongings. He hated to call Cane, but that was his only chance of getting a spare key and some clothes.

He was pissed the fuck off. What he had carefully tried to avoid happening to him had happened. He had gotten caught slipping. He hadn't bothered looking around for the Jack Boys nor had he scanned the parking lot because he had trusted Meka. He slipped on the first rule of making fast money: trust no one! He hated that he was going to have to explain this bullshit to Cane. As soon as Cane entered the room with clothes for him, he started telling him how Meka had set him up for the Jack Boys to rob him of two bricks and his jewelry. He didn't hold anything back from him. They were boys.

He could see the fire in Cane's eyes. He had to take the verbal abuse as Cane lit in on him for fucking with Meka from the start and for riding around in his truck with that much work on him. "You better be glad that it was the Jack Boys that robbed you and not the police that arrested you!" Cane said.

"My bad, Cane. I'm sorry."

"Your 'bads' and 'sorrys' always get you fucked up," Cane spewed. "Running around this hotel butt-ass naked because your ass was only thinking about some ass. You could have been killed all for a piece of ass. Now, I see what Tonya was talking about last night when she came crying to me. You running around here fucking everything that moves," he said, shaking his head in disbelief.

He didn't respond to Cane. He was thinking about Tonya coming home wearing only thongs under her coat. He had seen her car at Cane's house at two a.m. He had let it go because he knew her and Tina were really cool and maybe Tina was there also. But knowing now that Tina wasn't even home, his mind started piecing shit together.

"Cane, nigga, you ain't shit! You think that I'm stupid. You are fucking Tonya!" Calvin shouted as he flipped the fuck out.

"Man, what the fuck are you talking about? How do I look fooling around with your girl?" Cane said calmly, keeping his cool.

"Nigga, you fucked her! Stop this motherfucking truck!" he shouted as he punched the dashboard.

"Smoking all that weed and sniffing that cocaine got your head fucked up. You need to take a chill! You know me better than that."

"If she was with you last night, why did she come home only wearing a damn coat over her thong? I knew your ass was too good to be true. You want to play Mr. Perfect, but you ain't shit! I'm not playing with you, Cane. Stop this motherfucking truck!" he demanded.

"Nigga, you done lost your damn mind. Tonya is like a sister to me. I love Tina, and I would never do no shit like that. If she came home in only a thong, it's because she stopped and let another nigga do what you apparently have lost interest in doing with her!" Cane shouted.

"Stop the damn truck!" Calvin said again.

The truck stopped. Calvin hopped out and slammed the door so hard it nearly shattered the glass. He was pissed off as he started walking home. Just when he thought it was a lucky day, everything went to hell. He couldn't wait to get home and pack all of Tonya's shit to kick her ass out.

Chapter 40

Cane

Cane was worried since he had not heard from Calvin in three weeks. Every time he sent Shi and T-Lov to his house, he never answered his door. Every call and page he placed to him went unanswered or unreturned. He couldn't believe Calvin was really tripping. He knew for a fact that he didn't have sex with Tonya. At least Shi and T-Lov had his back because, after Trapp, they never condoned backstabbing or hating on anyone from their clique.

The whole clique was having issues. Shit most definitely had hit the fan from Redd's death, Calvin getting robbed, and this petty shit with Tonya. He felt the tension in the air. "I'm tired of this shit. Those motherfuckers killed my uncle and Redd. I am tired of waiting on the fucking police to catch up with them clowns. I'm going to be the judge, juror, and fucking executioner! I'm going to kill every one of them bastards, and when I get my hands on Trapp, he's going to wish he was never born," he spat out, mad as hell. "Come on, Shi. Let's roll the fuck out."

T-Lov saw the fire in his eyes, and he grabbed Cane by the shoulders, looking him in the eyes, letting him know that they were all still in mourning from both Redd's and Jack's deaths, but he had too much to lose. And although Jack and Redd were worth it, the Poison Clan wasn't worth them losing everything that they had worked so hard for and their own freedom. They were going to get theirs, but they had to do just as they planned: wait. Even though Redd was like a son to him, he didn't want to lose Cane over the same bullshit.

He was still fired up. He wasn't trying to sit around and let the Jack Boys kill off his entire crew, one by one. T-Lov agreed with him 100 percent, but he also let him know that he had a family who needed him. He told Cane that Terry Jr. would now be staying with him and that Trevia was six months pregnant. God had blessed him with a loving family and a loyal clique. He didn't want to lose any of them to those lowlifes.

Shi also told Cane that he had every right to be upset, but he was cut from a different cloth and was better than other motherfuckers. He let Cane know how much love he had for him for blessing him with his own detail shop. He expressed to him that he would take off his coat and let him walk on it before he got his shoes muddy.

He cheered up a little but was still weary with Calvin, hoping he hadn't done anything stupid.

"He's a grown-ass man, and he needs to stop being a fucking crybaby. He knows that you're a real-ass dude," Shi said.

"I hope so," he agreed with Shi.

"Shi, turn around and stop by the fruit stand so I can get my grandma some fruit. I most definitely have to get some green apples so she can make a nigga an apple pie." He rubbed his stomach as if he could taste it already.

"I wonder if I get some bananas, will she make me a pudding?" T-Lov asked.

Cane ignored him, knowing that was a stupid question because she would be glad to. They all bought baskets of fruits. Shi teased him about riding around in a Rolls-Royce with a truck full of fruit. He let Shi know that it didn't matter what kind of car he had, he was still the same nigga, with or without money.

They were heading to his grandmother's house to drop off the fruit. He had a new house built for her from the ground up three years ago. He never thought she would accept it, but to his surprise, she did and loved all 3,000 square feet of it.

"After the baby, I plan to build a house," T-Lov said, still mesmerized at the size of the house.

"Yeah, I'm thinking about selling my shit since Shelia wants to have another child. Bro, you don't want to have any kids?"

"Until recently, I never thought about it, but being around y'all and the way y'all talk about it makes me want to have some."

"I don't know what's taking you so long. You've got the best girl in the world, and y'all were made for each other."

"Yeah, I feel you, Shi, but we've talked about it. She knows it's something that is going to have to wait a few more years because when she gets pregnant, I'm out of the drug game."

T-Lov glanced at him like he was crazy. "Man, I admire you. You really have a good head on your shoulders. I love my child, but if I had it to do all over again, I would have waited until I had my shit one hundred. Knowing what I know now, I would have gone off to college. As good as I was, who knows, I might have been in the pros somewhere."

"May be too late to be in the pros, but it's never too late to go back to school. You've got your mini-me that will always be watching you, so set a good example for him. And make sure that Terry Jr. gets to live the life you always wanted," Cane said.

"Yeah, I know. That's why I'm stacking this paper, so he doesn't have to be in these streets like me."

Cane looked at them both, knowing that they should be millionaires by now, as long as they'd been in these streets, hustling crack cocaine, but they blew most of their money on jewelry, women, and material shit.

Gina ran outside with her cell phone glued to her ear. "There goes my favorite cousin in the whole wide world." She ended her call and then put her phone into her pocket. "Damn, that Rolls-Royce is nasty as hell. I want one!"

"You better be satisfied with the BMW I spent my hard-earned money on. Just like black folks, never satisfied."

"I love my car and my favorite big cousin." She smiled, giving him a hug.

He could tell that she wanted something. "What in the hell do you want?"

"Why did you say it like that?" She looked him in his eyes, giving him her puppy face expression. "I don't want anything from you except a little loan so I can open up a day care." She embraced him so he could loosen up.

He pulled himself away and then shook his head. "I'll think about it. Where's Grandma at?"

"In the house," she replied. "How long is it going to take you to think about it? Because the building may be gone soon."

He looked at her sideways and walked into the house. He gave his grandma a kiss on the cheek and said, "Now I know I can get an apple pie and banana pudding?"

"You sure can, baby." She smiled and then hugged him. She looked at the variety of fruits and said, "I take it that T-Lov wants the banana pudding and Shi the apple pie." All he could do was smile at her because she hit it on the nose.

"I'm your grandma, boy." She looked at him, smiling. "You can't pull anything over on me. Just like that so-called two-million-dollar lottery you claim to have won. I just don't argue what I can't prove," she said, raising her eyebrows.

"I told you, Grandma, beginner's luck."

"Boy, sometimes I wonder about you. But anyway, how's my baby doing? Let her know that Granny needs her wig done." She started patting her hair.

"All right, I'll let her know." He sat around and shot the breeze with her for about fifteen minutes and then hugged her goodbye.

"What's your rush? It ain't like you've got a job to go to," she kidded.

"I'm going over to Greenville Tech to enroll in school. I have been thinking I need to do something constructive with my life these days. I plan on starting a family eventually and want to give my children someone to look up to."

"Look at my baby, all grown up now," she said proudly. "If only your daddy and uncle could see how much of a man you've become."

He told her he had to go because he was going to the shop to surprise Tina. He didn't want to tell her that Shi and T-Lov were in the car waiting for him because she would have made them get out and had all of them in the house, reading scriptures, something she always felt the need to do when they were all together.

"Okay. Tell her what I said about my hair."

"I've got you," he said, planting a big kiss on her cheeks. She grabbed him back to her and kissed him again before throwing in a quick prayer for him before he walked out the door.

"Uhm, what about my loan?" Gina asked.

"How much do you need, girl?"

"I don't know. The building is going to cost me eight hundred dollars a month, and then I have to get the equipment—"

He cut her off. "Get together a proposal before you start asking for business loans, nigga, and then get with me," he said, nudging her with his arm.

"Ugh! Okay, I'll call you in about thirty minutes," she said.

He just looked at her and went to the car.

"Take me to the barbershop so I can check up on Reggie to make sure he's handling his business."

"Yeah, I need to do the same at the shop because I swear that Mike is scheming on me."

T-Lov was jealous because he hadn't invested his money into a business.

"I'm getting my cheddar right so I can open up a clothing store," T-Lov said, trying to save face so not to feel left out.

"That's what's up. I can see CMB taking over Greenville," Cane said, proud of his boys.

The entire barbershop was spotless. Reggie was on top of his game. He had kept all of the clippers clean and was always ready for business. Since everything was running smoothly, he decided to creep in on Tina.

She had a client in her chair as he crept behind her, blindfolding her eyes with his hands.

"Baby, you see me trying to do some work!" she cooed as he stared deep into her eyes. She could read through his eyes that he wanted to make love. "Re-Re, I'll be right back."

She walked with him outside. "Now, give daddy a kiss since I've got you all to myself now." He wrapped his arms around her waist, working them down her backside.

"Boy, stop it before you start something that you can't finish!" she moaned.

"Oh, I can finish it. Take the rest of the day off," he said, lightly sucking on her neck, trying to convince her to leave the shop. She felt the bulge growing in his pants.

"I can't, babe. I've got a shop to run." She felt his hands going down her pants. Her body trembled after his fingers hit her wet spot. She wanted to leave with him. Her moistness was seeping through her panties. She felt his steel pressing against her stomach. She yearned for him.

"That's what you've got employees for. The sign reads, 'Tina's Beauty Salon and CMB Barbershop.' You have ten stylists in there," he whined.

"Yes, that may be true, but I have my own clients who only like for me to do their hair. As much as I love you and want you, I have to get back to my clients, babe. I swear I will make it all up to you tonight."

"That's why we're meant to be together. You take really good care of daddy, and daddy wants to reward you!" He kissed her on the lips while he ground on her stomach, letting her feel his man tool.

"Well, mommy needs to get back to work. So, I'll come by your house after work, and make sure that you have that quiet storm CD playing and candles burning so we can make love all night long. And, if you're good, I'll reveal a big secret I've been hiding," she said, rubbing on his tool through his jeans.

"I can't wait to see you. I'll make sure I have your bubble bath run, and I'm going to rub your feet and massage your back."

"Well, make sure you wear your SCUBA diving gear because Ms. Pretty Pearl needs some loving." She moaned into his ear, followed by a kiss.

He hated to see her leave. They rarely saw one another because they both had hectic schedules. The thought of him giving up the game was becoming more real since he wanted to move her in and have a family with her. But then again, he wasn't sure if he really wanted to give up the fast money.

Chapter 41

DEA

The Bust

"Informant One, I'm Agent Jackson, and this is my partner, Agent Fernandez. I shouldn't have to tell you what to do. You should already be used to how we work since you've been working with us for some time, but I need to go through this with Ms. Fernandez in our presence for the records." He looked Informant One in his eyes. "All I need for you to do is sign statements on Curtis Griffin."

"What's in it for me?" he asked, rubbing his hands together.

"Motherfucker, cut the bullshit. You owe me your life. I was the one who kept you out of jail." He stood up over him, taking off his dark shades. "I gave you money and put you in a house and car."

"I know the funds run deep, and I need ten grand," he said as he licked his lips and then smiled at them both. He knew that Cane was worth every penny.

"Hell fucking no!" Jackson snapped, slamming his shades onto the floor. "You were the one that fucked up my investigation with Jack Griffin. I worked so hard to nail his ass, and I know that you had something to do with it because your friend, Raymond, signed statements on you." His face turned beet red as slobber flew from his mouth.

"And you're talking about you want ten thousand dollars. I've got your ass off six rape charges, you sick fucker! To make matters worse, I believe that you had something to do with Danny Jones being murdered. So don't play with me because I will start investigating your ass and have you never seeing the light of day again. I promise you that I'll fry your black ass if you don't write these statements on Curtis Griffin," he threatened, giving him a stern, straightforward look.

"Where do I sign?" He exhaled, defeated.

"I don't care where you sign, just write that you've received more than twenty-five kilos of cocaine from him."

Jackson gave Fernandez a wink followed by a smile as they entered investigation room number two where the informant was sitting. "We've already met several times, and I want you to meet Agent Fernandez. She'll be assisting me with this investigation," Jackson said as he looked over her files.

"I see that you've helped us out over the years, and I must say that you provided us with good information that led to some major drug busts. The government will continue to help you with a downward departure as soon as this investigation is over."

"But with the last bust, you said my peeps would be set free," she cried out in tears, feeling like she had been getting used and played by the government.

"Just calm the fuck down and be patient. We're working on it now. I just need your signature here, and I'll fill out the rest of the information as needed," he said, signing statements on Cane himself, using Informant Two's information. Fernandez gave him a stern look but kept her mouth closed.

Jackson was whistling as he opened the door for Fernandez, who stepped ahead of him, entering into the investigation room where Informant Three was pacing back and forth. "I'm Jackson, and this is my partner, Fernandez. We're very happy that you chose to come forth on your own to help out with this investigation." He shook her hand and then gave her a cigarette to calm her nerves.

"As soon as you sign statements on Curtis Griffin, you will be free to go, and the government will compensate you with twenty-five hundred dollars in cash." He gave her the pen as she signed away her soul to the devil.

Agent Jackson took off his shades while Fernandez sat next to him. "Informant Four, you're the one who can put the icing on the cake. All you have to do is sign and say Curtis Griffin, aka Cane, was the mastermind behind this drug war in South Carolina," he said as he slid his shades back over his eyes.

"I don't know if I can do that!" he stated, crossing his arms across his belly.

He slung his shades into the wall, breaking them into five pieces. "Look, motherfucker, we've already got your ass in pictures, tapes, and videos, bragging about having bricks coming from overseas. We heard you loud and clear." He took the folder out of Fernandez's hand. "Look." He smiled once he saw the facial expression on Informant Four. "Should I go on?"

"No, sir," he replied, feeling stupid that his cockiness and dick had gotten him into trouble as he was always told that it would.

"Well, with the information we've got on you, you are easily looking at a life sentence in prison. But truth be told, you're holding your own destiny in your hands. All you have to do is sign statements stating that Mr. Griffin is the ringleader and he's been selling drugs for over six years. I swear to you you'll never see a day of prison. I'll release you right now and compensate you for your cooperation." He smiled as Informant Four signed and recorded his statement into a recorder.

Jackson had his chest poked out and his head held high as he bragged to Fernandez about manipulating the system. "I promise you I won't let this Griffin get away like I did Jack, and I'll be damned if I let somebody fuck this up for me," he stated, heading to Chief Duncan's office so he could get an arrest warrant.

Fernandez was speechless as Jackson led the way. He presented him with Operation Major League, a drug ring that he'd been following for almost two decades, which included guns, trafficking of drugs, and murder. Curtis Griffin was now the leader after his uncle was killed, but Agent Jackson intended to make him hate that he was ever born into the family of Jack Griffin.

Chief Duncan reviewed each statement. "Agent Jackson, don't mess this up like you did with Jack Griffin," he snarled, grinding his teeth. "If you fuck this up, I'll make sure that you never work as an agent or officer in the United States again."

"Yes, sir. This case here is my mission to redeem myself for how I handled Jack's case. I've got this. I promise you. I won't mess this up. I got Mr. Griffin by the balls.

The only problem is that he's armed and dangerous, so I'm going to need an elite dream team to get his ass." He nearly pissed on himself when the chief gave him the arrest warrant.

Jackson went over the blueprint with five SWAT teams from upstate. He pointed out where he wanted them to be. He advised them not to worry about his yard and house alarms because they were the government. "Fuck his alarms. They will be disarmed before we even arrive."

He threw the blueprints up into the air. "I waited all of my life to get Jack Griffin, but he's dead now, so I'll settle for the nephew." He put his hands together. "Y'all are my umpires, and I'm the referee. Welcome to Operation Major League. The game will start at approximately three a.m., and y'all make sure that y'all don't be late because I don't want to start the game without y'all. But if I have to, I will because I want Curtis's ass so bad it makes my asshole itch," he said as everyone stood, applauding him and ready to be a part of going down in history as breaking up the biggest drug ring in South Carolina.

To Be Continued . . .

Kingpin Greenville: The Saga Continues

will be in a hood near you soon!

Chapter 1

Tina

She was furious about Cane getting arrested. She kept breaking down crying uncontrollably. She tried to stay strong for him, but her heart was hurting in a way that she couldn't explain. Her heart hurt for Cane, her, and their baby.

With all the shocking events going on, she didn't know who to call first—his boys or her girls. She most definitely wasn't going to call his grandma. She knew that she would've had a heart attack as soon as the words came out of her mouth.

She kept trying to call Tonya on her cell phone, but there was no answer. She looked down at her watch. *Damn, it's four in the morning. Who comes and arrests someone at this time of the morning?* She knew everybody was sleeping this time of the morning, but she didn't give a damn. Her man had been arrested, and she did not know where to start. Not knowing that Cane and Calvin had not spoken in a few weeks, she picked up the phone and called him. When a woman answered the phone, she hung up, thinking that she had dialed the wrong number and redialed the number. Again, a woman answered, and she again hung up. When her phone rang back, she noticed it was Calvin's number on the caller ID, and she answered, thinking it was the woman calling her back, but it was actually Calvin.

"Who was that who answered your phone?" He told her that it was his new friend. She couldn't believe the words that were coming from his mouth. She shouted, "How in the hell can you have another woman in your house when Tonya hasn't been gone two weeks?"

"I can mess with whoever I want and whenever I want to! Don't be questioning me about who I'm with. You need to be questioning your nigga and who he's messing with."

"Cane isn't with anybody but me!" she stated, defending her man.

He snapped, "You sure about that, Tina? Well, you better ask your best friend why was she at your man's house at two in the morning with no clothes on and why I put her out of my house!" he said as spit flew from his mouth.

She was shaking her head. "You are so damn crazy. You need to stay off them damn drugs because that shit got you fucked up!"

He lowered his voice. "Don't even go there! I'm far from being crazy. I know what I saw at Cane's house! That's why we fell out, and I put Tonya out! Guess neither of them bothered telling your ass that tidbit, did they?" Calvin stated matter-of-factly.

She started hitting her fist on the counter. "I'm not going to sit here and let you talk about Cane and Tonya like that!" He had her so frustrated that she forgot that she was calling to tell him that the Feds had come and picked up Cane. She hung up in his face. "I can't believe his stupid ass, making those kinds of accusations."

The more that she started thinking about what he said, she thought back on the night Tonya told her that she had gone to Cane's house late one night looking for her. Although she didn't say anything about it at the time, it didn't add up to her because Tonya knew that Tina was out of town that night. They had talked several times earlier that day, and she knew she wouldn't be back in town until early morning, but she shrugged it off and let it go because they were girls, and Tonya would never do anything like that to her and neither would Cane. She closed her eyes, getting that thought out of her head.

There wasn't any way that she was going to her apartment. She thought that the police were waiting on her so they could search her house. She wanted to be with Tonya, but she was not about to disrespect her parents' house at four a.m. She decided to go to Shi's and Shelia's house.

Traffic was very light as she cruised to the east side of town. She liked that side of town. The rich white folks always kept to themselves, and she had told Cane that she wouldn't mind moving to that side of town.

Shi and Shelia mixed in well in the neighborhood with their fancy cars that were not nigger-rigged. They both kept it simple with only the manufacturer rims and slight tint to keep the interior good, not for show. Tina was the same way with her Lexus GS 400. She wasn't with riding on twenties with loud music.

The only problem she had was her wardrobe. She was not a conservative dresser, and she loved wearing Baby Phat and revealing clothes. When she went out with the girls, that was their theme, "Baby Phat defines diva." She knew that Cane loved to see her in tight jeans, shorts, and skirts. That was what turned him on every time she walked, strutting her thing. She knew that her parents would kill her if they knew that she was dressing like a hoochie mama.

She was ringing the doorbell like there was no tomorrow. Every light from the bedroom to the living room came on. Shi came to the door in a black Sean John house coat with his eyes half closed.

"What brings you this way so early in the morning? I thought that you were the Jack Boys," he said.

She saw the shiny pistol in his hands. "I'm sorry to disturb you this early in the morning, but they got Cane!" she cried out. Her body was shaking with fear.

"Who got him, Tina? What are you talking about?" he asked.

"The DEA got him!"

He dropped his head, shaking it, and said, "Damn! What's going on?"

"I don't know, but they had guns drawn and everything!" She tried to keep her composure. "Shi, they took my baby away!" She broke down. He started throwing shit around the room in disbelief.

Shelia ran out of the back room to see what was going on. "What's wrong, baby?" she asked.

"They got my man. Baby, the damn Feds got Cane!" he hollered out.

"Calm down, Shi, before you wake up Shannon," Shelia said. He wasn't thinking about Shannon at the time, although that was his heart. He put down the gun and hugged Shelia.

"I'm sorry, baby. I'm sorry!" he cried.

He called Anderson, Greenville, and Spartanburg detention centers, looking for Cane, but there was no sign of him. "Tina, you sure that the Feds got him? It could have been the Jack Boys dressed in police suits that you saw!"

"I'm not crazy, Shi. I know what the hell I saw! I was there when they took him. I just don't know how this happened. It seemed like everything was going good. I told him that I was pregnant, and we were planning our life and future together when the police came from everywhere."

Shelia cut her off. "Did you just say that you were pregnant?"

"Yes," she replied.

Shelia started screaming. "Girl, come over here and sit down!"

Shi was still trying to get in touch with somebody about Cane and his whereabouts. He called T-Lov to let him know what was going on.

"How far along are you? And why didn't you tell me?" Shelia asked.

"I'm three months. I didn't want Cane to find out. I just didn't want him to get upset," Tina said. She knew that she should have told Shelia, but she didn't want Trevia to find out, and the only person who could hold water was Tonya.

Shi called Mr. Big who then called an informant at the DEA headquarters who told him that Cane was being held by the DEA under a federal investigation that couldn't be revealed until further notice. Shi called T-Lov back to let him know what was going on.

"Tina, you stay in the guest room tonight. We probably won't hear anything about Cane until later on today," Shi stated with water in his eyes.

Shelia walked with her to the room, hugging her. "Girl, everything is going to be all right!"

She just looked at Shelia, shaking her head. "I hope so, Shelia. Shit just seems so crazy right now. It just seems like a bad dream. One minute, I was telling Cane that I was pregnant, and he asked me to marry him, and then the next minute, it turned into a gangster movie, police every damn where!"

"Don't stress yourself because you will stress the baby."

"Easy said," Tina hmphed.

"He asked you to marry him?" Shelia asked, excited. "Oh, my gosh, you have so much to look forward to. I am so jealous. Hell, Shi hasn't even proposed to me yet!" she teased, trying to cheer up her friend.

She held up her eyebrows. "Shelia, stop tripping. You've got a good man too!"

"Yes, I do. That's when he's at home," Shelia replied, raising her eyebrows.

Tina knew exactly what she was going through because, in their line of work, Cane was never at home either. "I think that Cane is going to be all right. I'm going to pray for him and leave it in God's hands. I will let him take care of it."

"The best thing you can do is let the Lord take care of everything. I'm not going to keep you up any longer. You need to get some rest. We have a full day ahead of us," Shelia said as she hugged her and got up to leave.

She lay down, thinking about Cane. She couldn't get him off of her mind, but she knew that he was a strong warrior who could take care of himself and would want for her to do the same—stay strong.